A KISS AT MIDNIGHT

A KISS AT MIDNIGHT

Eloisa James

First published 2011
by Piatkus
This Large Print edition published 2012
by AudioGO Ltd
by arrangement with
Little, Brown Book Group

Hardcover   ISBN: 978 1 445 88341 0
Softcover   ISBN: 978 1 445 88342 7

British Library Cataloguing in Publication Data available

Printed and bound in Great Britain by
MPG Books Group Limited

This book is dedicated to the memory of my mother, Carol Bly. She didn't care too much for the genre of romance—or so she said. But she read my sister and me fairy tales over and over, enchanting us with princes who swept in on white chargers and princesses whose golden hair doubled as ladders. She gave me my first copies of Anne of Green Gables, Little Women, *and* Pride and Prejudice. *In short, Mom, it's all your fault!*

Acknowledgments

My books are like small children; they take a whole village to get them to a literate state. I want to offer my heartfelt thanks to my personal village: my editor, Carrie Feron; my agent, Kim Witherspoon; my website designers, Wax Creative; and last, but not least, my personal team: Kim Castillo, Franzeca Drouin, and Anne Connell. I am so grateful to each of you!

Prologue

Once upon a time, not so very long ago . . .

This story begins with a carriage that was never a pumpkin, though it fled at midnight; a godmother who lost track of her charge, though she had no magic wand; and several so-called rats who secretly would have enjoyed wearing livery.

And, of course, there's a girl too, though she didn't know how to dance, nor did she want to marry a prince.

But it really begins with the rats.

They were out of control; everybody said so. Mrs Swallow, the housekeeper, fretted about it regularly. 'I can't abide the way those little varmints chew up a pair of shoes when a body's not looking,' she told the butler, a comfortable soul by the name of Mr Cherryderry.

'I know just what you're saying,' he told her with an edge in his voice that she didn't hear often. 'I can't abide them. Those sharp noses, and the yapping at night, and—'

'The way they eat!' Mrs Swallow broke in. 'From the table, from the very plates!'

'It *is* from the plates,' Cherryderry told her. 'I've seen it with my own eyes, Mrs Swallow, that I have! By the hand of Mrs Daltry herself!'

Mrs Swallow's little shriek might have been heard all the way in the drawing room . . . except the rats were making such a racket that no one in that chamber could hear anything.

1

One

Yarrow House
The residence of Mrs Mariana Daltry; her daughter,
Victoria; and Miss Katherine Daltry

Miss Katherine Daltry, known to almost all as Kate, got down from her horse seething with rage.

It should be said that the condition wasn't unfamiliar to her. Before her father died seven years earlier, she found herself sometimes irritated with her new stepmother. But it wasn't until he was gone, and the new Mrs Daltry—who had held that title for a matter of mere months—started ruling the roost, that Kate really learned the meaning of anger.

Anger was watching tenants on the estate be forced to pay double the rent or leave cottages where they'd lived their whole lives. Anger was watching the crops wilt and the hedges overgrow because her stepmother begrudged the money needed to maintain the estate. Anger was watching her father's money be poured into new gowns and bonnets and frilly things . . . so numerous that her stepmother and stepsister couldn't find days enough in the year to wear them all.

It was the pitying glances she had from acquaintances who never met her at dinner anymore. It was being relegated to a chamber in the attic, with faded furnishings that advertised her relative worth in the household. It was the self-loathing of someone who can't quite bring herself to leave home and have done with it. It

3

was fueled by humiliation, and despair, and the absolute certainty that her father must be turning in his grave.

She stomped up the front steps girding her loins for battle, as her father himself would have said. 'Hello, Cherryderry,' she said, as their dear old butler opened the door. 'Are you playing footman now?'

'Herself sent the footmen off to London to fetch a doctor,' Cherryderry said. 'To be exact, two doctors.'

'Having a spell, is she?' Kate pulled her gloves off carefully, since the leather was separating from its lining around the wrist. Time was when she might have actually wondered if her stepmother (known to the household as Herself) was malingering, but no longer. Not after years of false alarms and voices screaming in the middle of the night about attacks . . . which generally turned out to be indigestion.

Though as Cherryderry had once commented, one can only hope.

'Not Herself, this time. It's Miss Victoria's face, I gather.'

'The bite?'

He nodded. 'Dragging the lip down, so her maid told us this morning. There's a swelling there as well.'

Sour as she felt, Kate felt a pulse of sympathy. Poor Victoria didn't have much going for her outside of her pretty face and prettier frocks; it would break her stepsister's heart if she were permanently disfigured.

'I have to talk to Herself about the vicar's wife,' she said, handing her pelisse to Cherryderry. 'Or

4

rather, the former vicar's wife. After his death, I moved the family to the far cottage.'

'Bad business,' the butler said. 'Especially in a vicar. Seems that a vicar shouldn't take his own life.'

'He left her with four children,' Kate said.

'Mind you, it's not easy for a man to get over the loss of a limb.'

'Well, now his children have to get over the loss of him,' she said unsympathetically. 'Not to mention that my stepmother sent an eviction notice to his widow yesterday.'

Cherryderry frowned. 'Herself says you're to dine with them tonight.'

Kate stopped on her way up the stairs. 'She said what?'

'You're to dine with them tonight. And Lord Dimsdale is coming.'

'You must be joking.'

But the butler was shaking his head. 'She said that. What's more, she's decided that Miss Victoria's rats have to go, but for some reason she banished them to your chamber.'

Kate closed her eyes for a moment. A day that had started out badly was only getting worse. She disliked her stepsister's pack of little dogs, affectionately, or not so affectionately, known to all as the rats. She also disliked Algernon Bennett, Lord Dimsdale, her stepsister's betrothed. He smiled too easily. And she loathed even more the idea of sitting down to dinner *en famille*.

She generally managed to forget that she had once been mistress of the household. After all, her mother had been bedridden for years before she died, and sickly most of Kate's life. Kate had grown

5

up sitting opposite her father at the dining-room table, going over the menus with Mrs Swallow, the housekeeper . . . She had expected to debut, and marry, and raise children of her own in this very house.

But that was before her father died, and she turned into a maid-of-all-work, living in the garret.

And now she was to come to dinner, in a gown that was out-of-date, and endure the smirking pleasantries of Lord Dimsdale? Why?

She ran up the stairs with a sickening foreboding in her stomach. Kate's stepmother was seated at her dressing table, examining her complexion. The afternoon light fell over her shoulder, lighting her hair. It had a glare to it, that hair, a fierce yellow tint as if the strands were made of minerals. She was wearing a morning dress with a pleated bodice of lilac net, caught under the breasts with a trailing ribbon. It was lovely . . . for a debutante.

But Mariana could not abide the fact that she was no longer in her thirties. In fact, she had never really accepted the loss of her twenties. And so she dressed herself to create an approximation of Mariana-at-Twenty. One thing you had to say for Kate's stepmother: She had a reckless bravery, a kind of fierce disregard for the conventions governing women's aging.

But of course if Mariana's costumes were the outward expression of her ambition, they were also the refuge of the failed. For no woman yet has appeared twenty in her forties, and a deliciously sensual gown cannot restore youth.

'I gather you finished your peregrinations amongst your friends and bothered to come home,' Mariana said acidly.

Kate took one look around her stepmother's boudoir and decided to remove a heap of clothes from what she was almost certain was a stool. The room was mounded with piles of light cottons and spangled silks; they were thrown in heaps over the chairs. Or at least where one presumed chairs to be. The room resembled a pastel snowscape, with soft mountains of fabric here and there.

'What are you doing?' her stepmother demanded as Kate hoisted the gowns in her arms.

'Sitting down,' Kate said, dropping the clothing on the floor.

Her stepmother bounded up with a screech. 'Don't treat my gowns like that, you stupid girl! The top few were delivered only a day or two ago, and they're magnificent. I'll have you ironing them all night if there's the least wrinkle, even the least.'

'I don't iron,' Kate said flatly. 'Remember? I put a scorch mark on a white gown three years ago.'

'Ah, the Persian belladine!' her stepmother cried, clasping her hands together like a girlish Lady Macbeth. 'I keep it . . . there.' She pointed a long finger to a corner where a towering mound of cloth went halfway to the ceiling. 'I shall have it altered one of these days.' She sat back down.

Kate carefully pushed the stack of gowns a little farther away from her foot. 'I must speak to you about the Crabtrees.'

'God, I hope you managed to shovel the woman out the door,' Mariana said, lighting a cigarillo. 'You know the bloody solicitor is coming next week to assess my management of the estate. If he sees that scrap heap of a cottage, he'll make no end of fuss. Last quarter he prosed on and on till I thought I'd die of boredom.'

7

'It's your responsibility to keep the cottages in good repair,' Kate said, getting up to open a window.

Mariana waved her cigarillo disdainfully. 'Nonsense. Those people live on my land for practically nothing. The least they can do is keep their own houses in good nick. That Crabtree woman is living in a pigsty. I happened by the other day and I was positively horrified.'

Kate sat back down and let her eyes wander around the room. The *pigsty* of a room. But after a moment she realized that Mariana hadn't noticed her silent insult, since she had opened a little jar and was painting her lips a dark shade of copper.

'Since her husband died,' Kate said, 'Mrs Crabtree is both exhausted and afraid. The house is not a pigsty; it is simply disorganized. You can't evict her. She has nowhere to go.'

'Nonsense,' Mariana said, leaning closer to the glass to examine her lips. 'I'm sure she has a bolt-hole all planned. Another man, most like. It's been over a year since Crabtree topped himself; she'll have a new one lined up by now. You'll see.'

Talking to her stepmother, to Kate's mind, was like peeing in a coalblack outhouse. You had no idea what might come up, but you knew you wouldn't like it.

'That is cruel,' she said, trying to pitch her words so that she sounded like the voice of authority.

'They have to go,' Mariana stated. 'I can't abide sluggards. I made a special trip over to the vicarage, you know, the morning after her husband jumped from the bridge. Bringing my condolences.'

Mariana preferred to avoid all the people working on the estate or in the village, except on

8

the rare occasions when she developed a sudden taste for playing the lady of the manor. Then she would put on an ensemble extravagantly calculated to offend country folk, descend from her carriage, and decipher in her tenants' startled expressions their shiftless and foolish natures. Finally she would instruct Kate to jettison them from their homes.

Luckily she generally forgot about the demand after a week or so.

'That woman, Crabtree, was lying on the settee crying. Children all over the room, a disgusting number of children, and there she was, shoulders shaking like a bad actress. Crying. Maybe she should join a traveling theater,' Mariana said. 'She's not unattractive.'

'She—'

Mariana interrupted. 'I can't abide idlers. Do you think I lay about and wept after my first husband, the colonel, died? Did you see me shed a tear when your father died, though we had enjoyed but a few months of matrimonial bliss?'

Kate had seen no tears, but Mariana needed no confirmation from her. 'Although Mrs Crabtree may not have your fortitude, she has four small children and we have some responsibility to them—'

'I'm bored with the subject and besides, I need to speak to you about something important. Tonight Lord Dimsdale is coming to dinner and you shall join us.' Mariana blew out a puff of smoke. It looked like fog escaping from a small copper pipe.

'So Cherryderry said. Why?' She and her stepmother had long ago dispensed with pleasantries. They loathed each other, and Kate couldn't imagine why her presence was required at

9

the table.

'You're going to be meeting Dimsdale's relatives in a few days.' Mariana took another pull on her cigarillo. 'Thank God, you're slimmer than Victoria. We can have her gowns taken in quite easily. It would be harder to go the other way.'

'What are you talking about? I can't imagine that Lord Dimsdale has the faintest interest in eating a meal with me, nor in introducing me to his relatives, and the feeling is mutual.'

Before Mariana could clarify her demand, the door was flung open. 'The cream isn't working,' Victoria wailed, hurtling toward her mother. She didn't even see Kate, just fell to her knees and buried her face in her mother's lap.

Instantly Mariana put down her cigarillo and wrapped her arms around her daughter's shoulders. 'Hush, babykins,' she crooned. 'Of course the cream will work. We just need to give it a little time. I promise you, Mother promises you, that it will work. Your face will be as beautiful as ever. And just in case, I sent off to London for two of the very best doctors.'

Kate was beginning to feel a faint interest in the matter. 'What kind of cream are you using?'

Mariana threw her an unfriendly glance. 'Nothing you would have heard of. It's made from crushed pearls, among other things. It works like a charm on all sorts of facial imperfections. I use it myself, daily.'

'Just look at my lip, Kate!' Victoria said, popping her head back up. 'I'm ruined for life.' Her eyes glistened with tears.

Her lower lip did look rather alarming. There was an odd violet-colored puffiness around the site that suggested infection, and her mouth had a slight, but distinct, list to the side.

Kate got to her feet and came over for a closer look. 'Has Dr Busby seen it yet?'

'He came yesterday, but he's an old fool,' Mariana said. 'He couldn't be expected to understand how important this is. He hadn't a single helpful potion or cream to offer. Nothing!'

Kate turned Victoria's head to the side so that the light fell on it. 'I think the bite is infected,' she said. 'Are you sure this cream is hygienic?'

'Are you questioning my judgment?' Mariana shouted, standing up.

'Absolutely,' Kate retorted. 'If Victoria ends up with a deformed mouth because you sloshed on some quack remedy you were swindled into buying in London, I want it clear that it's your fault.'

'You insolent toad!' Mariana said, stepping forward.

But Victoria put out an arm. 'Mother, stop. Kate, do you really think there's something wrong with the cream? My lip throbs terribly.' Victoria was a tremendously pretty girl, with a beautiful complexion and wide, tender eyes that always looked a bit dewy, as if she had just shed a sentimental tear, or was just about to. Since she shed tears, sentimental and otherwise, throughout the day, this made sense. Now two tears rolled down her face.

'I think that there might be some infection inside the wound,' Kate said, frowning. 'Your lip mended quickly, but . . .' She pushed gently, and Victoria cried out. 'It's going to have to be lanced.'

'Never!' Mariana roared.

'I couldn't allow my face to be cut,' Victoria said,

11

trembling all over.

'But you don't want to have a disfigurement,' Kate said, schooling her tone to patience.

Victoria blinked while she thought about that.

'Nothing will happen until the London doctors arrive,' Mariana announced, sitting back down. She had a wild enthusiasm for anyone, and anything, from London. Kate suspected it was the result of a childhood spent in the country, but since Mariana never let slip even a hint about her past, it was hard to know.

'Well, let's hope they arrive soon,' Kate said, wondering whether an infected lip created any risk of blood infection. Presumably not . . . 'Why do you want me to join you for dinner, Mariana?'

'Because of my lip, of course,' Victoria said, snuffling like a small pig.

'Your lip,' Kate repeated.

'I can't go on the visit, can I?' Victoria added, with a characteristic, if maddening, lack of clarity.

'Your sister was to pay a very important visit to a member of Lord Dimsdale's family in just a few days,' Mariana put in. 'If you weren't so busy traipsing around the estate listening to the sob stories of feckless women, you'd remember that. He's a *prince*. A prince!'

Kate dropped onto her stool again and looked at her two relatives. Mariana was as hard and bright as a new ha'penny. In contrast, Victoria's features were blurred and indistinct. Her hair was a delightful pale rose color, somewhere between blonde and red, and curled winsomely around her face. Mariana's hair had the sharp-edged perfection of someone whose maid spent three hours with a curling iron achieving precisely the look she

12

wanted.

'I fail to see what the postponed visit has to do with me,' Kate said, 'though I am very sympathetic about your disappointment, Victoria.' And she was, too. Though she loathed her stepmother, she had never felt the same hatred for her stepsister. For one thing, Victoria was too soft-natured for anyone to dislike. And for another, Kate couldn't help being fond of her. If Kate had taken a great deal of abuse from Mariana, the kind of affection that her stepmother lavished on her daughter was, to Kate's mind, almost worse.

'Well,' Victoria said heavily, sitting down on a pile of gowns about the approximate height of a stool, 'you have to be me. It took me a while to understand it, but Mother has it all cleverly planned out. And I'm sure my darling Algie will agree.'

'I couldn't possibly be you, whatever that means,' Kate said flatly.

'Yes, you can,' Mariana said. She had finished her cigarillo and was lighting a second from the first. 'And you will,' she added.

'No, I won't. Not that I have the faintest idea what you're talking about. Be Victoria in what context? And with whom?'

'With Lord Dimsdale's prince, of course,' Mariana said, regarding her through a faint haze of smoke. 'Haven't you been listening?'

'You want me to pretend to be Victoria? In front of a prince? Which prince?'

'I didn't understand at first either,' Victoria said, running her finger over her injured lip. 'You see, before Algie can marry me, we need the approval of some relative of his.'

'The prince,' Mariana put in.

13

'He's a prince from some little country in the back of beyond, that's what Algie says. But he's the only representative of Algie's mother's family who lives in England, and she won't release his inheritance without the prince's approval. His father's will,' Victoria confided, 'is most dreadfully unfair. If Algie marries before thirty years of age, without his mother's approval, he loses part of his inheritance—and he's not even twenty yet!'

Very smart of Papa Dimsdale, to Kate's mind. From what she'd seen, Dimsdale Junior was about as ready to manage an estate as the rats were to learn choral music. Not that it was her business. 'The doctors will take a look at you tomorrow morning,' she told Victoria, 'and then you'll be off to see the prince. Rather like the cat looking at the queen.'

'She can't go like *that*!' Mariana snapped. It was the first time that Kate had ever heard that edge of disgust applied to her daughter.

Victoria turned her head and looked at her mother, but said nothing.

'Of course she can,' Kate stated. 'This sounds like a fool's game to me. No one will believe for a moment that I'm Victoria. And even if they did, don't you think they'd remember later? What happens when this prince stands up in the church and stops the ceremony, on the grounds that the bride isn't the bride he met?'

'That won't happen, if only because Victoria will be married directly afterwards, by parish license,' Mariana said. 'This is the first time Dimsdale has been invited to the castle, and we can't miss it. His Highness is throwing a ball to celebrate his betrothal, and you're going as Victoria.'

14

'Why not just postpone your visit and go after the ball is over?'

'Because I have to get married,' Victoria piped up.

Kate's heart sank. 'You *have* to get married?'

Victoria nodded. Kate looked at her stepmother, who shrugged. 'She's compromised. Three months' worth.'

'For Christ's sake,' Kate exclaimed. 'You hardly know Dimsdale, Victoria!'

'I love Algie,' Victoria said, her big eyes earnest. 'I didn't even want to debut, not after I saw him at Westminster Abbey that Sunday back in March, but Mother made me.'

'March,' Kate said. 'You met him in March and now it's June. Tell me that darling Algie proposed, oh, say three months ago, just after you fell in love, and you've kept it a secret?'

Victoria giggled at that. 'You know exactly when he proposed, Kate! I told you first, after Mother. It was just two weeks ago.'

The lines between Mariana's nose and mouth couldn't be plumped by a miracle cream made of crushed pearls. 'Dimsdale was slightly tardy in his attentions.'

'Not tardy in his *attentions*,' Kate said. 'He's seems to have been remarkably forward in that department.'

Mariana threw her a look of dislike. 'Lord Dimsdale very properly proposed marriage once he understood the situation.'

'I would kill the man, were I you,' Kate told her.

'Would you?' She gave an odd smile. 'You always were a fool. The viscount has a title and a snug fortune, once he gets his hands on it. He's utterly infatuated with your sister, and he's set on marrying her.'

'Fortunate,' Kate commented. She looked back at Victoria. She was delicately patting her lip over and over again. 'I told you to hire a chaperone, Mariana. She could have had anyone.'

Mariana turned back to her glass without a comment. In truth, Victoria probably wasn't for just any man. She was too soft, too much like a soggy pudding. She cried too much.

Though she was terribly pretty and, apparently, fertile. Fertility was always a good thing in a woman. Look how much her own father had despaired over his lack of a son. Her mother's inability to have more children apparently led to his marriage a mere fortnight after his wife's death . . . he must have been *that* anxious to start a new family.

Presumably he thought Mariana was as fertile as her daughter had now proved to be. At any rate, he died before testing the premise.

'So you're asking me to visit the prince and pretend to be Victoria,' Kate said.

'I'm not asking you,' Mariana said instantly. 'I'm commanding you.'

'Oh, Mother,' Victoria said. 'Please, Kate. Please. I want to marry Algie. And, really, I rather need to . . . I didn't quite understand, and, well . . .' She smoothed her gown. 'I don't want everyone to know about the baby. And Algie doesn't either.'

Of course Victoria hadn't understood that she was carrying a child. Kate would be amazed to think that her stepsister had even understood the act of conception, let alone its consequences.

'You're *asking* me,' Kate said to her stepmother,

16

ignoring Victoria for the moment. 'Because although you could force me into the carriage with Lord Dimsdale, you certainly couldn't control what I said once I met this prince.'

Mariana showed her teeth.

'Even more relevant,' Kate continued, 'is the fact that Victoria made a very prominent debut just a few months ago. Surely people at the ball will have met her—or even just have seen her?'

'That's why I'm sending you rather than any girl I could find on the street,' Mariana said with her usual courtesy.

'You'll have my little doggies with you,' Victoria said. 'They made me famous, so everyone will think you're me.' And then, as if she just remembered, another big tear rolled down her cheek. 'Though Mother says that I must give them up.'

'Apparently they are in my bedchamber,' Kate said.

'They're yours now,' Mariana said. 'At least for the visit. After that we'll—' She broke off with a glance at her daughter. 'We'll give them to some deserving orphans.'

'The poor tots will love them,' Victoria said mistily, ignoring the fact that the said orphans might not like being nipped by their new pets.

'Who would accompany me as chaperone?' Kate asked, putting the question of Victoria's rats aside for the moment.

'You don't need one,' Mariana said with a hard edge of scorn, 'the way you careen about the countryside on your own.'

'A pity I didn't keep Victoria with me,' Kate retorted. 'I would have ensured that Dimsdale didn't treat her like a common trollop.'

17

'Oh, I suppose that you've preserved your virtue,' Mariana snapped. 'Much good may it do you. You needn't worry about Lord Dimsdale making an attempt at that dusty asset; he's in love with Victoria.'

'Yes, he is,' Victoria said, sniffing. 'And I love him too.' Another tear slid down her cheek.

Kate sighed. 'If I am pretending to be Victoria, it will create a scandal if I appear in a carriage alone with Dimsdale, and the scandal will not attach to me, but to Victoria. In short, no one will be surprised when her child appears on an abbreviated schedule after the wedding.'

There was a moment of silence. 'All right,' Mariana said. 'I would have accompanied Victoria, of course, but I can't leave her, given her poor state of health. You can take Rosalie with you.'

'A maid? You're giving me a maid as a chaperone?'

'What's the matter with that?' Mariana demanded. 'She can sit between you in case you lose your head and lunge at Lord Dimsdale. You'll have the rats' maid as well, of course.'

'Victoria's dogs have their *own* maid?'

'Mary-Downstairs,' Victoria said. 'She cleans the fireplaces, but she also gives them a bath every day, and brushes them. Pets,' Victoria added, 'are a responsibility.'

'I shall not take Mary with me,' Kate stated. 'How on earth do you expect Mrs Swallow to manage without her?'

Mariana just shrugged.

'This won't work,' Kate said, trying to drag the conversation back into some sort of sensible channel. 'We don't even look alike.'

18

'Of course you do!' Mariana snapped.

'Well, actually, we don't,' Victoria said. 'I—well, I look like me and Kate, well . . .' She floundered to a halt.

'What Victoria is trying to say is that she is remarkably beautiful,' Kate said, feeling her heart like a little stone in her chest, 'and I am not. Put that together with the fact that we are stepsisters related only by marriage, and there's no more resemblance between us than any pair of Englishwomen seen together.'

'You have the same color hair,' Mariana said, dragging on her cigarillo.

'Really?' Victoria said doubtfully.

Actually, Mariana was probably right. But Victoria's hair was cut in pretty curls around her head, in the very newest style, and fixed with a delicate bandeau. Kate brushed hers out in the morning, twisted it about, and pinned it flat to her head. She had no time for meticulous grooming. More accurately, she had no time for grooming at all.

'You're cracked,' Kate said, staring at her stepmother. 'You can't pass me off as your daughter.'

Victoria was frowning now. 'I'm afraid she's right, Mother. I wasn't thinking.'

Mariana had a kind of tight look about her eyes that Kate knew from long experience signaled true rage. But for once, she was rather perplexed about why.

'Kate is taller than I am,' Victoria said, counting on her fingers. 'Her hair is a little more yellow, not to mention long, and we don't have the same sort of look at all. Even if she put on my clothing—'

19

'She's your sister,' Mariana said, her mouth tight, as if the copper pipe had been hammered flat.

'She's my stepsister,' Kate said patiently. 'The fact that you married my father does not make us blood relatives, and your first husband—'

'She's your *sister*.'

Two

Pomeroy Castle
Lancashire

'Your Highness.' The prince in question, whose given name was Gabriel Albrecht-Frederick William von Aschenberg of Warl-Marburg-Baalsfeld, looked up to find his majordomo, Berwick, holding a salver. 'I've got this unguentarium all in pieces, Wick. Speak quickly.'

'Unguentarium,' Wick said with distaste. 'It sounds like a salacious item one might buy in Paris. The wrong side of Paris,' he added.

'Spare me your quibbles,' Gabriel said. 'This particular jug was meant for the dead, not the living. It used to hold six small bones for playing knucklebones, and was found in a child's grave.'

Wick bent nearer and peered at the pieces of clay scattered across the desk. 'Where are the knucklebones?'

'The knuckleboned Biggitstiff threw them out. In fact, he threw this little jug out too, since the child was poor, and he is only interested in ravaging the tombs of kings. I'm trying to see whether I can identify how the top, which I don't

20

have, was attached. I think there were bronze rivets attached to both these pieces.' He pointed. 'And the rivets were mended at least once before the unguentarium was put in the tomb, see?'

Wick looked at the pieces. 'Needs mending again. Why are you bothering?'

'This child's parents had nothing to give him to bring to the underworld but his knucklebones,' Gabriel said, picking up his magnifying glass. 'Why shouldn't that gift be honored equally with the trumpery gold Biggitstiff is after?'

'A message has arrived from Princess Tatiana's delegation,' Wick said, apparently accepting Gabriel's edict in regard to the knucklebones. 'She is now in Belgium and will arrive on schedule. We've had some two hundred acceptances for your betrothal ball, among them your nephew, Algernon Bennett, Lord Dimsdale. In fact, the viscount will arrive before the ball, by the sound of it.'

'Bringing the Golden Fleece?' Gabriel's nephew, whom he vaguely remembered as a boy with a fat bottom, had affianced himself to one of the richest heiresses in England.

'His Lordship will be accompanied by his betrothed, Miss Victoria Daltry,' Wick said, glancing at his notes.

'It's hard to believe that Dimsdale could have garnered such a prize; perhaps she has freckles or a squint,' Gabriel said, carefully aligning the clay fragments so that he could determine where the rivets originated.

Wick shook his head. 'At her debut this spring Miss Daltry was accounted one of the most beautiful women on the marriage market.' They had been in England for a matter of months, but he already had a firm grasp on relevant gossip among the aristocracy. 'Her adoration for her betrothed was also universally noted,' he added.

'She hasn't met me,' Gabriel said idly. 'Maybe I should steal her away before my own bride arrives. An English Golden Fleece for a Russian one. My English is far better than my Russian.'

Wick didn't say a word, just slowly looked from Gabriel's hair to his feet. Gabriel knew what Wick was seeing: black hair pulled back from a widow's peak, eyebrows that came to points over his eyes in a way that frightened some women, the shadow of a beard that never seemed to really go away. Something in his expression scared off the soft ones, the ones that thought to cuddle and wrap his hair around their fingers after sex.

'Of course, you could try,' Wick commented. 'But I expect you'll have your hands full trying to charm your own bride.'

Not his best insult, but pretty good.

'You make it sound as if Tatiana will run for the hills at the sight of me.' Gabriel knew damn well that the glimmer of ferocity in his eyes frightened ladies who were more used to lapdogs. But for all that, he had yet to meet the woman whose eyes didn't show a slight widening, a sparkle of happiness, at the prospect of meeting a prince. They liked to have a prince under their belt.

Still, this was the first time he would be trying to charm a wife, rather than a lover. One had to assume that women took the business more seriously than they did the occasional bedding.

A curse sounded in his head but died before reaching his lips. He turned back to the little pot before him. 'Perhaps fortunately, my betrothed has no more choice in the matter than I do.'

Wick bowed. He left as silently as he had arrived.

Three

Yarrow House

There was a moment of cool silence in the room, like the silence that follows a gunshot when hunters are in the woods.

Victoria didn't say anything. Kate took one look at her soft, bewildered eyes and saw that her mother's pronouncement had flown over her head.

'Victoria is my sister,' Kate repeated.

'Yes, so you bloody well better go there and make sure her marriage goes through before she's ruined. Because she's your sister.'

A little pulse of relief rushed through Kate's veins. She must have misunderstood, she had—

'She's your half sister,' Mariana clarified, her voice grating.

'But—she's—' Kate turned to Victoria. 'How old are you?'

'You know how old I am,' Victoria said, snuffling a bit as she rubbed her lower lip. 'I'm almost exactly five years younger than you.'

'You're eighteen,' Kate said. Her heart was thumping in her chest.

'Which makes *you* a ripe twenty-three,' Mariana said pleasantly. 'Or perhaps twenty-four. At your age, it's easy to forget.'

'Your husband, the colonel—'

Mariana shrugged.

23

Kate found herself struggling to breathe. She felt as if her whole life were unfolding in front of her, all the questions she never knew she had. The shock of her father coming home, just two weeks after her mother's funeral, and saying that he was planning to marry by special license.

Her mother lying in bed all those years, and her father popping his head in now and then to say cheerful things and toss kisses in her direction but never to sit by his wife's side.

Because apparently he'd been sneaking off to sit with Mariana. 'I feel as if I'm missing something,' Victoria said, looking from one to the other. 'Are you going to cry, Kate?' Kate recoiled. She had never cried, not since her father's funeral. 'Of course not!' she snapped.

There was another beat of silence in the room.

'Why don't you do the honors?' Kate said finally, looking at her stepmother. 'I'm agog to learn the particulars.'

'The particulars are none of your business,' Mariana stated. Then she turned to Victoria. 'Listen, darling, you remember how we used to see dearest Victor even before we came to live in this house?'

Victor! Kate had never thought for a moment that her father's name had any connection to that of her stepsister.

'Yes,' Victoria agreed. 'We did.'

'That would be because your mother was his mistress,' Kate said. 'I gather he *visited* your house for at least eleven years, before my mother died. Was there a colonel at all? Is Victoria illegitimate?' she asked Mariana.

'It hardly matters,' Mariana said coolly. 'I can

24

provide for her.'

Kate knew that. Her beloved, foolish father had left everything to his wife . . . and Mariana had turned it into a sweet dowry for Victoria, and be damned whether the estate needed the income. It was all Victoria's now.

Who was not only pregnant, but illegitimate. One had to suppose that the colonel, Mariana's putative first husband, had never existed.

Mariana got up and stubbed out her cigarillo in a dish overflowing with half-smoked butts. 'I am shocked beyond belief that the two of you haven't sprung to your feet and hugged each other in an excess of girlish enthusiasm. But since you haven't, I'll make this short. You will go to Pomeroy Castle, Katherine, because your sister is carrying a child and needs the approval of the prince. You will dress as your sister, you will take the bloody mongrels with you, and you will make this work.'

Mariana looked tough, and more tired than she usually did. 'In that case, you will keep the Crabtrees in their cottage,' Kate stated.

Her stepmother shrugged. She didn't really give a damn either way, Kate realized. She had launched the Crabtrees into the situation just in case the plea of blood relations failed.

'I've summoned the same man who cut Victoria's hair,' Mariana said briskly. 'He'll be here tomorrow morning to cut off all of that rot on your head. Three seamstresses are coming as well. You'll need at least twenty gowns altered.'

'You'll be at the castle for three or four days,' Victoria said.

She got to her feet, and for the first time, Kate recognized that her sister was indeed going to have a child. There was something slightly clumsy about the way she moved.

'I'm sorry,' Victoria said, walking over to stand before Kate. 'There's nothing for you to be sorry for!' Mariana interjected.

'Yes, there is,' she insisted. 'I'm sorry that our father was the sort of man he was. I'm not sorry that he married my mother, but I'm—I'm just sorry about all of it. About what you must think of him now.'

Kate didn't want to think about her father. She had tried not to think of him in the last seven years, since his death. It was too painful to think about the way he laughed, and the way he would stand by the fireplace and tell her amusing stories of London, reflected firelight glinting from his wineglass.

And now there was a whole new reason to not think of him.

She returned Victoria's embrace politely, then disengaged herself and turned to Mariana. 'Why must I come to dinner tonight?'

'Lord Dimsdale has some doubt that you two look enough alike to fool someone who might have met your sister.'

'But my hair—'

'It's not the hair,' her stepmother said. 'We'll put you in a decent gown and you'll see the resemblance soon enough. Victoria is known for her beauty, her dogs, and her glass slippers. As long as you don't indulge your churlish tongue, you'll pass.'

'What on earth is a glass slipper?' Kate asked.

'Oh, they're marvelous!' Victoria cried, clasping her hands together. 'I brought them into fashion myself this season, Kate, and then *everyone* started

26

wearing them.'

'Your feet are about the same size,' Mariana said. 'They'll fit.'

Kate looked down at her tired, gray gown and then up at her stepmother. 'What would you have done if my father had lived? If I had debuted when I was supposed to and people recognized the resemblance between myself and Victoria?'

'I didn't worry about it,' Mariana said with one of her shrugs.

'Why not? Wouldn't there have been the risk that someone would have seen the two of us together and guessed?'

'She's five years younger than you. I would have kept her in the schoolroom until you married.'

'I might not have taken. I might not have found a husband. My father would have . . .'

A smile twisted the corner of Mariana's lips. 'Oh, you would have taken. Don't you ever look in the mirror?'

Kate stared at her. Of course she looked in the mirror. She saw her perfectly regular features staring back at her. She didn't see Victoria's dewy eyes, or her light curls, or her charming smile, because she didn't have any of those.

'You're a bloody fool,' Mariana said, reaching out for her cigarillo case and then dropping it again. 'I'm smoking too many of these, which is entirely your fault. For God's sake, get yourself into a decent dress by eight this evening. You'd better go see Victoria's maid straight off; you're not fit to scrub the fireplace in that rag you're wearing.'

'But I don't want Algie to see my lip like this,' Victoria said, sniffing.

'I'll instruct Cherryderry to put a single

27

candelabrum on the table,' her mother said. 'Dimsdale won't be able to see a rat if it jumps on the plate in front of him.'

So it all came back to the rats, which was fitting, because that's where the story began.

Four

Kate knew quite well that the household was on her side. They couldn't help it; it was bred into the bones of the best servants. They were trained to serve ladies and gentlemen, not those of their own class. Obviously they had sensed that Mariana's origins were not genteel. For her part, Kate had imagined that her stepmother was a shopkeeper's daughter, who had married a colonel. She hadn't thought she was—

What she was.

A fallen woman. Her father's mistress. A trollop, by any other name.

No wonder poor Victoria found herself with child. Her mother was hardly qualified to steer her through the season. For that matter, Kate wasn't entirely sure how to behave in polite society either. She had been only twelve when her mother retired to bed, and sixteen when her mother finally died and her father remarried. Though she'd learned how to use cutlery, the finer nuances of behavior in polite society escaped her.

She'd had a year of dancing instruction, but it felt as if it had happened in another lifetime. Weren't there rules about talking to princes, for example? Did you have to back out of the room after speaking to one? Or was that a rule that applied only to kings and queens?

She found Victoria's maid, Rosalie, in Victoria's dressing room. Years ago the chamber had been designated for guests, but at some point Victoria had amassed so many dresses—and they had no visitors—that it had been transformed into a wardrobe.

Kate looked around with some curiosity. The room was lined with cherry cabinets clearly stuffed with gowns. Flounces of lace and corners of embroidered fabric poked from half-open drawers. The room smelled like roses and fresh linen.

'Cherryderry told me of the dinner tonight, and the seamstresses coming tomorrow,' Rosalie said, 'and I've been through all of Miss Victoria's gowns.' That would have been no small task, given that Victoria had half again as many as her mother, though they were more neatly arranged. 'I think you should wear this tonight, as it won't need more than a stitch or two around the bodice.'

She held up a gown of the palest pink silk. It wasn't particularly low-cut, but it looked to be tight until just below the bosom, when the overskirt was pulled up into curls and furbelows, revealing a dark rose lining.

Kate reached out a finger. Her father had died before they would have begun the visits to modistes to assemble a wardrobe for her debut. She had gone straight from funereal blacks to sturdy cambrics, reflective of her changed position in the household.

'*Couleur de rosette,*' Rosalie said briskly. 'I fancy it will set off your hair a treat. You won't need stays, being so slim.'

She started to unbutton her, but Kate pushed her hands away.

'Please allow me—' Rosalie began.

Kate shook her head. 'I've been dressing myself for years, Rosalie. You can help me put that gown on, if necessary, but I will pull off my clothing myself.' Which she did, leaving her in nothing more than an old chemise. She did own a pair of stays, but they were too uncomfortable to wear, as she was on horseback every day.

Rosalie didn't say a word, just looked at the tired chemise, and the way Kate had darned it (not terribly well), and the length of it (too short). 'Mr Daltry . . .' the maid said, and paused.

'Turning in his grave, et cetera,' Kate said. 'Let's get on with it, Rosalie.'

So the maid began pulling out hairpins and clicking her tongue like someone counting pennies. 'I never would have thought you had all this hair!' she said finally, having unpinned and unwound all of Kate's locks.

'I don't care to have it messing about,' Kate explained. 'It gets in my way while I'm working.'

'You shouldn't be working!' Rosalie cried. 'It's just wrong, all of this, and seeing you there in that chemise like a dishcloth. I didn't know.' She threw down her brush and pulled open a deep drawer. Inside were stacks of pristine white chemises.

Rosalie snatched one. 'Miss Victoria won't even notice, not that she would care because she isn't like her mother. She likes silk for her chemise,' the maid said, jerking Kate's chemise over her head and throwing it to the side. 'I prefer a nice cotton, as sweat stains these terribly. But there, if you aren't dressed properly to the skin, you aren't really a lady, when all's said and done.'

The chemise settled around Kate like a translucent cloud. It was trimmed with exquisite lace.

Had her father lived and had she debuted, she would have worn garments like this all the time, not fraying, tired garments in sober grays and blues that made her look like the poor relation she was.

Her mother had left her some sort of small dowry, but without the chance to meet any eligible men, it hardly mattered. For years she'd been telling herself to leave the house, to go to London, to find work as a governess . . . anything to escape. But that meant deserting the tenants and the servants to Mariana's haphazard and unfeeling oversight.

So she hadn't left.

An hour later her hair was curled and tousled and swept up into an approximation of Victoria's. Her face was dusted with rice powder, the better to approximate the pampered look of her sister's skin; she was swathed in pale pink, and her lips were painted to match.

She stood in front of the glass waiting for a moment of startled recognition. To realize that she really looked like Victoria, that she too would be accounted a great beauty.

Not only did she not resemble her sister, but she would be accounted a beauty only by a blind man. She looked too angular and the dress hung oddly from her shoulders.

Rosalie plucked at one sleeve. 'You're broader in the arms than Miss Victoria,' she muttered.

Kate glanced down at her offending limb and knew exactly what the problem was. She spent at least two or three hours a day in the saddle, trying to manage the estate the way her father's bailiff had done, before her stepmother threw him out of the house. Her arms were muscled, and lightly colored from the sun. She couldn't imagine that other young ladies faced that particular problem.

What's more, her cheekbones were too pronounced, her eyebrows too sharp. 'I don't look like Victoria,' she said, a bit dismally. She had vaguely hoped that fashionable clothing would transform her, making her as beautiful as her sister. A woman whom all the *ton* considered a diamond.

She looked more like a flinty stone than a diamond. Like herself.

'The style doesn't suit you,' Rosalie admitted. 'Pink wasn't the right idea. You need bold colors, more like.'

'You do know why I have to look like Victoria, don't you?' Kate knew perfectly well that Cherryderry had followed her up the stairs and positioned himself outside her stepmother's bedchamber, intent on hearing the entire conversation.

Rosalie set her mouth primly. 'Nothing that I shouldn't know, I would hope.'

'I am to accompany Lord Dimsdale on a visit to Pomeroy Castle, and I need to make everyone there think I'm Victoria.'

The maid's eyes met her own in the mirror.

'It won't work,' Kate said, accepting it. 'She's just too beautiful.'

'You're beautiful too,' Rosalie said stoutly. 'But in a different way.'

'My mouth's too big, and when did I get so thin?'

'Since your father died and you started doing the

32

work of ten people. Miss Victoria, bless her soul, is as soft as a pillow, but she would be, wouldn't she?'

Kate eyed the material draped over her bosom. Or rather, where her bosom ought to be. 'Can't we do something about my chest, Rosalie? In this dress, I don't seem to have one at all.'

Rosalie plucked at the extra material. 'You've a nice little bosom, Miss Kate. Don't worry. I can't do much for it in this dress, but I'll find others that will work better. Thanks be to God, Miss Victoria has more gowns in her chambers than a modiste would after a year's labor.' A moment later she had tucked two rolled-up stockings into the front of Kate's chemise, and that was that.

It was odd how her similar features resulted in such a different appearance from Victoria's. Of course, she was five years older. All ruffled and curled and made up, she looked like a desperate aging virgin.

Panic was a new sensation. Never having been offered the chance to dress like a lady, at least not for years, Kate had rather forgotten that her nubile years were passing.

She'd be twenty-four in a few weeks, and she felt as long in the tooth as a dowager.

Why hadn't she noticed that she wasn't rounded and charming and delectable anymore? When had bitterness entered her bloodstream and—and changed her from a young girl into something else?

'This isn't going to work,' she said abruptly. 'I don't have the faintest resemblance to a young debutante who took the *ton* by storm.'

'It's a matter of wearing the right clothing,' Rosalie said. 'You don't look your best in this gown, miss. But I'll find a better one for you.'

33

There wasn't much Kate could do but nod. She had thought . . .

Well, she hadn't thought much about it. But she knew that she wanted to be married, and to have children of her own.

A sharp pang of panic rose into her throat. What if she was already too old? What if she never—

She cut off the thought.

She would do this visit for Victoria, for her newfound sister's sake. After that, she would leave, go to London and parlay her modest inheritance, the money her mother had left, into a marriage license.

Women had done that for years, and she could do it as well.

She straightened her shoulders. Since her father died, she had learned what it felt like to be humiliated: to tuck your hands out of sight when you saw acquaintances for fear they would see the reddened fingers. To hold your boots close to the horse's side so that no one saw the worn spots. To pretend you left your bonnet at home, time after time.

This was just a new kind of humiliation—to be dressed as lamb while feeling like mutton. She would get through it.

Five

By the time Kate escaped to her room hours later, she was exhausted. She had been up at five that morning to do three hours of accounts, then was on a horse at eight . . . not to mention the emotional toll taken by the day's charming revelations. At dinner, Mariana had been snappy even with the viscount, and Victoria had wept softly through three courses.

And now the dogs—the 'rats'—were waiting for her, sitting in a little semicircle.

There was no more fashionable accessory than a small dog, and Victoria and Mariana, with their characteristic belief that twenty-three ball gowns were better than one, had acquired not one small dog, but three.

Three small, yapping, silky Malteses.

They were absurdly small, smaller than most cats. And they had a sort of elegant sleekness about them that she found an affront. If she ever had a dog, she'd want it to be one of the lopeared, grinning dogs that ran out to greet her when she stopped by the cottages on Mariana's lands. A dog that barked rather than yapped.

Though at the moment they weren't yapping. As she entered her small room, they rose in a little wave and surrounded her ankles in a burst of furry waving tails and hot bodies. They were probably lonely. Before the bite, they were always at Victoria's side. Perhaps they were hungry. Or worse, they might need to visit the garden. If only she had a bell in her room . . . but persons of her status had no need to call servants.

'I suppose,' she said slowly, thinking of the stairs and her aching legs, 'I have to take you outside.' In point of fact, she should be grateful that they had not urinated in her room; it was so small and the one window so high that the smell would last a month or more.

It took a few minutes to figure out how to attach

ropes to their jeweled collars, not helped by the fact that they had begun yapping, jumping up and trying to lick her face. It was hard not to flinch away.

She trudged down the back stairs that led to her room, her steps echoed by the scrabbling little claws of the rats. She was so tired that she couldn't even remember their names, though she thought they were all alliterative, perhaps Fairy and Flower.

'What do they eat?' she asked Cherryderry a few minutes later. He had been kind enough to accompany her to the kitchen garden and show her the area fenced off for the dogs' use.

'I sent Richard up to your chamber an hour or so ago; he fed them and brought them out for a walk. I will admit to disliking those dogs, but they're not vicious animals,' he said, watching them. 'It's not really their fault.'

They were all piling on top of each other, a mass of plumy tails and sharp noses.

'Caesar didn't intend to bite Miss Victoria,' he continued. 'You needn't worry that he'll bite you.'

'*Caesar?* I thought they were all named after flowers.'

'That's part of their trouble,' Cherryderry said. 'Miss Victoria never quite settled on names for them. She changed them every week or so. They started out as Ferdinand, Felicity, and Frederick. Currently they are Coco, Caesar, and Chester. Before that, they were Mopsie, Maria, and something else. The lead dog—see the slightly larger one? That one is Caesar. The other two are Coco and Chester, though Chester never learned to respond to any name other than Frederick or Freddie.'

'Why did Caesar bite Victoria, anyway? I never

36

thought to ask.'

'She was feeding him from her mouth.'

'*What?*'

'Holding a piece of meat between her lips and encouraging him to take it from her. Foolish business, coming between a dog and his meat.'

Kate shuddered. 'That is disgusting.'

'Princess Charlotte has trained her dogs to do the same by all accounts,' Cherryderry said. 'The princess has a lot to answer for.'

'So how do I keep them quiet at night?' Kate asked, longing for her bed.

'Just treat them like dogs, with respect, but firm-like. Miss Victoria made the mistake of thinking they were babies, and then she would get annoyed and send them down to the kitchen whenever they misbehaved, so they never learned better. I'll give you a little bag of cheese scraps. Give them a piece every time they do something right and they'll be fine.'

Back in her room Kate discovered that the dogs had their own personalities. Caesar was remarkably unintelligent. He seemed to believe that he was very large: He prowled and pounced and kept issuing promises to attack anyone who entered the room. In fact, he reminded her of an imperial general; his name befitted him.

Frederick was lonely, or at least that's what she surmised when he jumped onto the bed, licked her knee, and wagged his tail madly. Then he gave her a dramatically imploring look, quickly followed by a roll onto his back with his legs in the air. In short, he was silly and Freddie suited him better than Frederick.

Coco showed every sign of being remarkably

vain. Victoria had glued tiny sparkling gems into the fur around her neck, and rather than trying to scratch them off, as would any self-respecting mongrel, Coco sat with her paws perfectly aligned and her nose in the air. She showed no sign of wishing to approach Kate's bed, but arranged herself elegantly on a velvet cushion that had appeared on Kate's floor along with a bowl of water.

Kate pulled Freddie out of her bed and dropped him on the floor, but he jumped straight back up again. And she was too tired, too bone-deep tired, to do anything about it.

So she lay there for a moment thinking about her father, little pulses of anger going through her body. How could he have done this? He must have loved Mariana; otherwise, why would he marry his mistress?

It was a good thing that she never made her debut. She knew little of society, all things told, but she knew that no one would befriend a young lady whose stepmother was a woman of ill repute, even given that Mariana did marry her protector.

And yet Mariana and Victoria had simply marched into London, opened up her father's town house, and established Victoria as a beautiful young heiress.

There was a lesson there, she thought sleepily.

Six

The next morning

The French coiffeur and the two London doctors arrived together the next morning, one prepared to cut off Kate's hair and the others to lance Victoria's lip. Both sisters refused. Mariana had hysterics, waving her cigarillo around her head and shrieking like a fishwife.

But the session with Rosalie the evening before had cleared Kate's mind. She wasn't getting any younger, and her only crowning glory was her hair. She already looked too thin, almost haggard. Her face might look even worse without her masses of hair.

'I refuse!' she declared, raising her voice over Victoria's sobs.

The odd thing was that she had rarely refused anything. She had fought her stepmother tooth and nail in the past seven years: fought her when she sacked the house steward and told Kate to do the purchasing instead; fought her when she dismissed the bailiff and threw the books at Kate and told her to do them at night.

But she had never *refused* to do anything. She had taken up the estate books, and the bills, and the general management, said goodbye to her governess, to various maids, to the bailiff, and to the house steward.

She found it rather ironic that vanity was the point over which she discovered her backbone. 'I won't do it,' she repeated, over and over.

Monsieur Bernier threw up his hands, declaring

in a trilling French accent that a smart crop would make her look ten years younger, and (he implied) mademoiselle needed every one of those ten years.

Kate hardened her heart. 'I am grateful for your opinion, monsieur, but no.'

'You'll ruin it,' Mariana cried, her voice careening to the edge of frenzy and back. 'You'll ruin everything. Your sister won't be able to marry, and she'll have her child out of wedlock.'

Kate saw Monsieur Bernier's eyes widen and she gave him a look. Seven years of estate management had given her a quite effective glare; he flinched.

'It's all right, Mother,' Victoria put in, sniffling, 'Kate will simply have to wear wigs, that's all. She'll be hot, but it's a matter of only a few days.'

'Wigs,' Mariana said, with a kind of strangled gasp.

'I have them in all sorts of colors to match my dresses,' Victoria said. 'If Rosalie plaits Kate's hair every morning and then pins it flat, she would be perfectly fashionable and everyone will simply assume that I love my wigs.'

'True,' Mariana said, taking a hard draw on her cigarillo.

'I'll even give you my Circassian Scalp,' Victoria said.

Kate wrinkled her nose.

'No, it's lovely, an elegant pale blue wig that goes beautifully with gowns in blue and green. Plus there's a jeweled bandeau to wear with it, which will help it stay on your head.'

'Fine,' Mariana said. 'Now the doctors are going to lance your lip, Victoria, and that is the last I want to hear from either of you for the rest of the day.'

Victoria screamed and cried, but at last the grim

40

deed was done.

Mariana retired to bed with a headache; Victoria retired to bed with a weeping fit; Kate took the dogs with her on a visit to the Crabtrees.

Seven

Pomeroy Castle

'So what's the matter with the lion?' Gabriel asked Wick, walking quickly across the outer courtyard toward the makeshift menagerie that graced the back wall.

'I haven't the faintest idea. He can't seem to stop vomiting,' Wick replied.

'Poor old thing,' Gabriel said, coming to the lion's cage. The beast was crouched against the back wall, its sides heaving painfully. He'd had ownership of it for only a few months, but its eyes used to be full of light, as if it were longing to spring from the cage and eat a bystander.

It didn't look like that anymore. Its eyes were glazed and miserable. If it were a horse, he would have . . .

'It's not old enough to die,' Wick said, as if he heard Gabriel's thought.

'Augustus told me it wouldn't last more than a year.'

'The Grand Duke no longer wished for his menagerie so he may have exaggerated the beast's age. The lion is only five years old and should live many more, as I understand it.'

'How are the rest of them?' Gabriel walked past

the lion's cage toward that of the elephant, and found Lyssa swaying placidly in her cage. She had a sweet temperament; at the sight of him she blew some straw in a companionable sort of way. 'What's that monkey doing in there with her?'

'They became friends during the ocean passage,' Wick said. 'They seem happier together.'

Gabriel walked closer and peered at the monkey. 'Damned if I know what kind that is. Do you?'

'As I understand it, she's called a pocket monkey. The Grand Duke was given her by a pasha.'

'And the elephant came along with that Indian raja, didn't she? I wish people would stop giving animals as gifts. This courtyard smells.'

Wick sniffed loudly. 'True. We could move them to the gardens behind the hedge maze.'

'Lyssa would get lonely out there by herself. I don't suppose we can let her out of her cage now and then, could we?'

'I could ascertain whether we might build an enclosure in the orchards,' Wick said.

Gabriel stared at the unlikely pair for another moment. The monkey was sitting on the elephant's head, stroking a big ear with her knotty-looking fingers. 'Have you had any luck finding someone to care for the animals who actually knows something about elephants and the like?'

'No,' Wick said. 'We tried to lure a man from Peterman's Circus, but he refused to leave his own lions.'

'We can't have Peterman's lions along with our own, the poor sick bastard.' He walked back to the first cage. 'What the hell could be the matter with it, Wick?'

'Prince Ferdinand suggested that it might be

accustomed to a diet of human flesh, but I thought it best to ignore the implications of that comment.'

'In lieu of that, what have we been feeding it?'

'Beefsteak,' Wick said. 'Good stuff too.'

'Maybe it's too rich. What does my uncle eat after a bad night?'

'Soup.'

'Try that.'

Wick raised an eyebrow but nodded.

'On that charming topic, where *is* my uncle?'

'His Highness is working on the battle of Crecy this morning. He has commandeered the pigsty, which is happily free of occupants, and renamed it the Imperial War Museum. Forty or fifty milk bottles represent the various regiments and their leaders. His exhibit,' Wick added, 'is very popular with the servants' children.'

'He's happy then,' Gabriel said. 'I suppose—'

He was interrupted as a tall man with stork-like legs trotted into the courtyard. He had hair like thistledown, which stood straight in the air and waved slightly every time he moved. 'Speak of the devil,' Gabriel said, bowing.

'Same to you, dear boy,' his uncle Prince Ferdinand Barlukova said vaguely. 'Same to you. Have you seen my poor dog anywhere?'

Wick moved slightly behind Gabriel's shoulder and said quietly, 'There is some belief that the lion ate him.'

'Fur and all?'

'It might explain the beast's current plight.'

'I have not seen your dog,' Gabriel told his uncle.

'Just yesterday he ate a whole plate of pickled crab apples,' Prince Ferdinand said, looking a bit tearful. 'I have him on a pickled diet, everything

43

pickled. I think it's much better for his digestion.'

The pickled apples might not have agreed with the dog—or, secondhand, with the lion. 'Perhaps he ran away,' Gabriel said, turning toward the great arch that led back to the inner courtyard. 'He may have not appreciated your dietary innovations.'

'My dog adores pickled food,' Ferdinand stated. 'Adores it, especially pickled tomatoes.'

'Next time, try pickled fish.' From the corner of his eye, Gabriel could see two aunts approaching, out for a perambulation, waving their fingers in his direction, smiling archly. He started moving more quickly, avoiding the cook's child at the last minute, striding finally into his chamber with a feeling of having narrowly escaped.

The problem with having a castle was that a castle filled with people. And they were all *his* people, one way or another: his relatives, his lion, his elephant, his servants . . . even the pickle-eating dog was his responsibility, though it sounded as if it might have escaped to the great hunting ground in the sky. Probably gratefully.

'I'll take a gun out and look for birds,' he told his man-servant, a lugubrious man named Pole, who had been jettisoned from his brother's court because he knew far too much about the sexual proclivities of every courtier.

'Excellent,' Pole said, putting out a riding coat and breeches. 'Young Alfred could do with some fresh air. Mr Berwick is training him in service *à la française* and he's not taking to it easy-like. He will do to carry back the birds.'

'Right.'

'May I suggest that you ask the Honorable Buckingham Toloose to accompany you?' Pole said, placing a pair of clean stockings precisely parallel to the breeches.

'Who in the world is that?'

'He arrived yesterday, with a note from Queen Charlotte. You would have met him this evening, but I gather the meal will be *en famille*, given the imminent arrival of your nephew. So it would be polite to greet the gentleman now.'

'And he is of what sort?'

'I would suggest that he is of a proselytizing nature—'

'Oh no,' Gabriel said. 'My brother's court was overrun by religious types. I don't want any of those here. *You* don't want that, Pole. If I turn into my brother, you and the lion would be out in the cold.'

Pole smiled in a slightly detached way, as if he had been told a joke of extreme indelicacy. 'I have faith that Your Highness will not succumb to the delectations of a roving preacher, as did His Majesty Grand Duke Augustus. Mr Toloose proselytizes in a different arena. I have warned all the younger maids to stay away from the east wing. He has a quite amusing way about him; he was exerting it on the Princess Maria-Therese this morning, but I fancy she was unmoved.'

Gabriel brought to mind his beetle-browed, sixty-year-old aunt, as sturdy and ethical as a German-built boat. 'I fancy you're right about that,' he agreed. 'And what is Mr Toloose looking for in my household?'

'My guess would be that he is rusticating due to debts in London,' Pole observed. 'His stockings are quite interesting—a brilliant orange, with clocks—and his coat is worth more than a moderate-sized emerald.'

If Pole said that, it was true. Pole knew all about emeralds.

'All right,' Gabriel said. 'Tell Berwick I'm in the gun room and send a note to Toloose requesting his company. I believe my uncle might like to go as well.'

Down in the gun room, he set to polishing the barrel of his Haas. It was a lovely tool, one of the only air guns he'd seen with seven rifling grooves, allowing a man to switch in a moment from hunting deer to hunting pheasants.

The German hunting air gun was everything life wasn't: beautifully designed, spare, decorative. He didn't actually care to hunt anything other than game birds and rabbits. But that didn't mean he scorned the beauty of a Haas, its barrel etched with the coat of arms of the Duchy of Warl-Marburg-Baalsfeld.

His older brother's coat of arms, to be exact.

A pulse of relief, so old that it felt as familiar as his morning beard bristles, panged in the area of his heart. He'd decided years ago that it was far better to be a prince than a grand duke.

For all that Gabriel thought his older brother was a dried-up old stick, he felt sorry for him. It wasn't a pleasant task, ruling a small principality, especially given the three brothers who stood between Gabriel and Augustus, each of whom rather thought they'd like to have a crown as well.

And if not a crown, an heiress. He'd had a letter the other day implying that Rupert, the most handsome of his brothers, was toying with the sister of Napoleon.

His mouth tightened. If Augustus hadn't lost his mind a few months ago, Gabriel would be in Tunis this very moment, quarreling with his old professor Biggitstiff over excavation of the legendary city of Carthage.

He wouldn't be sitting in a damp castle in a puddle of summer rain, surrounded by elderly family members and debtridden courtiers . . . he'd be sweating in the sun, making sure the dig didn't turn into a greedy ransacking of history.

Gabriel looked down to discover that he was polishing the Haas's barrel so hard that he was likely to obliterate the duchy's coat of arms.

Damned Augustus and his damned ideas. Gabriel had been on the very eve of leaving for Tunis when his brother's religious fervor burst into flame, inspiring the Grand Duke to expel from his court everyone he considered corrupt, infirm, awkward, or mad.

In short, practically everyone, and all to save Augustus's selfrighteous little soul.

One by one, each of his elder brothers had refused to intercede, either because he was toadying up to Augustus or because (like Rupert) he just didn't give a damn.

Finally it was left to Gabriel. He could accept a god-forsaken castle in England, big enough to house all those deemed too imperfect to grace Augustus's court, or he could leave for Tunis and never look back.

Put Wick and Ferdinand and the pickle-eating dog and all the rest of them out of his mind.

He couldn't do it.

So . . . rain rather than blinding sun. A bride on her way from Russia, with a dowry to support the castle. And a castle full of miscreants and misfits, rather than an excavation site full of crumbled

47

rocks and bits of statuary that might, eons ago, have been the magnificent city of Carthage.

Not that he believed it was Carthage. He had wrangled his way into the excavation because he didn't believe in Dido, the famous Queen of Carthage, or even the existence of the city, for that matter. It was all a myth, made up by Virgil.

And now Biggitstiff was out there in Tunis chortling and labeling half the rocks in the countryside 'Carthage.' Hell, by now he'd probably identified Dido's supposed funeral pyre. The next step would be articles detailing his sloppy assumptions and sloppier fieldwork. Gabriel's jaw clenched at the thought.

But he had no choice, not really. He wasn't Augustus, with his religious principles unleavened by a sense of humor. He couldn't watch everyone he grew up with, from his cracked uncle to his father's jester (seventy-five, if he was a day), be thrown into the street because Augustus deemed them likely to tarnish his halo.

The only thing he could do was pray that Augustus's choice for his bride—probably pious and whiskered, as virtuous as she was virginal—had enough backbone to run the castle, so that he could leave for Carthage.

He didn't really care who she was, as long as she could manage the castle in his absence. Beddable would be nice; biddable was a necessity.

He bent back over the Haas.

Eight

After four hours in the carriage with Lord Dimsdale, Kate decided that the most interesting thing about Algernon was that he wore a corset. She'd never dreamed that men wore stays.

'They pinch me,' Algernon confided. 'But one must suffer to be elegant; that's what my valet says.'

Since Kate disliked suffering, she was very glad that the seamstresses had not had time to alter one of Victoria's traveling costumes to the point of elegant pinching. The one she was wearing bunched comfortably around the waist.

'The padding doesn't help,' Algernon said fretfully.

'What have you padded?' Kate asked, eyeing him. He swelled in the chest and shrank down at the waist so she had a good idea.

'Everyone's costumes are padded these days,' he said, avoiding the particulars. 'At any rate, I don't want you to think that I'd ordinarily discuss such a thing with you, except that you are my family. Well, almost my family. Do you mind if I begin calling you Victoria immediately? I'm not very good with names and I don't want to become confused in company.'

'Not at all,' Kate assured him. 'How does my sister address you?'

'Oh, as Algie,' he said, cheering up. 'You should as well. That's one of the things that I love about Victoria. She never stands on ceremony . . . she started calling me Algernon directly after she met me, and then she shortened it to Algie. That's how I

49

knew,' he added, somewhat mysteriously.

'Knew what?'

'Knew that she was the one for me. It was fated, really. We felt a wonderful closeness and we both knew.'

It was fated due to the lack of a governess, to Kate's mind. Victoria's charming intimacies—verbal and otherwise—were the result of inadequate guidance. She would even guess that Mariana had encouraged various improprieties.

Kate would rather slay herself than marry Algie, but she could see why Victoria adored him. He had a coziness, a kind of sweetness around his mouth and eyes that was a soothing antidote to Mariana's bitterness.

'I just wish we'd arrive at the castle,' he said tetchily. His collar was so high that it was chafing his ears, Kate noticed. She herself was lounging back on the padded carriage seat, so comfortable that she could hardly move. Normally by this time in the day she would have already been on a horse for hours.

'Are you worried about meeting your uncle?' she inquired.

'Why should I be? He comes from a little backwater, a principality they call it over there, but in England it wouldn't be more than a small county. Hardly a kingdom. I can't imagine why he has a title. It's absurd.'

'I believe there are many small principalities on the Continent,' Kate said, with a touch of doubt. Mariana didn't believe in taking a newspaper, and her schooling, such as it was, had come from filching books from her father's library, not that her stepmother had ever noticed their absence.

'I would just introduce you, and then we could leave in the morning, but the prince insisted that you attend his ball. Most clear, his letter was. I expect he's worried that he won't be able to fill the ballroom.' He eyed her. 'My mother suspects that he might be making a play for you.'

'Not for me,' Kate corrected him. 'For my half sister.'

'And isn't that a turn-up for the books,' Algie said gloomily. 'I must say that I thought the colonel existed. I couldn't believe it when Mrs Daltry told me the truth of it last night. You'd never know it from looking at her, would you? If my mother ever finds out, she'll explode.'

Kate thought that one *would* know it from looking at her stepmother, but she nodded, out of some vague sense of family loyalty. 'There's no reason your mother need ever discover the truth. I certainly won't tell anyone.'

'At any rate, I love Victoria, and I must marry her, and my mother wants me to have the prince's approval, and that's that.'

Kate gave Algie an approving pat on the knee. It must have been difficult to get so many thoughts in logical order and she certainly didn't want to ignore his accomplishment. It was interesting to see what a healthy fear he had of his mother; that might explain why Mariana's demand that he marry Victoria had instantly borne fruit.

'We should be entering his lands now,' Algie said. 'The man owns an awful amount of land in Lancashire, you know. My uncle thought it was an abomination, turning good English soil over to a foreigner. For all he went to Oxford and so on, the prince still has foreign blood.'

51

'As do you,' Kate pointed out. 'You are related to him through your mother, no?'

'Well, my mother . . .' Algie said, letting his voice trail off. Apparently he didn't consider her blood to carry the foreign taint. 'You know what I mean.'

'Have you ever met the prince?'

'Once or twice, when I was small. It's rubbish, his being my uncle. He's not that much older than I am: perhaps ten years or a bit more. So why should I be forced to parade my bride in front of him? It's not as if he's a king. He's just a spare prince.'

'It will be quickly over,' Kate said.

'He's desperate for funs, of course,' Algie reported. 'I heard that his betrothed is—'

But whatever bit of hearsay he was about to pass on was lost in a welter of noise. The coachman suddenly bellowed and pulled the carriage to the right; the wheels squealed as they careened across the road; the dogs lost their breath expressing their opinions. Mercifully the vehicle came to a stop without toppling over, and the second carriage (carrying trunks, Rosalie, and Algie's valet), managed to avoid bowling them over.

Algie pulled down his waistcoat, which had got rucked up in the disturbance. 'I'd better see what happened. This will take a man,' he said, looking not a day older than his eighteen years. 'You stay here where it's safe. I've no doubt but that we have a bit of trouble with the axle or some such.'

Kate gave him a moment to exit from the carriage and then straightened her traveling bonnet and followed him.

Outside, she found the groomsman soothing the horses, while Algie himself was bowing so deeply that she expected his ears to touch his knees.

52

A man who had to be the prince was seated on a great chestnut steed, and for a moment she could see only his dark silhouette against the sun. She had the confused impression of his motion and power, easily controlled: an aggressive body, with big shoulders and muscled thighs.

She raised her hand to her eyes to shade the sun just as he leaped from his horse. Dark hair swirled around his shoulders as if he were one of the actors who came through the village to play King Richard or Macbeth.

Her eyes adjusted and she changed that idea. He was no Macbeth . . . more the king of the fairies, Oberon himself, eyes at a slight, wicked tilt, with just a hint of the exotic. His 'foreign blood,' as Algie had it.

He had an accent, a delicious smoky accent that matched his eyes and his thick hair, and there was something else about him, something more *alive*, more powerful and arrogant than the pallid Englishmen she met every day.

She realized her mouth had fallen open, and snapped it shut. Thank goodness, he hadn't noticed her.

Groveling probably happened before the prince all the time. His Highness was nodding to Algie. His retinue had dismounted and were standing about him. The man to the left was precisely what Kate imagined courtiers should be, all curled and colorful like a peacock. There was even a boy in splendid red livery. Apparently they were out shooting, a royal shooting party.

Then he did notice her.

He surveyed her coolly, as if she were a milkmaid at the side of the road. There wasn't a

53

spark of interest in the man's eyes, just a haughty calculation, as if she'd offered to sell him milk and he found it curdled. As if he were mentally stripping off her too-large traveling costume and staring at the stockings rolled up inside Kate's corset.

She inclined her head a fraction of an inch. She'd be damned if she'd rush forward and curtsy, there in the dust and the road, to a prince whose self-importance mattered more than his manners.

He didn't react. Didn't nod, didn't smile, just looked away and turned back to his horse, swung onto the saddle, and rode away. His back was even larger than she'd at first thought, larger than the smithy's in the village, larger than . . .

She'd never met anyone so rude in her life, and that included the smithy, who was often drunk and so had an excuse.

Algie was snapping at the footman, telling him to open the carriage door and make it quick. 'Of course it wasn't the prince's fault that our horses were startled by his party,' he said. 'Now get us back on the road and be quick about it.'

'Caesar!' Kate called. The little dog was busy yapping at the heels of a horse who could brain him with one restless movement. 'Come!'

Algie motioned to a footman, but Kate stopped him. 'Caesar has to learn to obey,' she said, taking out her bag of cheese.

Freddie and Coco crowded against her skirts, acting like the ravenous little pigs they were. She gave them each a piece of cheese and a pat, and then all of a sudden Caesar realized what was going on. 'Come!' she called again.

He came, and she gave him a piece of cheese.

54

'Tedious business,' Algie remarked.

'Yes,' Kate agreed with a sigh.

'But they do seem to be less noisy. I'm afraid Victoria has too soft a nature. Just look what happened to her poor lip.'

Once they were seated Algie said, rather unnecessarily, 'That was my uncle. The prince.' His tone was reverent and hushed.

'He seemed princelike,' Kate agreed.

'Can you imagine what His Highness would make of Victoria's background?' He sounded horrified at the thought.

'I wonder what his bride will be like,' Kate said, again picturing the prince silhouetted against the sun. He was the sort of man who would marry a glimmering princess from a foreign land, a woman wrapped in ropes of pearls and diamonds.

'Russian women are dark-haired,' Algie said, trying to sound as if he knew what he was talking about. 'I might have introduced you, but I thought it was better that he not notice you until . . .' He waved a hand. 'You know, until you change.'

As far as Kate could tell, he hadn't minded a bit that Kate didn't look as pretty as Victoria—until now.

'I'm sorry,' she told him.

He focused, blinking a little. 'For what?'

'I'm not as much fun to have on your arm as Victoria. The prince would surely have noticed how beautiful she is.'

Algie was too young to dissemble. 'I do wish she were here,' he said. 'But it's probably better this way, because what if she saw him and she decided . . .' His voice trailed off.

'Victoria adores you,' Kate told him, feeling very

55

pleased with herself for suppressing an impulse to add 'more the fool she.' They were perfectly matched, Victoria and Algie: both fuzzy and sweet and awed by anyone with two thoughts to knock together. 'And remember, the prince would never in a million years marry someone like Victoria. I expect that he's too high in the instep for even a duke's daughter, let alone someone like my stepsister.'

Caesar growled out the window at a passing carriage. 'On the floor,' she said sternly, and he hopped down. But Freddie put his front paws on the seat and whined gently, so she let him jump up and sit next to her. He leaned his trembling little body against her and then collapsed, chin in her lap.

'I say, that's not fair,' Algie pointed out.

'Life isn't fair,' Kate said. 'Freddie is being rewarded for not barking.'

'He's brilliant,' Algie said, rather unexpectedly. Kate blinked down at Freddie, who was decidedly *not* brilliant.

'I mean the prince. My mother said that he actually took a degree at Oxford. I didn't even bother going to university. But he took a top degree in ancient history. Or something like that.'

The prince had not only arrogance and royal blood and a truly beautiful riding coat, but *brains*?

Not so likely. Weren't all those princes inbred? 'Likely they give every prince a top degree just for gracing the door of the university,' she pointed out. 'After all, what else could they say? "I do apologize, Your Highness, but you're as stupid as a hedgehog, and so we can't give you a degree"?'

As they trundled the last miles to the castle, she

carefully nurtured that sprig of disrespect for a man whose hair curled wildly around his shoulders, who spent his time careening about accompanied by scented courtiers, and who didn't bother to greet her.

He counted her beneath his notice, which was humiliating but not exactly unexpected. She *was* beneath his notice.

In fact, thinking about the way he looked at her was almost amusing, in retrospect. She just had to get through the next few days. Then she could take all her newly altered clothing and go to London and find just the sort of man she wanted.

She could see him in her mind's eye. She didn't want a man like that prince; what she wanted was someone more like Squire Mamluks, whose property ran close by Yarrow House. He was a sweet man who doted on his wife. They had nine children. That's what she wanted. Someone straight and true, decent, and kind to the bone.

The very thought made her smile, which caught Algie's attention. 'Did you see the waistcoat Mr Toloose was wearing? He was the tall one, with the striped costume.' Obviously Algie had been experiencing some anxiety.

'Yours is very nice,' she assured him.

Algie looked down at his padded chest. 'I thought so, I mean, I do think so. But that waistcoat . . .'

They had both found something to desire.

Nine

Kate didn't know much about castles; she had only seen engravings in one of her father's books. She had thought Pomeroy Castle would have airy flounces and furbelows, slender turrets, a pile of rose-colored brick in the setting sun.

Instead it was four-square and masculine, with the aggressive look of a military fortress. The two turrets were round and squat. There was nothing lyrical about it. It bristled, its walls thick and bossy, like a stout watchman with someone to scold.

The carriage trolled down a gravel drive, through the stone archway and into a courtyard. The door to the carriage swung open and Kate stepped down, taking the hand of one of Mariana's groomsmen, to find that the courtyard was so crowded with people that she was tempted to turn and peer under the carriage to see if they had accidentally run someone over.

A confused stream of persons was clattering in every direction, heading for arched passages on all sides. As she watched, a donkey cart piled with sacks of laundry narrowly avoided a man holding a stick, from which hung at least ten fish, bound for the kitchens, no doubt. He was followed by a man carrying a crate of live chickens, their heads poking between the slats. Two boys were carrying bunches of roses bigger than their heads, and narrowly missed being drenched as a maid tossed out what one could only hope was nothing worse than dirty water.

Castle footmen, dressed in elegant, somber

livery, quickly ushered them over the flagstones and through a second archway, into a second courtyard . . . where everything was transformed. Here was a quiet, beautiful space, as if the castle fiercely repelled those outside the walls, but celebrated its own occupants.

The last rays of the sun caught Kate's eyes and dazzled them, making the windows look like molten gold, and the people strolling through the inner courtyard like denizens of the French court: beautiful, relaxed, noble.

The castle was sober outside, and drunk on champagne inside.

She felt a flash of pure fear. What on earth was she doing, descending from a carriage in an ill-fitting traveling costume, pretending to be—

She glanced at Algie and saw the tight anxiety in his eyes and knew that he didn't belong here either: that this gathering of people shouting at one another in French and German, so carefully elegant and carelessly beautiful, was more than he had experienced before.

And he was her family, or he soon would be. 'You look splendid,' she said warmly. 'Just look how unfashionably that gentleman is dressed!'

In fact, she had no real idea what was fashionable and what wasn't, but it was a fair bet. The man in question had almost no collar at all, whereas Algie had three.

He followed her gaze and immediately brightened up. 'Dear me, just look at those buttons,' he remarked.

They were greeted by a Mr Berwick, who introduced himself as the majordomo of the castle. He announced that he would personally escort

Kate, trailing Rosalie, to a bedchamber in the west wing, and sent Algie and his man off in the charge of a footman.

They walked through long, quiet corridors illuminated by the deep eyes of slitted windows open to the outside air, and then through a room hung with a worn tapestry depicting two knights on horseback.

It all fascinated Kate. How did one keep the castle warm in the winter, when most of the outside windows seemed to have no glass? And what happened when rain drove through those narrow slits, as it sometimes must? She paused for a moment and peered through one of the little openings onto the courtyard. She found, to her delight, clever gutters built to drain away water. The wall was extraordinarily thick, at least the length of her arm.

Berwick had waited for her. 'I was just investigating the gutters,' she told him.

'The windows are slanted to reduce wind pressure,' he told her, setting out again. 'The west wing is just ahead. This is the main gallery. All chambers in this wing lead from this hall; yours is the second from the end on the left. I have given you a room facing the courtyard, as even in this clement weather, those facing the outside can be a trifle chilly at night.'

The gallery was punctuated at regular intervals by doors, on either side of which sprouted pilasters. After one glance, Kate broke out laughing; at the top of each pilaster was a cherub, a frivolous, laughing cherub. And they were all different. On one side of her door was a naughty child with flower petals in his hair, and on the other, an irritable little priest with starched wings instead of a neck cloth.

Kate stood in the middle of the corridor, turning around to make sure that she saw every one. Finally she glanced down again to see Berwick patiently waiting, not in the least annoyed.

'How on earth did this come about?' she asked.

'As I understand it, a young son of the Pomeroy family traveled in the 1500s to Italy and found himself enamored of Italian sculptors. So he stole one and brought the poor man here. The sculptor was so irritated by his kidnapping that he turned everyone in the household into a cherub, and when he was finished, escaped in a butter churn and was never heard from again.'

'He absconded with a sculptor?' Kate asked, fascinated.

Berwick nodded. 'This is your chamber, Miss Daltry. Please do not hesitate to ring if there is anything we can do to further your comfort.' And he showed them where the bell cord was to summon Rosalie, and how the tin bath was cleverly secreted under the tall bed.

He cast one look around the room, frowned at a vase of roses as if warning them not to droop, and took himself off.

'Oh miss,' Rosalie said, 'didn't it take us an hour to walk here, then? And that cold stone went straight through my slippers. My, but I'd hate to live here.'

'Really?' Kate said. 'But it's so interesting. Like living in a fairy tale.'

'Not a fairy tale I'd like,' Rosalie said. 'The place must be horribly damp in the winter; just feel the stone over by the window. Ugh. And I expect it smells when it rains too. I prefer Yarrow House, with nice wood paneling to keep a body warm, and a proper water closet. I do love a water closet.'

'But this is the kind of place that people committed crimes to build,' Kate said, rather dreamily. 'I wonder what the Pomeroy family was like. From what I saw of one portrait we passed, the men had long upper lips and hawk noses. Perhaps he was the one who stole the Italian sculptor.'

'That's not a nice thing to do,' Rosalie stated. 'Though I did see an Italian at the fair once that was so small he would probably fit in a butter churn easy-like. When do you suppose those footmen will be bringing up your trunks, then? I'll say this, the room has wardrobes enough for Miss Victoria's garments, and that's handy.'

Berwick was nothing if not efficient; there was a brisk rap on the door and in came a string of footmen carrying the trunks, as well as cans of hot water ready to be poured into the tin bath.

A few minutes later, Kate settled into that bath with a sigh of pure joy. All in all, she'd done less so far that day than she had for years, since her position was not the sort that allowed one to relax of a Sunday—or even Christmas Day, for that matter. But somehow it was as exhausting to travel in a coach as it was to ride a horse.

'I don't wish to hurry you, Miss Katherine,' Rosalie said after a time. 'But Mr Berwick said that once the bell rings, you must make your way down all those stairs to the silver drawing room, wherever that is, though I believe he left a footman to guide your way. Still, I'm worried about the fit of this gown.'

So Kate reluctantly climbed from her bath, though she wouldn't allow Rosalie to dry her.

'I'm not a child in the nursery,' she said, positively wrestling the maid for the toweling cloth. 'I'll do it myself.'

'It isn't proper,' Rosalie said, yielding.

'Why on earth not?' Kate demanded. 'Why shouldn't a lady dry her own body? If you ask me, the impropriety is in having someone touching you all over.'

'You'll just have to accept it,' Rosalie said. 'Ladies don't towel themselves. Not ever.'

'Lord almighty,' Kate said with a sigh. 'I suppose it's too late for me to try to become a lady. It would take a magic wand at this point.'

'You *are* a lady,' Rosalie said stoutly. 'It's in your blood.' She braided Kate's hair and pinned on a frizzled wig in a delicate shade of violet, with a jeweled comb to hold it in place.

Her gown was cream-colored and sewn all over with pearl embroidery. Rosalie had stitched pockets into the bosom and filled them with mounded wax, so Kate looked miraculously endowed in the front.

'It's not terrible,' Kate said, viewing herself in the glass.

'How can you say that?' Rosalie demanded. 'You look wonderful, miss. Just beautiful!'

Kate turned to the side. The gown was caught up under her jutting (wax) breasts and the cloth fell lightly to the ground, with just the tips of her slippers showing. They too were embroidered with pearls.

'I'd put you in a pair of glass slippers,' Rosalie said, almost to herself, 'but they're only good for one night, and it's just a family dinner. They won't be inspecting your toes.'

Kate turned herself square to the glass and

forced herself to look critically. 'I look like my stepmother,' she said finally.

'You don't!'

'I look as if I'm trying to be young. Virginal.'

'Well, but you—' Rosalie stopped. 'You're no old biddy, miss! You should be—'

'No,' Kate said flatly. 'I look as if I'm past my first blush, which I am. I don't even mind that, but I don't want to look as if I'm pretending. Do you see what I mean, Rosalie? The way my stepmother pretends to be thirty.'

'You make yourself sound haggish!' Rosalie protested. 'You've no more than what, twenty years?'

'Twenty-three,' Kate said. 'And I'm tired. I suppose there are some twenty-three-year-olds who would carry this off with aplomb, but I'm not one of them. I look . . . wrong.'

'Well, miss,' Rosalie said, 'one of the seamstresses spent four hours altering that gown, and I shaped the wax inserts myself, and that's what you're wearing.'

Kate gave her a swift hug. 'I'm being a beast, and I apologize. It doesn't matter anyway, does it? I just need to simper at the prince, so that he will approve Victoria's wedding.'

'And go to the ball,' Rosalie said. 'I brought three ball gowns, but I hadn't yet—'

'We'll discuss that when the time comes,' Kate said firmly. She'd already made up her mind there would be no wax breasts at the ball. But why give Rosalie a sleepless night worrying over it?

Ten

'I saw Dimsdale's Golden Fleece this afternoon,' Gabriel told Wick just before the evening meal, 'and we can forget the idea of trading my Cossack Fleece for his English one.'

'Really?' His majordomo cocked an eyebrow. 'After meeting your esteemed relative, I cannot help but think that the young lady may succumb to your charms, impoverished though they are.'

Gabriel gave him a wry smile. 'I'm not that desperate. My uncle nearly ran down their carriage because he thought he heard his dog barking. The yapping came from a pack of mongrels the size of fleas. And the Fleece was as unattractive as her dogs: overdressed, overly bold with her eyes, and overly gaunt. I have minimal standards, but I have them.'

'I like her,' Wick said thoughtfully. 'And she has only three dogs.'

'They're the kind that spin in circles and bite their own tails. Which is what I would do if I had to spend much time with her. She looked at me as if I were a disreputable banker. I think she didn't like my hair.'

Wick grinned. 'Now we're getting somewhere. Disapproved of you, did she?'

'Soundly.'

'Well, you'll have to get through dinner with her, because I've put her at your right and I'm not switching places at this point. I have you dining in the morning room and the rest of the horde in the dining room proper. There are more arriving

65

tomorrow, so I'll have to switch to the great hall for meals.'

'You don't mind all of this, do you?' Gabriel asked, looking at the boy he'd known his whole life, now grown to a man.

'I was made for it.'

'Well, I'm glad I got a castle for you to muck about in.'

'You should be glad for yourself,' Wick pointed out.

'I'm not,' Gabriel said. 'But I have a brotherly pride in the fact I spared Augustus the sight of you.'

'Not very nice of the Grand Duke,' Wick said, pouring himself a small glass of brandy and tossing it back. 'Throwing out his own brothers like that.'

'Augustus would prefer to forget that our father left quite so many counterfeit coins with his own face around Marburg.'

'I don't look like Augustus,' Wick said, revolted.

'That's because he resembles my mother, whereas the two of us take after the old devil himself.'

Wick's mother was a laundress, and Gabriel's a Grand Duchess, but the distinction never bothered either of them much. They were born mere days apart, and their father had promptly brought Wick into the nursery to be raised with his legitimate children, not to mention a pack of other assorted half siblings.

'He was a ripe one,' Wick said. 'I always liked our papa.'

'Did we see him enough to judge?' Gabriel asked. 'Here, give me some of that brandy.'

Wick handed over a glass. 'We saw him the right amount, I'd say. Look what happened to Augustus,

66

after he had to spend every day with him.'

It was true. Gabriel and Wick shared a bone-deep conviction that being the last son and an illegitimate son were far better fates than anything closer to the crown.

'I know why you're brooding over Dimsdale's fiancée,' Wick said. 'It's because you're nervous about the impending arrival of your own.'

'She's got the look of a shrew,' Gabriel said. 'I'll admit, it gave me a qualm about Tatiana.'

'I know,' Wick said, 'you want beddable and biddable.'

'It's not as if you're looking for anything different,' Gabriel said, stung by something in Wick's voice.

'I'm not looking for a wife at all,' Wick said. 'But if I were, I wouldn't want biddable.'

'Why?'

'I'm easily bored.'

'I wouldn't mind a bit of shrewishness,' Gabriel said. 'But the Fleece has no figure. I could tell, even though she was bundled in a shaggy traveling costume. She doesn't look as if she'd be fun.'

'Wives aren't supposed to be fun,' Wick said, putting down his glass and straightening his neck cloth. 'Time to go down and jockey everyone into the proper places. The cook that we brought over is threatening to leave. Plus I had to hire three more downstairs maids. Thank God your bride is on the way; I don't think we can afford another such event.'

'We've got enough money without her,' Gabriel said, stung.

'More or less. I have a bad feeling that repairs to this castle won't come cheap.'

After Wick left, Gabriel sat for a while, staring at his desk. It was inestimably better in England than in Marburg. There he was in constant danger of being dragged into some sort of political intrigue, or any of the other military frivolities that kept his brothers' eyes bright and shining.

It was wonderful to own a castle. It really was.

Without really noticing, he pulled over the copy of *Ionian Antiquities* that had arrived two days before and started reading it. Again. Which was foolish because he had the whole issue memorized.

Of course he couldn't run off to Tunis. He tried to wrench his mind back to the present. He had to go to his chambers and submit to Pole's ministrations, put on an evening coat, and greet his absurd nephew. He should be *happy* to have an estate, and be able to house the menagerie, and his uncle, aunts, illegitimate half brother, the court jester . . .

If only he could stop dreaming of being in the heat of Tunis, finding out for himself whether that dig truly held the remains of Dido's city. He had loved the story of Carthage as a schoolboy, caught by the determination of Aeneas sailing away to found Rome, leaving Dido behind, and then living with guilt after she threw herself on a funeral pyre.

Ionian Antiquities would publish again in a mere . . . in a mere twenty-three days.

He got up with a sigh.

Time for dinner.

Eleven

'We're eating with the family,' Algie said nervously.
' "In family" they call it.'

'*En famille,*' Kate corrected him.

'I suppose that's the language they speak over in Marburg. I probably won't understand a word.'

'Actually, that's French,' Kate said.

'French? I learned that at Eton.' There was a pause. 'More or less . . . do you suppose that's what they speak at the table?'

'I shall translate, if need be,' Kate told him, thinking that it was a good thing she had come rather than Victoria, who didn't speak a word of French. Thankfully, she herself had learned the language before her father died. 'Do you know anything of the prince's entourage?'

But Algie knew nothing of his mother's family and had never, it seemed, bothered to inquire.

The meal was served in a delightful room that, although Berwick referred to it as the 'small morning room,' was bigger than any single chamber at Yarrow House.

The prince himself sat at the head of the table, of course. He was wearing a midnight-blue evening coat over a violet waistcoat with gold buttons. In fact, her wig and his waistcoat would go very well together. All in all, he looked magnificent and outrageously expensive. And bored.

She wouldn't have minded watching him from afar, but in fact, Kate was rather horrified to find herself seated at the prince's right hand. She sat down in a haze of embarrassment, acutely conscious

69

of her diamond necklace and diamond-encrusted comb. She was tarted up like the daughter of a rich cit, thrusting herself into company in the hopes of a wealthy husband.

Which, she reminded herself, I am not. My father was the younger son of an earl. An *earl*. And never mind the fact that her father had died without leaving her a dowry, or that he had married a woman of ill repute, or that . . .

Or all the other ways in which her father had disappointed her. Blood is blood. I am an earl's granddaughter, she told herself.

With that, she raised her chin and straightened her shoulders. The prince was talking to a stout lady on his left, who was discoursing with deep earnestness on . . . something. Kate listened hard, only to realize that the lady was speaking German, and he was responding in French. The gentleman to her right was occupied, so she nibbled her fish and listened to the prince's French replies.

The lady said something; the prince characterized her comment as a wild guess. The lady replied; the prince broke into German, so Kate watched him under her eyelashes, since she couldn't understand enough to eavesdrop.

The first thing one noticed about him was that he was a prince. That was stamped on his face. She couldn't call it simple arrogance, though he was certainly arrogant enough, she thought, cataloguing the harsh line of his jaw.

She thought it had more to do with the way that he looked so easily commanding, as if he'd never seen anything in the world that he couldn't have for the asking. She considered it for a moment. A prince would never have done any of the things she had found herself doing in the past years. The time she'd helped with the birth of a calf came to mind as a particularly odiferous and unpleasant chore.

A prince would not have three small dogs locked up in her chamber at this very moment.

A prince . . .

She took another bite of fish.

'What are you thinking about?'

His voice was like velvet, accented and deep.

'I am contemplating the fish,' Kate told him, dishonestly.

And he knew it. There was a devil in those eyes, and they registered her fib. 'I would guess,' said he, 'that you are thinking of me.'

Everything English in her rose up in protest at his effrontery, at the nerve of him saying such a thing.

'If it will make you happy,' she said sweetly, 'I was indeed.'

'Now you sound like my majordomo.'

'Ah, Berwick is English, is he?'

That caught his interest. 'As it happens, Berwick grew up with me and I've known him my whole life. But what would it mean if he were English?'

Kate shrugged. 'We never ask people if they are thinking of us.'

'Why not? Since you are unable to inquire, I was thinking of you.'

'Really.' Kate gave the word all the coolness with which she addressed the baker after he overcharged for loaves of bread.

'Your wig,' he said, with another one of those wicked, sideways smiles. 'I've never seen a purple wig before.'

'You must not often travel to London,' she told

him. 'Or Paris. Tinted wigs are all the fashion.'

'I think I would prefer you without a wig.'

Kate told herself to be quiet, but she simply couldn't. 'I can't imagine why you think that your preferences are of any interest when it comes to my hairstyle. That would be as odd as you assuming that I have interest in *your* hair.'

'Do you?'

The effrontery of the man knew no bounds! Kate felt all the irritation of the dispossessed. Just because he was a prince, he apparently assumed that everyone was fascinated by him.

'No,' she said flatly. 'Your hair is just—hair.' She glanced at it. 'Rather unkempt and slightly long, but one must make allowances for a man who clearly has no interest in fashion, and does not travel to London.'

He laughed, and even his laugh had a slightly exotic sound, like his accent. 'I had the impression on our first meeting that you disapproved of it. Having exhausted the subject of our respective hair, Miss Daltry, may I inquire how you are finding Lancashire?'

'It seems quite lovely,' Kate said. And then, before she stopped herself, she asked, 'How is it different from your home in Marburg?'

Of course, he smiled. She'd done the expected and turned the conversation to himself. She let a shadow of contempt steal into her eyes, though she doubted he would even catch it. Men like that didn't recognize scorn directed toward themselves.

'It's much greener here,' he said. 'It occurred to me while I was out riding that the English countryside is the opposite of the English people, really.'

72

'How so?' Someone had taken her fish while she wasn't looking and replaced it with another plate, which made her suspect that this was one of those dinners she had only read about, with twenty-four removes, and fifteen sweet things to finish. A royal table indeed.

'The English are so restrained in their fertility,' he said, smiling at her. 'Whereas the plants are all bursting with reproductive fervor.'

Kate's mouth fell open. 'You—you shouldn't speak of such things with me.'

'What an instructive conversation this is for me. Apparently nature falls into the same category as hair: not to be discussed at mealtimes in England.'

'*Do* you discuss fertility with young ladies in Marburg?' she asked, keeping her voice rather low in case the sturdy dowager across from her caught the question.

'Oh, all sorts of fertility,' he said. 'A court simply bubbles with passion, you know. Most of it of a very short nature, but all the more intense for its brevity. Though not my brother's court, at the moment.'

Despite herself, Kate was fascinated. 'Why on earth not? Has the Grand Duke suppressed his court somehow? You seem so—' She caught herself once again. It wasn't for her to characterize men of his stripe.

'How I'd love to know what I seem to be. But fearing you will cut me off, I'll just say that last year my brother welcomed a desperately pious preacher to the court, and within a matter of a week or two, the man had convinced most of the court to give up any frolicking not approved by the church.'

'I suppose you were the exception,' she said. And then realized she'd given him an opportunity to talk about himself *again*. It must be a gift given to princes: to draw all conversation into their own orbit.

'I turned out to be impervious to Friar Prance's rhetoric,' he said, grinning. 'It was rather unfortunate, particularly when it became clear that my brother Augustus thought that the friar's ideas were, shall we say, divinely inspired.'

'What precisely did Friar Prance recommend in place of frolicking?'

'He was particularly disturbed by what he called "smock treason," which was essentially anything that women and men might choose to do together. So he established a board in the drawing room with a sort of point system. The reward, naturally enough, was life everlasting.'

Kate thought about that as she ate her venison. 'I've heard rhetoric of that sort from the pulpit.'

'Yes, but priests tend to be so vague . . . a reference here or there to Pearly Gates and perhaps clouds. Friar Prance had the courage of his convictions; his promises were quite explicit. Furthermore, his point system allowed one to earn little rewards for memorizing parts of the Bible.'

'And those awards would be?'

'The right to wear robes of spun silver rather than plain white was a particular favorite among the ladies. In fact, the question of fashion was an irresistible temptation for those who might otherwise be inclined to disbelief. It became quite a competition around the court, only exacerbated when he agreed to give extra points to those who recited their verses in public.'

'I'm training my dogs with a system quite like that,' Kate said. 'Of course I'm using cheese instead of heaven as the ultimate reward, but for them, it's likely the same thing.'

'Well, that's probably why I was such a failure. I dislike cheese.'

Back to himself, Kate thought. She ate another bite rather than return to his favorite subject.

'Aren't you curious about my particular failures?' he persisted.

'I haven't got all night,' she said, favoring him with a smile. 'If you wouldn't mind terribly, I'd rather hear more about your brother's court. Did everyone eagerly submit to the system?'

'They tried, after Augustus indicated a keen interest. That's the nature of a court.'

'It sounds tiresome.'

'Augustus's newly acquired piety was a blow, I'll admit. But you see how well it turned out: He pitched everyone out of his court who couldn't drum up the necessary enthusiasm for the scheme, and that's how I ended up here.'

'Does your court operate on the same principle?'

'Mine? I don't have a court.'

She looked around. 'Tall stone walls, and tapestries that must go back to the days of Queen Elizabeth herself. Lovely courtyard. Loads of servants. Why, I do believe I'm in a castle!' Considering her point made, she smiled at the footman standing to her right. 'Yes, I am finished with this venison, thank you.'

'A castle is not the same thing as a court,' the prince said.

'Dear me, *Your Highness*,' she said sweetly. 'Of course you're right, *Your Highness*.' It was actually quite fun to see his jaw go a little rigid. The poor prince . . . obviously so used to people kissing his

75

toes that he couldn't even be playful.

'A court serves a useful purpose,' he pointed out. 'The king or grand duke, as in my brother's case, rules his lands. I rule no one, Miss Daltry. Therefore, this is no court.'

'Then you are doubly lucky. You needn't worry at all about whether you are useful or not,' she replied.

'I suppose you would say that I am not?'

'You yourself said that you were a prince without subjects. Of course you are not useful, but that is hardly your failure. It's a matter of birth, and your birth, Your Highness, means that you need never be useful. Or question the market value of anything, which I would consider an even better inheritance.'

'You believe a prince is someone who knows the price of nothing?' There was something in his smile, something a little dark and sardonic that made Kate suddenly wonder if she was over her head, being too clever.

'I expect,' she said more delicately, 'that you know the value of a great many things, if not their prices.'

He stared at her for a moment, and then leaned just a trifle closer. 'I did hear somewhere that the price of a woman, my dear Miss Daltry, is above that of rubies. Or was that the price of a *good* woman? How unfortunate that Friar Prance is not here to settle the question.'

'It was indeed a good woman,' she told him.

The prince smiled at her, the calculated, tigerish smile that he probably used to seduce wayward ladies. 'And are you a good woman?'

She returned the favor, giving him the gentle

76

smile one gives to a deluded infant. And in case he
didn't entirely understand, she patted his arm. 'If
you don't mind a word of advice, one never asks
a lady to set her own price. If you have to ask, the
answer will always be more than you can afford.'

The elderly man on her right turned his head
at that moment. 'Do tell me more about your war
museum,' Kate said to him. 'I've always thought
that milk bottles were remarkably versatile. No, no,
you're not interrupting anything. His Highness and
I are boring each other silly.'

Gabriel felt like laughing aloud as he blinked
at the back of Miss Daltry's head. It served him
right for jumping to the conclusion that all women
wanted to be princesses. Or that any Englishwoman
would like him simply because he *was* a prince.

This Englishwoman had decided within seconds
that he was a self-important ass. He'd seen it in her
eyes, in the way she looked down her straight little
nose.

Perhaps her nose was a little too long. Wasn't
Dimsdale's fiancée supposed to be a raving beauty?
He didn't think she was. There were dark blue
shadows under her eyes, for one thing. Beauties
were supposed to have glowing skin the color of
peach blossoms.

A lady of the court would have plucked her
eyebrows to high, airy peaks . . . hers slashed
over her eyes, giving them punctuation. Rather
extraordinary eyes, he had to say. They suited that
foolish purple wig of hers.

Another question: What color was her hair under
that wig? Her eyebrows suggested a warm brown,
perhaps a chestnut brown. Perhaps she had one
of those short cuts that he hated, but could quite

imagine on her. It would highlight her cheekbones and—

He realized his aunt was clearing her throat ominously. What on earth was he doing? Likely Wick was right, and he was obsessing over his nephew's betrothed simply out of dread of his own.

Tatiana probably had a perfect short nose. And sweet eyes that would look at him with approval.

The thought came into his head, willy-nilly: Miss Daltry was the epitome of *beddable*.

But biddable?

He turned to his aunt with a lavish smile.

Never.

Twelve

'Do you truly plan to go to bed?' Algie inquired, when the party had finally moved to a drawing room. 'I know that you haven't been out much, but it's outrageously early.'

Not been out much was a nice way of summing up Kate's life in Mariana's house. 'You stay here,' she told him. 'The less I'm in company, the better. Apparently Mr Toloose met Victoria last spring. We were lucky that he wasn't offended when I accidentally snubbed him a minute ago.'

Algie shrugged. 'You should smile at everyone, just to be sure. The important thing is that the prince seems reasonably pleased with you. Who would have thought that so many people would be here? Lord Hinkle just told me that the *ton* is dying of curiosity about my uncle.'

The way he said *my uncle* was entirely different

78

now that he'd met the man in question. Kate had the definite impression that Algie would be dining out for years to come on his relationship to royalty.

'I'll see you tomorrow morning,' she told him, turning toward the door of the drawing room. The room was thronged now, and the air filled with the clamor of fifteen simultaneous conversations. Kate was almost at the door when an extraordinary woman blocked her path.

She was probably forty years old, and stunning in an opulent, deluxe sort of way. Unlike most of the women in the room, she hadn't shorn her hair; instead, she'd piled it on top of her head and then powdered it strawberry color. It clashed madly with her dark blue eyes, but, somehow, the effect was marvelous.

'You!' she said.

Kate was trying to slide sideways, but at this command she stopped.

'I know you.'

She could hardly say, 'You must know my sister,' so she plastered on a rather mad smile and said, 'Oh! Of course, how are you?'

'Not know you that way,' the woman said impatiently, waving a jeweled fan in the air. 'Now who are you? Who are you?'

Kate curtsied. 'I'm Miss—'

'Of course! You're the spitting image of Victor. Devil's spawn that he was.' But she said it affectionately. 'You've his nose and his eyes.'

'You knew my father,' Kate said, stammering a bit.

'*Quite* well,' the woman said, grinning. It was the sort of grin one didn't expect from a lady so obviously well-born. 'And your name is Katherine.

79

How do I know that, you might ask?'

Kate suddenly realized with a pulse of alarm that anyone might overhear the conversation. 'Actually—' she began, but was interrupted.

'Because I'm your godmother, that's why! My goodness, it's been forever. Appalling how the years go by. You were just a wee thing last I saw you, all plump cheeks and big ears.' She peered closer. 'Look at you now. Just like your father, though that wig does nothing for you, darling, if you don't mind my saying so. You're lucky enough to have his eyes; for God's sake don't pair them with a purple wig.'

Kate felt a little flush rising up her neck, but her godmother—*her godmother?*—wasn't done surveying her. 'And that padding in front isn't doing you any favors either. There's too much of it. It looks like you've got two pudding bags suspended from your neck.'

The flush was up to her ears. 'I'm just retiring for the night,' Kate said, dropping another curtsy. 'If you'll forgive me.'

'Offended you, have I? You're looking a bit feverish. Now that was one thing that Victor had control of: his temper. Didn't control anything else, but I never saw him blow his dickey, even when he was three sheets to the wind.'

Kate blinked. *Blow his—*

'Offended you again,' her godmother said with satisfaction. 'Come along, then. We'll go to my chambers. The butler put me in one of the towers, and it's utterly heavenly, like being stuck in the clouds except for the pigeons crapping on the windows.'

'But—I don't—what is your name?' Kate finally asked.

She raised one perfectly shaped eyebrow. 'Didn't your father ever tell you about me?'

'I'm afraid that he died before he had a chance.'

'The old sod,' she said. 'He swore that he'd tell you all about me. I'll give you the story, but not here. This castle is crammed with people longing for gossip and making it up as fast as they can. No need to feed the blaze.'

Kate held her ground. 'And you are?'

'Lady Wrothe, though you might as well call me Henry, which is short for Henrietta. Leominster, my husband, is over there getting drunk with the Prince of Württemberg. Poor Leo simply can't bear to let a glass of brandy pass him by.' She reached out and took hold of Kate's wrist. 'That's enough of an introduction; let's go.'

She towed Kate up stairs, through corridors, up more stairs, and finally into her chamber, pushed her onto the bed, and plucked off her wig. 'You've got Victor's hair. You're a beauty, then, aren't you?'

Kate felt as if a whirlwind had come out of nowhere, picked her up, and deposited her in the tower room. 'Did you know my father well?'

'I almost married him,' Lady Wrothe said promptly. 'Except that he never asked me. I still remember meeting your father for the first time. It was at the Fortune Theater, during an interval of *Othello*. I knew instantly that I'd love to play Desdemona to his Moor.'

'Was my mother there?' Kate asked, feeling a surge of loyalty for her poor mother, who appeared to have been overlooked not only by Mariana, but by Lady Wrothe as well.

'No, no, he hadn't met her yet.'

'Oh,' Kate said, feeling better.

'We had the most delicious flirtation,' Lady Wrothe said, looking a bit dreamy. 'But your mother already had her eye on him, and within a few months her father—your grandfather—had reeled Victor in like a half-dead trout. Victor was fantastically poor,' she explained.

'Oh,' Kate said again.

'Luckily for him, he was a handsome beast of a man, all that dark buttery hair and your eyes, and then the cheekbones . . . if things had been different, I would have married him in a moment.'

Kate nodded.

'Of course, he would have been unfaithful to me and then I'd have shot him in a private area,' Lady Wrothe said thoughtfully, 'so it's just as well.'

A giggle escaped Kate's mouth. It was wrong to laugh, just wrong, when she was listening to tales of her father's rampant infidelity.

'He just couldn't help it. Some men are like that. I suppose you've met the prince? He's one of them. No woman will be able to keep that man at home, and though they're delightful to play with, it's best to avoid them. I've been married three times, darling, so I know.'

'So my godfather must be dead,' Kate said. 'I'm sorry for your loss.'

'It was a long time ago,' Lady Wrothe said. Then she gave Kate a lopsided, secret smile. 'Your father and I—he—'

'You had an *affaire*,' Kate said, resigned.

'Oh no. Perhaps it would have been better for both of us if we had. We were young and foolish when we met, which meant that it was all talk of love and roses, rather than beds. And Victor couldn't marry me because my dowry wasn't large enough.'

The more she learned of her father, the less she liked what she heard.

'Classic Romeo and Juliet,' Lady Wrothe said, 'but without all the stabbing and poison, thank you very much. Instead your father simply married your mother, and that was the end of it.'

'Did you know her as well?'

Lady Wrothe sat down at the stool before her dressing table, so Kate couldn't see her eyes. 'Your mother hadn't been strong enough to have a proper season, so I didn't meet her until your baptism.'

'I have wondered how my mother and father managed to meet, since my mother was so frequently abed,' Kate admitted.

'Oh, they didn't. She saw him passing in Hyde Park, and inquired about his name. From there, her father took over.'

Kate felt even more depressed at that revelation.

'And of course I married as well,' Lady Wrothe said, swinging around to face Kate again. 'You mustn't think it was all sackcloth and ashes. I fell in love with my husband and I daresay Victor did the same with your mother. Over the years we saw each other occasionally. *Not*, I hasten to add, in any sort of clandestine fashion.'

Kate nodded.

'A few years later, I found myself dancing with him at Vauxhall. I had just lost another child; I was never able to carry a babe. I wept all over his shoulder.'

Kate would have patted her hand, but somehow Lady Wrothe was not the sort of woman one consoled in that fashion.

'Next thing I knew, Victor had wrangled it so that I and my first husband were your godparents.'

Kate smiled weakly.

'I wanted to kill him. Oh, we did the ceremony, of course. How could we not? But I was so angry at his blindness, thinking that godmothering his child with your mother would somehow make up for my own lost children. *His* child of all people!'

'My father was not very perceptive,' Kate said, remembering how cheerfully he had told her that he was bringing home a stepmother, at a time when she was still grieving her mother's death. 'But surely he was well-meaning?'

'Of course . . . but at the time I was so heartsick about losing another babe that I couldn't see it. I'm afraid that I put you out of my mind after the ceremony. In fact, in a fit of pure spleen, I pretended you didn't exist. But here you are!'

Which reminded Kate. 'I'm not actually here as myself,' she confessed.

'Really?' Lady Wrothe glanced at her reflection and then powdered her nose reflectively. 'I wish I weren't, too. Sometimes I get so tired of Leo. I'd love to be someone else, although if it meant I had to wear a purple wig, I might rethink it.'

'The purple wig is part of it,' Kate said. 'I'm here as my half sister, Victoria, who . . .' and she blurted out the whole story, largely because Lady Wrothe didn't look in the least sympathetic, but just kept nodding and saying things like 'Victor, what a loose fish,' in a tone that didn't seem judgmental, just definitive.

She neatly summed up the situation. 'So at the moment you're playing Victoria, who's betrothed to a fatheaded man named Algernon, who's dragged

84

you here because he needs the prince's blessing for the wedding that has to happen because Victoria is as much of a light frigate as her mother.'

'That makes her sound like a trollop,' Kate protested. 'She's not, she's just in love.'

'In love,' Lady Wrothe said moodily. 'For God's sake, don't ever fall in love before you get married. It's just too messy and leads to appalling consequences. The only time I ever fell in love out of wedlock was with your papa, and that's because I couldn't stop myself, though I fought it tooth and nail.'

Kate smiled. 'I'm not planning to fall in love, Lady Wrothe.'

'Henry.'

'I can't call you Henry,' Kate protested.

'Why not? Because I'm too old?'

'No—well—'

'I'm old enough to demand a name I prefer,' she said, waving a diamond-encrusted hand in the air. 'Forget this talk of love; it's all a pile of nonsense. I wish Leo and I had been in London for the season, rather than on the Continent. I would have met your trollopy relatives and demanded to know where my goddaughter was. At any rate, the real question is whom *you* should marry. After you finish this little charade, of course.'

Kate felt a great easing in the area of her chest. There was something about Henry: She was all luxurious curves with a great expanse of white bosom, but her big blue eyes were steady. You could trust her.

'You aren't going to cry, are you?' Henry demanded, looking suspicious. 'I can't abide tears.'

'No,' Kate said.

'So whom do you want to marry, then? I trust you're not planning to steal away your sister's Algernon. He doesn't sound like much of a bargain.'

'I know just whom I'd like to marry,' Kate said promptly. 'That is, I don't know *precisely* who, but I know the sort of man. Someone like my father, but not, if you see what I mean. He wasn't home much, and I'd prefer someone who likes the country. I loved our house in the country. It's beautiful, and just the right size, big enough for lots of children.'

'You want your father but without the wandering eye,' Henry said, going straight to the heart of it. 'Victor had a snug estate, thanks to your mother's dowry, but nothing—'

'It's just the right size for me,' Kate interrupted. 'I don't want to marry an earl or anyone like that. Just a squire would be lovely. Or even a merchant who'd moved to the country.'

'No goddaughter of mine is marrying a merchant,' Henry stated. 'For goodness' sake, girl, you're the grand-daughter of an earl. And your mother was no country bumpkin, for all that she couldn't get out of bed. She was a lady and so are you.'

Kate hadn't been a lady for years, not since her father died and Mariana moved her into the attic. She felt her throat tighten. 'I'm sorry,' she said. 'I *am* going to cry.'

'Ah well, happens to the best of us,' Henry said philosophically. She got up and went over to a little silver tray and poured out glasses of pale liqueur. 'I cried buckets after your baptism. I was so convinced that you should have been my child, you see.'

86

'You did?' Kate mopped up her tears and tried to concentrate.

'After that I turned my back on Victor and never spoke to him again.' She added, a little gruffly, 'I didn't stop thinking of him, though. Devil that he was.'

'I'm sorry,' Kate said. 'He really didn't have a very good moral character, as it turns out. I'd rather my husband was quite different in that respect.'

'Here, drink your liqueur,' Henry said, tossing back her drink. 'I carry it with me everywhere because it's the only kind of drink that Leo doesn't like, so there's a chance I'll still have some tomorrow.'

Kate sipped hers. It tasted like lemons, fierce and cruel to the nose.

'Limoncello,' Henry said with satisfaction. 'Isn't it brilliant? I learned of it from a man I knew in Sorrento once, Lord Manin. I left him behind, but I've brought limoncello with me ever since.

'So you want a gentleman with a snug estate and a righteous nature. It shouldn't be much of a problem. I've tended that way myself, though I must admit that I choose men with rather more than a *snug* estate. Still, if there's any wandering to be done, I always do it myself. That way I know no one will get hurt.'

Kate sipped her limoncello again, and found herself smiling at her godmother. She was so funny and frank. 'I don't have a dowry,' she said. 'That is, I have a small nest egg left to me by my mother, but it's nothing much.'

Henry put her empty glass down. 'That doesn't sound right, Katherine. *Are* you a Katherine? Somehow it doesn't quite suit you, any more than

87

Victoria did.'

'My father called me Kate.'

'Brilliant. Of course. So what's this nonsense about your dowry, and while we're at it, what's happened to you? I've just worked out that you must be at least twenty-three, so why aren't you already settled with two or three squalling brats on your knee? Your wishes are modest enough, and you're beautiful.'

Kate finished her glass. 'As I told you, my father married again, but he died shortly thereafter. And he left all his money to his new wife.'

'That's just the kind of stupid thing that Victor would have done. Probably neglected to make a will. But his estate was beans . . . nothing compared to your mother's.'

Kate's mouth fell open. 'What?'

Henry had a sleepy kind of smile, but her eyes shone. 'He never told you?'

'Told me what?'

'Your mother was an heiress. Your grandfather wanted her married, so he bought your father, and he . . . well, I'm afraid that Victor wanted her guineas.'

'He must have spent it,' Kate said, deflating. 'Because I have only a very small income from my mother. If he didn't spend it, my stepmother would have.'

'I don't know,' Henry said dubiously. 'How would she get her hands on that money? I vaguely remember Victor complaining that he couldn't touch it. I'll have Leo look into it.'

'Even if Mariana took it illicitly,' Kate said, 'I couldn't do anything about it. I don't like her, but—'

'Well,' Henry said, interrupting, 'It doesn't matter.'

'It doesn't?'

'Your father gave you to me, Kate. And though I was ungrateful for the present at the time, I feel differently now.' Henry reached forward and put a hand on Kate's cheek, for just a second. 'I'd like to try being a proper godmother to you, if you wouldn't mind.'

Kate's vision blurred again. 'I would be most honored.'

'Good!' she said, standing up. 'Now you must run off because I've learned that if I don't have my beauty sleep I'm a total beast in the morning. There's nothing wrong with that, but since Leo is downstairs drinking brandy, it would make two of us. And that's two more than this castle can bear.'

Kate stood up too and then hesitated for a second.

'Come here,' Henry said gruffly, and held out her arms.

Kate's mother had been rail-thin and smelled like lemons; Henry was curvy and smelled like French perfume.

But for the first time since her mother died, Kate felt safe.

Thirteen

When Kate got back to her room she eyed the cord that would summon Rosalie to prepare her for bed, but she didn't feel sleepy in the least.

Images were jumping through her mind, memories of her mother's wistful face at the sight of her father, of her father's polite courtesy toward his wife. Could it be that he was still in love with Henry? Or did he then fall in love with Mariana?

Her heart felt wrenched between her mother's sadness and Henry's, between the romance of young love and irritation at her father for allowing himself to be bought.

Finally she decided to take the dogs out for a walk. She calmed Caesar by fixing her eye on him, and then gave him a cheese bit once he stopped barking.

The great drawing room was still blazing with light as she entered the inner courtyard, the dogs pulling ahead. She walked the other direction, stumbling across the cobblestones.

The outer courtyard was only dimly lit, but there seemed to be a set of large cages lined up against the wall. The dogs were straining at their leashes, so she remembered Cherryderry's advice and stopped walking until they calmed down. Then she gave them a round of cheese, and this time they stayed quite politely at her side.

'If you're good,' she told them, 'I'll bring you into company tomorrow.' She had to do that in any case; Victoria had carried those dogs with her everywhere, and Mariana considered the dogs to be an essential part of her disguise.

They all looked up at her the moment she spoke. She was getting a bit fond of them, especially of Freddie. He was afraid of everything from a random fly to a dark shadow, but bravery is not a required virtue for dogs. Plus he was very nice to sleep with.

The cages were frightfully large. Light from the single lantern hanging on a hook on the wall didn't reach past the bars. The dogs stopped short of the first cage, sniffing intently at the dark enclosure. Kate peered inside, but couldn't see anything. There was a rather fierce smell, though.

'What on earth would a prince keep in a cage?' she said out loud. Caesar gave a little woof in reply, but kept his eyes focused on the cage. Freddie was huddled against her leg, showing no inclination to learn more. She reached up toward the lantern— when a big hand reached over hers and took it first.

'Who's—oh!' She swallowed the word in a squeak. It was the prince himself, looking even more sulky and brooding in the wavering light from the lantern. His unruly hair was falling out of its ribbon and his mouth looked haughty. Thin-lipped, she told herself, raising her chin. Everyone knew royals were inbred.

'I keep a lion in this cage,' the prince said, matter-of-factly. 'There's an elephant over there, with her companion, a monkey. And there was an ostrich, but we moved her into the orchards along with some Himalayan goats.' He raised the lantern, and Kate saw a slumbering form in the back of the cage. As the light fell on it, one contemptuous eye opened, and the lion yawned, showing off rows of efficient-looking teeth.

91

'*Teeth* isn't really the right word for those,' she observed.

'Fangs,' the prince said with satisfaction.

The lion closed his eyes again, as if his observers were too boring to contemplate. Kate realized that Freddie was trembling against her ankle, and even Caesar had moved behind her, showing the first sign of real intelligence he'd displayed since she met him.

'You'd better keep those dogs out of the cage,' the prince remarked. 'The lion threw up all day yesterday after eating my uncle's dog.'

'Not the pickle-eating dog?' Kate said. 'What a shame. Your uncle told me that he is quite convinced his dog will return soon.'

'Would you, given that diet?'

'It wouldn't make me leap into a lion's cage,' she pointed out.

'I doubt anything would make you so reckless.'

That was the kind of comment she hated because it implied something about her personality—but what exactly? She certainly wasn't going to ask Prince High-and-Mighty himself for elucidation, so she just walked off in the direction of the elephant's cage.

He followed her with the lantern. 'The elephant's name is Lyssa. She's too big for the cage, so we're making her a pen in the orchard. But if we put her out there, her monkey might run away.'

The monkey was sleeping at the elephant's feet, one long arm curved around her leg. 'I doubt it. It looks like love to me.'

'If that's love I want nothing to do with it,' the prince said, and his eyes laughed.

'I know just what you mean,' Kate said, a giggle

escaping her. 'You'll never catch me sleeping at someone's feet.'

'And here I thought you were desperately enamored with my nephew.'

'Of course I am,' Kate said, sounding insincere even to her own ears.

'Ha,' the prince said. 'I wouldn't want to stake out poor Dimsdale in the orchard and hope his presence would keep you in bounds.'

He was rather terrifyingly attractive, when he wasn't smoldering in a princely way, but laughing instead. 'Algie would never allow himself to be put out to pasture,' she said, trying to think of a magnificent set-down.

But he cut her off. 'Toloose says you've been ill. What happened?'

For a moment Kate's mind boggled, and then she remembered Victoria's sweetly plump face and her own angular cheekbones. 'Nothing much,' she said.

'Other than a brush with death?'

'I hardly look *that* bad,' she said sharply.

He tipped up her chin and studied it. 'Shadowed eyes, thin face, something exhausted about you. You don't look good.'

She narrowed her eyes. 'You're terribly impolite for royalty. I would have expected that you were trained to be diplomatic in every circumstance.'

He shrugged. 'It must be your beauty. It brought out that rare moment of truth in me.'

'Just my luck,' she said crossly. 'You bolt from diplomacy just in time to tell me how dreadful I look.'

He put a finger on her lips and she stilled. It was as if she suddenly saw him again for the first time:

93

all that restless energy and gleaming sensuality bound up with huge shoulders and a sulky mouth. 'You, Miss Daltry, are talking rot and you know it. I can only imagine what you looked like with a little more meat on your bones, but you're exquisite.'

His finger dropped away and she felt her mouth curling into a smile, like a fussy child soothed with a boiled sweet. He was leaning against the cage now, looking pleased with himself, as if he'd taken care of yet another little problem.

'What are you doing out here in the dark?' she asked. 'Don't you want to return and be fawned over some more? Life is so short.'

There was a moment of silence after she issued this appallingly rude statement. Then he said, rather slowly, 'I actually came out to see if the lion was still vomiting up bits of pickled dog. And the English do not fawn, in my experience.' He turned away to hang up the lantern, so his voice issued from a patch of darkness. 'How did you meet my nephew, if you don't mind my asking?'

'We met in a cathedral and fell in love immediately,' Kate said, after a second's pause in which she wracked her brains to remember the story.

'In love,' the prince said. 'With Dimsdale. Whom you affectionately refer to as Algie, I notice. Rather like some sort of pond life.'

'Yes,' Kate stated. 'In love.'

'If you knew what love is, you certainly wouldn't be marrying my nephew.'

'I love Algie,' she repeated.

'You'll eat him alive by the time he's twenty,' he said unemotionally. 'You know he's younger than you are, don't you? Still wet behind the ears, the

94

poor little viscount. Though perhaps you like it that way.'

'You are an odious man,' Kate said, shading her voice with just the right amount of cool disdain. 'I am glad for your sake that your betrothal was a matter of imperial alliances, because I doubt you could catch a wife on your own.' Which was a rotten lie, because she couldn't think of a woman who wouldn't slaver to marry him. Except herself, of course.

She walked off, then turned and said acidly, 'Your Highness.'

There was a flash of movement and an arm wrapped around her waist from behind. He was hot and incredibly large and she could feel his heart beating. He smelled wonderful, like a bonfire at night, smoky and wild and out of bounds.

'Say that again,' he said, his breath touching her neck.

'Let me go,' she said steadily, fighting the impulse of her body to relax back against him, turn her chin, invite—invite a kiss? She'd never been kissed, and she didn't intend her first kiss to be given by an arrogant and unruly prince who was irritated because she didn't fawn over him.

His voice was a smoldering, smoky demand. 'I just want a taste of you, Miss Victoria Daltry.' His lips touched her neck, and the feeling of it shivered down her spine.

With one swift gesture she raised her pointed, jeweled heel and slammed it down in the spot where she guessed his foot had to be, twisting and wrenching away from him.

They had moved close enough to the walls that she could see him in the light from the windows.

'You are an ass,' she said through clenched teeth.

'Did you have to be quite so violent? These are my favorite shoes,' he said. 'And I don't think I'm *always* an ass.'

She backed up a few more steps. 'While I might pity you for your faulty thought processes, you have so many other attributes that command pity that I won't bother.'

'If I am an ass,' he said, 'what does that make you?'

'Uninterested,' she said flatly.

'A snappish little shrew,' he retorted.

His eyes were narrowed, and for the first time since she met him, he looked angry. Against all odds, the look of him made her laugh. 'You look like a grocer whose daily allotment of potatoes didn't arrive.'

'Potatoes,' he said. 'You compare yourself to a potato?'

'Look, you just can't go and kiss English ladies whenever you feel the urge,' she said. 'Here, Caesar! Come back.' Caesar had apparently realized the lion was asleep and had started sniffing at the cage bars again. 'I don't want you turned into the lion's supper.'

'Why can't I?'

A mop of hair had fallen over his eyes and she had to admit that he looked like the sort of man who *could* kiss anyone he pleased. He looked explosive and utterly sensual and dangerous. Henry's assessment of him came back into her mind at that very moment: He was just like her father, the sort of man who would never be faithful.

Her smile turned bittersweet. 'Because you're not for every woman,' she explained, trying to put it kindly. 'For goodness' sake, are all princes like this?'

He walked closer and she eyed him, but he didn't look lustful as much as curious.

'You can't tell me that a woman simply enters a royal court in Marburg or wherever it is you're from and expects to be kissed by any prince who happens upon her.'

'Of course not!'

'Well, why on earth would you think I am available for kissing?'

'To be honest, because you're here in the dark,' he said.

It was a fair point. 'I'm here only because of my dogs,' she said defensively.

'You spoke to me for quite a while. You have no chaperone with you. Wick tells me that you arrived with a single maid to attend you.'

Damn Mariana for throwing their governess out of the house. 'I would have brought my maid downstairs with me but she has indigestion,' Kate said.

'I think you forgot to summon her. I assure you that young ladies in the court never forget their maids, and they are never alone,' he stated. 'They travel together, like flocks of starlings. Or packs of dogs,' he added, as Caesar growled at the lion.

She could hardly explain that her governess had been dismissed the day after her father died, and consequently she had never learned to travel in a flock. 'I should have been accompanied by my maid,' she said, 'but you mustn't assume that every woman wishes to kiss you.'

He stared at her.

'This is a ridiculous conversation,' she muttered.

'Caesar, come here! It's time to go.' The dog stayed at the cage, growling.

'Absurd animal,' she said, scooping him up.

'I thought,' the prince said, 'that I might seduce you.'

She turned around, mouth open. 'You can't go about trying to seduce young ladies!' she squeaked.

'If I weren't betrothed already, I would consider marrying you.'

Kate snorted. 'You might consider it the way you would consider a case of the measles. No, you wouldn't, and you shouldn't imply that you would.'

He took one step and looked down at her with his midnight eyes. Some dim part of her mind registered that his lips weren't thin at all. Quite the opposite, really.

'I'm a shrew, remember?' she told him. 'Look, what are you doing? You're a prince. This is a remarkably improper conversation, and you shouldn't try to do it with other young ladies or you *will* be forced to marry someone, likely at the end of a dueling pistol held by her father.'

'Your father?' he asked, still staring down at her.

'My father is dead,' she said, feeling a queer thump of her heart. 'But you and he had a great deal in common, and I'm afraid that that has given me immunity to your particular charms.'

'Not to mention, you're in love with Dimsdale. Did your father want you to marry him?'

'My father died years ago. He doesn't belong in this conversation. Anyway, you're quite mad. You couldn't marry me, and it's unkind of you to raise my expectations. What if I believed you? You are marrying a Russian princess, by all accounts.'

'It's true that I need to marry an heiress,' the

prince said casually. 'You're one, by all accounts. I don't necessarily want someone well-connected. I just want someone rich.' His eyes drifted over her bosom. 'Beddable.'

Kate hoisted Caesar a little higher, so the dog almost covered her wax breasts. 'This is the most improper conversation I've ever had in my life,' she observed.

'It must be your age that inspires my impropriety,' he said. 'I've had many improper conversations, though not, I admit, with nubile maidens.'

She felt that like a sting, though she didn't quite work out whether he was implying she was young or old. 'Do you often confess your desire to marry a woman for her money, then?'

'Generally we speak of other desires.'

'I can just imagine,' she muttered. 'This has been absolutely charming. Just so you know, I'm not available for marriage. And I'm not rich either.' She buried the memory of Henry's belief in her mythical dowry. It was too fantastical for truth.

He cocked an eyebrow. 'You're not? Does Dimsdale know that? Wick seems to think you have a healthy inheritance.'

'Absolutely,' she said. 'Algie loves me anyway.'

'Interesting. My nephew strikes me as the sort who would put adoration a strong second to monetary policy.'

'Unlike you, who would apparently put it at the bottom of the list.'

'As would you,' he said cheerfully.

'Does this mean that I can walk my dogs without fear that you'll leap out at me from a dark corner?' she asked, putting Caesar back on the ground.

'One would certainly think so,' he said. 'But then . . . you're extraordinarily beautiful.' And while Kate was still registering that comment, he gathered her up in his arms in a business-like fashion and lowered his head to hers.

And then he wasn't businesslike anymore. All that rest-less, wild energy she felt in him poured into his kiss, into a demand that she had no hope of denying. She thought kissing was about a brush of the lips, but this . . . this was about tasting and feeling. He felt like silk and fire.

He *tasted* like fire. She leaned into it, opened her mouth, feeling a tremor go down her back again. He murmured something into her mouth, something hot and sweet. She dimly remembered that she meant to give him a lesson, to teach him not to kiss any lady he met.

She ought to give him a slap.

But then he might take his lips away, or his large warm hand from her waist, or . . . it was only innate self-preservation that saved her. His kiss had started out with a question, but it was quickly turning into a demand, and inexperienced though she was, her whole body was answering in the affirmative.

Yet one rather small, cool voice in her head reminded her exactly who she was, and whom she was kissing.

She pulled back; he resisted for one second, one glorious blazing second, and then it was over.

Her first thought was utterly irrelevant: that she'd never noticed how thick his eyelashes were. Her second was that she'd done nothing more than feed his absurd conceit, and now he would think that he was irresistible even to Englishwomen.

100

In that split second, she drew on years of composure honed in Mariana's presence. She opened her mouth to say something that ought to shrivel his self-esteem, but he spoke first.

'Oh damn,' he said, and there was a kind of hoarse hunger in his voice that spoke of truth, 'I wish you were my Russian princess.'

And just like that, her irritation with his pompous princely self drained out of her and she started gurgling with laughter. 'You're—' She stopped. Did she really want to compliment him, to add to his already monumental self-regard?

It was only fair.

She leaned forward and brushed her lips across his. 'If money could buy kisses like that, I wish I were an heiress. I'd even go so far,' she added, 'as to wish myself a princess's pedigree.'

His hands came up and cupped her face. 'I have to taste you again,' he said with a queer kind of groan in his voice.

They were thinking the same things, she thought dazedly, about tasting—but then she *was* tasting, and he tasted like dark honey and something smoother and wilder, something that made her tremble and—

And then he put her away.

'You are dangerous,' she said slowly.

His smile told her that she'd said the wrong thing, fed that monumental self-conceit again.

'Princes,' she said with a sigh. 'I suppose you do have some usefulness after all.'

That stung, and she noted it with satisfaction because her knees were trembling and her—her legs—

'No,' he said, a bit harshly. 'I have little utility, I

assure you. Now, unless you wish to be caught and kissed by another stranger, Miss Daltry, I strongly suggest that you return to your room post-haste, and do not emerge again unchaperoned.'

Fourteen

The next morning Kate took the dogs down for a constitutional, this time accompanied by Rosalie. It was only just after dawn, but she was used to waking up early and couldn't seem to sleep in, even when Freddie whined and tried to hide under the covers. The moment her eyes opened she remembered the evening before—and that was that.

'Come on,' she told them. 'You three are going out without a leash. We'll visit the lion in daylight; if you don't behave, you'll be down his gullet, so keep that in mind.'

The courtyard echoed emptily as she and Rosalie walked across the flagstones. Last night it had been a warm, velvet enclosure. This morning it looked hundreds of years old, chilly, and capable of existing far past their lifetimes. Kate shivered and walked a little faster.

The lion was awake. He yawned at the sight of them and padded forward. She fell back a respectful step.

He was far shaggier than she would have thought. She had a vague idea that lions were glossy, but this lion looked time-worn, like a battered hearth rug. He gave them a disgusted look and walked to the rear of the cage, turned around, and walked forward again, shaking his mane as if his head was too heavy.

'Oh, miss!' Rosalie squealed.

Caesar had pranced forward and was sniffing the bars. Kate snapped her fingers and he moved back, so she gave him some cheese.

'All the servants are talking about that lion,' Rosalie said. 'The beast has eaten half the household pets, they say. We'll be lucky to leave with all three dogs.'

'I expect he'll get Caesar first,' Kate said ruthlessly.

The lion came to the bar and looked hungrily at the dogs, so she threw him some cheese instead. He sniffed disdainfully but ate it up.

'That animal gives me the shivers,' Rosalie said. 'Just look at Freddie. He's scared to death. We'll visit the elephant. Come on, Freddie; let's get away from this nasty cat.' She headed around the corner to the other cages, but Kate stayed where she was, staring at the enclosed lion.

'Good morning, Miss Daltry,' came a voice at her shoulder. She turned to find the prince's majordomo smiling at her.

'Good morning, Mr Berwick,' she said. 'I do believe we're the only people awake in the whole castle.'

'I came out to see how the lion's holding up. He seems better.'

Berwick didn't seem to be in a hurry, so Kate ventured a question. 'Would you mind if I asked you some details about the castle?'

'Not at all,' he said, leaning against the bars of the cage.

'I estimated last night that you must be taking in at least two hundred wax candles a week. So does the castle have its own chandler? I know you must have a baker, but what about all the sort of things one usually finds in a village, such as a smithy?'

Berwick wore beautiful livery with frogged buttons and a high collar. He looked precisely like the very best sort of servant, but just for a moment, his eyes twinkled at her and she felt . . .

Absurd. As if she knew him, or had at the least met him before.

'The castle does include its own chandlery,' he replied. 'But you've underestimated the candles, Miss Daltry. In a normal week, I have more than three hundred burning throughout the castle, and we also employ Argand lamps in some rooms. With the ball, of course, I've ordered quite a lot more to make sure that the candelabra are fully lit till dawn.'

'Fascinating,' Kate said. 'What about servants? How many are there, overall?'

He paused for a moment, obviously calculating. 'I just hired four and let go one, so with a net gain of three, we currently employ one hundred thirty-seven in and around the castle.'

'Does most of the income come from rents?' she asked, before she thought. Then she colored. 'I do apologize; that was a remarkably improper question.'

He cocked an eyebrow. 'The English are more prudish than we are about matters of money. The castle is surrounded by farms, of course, and they bring in rents, which support the castle in a minimal fashion. The prince doesn't feel they are sufficient, given the number of people living here.'

Kate felt pink rising in her cheeks. 'I certainly

didn't mean to inquire about the prince's financial situation!'

'Why not?' he said, shrugging. 'Impecunious princes are thruppence a dozen in Marburg, I assure you. Prince Gabriel is singular in that he has a castle to oversee.' Berwick's hair was tied back in a proper queue, but as he shrugged, part of it fell over his brow.

Then, as if a mirror appeared before her, she saw the prince's face—in Berwick's. Cast in the same mold, as it were. Twin sides of two coins.

Her mouth fell open.

The majordomo met her eyes and clearly diagnosed her stunned look. His sideways smile was a precise copy of his master's.

'Ump,' Kate said, recovering herself.

'Today we will have a picnic al fresco in the gardens behind the castle,' Berwick said, without flickering an eyelash. 'Several ladies have expressed an interest in seeing the rest of the menagerie, which is housed behind the hedge maze. Punting on the lake can also be very enjoyable.'

The lion had gone back to sleep. 'Don't you think that that beast needs a bigger cage?' she asked. The realization that Berwick must be intimately related to the prince made him somehow easier to speak to.

'How much bigger would you advise?'

'Well, think about pig enclosures. You could put a large sow and all her piglets in a six-by-six enclosure, but I believe most farmers consider a larger space preferable. This lion has less space than a fallow pig. That can't be right.'

She looked up at Berwick to find that he was blinking down at her in a puzzled sort of way. 'I shouldn't know the size of a sow's sty,' she said, sighing.

'Who is to say what one should and shouldn't know?' Berwick murmured. 'But I will admit that the few English ladies I encountered during my time at Oxford appeared to find an extraordinary number of topics indelicate.'

'Oh, were you at Oxford as well?' she asked. 'Or were you there as the prince's attendant?'

'As myself,' Berwick said cheerfully. 'And myself attends the prince, so it worked out very well for both of us. I studied philosophy and he studied history and we both studied women. We were very young, you understand.'

Kate grinned at him. 'Does philosophy help you in your current position?'

'You can have no idea,' Berwick said. 'I resort to philosophical reasoning on a daily basis when things get sticky.'

'Matters of precedence and such?'

'The prince's relatives,' he said with some vehemence, 'are an unruly lot. Did you meet Mr Tippet last night?'

Kate frowned. 'Rather pale and a bit plumpy?'

'That's he. Mr Tippet is a reader attached to one of His Highness's aunts. You might remember Princess Sophonisba by her penchant for wearing plumes.'

Kate brought to mind a fierce-looking woman with a bosom like a plow. 'How nice that she has someone to read to her,' she said politely.

'Tippet reads palms. Or so he says,' Berwick added with an elegant touch of doubt. 'At any rate, he is being driven quite mad by Prince Ferdinand, who demands that he read his palm over and over, searching for a better answer.'

'The idea that one's palm might change moment to moment seems to invalidate the whole idea,' Kate observed.

'Mr Tippet has already informed the prince that he will marry a dark-haired lady, and live to one hundred and twelve, and any number of other interesting fortunes, but none of them are good enough.'

'So you call upon your philosophical training to manage the travails of your—' And caught herself up.

Whether Prince Ferdinand was indeed Berwick's relative was none of her business.

'Exactly,' he said smoothly. 'Miss Daltry, may I point out what an extraordinary young lady you are?'

'Ah well,' she said, and then, realizing that she really liked him, 'royalty aren't the only ones who have oddly shaped families, you know.'

He nodded, his eyes resting thoughtfully on her. At that moment, Rosalie came back around the corner.

'You must come and see the elephant, Miss Katherine,' she cried, not noticing that she was using the wrong name. 'She has the sweetest monkey clinging to her leg. I've never seen anything so darling in my life.'

'The monkey is a castle favorite,' Berwick commented.

Kate glanced at him to see if he had caught Rosalie's mistake, but he showed no sign of it.

It turned out that Caesar, who showed proper caution around the lion, had no such sense when it came to the elephant. He rushed between the bars of the cage, yapping madly, trying to catch the monkey.

The elephant looked uneasy and began shifting back and forth.

'Elephants don't like mice, and that dog is not much bigger,' Berwick pointed out, sounding entirely unconcerned. 'She might stamp on him.'

'Caesar!' Kate cried. 'Please come out of there!' She waved a piece of cheese desperately.

But Caesar was as dimwitted as he was brave, and he seemed to think the monkey's tail would drop into his mouth if he barked loudly enough.

Berwick sighed. 'Excuse me, ladies.' He pulled open a small box attached to the cage, took out a key, and unlocked the door. One step inside the cage and he scooped up Caesar.

'I'll have to keep him on a leash,' Kate said. 'I'm afraid that he's quite fearless. He has no brains.'

'None?'

Kate shook her head. 'Absolutely none that I can ascertain. It's like that sometimes.'

Berwick raised an eyebrow.

She smiled at him, just as if she were at home, funning with Cherryderry. 'He's male. I've noticed that sometimes the brains simply get left out of the package.'

She and Rosalie left the courtyard to the sound of the majordomo's laughter.

Fifteen

The picnic and punting took place in the late afternoon, in the gardens stretching behind the castle. The gardens were laid out very formally, stretching from the bottom of a vast flight of white marble steps. There was a hedge maze, and a lake with swans, and everything imaginable a self-respecting castle's garden should have, including an orchestra, scraping away on a marble terrace.

Kate wore a cherry-tinted wig to match her gown, a lovely tunic with overskirts in cherry, cut back to reveal two layers, one in a paler cherry and another in cream. She had a little argument with Rosalie over the wax inserts, but her maid had insisted that the cherry dress would be disgraced by Kate's natural shape. Or, more to the point, by her lack of natural shape.

'They may melt, and then where would I be? What if I grow hot, and they change shape? What then?'

'Do not grow hot,' Rosalie had said, with impeccable logic.

Algie and Kate strolled to the top of the long flight of stairs leading down to the garden and paused.

The orchestra was playing something delicious, a waltz perhaps . . . She'd heard of waltzes and their decadent influence on dancers. The music made her want to pick up her skirts and dance.

'Wonder how they keep those fountains going,' Algie said. Water was shooting into the air out of the mouths of great stone sea monsters.

'You might ask Mr Berwick,' Kate suggested. 'I find he's remarkably knowledgeable about the castle.'

'I certainly will not have a conversation with a servant,' Algie said, appalled. 'For God's sake, Kate, remember that you're Victoria, will you? My wife would never lower herself in such a manner.'

'If you want to know something, why not ask?' retorted Kate. 'I do think that you're being a snob, Algie. The prince won't be able to answer your question.'

'As if I would ask *him*!' Algie cried, insulted all over again.

Kate sighed and began walking down the steps. There were more people in the gardens than she had seen in the drawing rooms yesterday; apparently guests were already arriving for the ball. 'Don't leave me, Algie,' she told her sulky fiancé. 'I'm quite likely to see people whom Victoria knows. I'll smile at everyone, but you must handle introductions.'

Algie took a quick look at her and said, 'You look more like Victoria today, which is lucky.' Then, suddenly aware of a crucial detail, 'Where are the dogs?'

'I left them with Rosalie,' she said. 'I thought—'

'No, you must have them,' Algie said, snapping his fingers at a footman in a way that Kate considered contemptible. 'Victoria takes them with her everywhere; they're her signature. Bring the dogs from Miss Daltry's chamber,' he commanded the footman. 'And be quick about it. We'll wait here.'

The wait gave Kate the opportunity to discover exactly where the prince was. He wasn't hard to find, as he was surrounded by a veritable flowerbed of young ladies, and wearing a costume of dull yellow silk. At least she knew in which direction not to go.

'Just look at that,' Algie said in an awed voice.

'What?' Kate asked, pretending she had been examining the lake.

'Mr Toloose's coat has five seams down the back, rather than three.' He twitched his own sleeve.

'I find it remarkable that you are able to see such minute detail from here,' Kate said, and then, turning to the young footman, 'Thank you! That was very kind of you.' She gave each dog a stern look in turn. 'Caesar, no barking. Coco, stay away from the water. And Freddie . . .' She paused and looked down at Freddie's silky little ears and sweet eyes. He looked so happy to see her. 'Well, you're perfect as you are. Come on, then.'

They all pranced down the steps together, Algie in the lead, and she was so busy complimenting the dogs for not pulling on their leashes that she didn't realize that the prince had shaken off his coterie of admirers and was waiting to greet them at the bottom of the steps.

'Miss Daltry,' he said solemnly, as if the previous night had never happened.

'Your Highness,' said she, dropping into a deep curtsy.

'Nephew,' he said, turning to Algie.

Algie obviously wrestled with the question of what to say in response; he finally blurted out, 'Your Highness, Uncle,' and bowed so deeply that his nose likely brushed his breeches.

'I insist that you come with me for a turn on a punt,' the prince said, raising Kate's hand to his lips.

It really wasn't fair to the rest of mankind that a prince should have eyes like that. More accurately, it wasn't fair to womankind.

'Perhaps I will, at some point,' she said, retrieving her hand.

'Now,' he said, sweeping her across the lawn without another look at Algie.

'What are you doing?' she hissed, trying to keep the dogs' leashes from tangling with her skirts.

'Taking you out on the lake, of course.'

Mere seconds later they were on one end of a long boat the approximate shape of a green bean, with a footman punting them along from the other end.

'Algie—that is, my darling fiancé—won't like this,' she said, wondering if she could take off her gloves and trail her fingers in the water. It was so beautiful, clear and dark blue.

'Yes, take them off,' the prince said, guessing her thought. 'We're far enough out that no one will see.'

'What on earth do you mean by taking me out in this boat?' she demanded, though she did pull off her right glove.

'Do you know what that group of women over there is talking about?' he said, jerking his chin toward the fluffy cloud of silks and satins in which she'd first spied him.

'No. Here—' She handed him Caesar's leash. 'Can you take care of him? Freddie will be fine, and Coco is actually quite well-behaved, but I wouldn't put it past Caesar to topple in if he sees a fish.'

'I dislike dogs,' the prince said, looking disdainfully at Caesar's fluffy tail.

'So do I,' she said cheerfully, and then remembered whom she was pretending to be. 'Except for my own sweet doggies, of course.'

'Those women are discussing the extraordinary way you've changed since they last saw you in London, two months ago,' the prince said, leaning back and regarding her with a wicked gleam in his eye. 'By all accounts, you were *much* more attractive a matter of a few months ago, rounded in all the right places, et cetera.'

'How churlish,' Kate said. 'Very mean-spirited of them to be so critical after my illness. Kind of you to warn me, though.'

'So who are you?' the prince said, leaning in.

'Look, I think I see a fish, right there!'

'You are not Miss Victoria Daltry.' He reached out and took her hand, turning it over. His thumb rubbed slowly over her palm and her eyes rose to meet his. 'Calluses. The darling of the *ton* would not have calluses. Not even after an illness.'

'Well,' Kate started, and stopped.

'Let me guess,' the prince said, with the kind of tempting smile that really ought to be outlawed. 'Wick and I discussed it at length earlier this afternoon.'

'Wick?'

'My brother Berwick. He says you ratted to the fact that he's my brother.'

'I may have surmised—' Kate begun.

'I surmise the same,' the prince said triumphantly. 'In short, you are not Victoria Daltry. You are an illegitimate twig of the family, who for some unknown reason has replaced Victoria, thereby explaining many mysteries: your hands, your apathy toward both your dogs and my poor

113

sod of a nephew, your lack of resemblance to the plump and powdery Victoria, and your knowledge of the sufficient area of a sow's sty.'

'Plump and powdery?' Kate repeated, desperately wondering what she should say. To protest her legitimate birth seemed rather foolish, under the circumstances.

'One of the sharpest-tongued of the young ladies expressed grief over the fact that a doctor must have forced you to spend time in the sun, because you used to have the most beautiful skin.'

'She was distracting you, in the hope that you wouldn't notice her cloven hoof.'

'Could be,' the prince said, grinning madly.

'I can see you're finding this a great deal of fun,' she said crossly.

'Well, you *are* family,' he said. 'That is, once Algernon has married the undoubtedly delectable Victoria, you'll be part of my extended family.'

'Won't that be lovely,' Kate said, scooping up a water lily. She stole a look at the footman standing in the punt's stern, but he seemed to be preoccupied with avoiding the other boats skewing recklessly across the lake. 'Related to a prince. On my list of things to achieve in life, I assure you.'

'Quite like the homeland, where, I assure you, half of the population is related to me on one side of the blanket or the other,' the prince said. 'So what's your name? Wick thought it might be Katherine, but he wasn't sure.'

So Berwick *had* heard Rosalie's slip of the tongue. 'Katherine,' she admitted. 'Though generally people call me Kate.'

'Gabriel,' he said.

'Though generally people call you Your

114

Highness,' she pointed out, 'and so shall I.'

'No one can hear us out here.' He leaned back looking rather happy, and she realized with a start that for the first time, he wasn't looking at her mockingly. 'What happened to plump and powdery Victoria?'

'Caesar bit her,' Kate said.

He glanced down at Caesar, who was standing with his front paws on the side of the boat, watching the water keenly in case he saw a reason to attack it.

'He may look tame, but he has a wild side,' she added.

'Shall I push him over?' Gabriel asked helpfully. 'With all that hair, he would sink like a stone. Though not as fast as that little one. Are those jewels glued to her coat?'

'Not real ones. They're glass.'

Gabriel leaned over and examined Coco more closely. 'Actually, they are star sapphires. Although as a prince, I may not know their *price*, I can tell you that the value of that dog, jewels included, is approximately the same as a small cottage on the outskirts of this estate.'

Kate looked down at Coco with some dismay. 'No wonder she's so proud of herself.'

'Yes, she's like one of those circus dancers who carry a dowry in her navel,' Gabriel said. 'Obviously I truly missed an experience when Victoria was unable to come. She and I would have so much to talk about.'

'Do you decorate your dogs as well?'

'I have no dogs, but I'm willing to consider the lion as a substitute.'

'Your lion is desperate for a larger cage,' Kate

said, scowling at him.

'Dear me,' the prince said lazily. 'I'm afraid that we're attracting quite a bit of attention.'

Kate looked up to discover that the lake was now positively littered with boats, and most of them seemed to be filled with aristocrats craning their necks in the direction of the prince's punt. 'Damn and blast,' she muttered. She shook the water off her hand, but there was nowhere to dry it. 'Do you have a handkerchief?' she asked.

'No,' the prince said, looking amused.

'I suppose you have servants who carry around that sort of thing in case you sneeze,' she said.

'You aren't carrying one either,' he retorted.

'I don't have room; my reticule is full of cheese.'

'I thought you had an interesting smell! Most ladies smell rather French.'

'Whereas I smell of the dairy,' she said, resigned. 'How do French ladies smell?'

'Like flowers,' he said, grinning. 'Or sweat. It all depends.'

Kate wasn't really listening. She couldn't dry her hand on the cherry silk of her dress because it would spot. 'Don't look,' she told him, and hastily pulled up the cherry silk, and the two layers of silk underneath, until she reached the delicate linen of her chemise.

He looked.

Of course he looked.

She felt his eyes and looked up. He had the oddest little smile.

'You shouldn't!' she said, twitching her skirts over her ankle.

He leaned forward. 'I like your slippers.'

They too were cherry silk, with small heels, and

116

quite irresistible.

'Thank you,' she said sedately. She was fairly sure that a gentleman was not supposed to see a lady's ankles, but surely shoes were meant to be admired?

He picked up her hand, still ungloved, and raised it to his lips. His eyes glittered at her, a kind of wild invitation, a temptation. 'Though not as much as your ankles. Ankles like that . . .'

'They're just ankles,' she said.

'Yes, but you should never let a man see your ankles.'

'I know that,' she said, tugging at her hand. 'I wasn't raised in a barnyard, you know.'

His eyes were laughing now, but there was a sultry burn in them, a heat that made her stomach curl with . . . something. 'You should never let a man see your ankles,' he repeated, 'because if they are as finely and beautifully knit as yours, it tells him a great deal.' He turned her hand over and put her palm against his lips, for just a split second.

'About what?' she asked, unable to stop herself.

He leaned forward. 'About the rest of a woman's body. The curve of an ankle talks of the curve of a waist, the curve of a woman's thigh, the slope of her back . . . other places as well.' His eyes lingered on her bosom.

Before she could stop herself, a giggle escaped from Kate's mouth. She clapped a hand over her lips.

'You are laughing at my compliment?' His face was utterly unreadable.

'I'm so sorry,' she said, but she couldn't help herself. 'I suppose I am.'

'Why?'

Kate straightened her back, which made the wax that was propping up her real bosom jut forward.

He looked puzzled.

'Did you know that Algie pads his chest? Do *you*?' She eyed his coat and realized that he didn't. His chest was twice as large as Algie's, but it was pure muscle.

'No.'

'Algie also has little pads sewn into the thighs of his breeches,' she said patiently.

'He used to have a very fat bottom; he must have lost all that flesh somehow,' the prince said. 'What does that—oh!'

His eyes fastened directly on her bosom.

She grinned at him. 'A word to the wary, Your Highness: I would not consider the curve of an ankle to be an altogether reliable forecast of a woman's curves.'

He looked up from her bosom and, to her surprise, smiled with that fierce spark of desire in his eyes, the one that made her feel instantly hot.

'Don't do that,' she snapped. 'You look like an old goat.'

'You practically instructed me to look at your breasts.'

'What you are looking at only nominally fits the label,' she pointed out.

He snorted. 'There may be some sort of padding underneath, Kate, but what I see is utterly desirable, secious, creamy . . .'

Kate couldn't help smiling. 'You know, just because I'm not Victoria doesn't mean that I'm available for seducing.'

'I know that,' he said, sitting back. 'I'm not seducing you, either.'

'I'm glad to know it,' Kate said. 'Otherwise I might be quite confused. Your being a prince and all, and likely expecting women to fall into your arms. You might decide I was a dairymaid, given my lovely *parfum de fromage*.'

He laughed. 'I did consider trying to steal you from Dimsdale, but that was when you were Victoria, with all the money to lavish on her dogs.'

'Why do you need an heiress?' she asked. 'Berwick—'

'Wick,' he put in.

'Wick implied the castle might be able to support itself.'

'In a nip-cheese fashion that would make my aunts unhappy. One can never have too much money.'

Kate looked at him. It was four o'clock now, and the sun's rays were slanting golden across the lake. Gabriel's hair was falling from its tie, and a strand or two curled against his cheek. He was arrogant, and regal, and utterly triumphant to have found out her secret.

He didn't look greedy.

Just arrogant.

Her silence seemed to prick him and he said, 'Money can buy you freedom.'

'Freedom,' she echoed. 'Freedom from what? You're not the lion—'

'Oh for God's sake, shut up about the lion,' he snapped.

She raised an eyebrow.

'I never speak to anyone that way,' he said, with the sweet ruefulness of a boy.

'Obviously I bring out your worst side.'

'Yes, let's blame it on you. At any rate, I would

119

like to have so much money that I could leave my wife in charge here, with all the aunts and uncles and the lion and all, and go off.'

'Go? Go where? Back to Marburg?'

'No!'

'Then?'

'Have you ever heard of Dido and Aeneas?'

She shook her head. 'Are they historical or literary? I have to admit that I'm shockingly ill-educated. I can speak some French, and I did read most of Shakespeare, but otherwise I'm an ignoramus.'

'Who happens to know the size of a pigsty,' he said, his eyes thoughtful.

'Yes, I'm full of charming knowledge of that sort,' she said. 'What about Dido, then? She has a very unattractive name, I must say.'

'She was the Queen of Carthage. She fell in love with Aeneas, but he was bound by the gods to continue his journey and found the city of Rome . . . so he did. And she threw herself on a funeral pyre in grief when he left.'

He stopped.

'She burned herself for love?'

He nodded.

'Fiction,' Kate declared. 'No woman would ever be so foolish. Do you think the footman would consider it improper if you buttoned up my glove? I'm afraid that I can't do all these buttons myself.'

'It's not the footman who's the problem; it's the other boaters. You'd better sit next to me so I can do it without anyone's being able to see.' He moved to the right side of his bench.

So Kate stood up and then quickly turned and sat down next to him. He was very large, and his leg

120

pressed directly against hers. She could feel color rising in her cheeks.

That spark was back in the prince's eyes. 'Well?' he said. 'Let's have the glove, then.'

Reluctantly Kate turned over her right hand. The tiny pearl buttons on the glove went past her elbow. The prince bent over her arm. His hair wasn't as dark as she had thought. It was chestnut streaked with lighter strands, the color of earth that's been turned over for tilling.

A not very romantic comparison, now she thought of it.

'You do know,' he said, fastening the last pearl, 'ladies never sit next to gentlemen.'

'Even princes?'

'Only if they're hoping to become princesses.'

'I'm not,' she said quickly. She was glad to hear the ring of truth in her voice.

'I know that,' the prince said. 'Kate?'

'Yes, Your Highness.'

'Gabriel. Don't you want to know more about Dido?'

'Not particularly. She sounds like an extraordinarily foolish woman.'

'Dido *was* literary,' he said, ignoring her reply. 'But she may well also have been historical. And at this very moment a former professor of mine, Biggitstiff, is excavating an ancient city that might have been her city of Carthage.'

If there had been a ring of truth in her voice when she talked of marriage, there was a ring of true longing in his when it came to Carthage. 'Well, go then,' she said, startled.

'I can't. I have this castle.'

'So?'

'You don't understand. When my brother Augustus cleaned his stables, metaphorically, he threw out everyone and anyone whom he considered to be less than godly.'

'Including the lion and the elephant?' Kate asked. 'I could see if he were talking about Coco, since she clearly has no gods before herself, but the elephant? And the monkey?'

'I think that was just because his wife was tired of the smell. But everyone else . . . out they went, bag and baggage, into my care.'

'Are you saying that you are marrying a Russian princess in order to support all of them?'

'Yes,' he said bluntly. 'Not only is her dowry essential, but I can leave her here to run the castle.'

Kate stood up with one quick movement and sat back down opposite him. 'I think we should head for shore,' she said. And then: 'I just want to make sure that I understand you. You're planning to marry so that you can support your motley family, and then you will promptly leave your wife in charge of the lot of them and go to Carthage, wherever that is? I assume it's not in Lancashire, because Englishwomen *never*, even in literature, burn themselves for love.'

'You make it sound rather self-serving,' he said, cheerfully enough, 'but that's marriage, isn't it?' He waved at the footman and gestured toward shore. 'After all, she will gain my title. And with my inestimable gift for ascertaining value, I can tell you that the value of being a princess is high. For all that you show no interest.'

'I can't believe that you ever considered seducing Victoria out from the very arms of her betrothed,' Kate said. 'She's terribly in love with Algie, you

122

know. And he's your *nephew*.'

'Yes, but it's so hard to feel loyalty to him,' the prince said ruefully. 'Though I suppose now that I've met you, I should.'

'I'm no relation to Algie.'

'But if my guess about your parentage is right, you're his sister-in-law, or you will be,' he pointed out.

'So you'll approve the marriage, then?' she asked, deciding not to comment on the question of her parentage. 'Algie will be very happy. If it's all right with you, we'll leave this afternoon, because what with all the ladies who've noticed my less-than-delectable figure, this is a quite nerve-wracking visit.'

'No.'

She blinked at him. They were gliding into shore now, the punt knocking against the marble ledge circling the lake, and she thought perhaps she misheard him. 'Did you say no?'

'You'll stay for my ball.' He folded his arms and looked mulish.

'Don't be absurd. Someone might realize that I'm not Victoria, and now that you know the truth, there's no reason to stay.'

'You'll stay because I wish you to.'

'*You* can say whatever you please,' she snapped, 'but—'

He leaped onto shore and held out his hand. She stepped from the boat, fuming, and he said in her ear, 'Dimsdale will never cross me, Kate.'

Of course he was right, blast him. She turned and thanked the footman, who was handing out her dogs. 'Well,' she said. 'Do run along and be a prince now, Your Highness.'

123

'Come and dance,' he said, holding out his hand.

'You must be mad. Caesar, behave yourself!' One of the swans was swimming perilously close to the shore, at least from Caesar's point of view. Thank goodness none of them had swum up to the boat to greet them.

'Do come,' he said.

'Your Highness—'

'Call me Gabriel!' He said it between clenched teeth.

Kate took one look at his fierce eyes and rolled hers. 'Gabriel,' she said in a near-whisper. 'I'm the dairymaid, remember? I had a governess for only three or four years, and I'm not sure I remember how to dance. I certainly don't want to stumble around in front of Victoria's acquaintances.'

'What are you planning to do at the ball?'

'I'll wrap a scarf around my ankle and pretend Caesar tripped me.' That scapegoat was pulling at the leash like the little monster he was. 'Caesar!' He turned and looked at her, so she made him sit, then rewarded him with a piece of cheese from her reticule.

'Your Highness,' Wick said, appearing before them. 'Miss Daltry.' It wasn't her imagination that he gave her name just the slightest, mischievous emphasis. 'I do hate to interrupt Your Highness, but the Countess Dagobert has arrived and she wishes to greet you.'

'Wait here,' Gabriel said to Kate, moving away without looking back.

'Sod that,' Kate muttered. 'Come on, dogs.' She took off in the opposite direction, Coco prancing ahead. The sapphires glued to the dog's coat caught the setting sun and made it look as if she had a

124

gleaming halo around her neck.

There's the money that should have gone into refurbishing the cottagers' roofs, Kate thought. And her dowry. She didn't believe for a moment that Mariana hadn't got her hands on it.

She had taken it—and glued it to a dog.

Sixteen

Kate heard someone squawking her name—her actual name, not Victoria's—and turned around to find Lady Wrothe waving from the edge of the maze. Henry was wearing a madly fashionable violet and green striped day dress with a little ruff edging the bodice. As Kate came closer, she saw that it was a good thing that ruff existed, or Henry's breasts would be entirely open to the air.

'Darling!' Henry called. 'Come here this minute . . . what on earth are you doing cavorting out on the lake with that prince? Your little turnip of a betrothed is wandering around looking like a dog who's lost his bone and that, as much as anything, has convinced them all that you're really your tart of a sister. Of course, they think the prince is trying to steal your virtue.'

'Hush,' Kate said. 'Someone will hear you!'

'You can't hear a thing out here,' Henry said. 'Haven't you noticed? I think it's all the water. I was desperately trying to eavesdrop on Lady Bantam warring with her husband, but I couldn't hear more than a few insults about her beard and his floppy poppy, as if we didn't know all that already.'

'Does she really have a beard?' Kate said. 'Come

along, Caesar. We're going to walk this direction.'

'*Dogs*,' Henry said, noticing them for the first time. 'Do tell me they're part of the costume, darling, because I just can't abide the beasts. I refuse to have them in London when you come to live with me.'

'They belong to Victoria,' Kate said.

'No!' Henry shrieked. 'I forgot the animals that tried to gnaw your sister's nose off!' She stared down with horror. 'I have a jeweled dagger, you know. I can give it to you so that you can ward off a sudden attack. I generally stick it in my bosom to draw attention, but the end is quite sharp.'

Freddie was looking up at Kate with his usual expression of complete adoration.

'This is Freddie,' Kate said, 'and that one with the jewels is Coco. And Caesar is that tough little customer there.' Caesar was growling at a sparrow, presumably keeping himself in practice.

'Well,' Henry said after a moment of peering at them, 'they don't look like ferocious beasts. I rather like that one.' She pointed to Coco. 'She has a way about her. She looks as if she knows her own worth, and believe me, darling, that's a woman's most important asset.'

'Coco is utterly vain,' Kate said, laughing.

'Vanity is just another word for confidence,' Henry said, waving her fan in the air. 'There's nothing more enticing to a man. Is she prinked out in jewels or glass?'

'Jewels,' Kate said.

'And she belongs to the feather mattress herself, Mariana? Oddly enough, we seem to have more in common than just your father. I like the idea of a bejeweled dog. Perhaps I'll get one of those

126

great Russian dogs, the ones that the nobility have over there, and paste him all over with emeralds. Wouldn't that be pretty?'

'Let's try the maze,' Kate said, wanting to be out of earshot of the party. She moved toward the entrance.

'There's no need to be quite so energetic,' Henry said. 'I was only standing here to keep out of the sun. My heels are extraordinarily high, and not designed for prancing through shrubbery.'

'They sound very uncomfortable.'

'But they show off my ankles. It's absolutely horrible getting older, so one simply has to make the best of what doesn't change.'

'Ankles?'

'And breasts,' Henry said, nodding. 'I expect they would have turned into sagging oranges if I'd been lucky enough to have a child. No baby, so I still have a fabulous bosom, while my friends are wrinkled like old prunes.'

'I don't have one at all,' Kate said. 'Just in case you're wondering, these are wax.'

'As I pointed out last night, they are far too large for your figure. Mine are mostly wax too, of course. I call them my bosom friends.' She had an enchantingly naughty giggle. 'Anyway, as far as men are concerned, it's all about what shows on top. Now, I've found the perfect man for you.'

Kate stopped. 'You have?'

'Yes, wasn't that brilliant of me? He's a second cousin once removed on the side of my second husband, Bartholomew, but then he's connected as well somehow through Leo—who is already three sheets to the wind, by the way. I stowed him in one of those boats and told the footman not to bring

127

him back to dry land until suppertime. That way he should be steady enough to take me in for the meal.'

'Do you mind?' Kate asked.

'Not particularly,' Henry said. 'I knew he wasn't perfect when I married him, but he's perfect enough. He drinks a bit too much, but so far'—she cast a saucy look at Kate—'he manages to perform when required.'

Kate snorted.

'Well, thank God, you get a joke. One never knows with virgins.'

'I haven't been very sheltered in the last few years,' Kate confessed.

'Don't worry about it,' Henry said. 'As long as you're not as much of a fool as your sister, there's no need to fuss about a bit of liberty before marriage. Just squeak loudly on your wedding night and your husband will never know.'

'Oh! I didn't mean *that*,' Kate protested.

Henry shrugged. 'It's fashionable to be a maid when you're a bride, but if you actually bet the wedding cake on most of our *ton* nuptials, there'd be a lot of champagne and no cake.'

Kate thought that one through. Her mother used to tell her gently that a woman's virtue was her only true possession. Henry certainly had a different point of view. 'I wouldn't want to end up like my sister.'

'Victoria is notable only for the fact that her mother was such a fool that she taught her nothing about babies,' Henry said. 'Otherwise, she did quite well for herself, all things told. That gaudy young man of hers has a sweet estate. And he certainly is infatuated with her.'

128

'Algie didn't offer marriage until my stepmother cornered him and told him of the baby.'

'Your sister was a fool to have given him what he wanted without getting a proposal first, but as it happened, she managed to tie him down anyway.'

'With my luck, I'd find myself in Mariana's situation, raising a child in the country, pretending to have a dead colonel for a husband,' Kate pointed out.

'You have wonderful luck,' Henry said bracingly. 'You have *me*. I informed Dimsdale a few minutes ago that I had recognized you, and he gave me an earful about how wonderful his Victoria is. I'm afraid you're not living up to his fiancée, darling. He's all fretful because you were out there on the lake blackening his future wife's reputation. You should sleep with the pretty prince just to fret the man.'

'That's going a bit far merely to annoy my brother-in-law.'

'Well, you can't pretend that it would be indentured labor,' Henry said. 'The man glitters like a hot day in Paris.'

'Too much,' Kate said. 'He keeps saying he's not seducing me, but—'

'Of course he is,' Henry said. 'And why shouldn't he? He's a prince, after all.'

'That doesn't give him the right to bed whoever crosses his path,' Kate said. 'Caesar, get away from there!'

They had somehow come through to the other side of the maze without finding the center, and found the rest of the menagerie instead. There was a pen full of hairy, malodorous goats, and another that housed an ostrich.

'Just look at that bird,' Henry said. 'It looks like a short man craning his neck to look down someone's bodice. We really ought to get back to the lake and find the husband I picked out for you.'

'What's his name?' Kate asked, pulling sharply on Caesar's leash. 'Come here, you miserable little beast.'

'Your future husband? Dante. Why don't you let that dog go? The ostrich has an eye on him, see? It's probably like those snakes, the ones that swallow rabbits. Caesar could feed it for days.'

'Caesar may not be lovable, but I've grown rather fond of him,' Kate said, hoping that saying it aloud made it true.

'Well, in *that* case,' Henry drawled, making it quite clear that she saw through the lie. 'Why don't you let me take the bejeweled one for a bit, and you drag along Freddie and Caesar the Lion. I loathe dogs, of course, but perhaps that one is acceptable.'

So Kate handed over Coco. They met a few people on their way back through the maze, but Henry introduced Kate—as Victoria—with such a crushing air of familiarity that no one dared say a word about her miraculous weight loss.

'How can you introduce me to your cousin?' Kate asked. 'You'll have to call me Victoria, and that won't do.'

'Oh, we'll tell him the truth,' Henry said. 'And make it seem as if we need his help. He's the sort who couldn't resist the chance to jump to your rescue. He won't approve, not entirely—because, darling, you *did* say that you wanted someone who won't ever stray. Dante didn't even cheat at conkers when he was a boy. And don't think he's Italian because of his exotic name; he should have

130

been called John or something, because he's not flamboyant.'

An image of the restless, glittering prince flashed into Kate's mind and she shook it off. 'He sounds perfect,' she said firmly. 'I don't want anyone flamboyant.'

'He doesn't need money either, so you needn't worry about his being a fortune hunter.'

'I'm not worried, because I'm quite sure you're wrong about my dowry,' Kate said, giving her godmother an apologetic glance. 'I thought about it last night. If my mother had left me all that money, she would have said something to me. All those afternoons when my father was in London, while she and I sat together. She taught me how to do embroidery, and how to curtsy to a queen, and how to hold my fork and knife.'

'She was sick such a long time, poor thing,' Henry said. 'She didn't have time.'

'She just got weaker and weaker,' Kate said, around a lump in her throat. 'Still, I didn't think . . . I just came in one morning and she was lying there, but she was gone.'

'You're going to make *me* cry,' Henry said bracingly.

'I just—' Kate took a deep breath. 'She would have told me.'

'She thought she had time,' Henry said. 'We all think we have time, you know. It's this miracle substance and there seems to be so much of it, and then all of a sudden, it's gone.' Her voice had an edge that made Kate bite her lip.

'My first husband was older than I was, and I gallivanted around town and generally carried on the way a young wife shouldn't, but that didn't mean I didn't love him. I did. When he died, I howled for days. Absolutely howled. I hated myself for every moment I'd spent with anyone else.'

'I'm sorry,' Kate said, touching her arm.

'But that's it,' Henry said, turning her head. Her eyes were bright and quite dry. 'We never know how much time we have with each other. Even your supposed fiancé, who's all bursting with self-importance in his lovely purple waistcoat, could be gone tomorrow.'

'Victoria would be—'

'Of course she would,' Henry interrupted. 'But my point is that we can't—we don't—live like that, remembering that the end is coming. Your mother didn't count her time because she loved being with you. She let herself forget that death was coming, and what a gift that was. So she never told you about the money; she knew it was there. More interesting is why your father never said anything to you.'

'He actually told me after she died that my mother had left me a dowry, but I was wretched and didn't want to talk about it. And then he went off and brought home Mariana. The next thing I knew, he was dead as well.'

'Typical of a man,' Henry said. 'They always die inconveniently.'

They broke out of the seclusion of the maze to find that the gardens were thronged with elegant gentlepersons. 'Now, Dante is very like Bartholomew,' Henry said. 'That would be my second husband, the one before Leo. He was decent through and through. We just have to find Dante, and I'll drag the two of you into a hedge or something and tell him the story.'

132

'Wait!' Kate said, grabbing her arm. 'I don't want to meet him like this.'

'Well, then, how do you want to meet him?'

'Not in this wig,' Kate hissed at her.

'It's better than yesterday's,' Henry said. 'I've never seen that cherry color, and at least it makes you look fashionable.'

'Can't we wait and meet him at a later date, when I'm myself?'

'No,' Henry said, 'we can't. He's on the verge of declaring himself for Effie Starck. She's practically an octogenarian, at least twenty-two.'

'I'm twenty-three!' Kate said.

'I forgot that. Look, she's so desperate that she went for Lord Beckham under the table, and he stuck her with a fork. Or no, she stuck him. Later he told everyone that he thought there was a mongrel under the table gnawing at his trousers. I don't want her anywhere near poor Dante.'

'I would still rather not meet him until I'm in London.'

Henry turned and looked at her.

'I just want to look better than this when I meet your—when I meet Mr Dante,' Kate confessed.

'He's not Mr Dante,' Henry said in an offended kind of way. 'I would never pair off my goddaughter with an Italian merchant. He's Dante Edward Astley, Lord Hathaway.'

'I'm fairly sure that my breasts, the wax parts, are melting,' Kate said desperately, 'because my wig is so hot that I'm sweating. Plus I'd rather not have the dogs with me.'

Henry looked her over. 'You do look rather hot. The cherry-colored wig doesn't help.'

'I'm going to my chamber,' Kate said, making up

133

her mind. 'Here, give me Coco.'

'I'll keep her,' Henry said, rather surprisingly. 'I like the way she walks. You can tell just by looking at her that she'd rather be out here showing off her jewels than closed up in your chamber.'

Kate looked down to find that Coco had positioned herself just next to the hem of Henry's gown, as if she knew how well her multicolored look complemented striped silk. 'Send her back whenever you wish.'

'Wear a different wig this evening,' Henry said. 'I'll have that handsome devil Berwick seat us together with Dante. Do you have a wig that you actually like?'

'No,' Kate said. And then she added, a little desperately, 'My hair is my only asset, Henry. Please, could I just avoid Lord Hathaway until I can meet him as myself?'

'Your hair is your only asset?' Henry snorted. 'Look at Coco.'

Kate looked.

'She's the most vain scrap of animal I've ever seen, and she's utterly irresistible as a result. No one's going to undervalue her. Do you suppose that she thinks she has only one asset? But you . . . if you tell yourself that hair is all you've got, then that's all you've got. Among other things—and I don't have time to enumerate them all—you have utterly devastating eyes. That's Victor's color, of course; he had gorgeous dark yellow hair, like some sort of lion, and then the green eyes. He was a sight to behold.'

'Victoria sent along a pale green wig that looks better with my eyes than this red one,' Kate offered.

'Wear that one, then. I'll deal with Berwick, and

you screw your courage to the sticking point. Dante is ripe for the plucking and I don't want Effie to grab him before you.'

Seventeen

Gabriel was fantastically annoyed. He had tramped off to meet Lady Dagobert, and managed to extract himself from a crowd of ladies only after a young woman practically importuned him on the spot. She'd powdered her face so heavily that her eyes glowed like bits of coal, desire smoking from her white face.

He only managed to escape by grabbing Toloose's arm as he strolled by and pretending that they were bosom friends.

'Miss Emily Gill,' Toloose said. 'You can't blame her, poor thing. She got her materialistic side from her father, and the jowls from her mother.'

'I didn't even notice any jowls,' Gabriel muttered, walking fast. 'Her eyes had me backing up until I was about to fall into the lake.'

'She made a dead set for me last year,' Toloose said cheerfully. 'She gave up only after I told her that I was planning to leave all my money to the deserving poor.'

'Do you have money, then?' Gabriel asked.

'Yes, isn't that lucky for me? Not much at the moment, but someday I'll be a viscount, though I fully expect my papa to live to one hundred. That gets me the attention of ladies like Emily Gill; she looks at me and sees a pile of golden ducats. 'Course, she looks at *you* and sees ducats with

135

crowns on them, so you'll have to be even more repellent than I was, at least until you are safely married to your princess.'

'Have you seen Miss Daltry?'

'She disappeared into the maze with Lady Wrothe. I have to say, I do like Henry. She's inexpressibly vulgar, but it's the kind of vulgarity one expects in a queen. Too bad she's not twenty years younger; she'd make a great princess.'

'Let's go through the maze,' Gabriel said.

Toloose raised an eyebrow.

'Don't give me any more of your clever comments,' he growled. 'This castle is crammed with people making witty comments.'

'Simpering cleverness is our ladies' stock-in-trade,' Toloose said, turning obediently toward the maze.

Which explained, to Gabriel's mind, why Kate was so fascinating. She wasn't sugary, or simpering, or particularly pretty, especially in that ridiculous red wig she was wearing today. She wasn't a lady, either.

So why was he pursuing her into the maze? He wouldn't—would he?—make her his mistress after her absurd masquerade was over?

She wouldn't want to be his mistress. She was too fierce and sharp-tongued to settle into a lush little country house somewhere. And yet he could see himself riding there, throwing himself off the horse, throwing himself onto her . . .

By the time they reached the center of the maze he was walking so fast that he'd left Toloose behind. But there was no one there, only a quiet patch of sunshine housing a little fountain. Water splashed from the mouths of the laughing mer-horses ringing

136

its edge.

He sat on the marble rim, in a patch where he wouldn't be sprinkled by the horses, and wondered what had come over him.

Of course he wouldn't make the illegitimate sister of his nephew's fiancée his mistress. Not that she had shown the faintest interest in that position. He considered himself a decent man, on the verge of marriage.

The sooner Tatiana showed up, the better. A wife would stop him from hungering after women with fierce smiles and laughing eyes, women who adorned themselves in red wigs and pretended to be debutantes.

Toloose finally strolled into the clearing and gave the fountain a disappointed frown. 'I would have hoped for something far more decadent after all this walking,' he said, pulling off his gloves and then his coat. 'Christ, it's hot.'

'What sort of decadence did you envision?'

'A few chaises longues wouldn't go amiss, even if they were made out of stone. With lounging beauties, *not* made from stone.'

'You're talking bachelor fare,' Gabriel said. 'I'm taking a wife.'

'I hear tell there are wives who take to a bit of decadence,' Toloose said.

'Are you looking for a wife?'

'Absolutely not,' Toloose said, throwing himself down on the broad marble ledge around the fountain. 'Lovely, the spray's blowing on my face. I don't see what you're doing trolling amongst our English maidens anyway. Though I hate to mention it, you *are* holding a betrothal ball for yourself in a few days.'

137

'I know,' Gabriel said, unaccountably depressed. 'My fiancée should be arriving tomorrow or the next day.'

'Were you sent a miniature?' Toloose inquired.

'No.'

'So you have no idea what your future wife looks like? That's so desperately medieval. I shouldn't care for it.'

'I don't,' Gabriel said. 'My brother fixed it all up after I sailed for England.'

There was a moment of silence. 'Looks aren't everything,' Toloose offered. 'Take Miss Daltry as an example. When I first met her, I thought of her as a fluffy, giggly type. But that illness must have given her backbone. She's far more appetizing now, even though she's little more than a twig. You should have seen how juicy she was a few months ago.'

'No,' Gabriel said. His voice came out a rumble, from somewhere deep in his chest.

Toloose didn't notice; he was waving his hand happily through the fountain spray. 'I take it that you're perfectly aware of her charms, given the way you sprinted through the maze after her. She must have been at death's door, the difference is so marked. Only thing still the same is her bosom, which makes me suspect—'

Without thinking Gabriel lunged over and pinned the man flat against the marble. 'Her bosom is not for you.'

Toloose froze. 'Let me go,' he said slowly.

Feeling a bit foolish, Gabriel raised his hand.

'Jesus Christ,' Toloose said, sitting up. 'If you plan to steal your nephew's bride, then do it. There's no need to play Wild Prince from the

138

Steppes. I saw that play and didn't like it the first time around.'

'I'm an ass,' Gabriel said. 'Sorry.'

Toloose got to his feet and retrieved his coat. 'You just surprised me, going all masculine and provincial.'

'Surprised myself as well. And I'm not stealing my nephew's bride.'

At that Toloose turned around and stared at him. 'Why bother defending her bosom, if not?'

It was a good question. Just some sort of madness induced by Kate, he decided. 'She doesn't like me.'

'I hate to destroy your illusions,' Toloose said acidly, 'but she's probably not the first person you've met who would fall into that category.'

Gabriel gave him a rueful grin; it was no more than he deserved. 'Perhaps I'm having a nervous reaction to Miss Gill's pursuit.'

'From here, it looks more as if you're having a quite different reaction to Miss Daltry's proximity.'

Gabriel didn't know what to say to that, so they set off through the maze without another word.

Eighteen

'What do you mean, I have to sit with the Lady Dagobert?' Gabriel said. 'I don't want to.'

Wick lit a cheroot and glared at him over the trail of smoke. 'You're acting more like a four-year-old child than a grown man. Of course you're sitting next to the countess. She's the highest-ranking individual in the castle barring yourself; she has known you since you were a child; she will be to your right.'

'I want to sit next to Kate,' Gabriel said, ignoring the truth of Wick's statement. 'Like last night. I'll dine *en famille*.'

'You will not,' Wick stated. 'Miss Katherine Daltry, sometimes known as Victoria, is to sit with her godmother, Lady Wrothe, as well as Lord Hathaway. I don't want to puncture whatever pleasant dream you've having of transforming the illegitimate swineherd's daughter into a princess— or something less respectable—but her godmother is clearly planning to match her to Lord Hathaway.'

'Kate can't marry a lord. She's illegitimate.'

'All I can say is that Lady Wrothe gave me two guineas to put them together, and since she's not a brothel keeper, my guess is that she's found some way around Kate's irregular birth. It could be that she's not as illegitimate as I am.'

'Nothing about Kate makes sense,' Gabriel said. 'Why are her hands callused if her godmother is Lady Wrothe?'

'The only thing completely clear about the situation is your infatuation,' Wick said. 'Let me sum it up for you: Kate, very sensibly, shows no interest in you. Frightened by the imminent arrival of your bride, you are now running shrieking in the direction of the one woman who not only doesn't want you, but isn't eligible. Really, could you be a bit more original?'

'I almost took off Toloose's head for an ill-considered remark about her bosom,' Gabriel said moodily. 'He was decent about it, but he was angry to the bone. Damn it, and I like him.'

'Then stop this ridiculousness,' Wick said.

'You're chasing the girl to distract yourself. It's not kind to her, since you couldn't marry her anyway. She's already got competition; Lady Starck gave me four guineas to put her daughter and herself next to Hathaway, so the man's in demand. Kate will need all her wits about her.'

Gabriel frowned. 'Lady Starck, whose daughter is Miss Effie Starck? She's no competition! Kate will crush her into the parquet.'

'Miss Starck is presumably of excellent birth, and likely has a dowry,' Wick pointed out.

'I'll give Kate a dowry,' Gabriel said instantly.

'One minute you want to seduce her, and the next you're championing her marriage to Hathaway? And just where do you plan to get the money for a dowry? I'm worried about feeding the lion, for God's sake.'

'I'm just saying that Effie Starck is a monkey's arse compared to Kate.'

Wick sighed. 'Forget Kate.'

'*You* should dower her,' Gabriel said moodily. 'Six guineas from that table alone . . .'

'The going rate is much higher to sit at your table,' Wick said, grinning. 'I gather all the young ladies are hoping Princess Tatiana's ship will founder.'

'So it's to your benefit to keep me unwed.'

'I know you don't really want your Russian bride, Gabe,' Wick said, his voice softening.

Gabriel glanced up at his brother. Wick never called him Gabe anymore; it was always Your Highness or, more often, Your Heinous, occasionally varied with Your Knaveness. 'It's not that I don't want Tatiana. I don't want any bride.'

'So run off to Carthage. We'll all survive here,

141

and you wouldn't be the first bridegroom to flee before your wedding night.'

For a split second Gabriel actually considered it, imagining himself dropping all responsibilities and promises, running for Carthage like a man with a devil on his tail.

Then he shook his head. 'Promises were made, and we need the money,' he said, hoisting himself up. 'I'm aiming to be a prince rather than a total ass. I'd better hie myself off to Pole. He gets twitchy if I don't give him at least an hour.'

*   *   *

As the castle now held nearly one hundred gentlepersons, Wick had removed the vast oak table that usually spanned the dining hall, and placed tables for six and eight around the room instead. He himself met every person at the entrance to the hall, and with the seating arrangements safely stowed in his head, dispatched them to the appropriate table in the tender care of a footman.

The whole system was working more smoothly than did most military regiments, Gabriel thought, moving to the head of his particular table, Lady Dagobert on his arm. 'What a pleasure to meet your daughter, my lady,' he said, bowing to Lady Arabella.

Arabella smiled at him with the guileless charm of a young lady trained to bag eligible gentlemen at fifty paces. He sighed and let the conversation wander where it would, and the table was quickly embroiled in a discussion of the French blockade's influence on hemlines.

He didn't let himself look over to Kate's table.

Not even when he actually heard her laughing. One had to assume that Lord Hathaway was amusing.

Lady Arabella gave him a startled look when she heard the low growl that came from somewhere in his chest, but he controlled himself and smiled at her, and she melted.

Like snow hitting a steaming pile of horseshit, he thought to himself.

Across the room, Kate would have agreed that Lord Hathaway was amusing. He wasn't a wit, not in the way that Mr Toloose seemed to be. But she liked him.

She liked the sturdy set of his shoulders, and the way his hair curled over his forehead, as if he were a little boy. He was charmingly boyish, really, while managing to be very much a man. The only problem was Miss Effie Starck, who was seated to his left.

As Henry had warned, Effie was making a dead set for Lord Hathaway. And it looked to Kate as if she was likely to succeed, given the way she kept putting her hand on his arm, as if they were as close bosom friends as Henry and her wax companions.

Effie was quite pretty, in a mouse-eyed kind of way, Kate thought uncharitably. She had soft yellow curls, a round chin, and straight little teeth. She wasn't stupid either.

'You're very fortunate,' she said, smiling lavishly at Kate, who, of course, she thought was Victoria. 'I wish I were celebrating my betrothal in a castle. It's just so romantic!'

'I am very privileged that my uncle is so kind to me,' Algie put in, just to make sure that everyone remembered his relationship to royalty.

'Of course,' Kate said a bit sheepishly. Victoria

143

would have loved to sit at this table, accepting accolades for her betrothal. She felt as if she were stealing flowers that had been sent to her sister.

Effie turned to Lord Hathaway. 'Do tell me more about the blackbirds, Lord Hathaway.'

Kate blinked.

'That came out of the blue, didn't it?' Lord Hathaway said, his eyes twinkling.

'Yes,' Kate said. 'It's oddly fascinating, though. For example,' she said to Effie, 'if you had said, *Tell me more about the crows*, it would have a rather sinister tone, whereas blackbirds make one think about pies.'

'And queens and counting houses,' Lord Hathaway said. 'Now what if Miss Starck had said, *Tell me more about the Minotaurs*. What would you think of me then?'

Kate laughed, and Effie tittered uncertainly. 'I'd think that Miss Starck was five years old, and you were telling her fairy tales. But not everything fantastic would have the same ring. What would you think if she asked, *Tell me more about the giant*?'

'I wouldn't think about children's stories,' Hathaway said, 'but about the men who wrestle each other at the fair.'

'But *Tell me more about the giantess*?'

'I'd think you were talking about Lady Dagobert,' Henry put in, with a wicked grin. The countess could not be described as slender.

Lady Starck shifted uneasily; her own figure rather resembled Lady Dagobert's. 'I think,' she interjected, 'that my dear Effie was merely fascinated by your account of a plague of blackbirds, Lord Hathaway.'

'A plague of blackbirds,' Kate said, before she could stop herself. 'It sounds like divine retribution, which is ominous. What have you been up to, Lord Hathaway?'

Hathaway laughed again, and Kate thought about how very *nice* he was. 'It may be divine retribution,' he said, 'but if so, I'm not sure to which of my many sins to attribute it. And it wasn't a plague of frogs, may I point out.'

Effie turned to Kate, her eyes cool. 'The blackbirds are causing a serious inconvenience to Lord Hathaway, Miss Daltry. They are roosting in his eaves and diving at the servants when they enter the kitchen gardens. And now they've started attacking his guests.'

Kate couldn't suppress the little cynical smile on her face. It was one thing when birds attacked servants . . . but *guests*? 'It's unlike blackbirds to be so aggressive,' she said to Lord Hathaway. 'They're acting like bluebirds. Could you have disturbed their nests somehow so they had to relocate to the eaves?'

'I don't think so,' he said. 'I hate to admit it, but I never gave the birds much thought, though there were some complaints from the housekeeper. But last week the vicar came to call and I'm afraid that . . . well . . .'

'What?' Effie asked, confused. 'Did a blackbird swoop at his head?'

Lord Hathaway had turned a little red.

'I suspect they shat on the vicar,' Kate told Effie, putting His Lordship out of his misery. 'All that black, marked with white. The man must have looked like a chessboard.'

Lady Starck drew in her breath with an audible

sound of displeasure. 'Well, I never!' she said.

Effie's pink mouth formed a tiny, startled circle, but Henry laughed and said, 'It proves that the plague of blackbirds wasn't the work of heaven. I assume that the vicar did not react in a pious manner.'

'This is a remarkably vulgar conversation,' Lady Starck said, her eyes fixed on Kate.

'I shall make the birds into a pie,' Lord Hathaway said, coming to the rescue. 'Thank you for that suggestion, Miss Daltry.'

'Oh, I didn't mean it,' Kate cried, feeling a pang of guilt. 'You mustn't shoot at them, Lord Hathaway. The creatures have no idea they were upsetting your servants; they were probably just protecting their babies. Nesting season must be over, so you could send up a man to clean out the nests.'

'They'll build them again,' Algie said, affecting as authoritative a voice as his eighteen-year-old self could muster. 'You'll have to take a gun to them, though of course the young ladies will dislike the idea. My betrothed has very delicate sensibilities,' he stated, staring hard at Lady Starck.

Kate gave him a rather surprised smile; it was nice of Algie to come to her defense.

'Would you feel the same if I had suffered a plague of frogs?' Lord Hathaway inquired. 'The French eat frogs as a daily affair, you know. They would likely count a rain of them as offerings from heaven.'

'I think,' Kate said, 'that you should cook up any frogs that hop—or fall—onto your property, Lord Hathaway.'

She added with a grin, 'Just please don't invite

146

me to supper.'

'I don't think the French put frogs into pies,' Effie said seriously.

Lord Hathaway looked at her and smiled. It was clear that he liked her earnestness. 'In point of fact, I don't like the idea of shooting around my house.'

Effie gave a little squeal. They all looked at her. 'Well,' she said, 'you might strike someone dead.'

'He'd presumably use birdshot,' Kate told her. 'One of my footmen took a load of birdshot and he couldn't sit down for two weeks, which caused a great deal of amusement in the household. His name was Barsey and—' She broke off.

'You have a lively sense of humor, Miss Daltry,' Lord Hathaway said, showing that he had realized exactly how close *Barsey* was to *arse*.

'I don't inquire as to the names of my footmen,' Lady Starck said loftily. 'I call them all John, which suffices well enough.'

Kate was appalled, but she bit her tongue. It was the last seven years, of course, living as half a servant and half a family member . . . it had changed her attitude toward the household. It took an effort of will not to snap at Lady Starck.

'I know all our footmen's names,' Miss Starck said, showing that she wasn't nearly as blind as her mother. She curled her hand around Lord Hathaway's arm again. At this rate the man was going to start feeling as if he were wearing a mourning band. 'Don't you think that it is our providential duty to care for all those below us, whether they be birds or unfortunate degenerates?'

'Are your footmen unfortunate degenerates?' Henry put in cheerfully. 'The only one of those in my household is my darling Leo.'

147

They all glanced over at Henry's husband, seated opposite her. Leo gave Kate a naughty wink and said, 'It takes a degenerate to keep track of my wife, I assure you. No one else would have the imagination.'

Lady Starck sniffed in horror, but Kate liked Leo, for all Henry's complaints about his drinking. True, he seemed to be enjoying the champagne more than the fish, but for that matter, so was she.

Nineteen

The evening's entertainment was announced by Berwick; it was to be a display of naval prowess on the lake, designed by Prince Ferdinand.

'The gardens in the dark?' Lady Starck said, sniffing again. 'My daughter will certainly not participate. We shall retire.'

'When one is older, one simply *must* rest one's bones,' Henry said. 'If you wish, I will chaperone your daughter for you.'

Lady Starck took a deep breath, which had the unfortunate effect of swelling her more-than-ample bosom.

'Darling,' Henry said kindly, 'I'm afraid you've suffered a wardrobe malfunction.'

Lady Starck glanced down at her right nipple, which was staring like a fish eye over the ruffle edging her bodice, and slapped her napkin over her chest, surging to her feet. 'Effie, come!' she said, with all the authority that Kate tried to use with Caesar.

148

It worked about as well for Her Ladyship as it did for Kate. 'Mama, I should dearly love to see the naval display,' Effie said, her voice soft but firm. 'I shall be perfectly safe under the chaperonage of Lady Wrothe.'

'We shall guard your treasure very carefully,' Lord Hathaway said. He was standing, of course. As soon as Lady Starck's nipple made its appearance, all the gentlemen leaped to their feet, though Kate knew that it was ostensibly in response to the lady's departure.

'I doubt it will be a long performance,' Henry put in. 'We'll all trot back to the house in a few minutes.'

'Very well,' Lady Starck said, her napkin still clutched to her breast. 'Effie, I expect you to come to my chamber the very moment this naval spectacle is finished.'

'I will, Mama,' Effie said, sounding very cheerful.

'I don't think you have that story right,' Kate whispered to Henry as they strolled from the dining room. 'Effie can't possibly have groped Lord Beckham under the table. She's not that sort of woman.'

'She wouldn't know what she was groping for, would she?' Henry said. 'It must have been someone else. But I'm right about the fact that Dante is ripe for plucking *and* that the two of you are quite suited. Don't you see what will happen to him if he marries her?'

'He'll be happy,' Kate said. 'She's quite sweet, in a somber kind of way.'

'She never laughs unless someone else gives her a cue,' Henry said, sounding genuinely dismayed. 'And I like Dante. He's grown into a very decent fellow. When he was just five years old, he used to lean on my knee and ask me to tell him another story.' She narrowed her eyes. 'Of course, I was a mere toddler myself. If you ever tell anyone that I am old enough to have told Dante stories, I'll be forced into an act of violence.'

'What kind of violence?' Kate inquired, fascinated.

'I've got the measure of you,' Henry said. 'You don't like dogs, but you're doing your best with those little mongrels of your sister's. You don't care for lions, but you're championing for a bigger cage. You wouldn't even let the nasty blackbirds be made into a pie in order to restore the dignity of the vicar. It would be easy to put you under my thumb; all I'd have to do is threaten to throw Coco onto the King's highway.'

'I would save Coco only because my dowry is glued to her neck,' Kate said. The disconcerting thing was that Henry was right, of course. That was how Mariana had kept her under her thumb all these years: by threatening to dismiss a footman, or the housekeeper, or even dear Cherryderry.

They were walking out the back of the castle now. Stretching before them were the pale marble steps descending to the lake. They shimmered the color of pearl in the light of torches that lined the stairs.

'What on earth have you done with Coco, by the way? She never came back to my room.'

'She's right here,' Henry said smugly. 'And what a good girl she is; no one heard a peep from her during the meal.' She turned around and crooned, 'Come on, darling.' Coco pranced out before them, her tail waving.

150

'What's she got around her neck?' Kate asked. 'And on her leash?'

'Ribbons and flowers to match my gown, of course,' Henry said. 'Her jewels are all very well, but a lady needs a new *toilette* in the evening. So my maid soaked off the jewels and replaced them with a flower called lupine, which sounds like a half-deranged wolf, but is actually beautiful and matches my costume perfectly.'

'She looks as if she's stuck her head through a funeral wreath,' Kate pointed out.

'Coming from a woman wearing a wig the color of a gooseberry, that means little,' Henry retorted.

'I have to wear a wig,' Kate said firmly. 'I'm incognito.'

'You make it sound as if you're working for the Foreign Office,' Henry said. 'Now what are you going to do to dislodge Effervescent Effie from Dante's arm? She's attached like a limpet.'

Kate shrugged.

'No wonder you're unmarried at the ripe age of twenty-three,' Henry said. 'Leo, come here!'

Her husband, who was ambling along behind them, looking just slightly tipsy, stepped forward next to Kate. 'Yes, love?' he said.

Kate liked that. She could tolerate a husband who drank too much if he called her love and looked at her the way Leo looked at Henry. As if he'd be there for her, always.

'Can you shake some sense into my goddaughter? She's practically as old as I am, and yet she's lazy when it comes to marriage.'

Leo twinkled at Kate. 'Henry likes marriage,' he said, taking her arm. 'That's why she's done it so many times.'

'I wouldn't have had to if men lived longer,' Henry said.

'Is there anyone you'd particularly like to marry?' Leo asked Kate.

The prince, Kate thought—and quelled the thought in horror. What on earth was she thinking? It was just that kiss . . . that kiss. . .

'No one in particular,' she said firmly.

'What about Toloose? He's a decent chap,' Leo said. 'My house at Oxford and all. Going to be a viscount someday.'

'You went to Oxford as well?' Kate inquired.

'A double first in philosophy and history,' Henry put in. 'Never marry anyone with fewer brains than yourself, darling. It always ends badly.'

'If my wife had gone to Oxford, they would have had to create a triple first,' Leo said.

'What did you say?' Henry asked.

'In seduction,' he whispered.

Kate giggled, and Lord Hathaway turned around and looked back at them. It might have been her imagination, but he looked as if he were longing to know the joke.

'Kate can't marry Toloose,' Henry said. 'For goodness' sake, Leo. The man's got a wandering eye. I can assure you of that.'

'All eyes wander in my wife's direction,' Leo sang tunefully.

Henry reached past Kate and poked him. 'But they don't wander into your wife's bed, so be happy with that. Now, my idea is that Kate should marry . . .' She nodded at Lord Hathaway's back.

'Really?' Leo said, a trifle doubtfully.

'Why not?'

'I was listening to the dinner conversation,' Leo

said, 'and it seemed to me that Miss Kate has a great deal of wit, as my grandmother would say. She reminds me of you, m'dear.'

'Well, I did hold her during her baptism,' Henry said. 'Maybe I rubbed off on her.'

'And *you* would not be happy in such a marriage,' Leo continued. 'The man in question is a brave and gentle soul, no doubt. But in a matter of ten years he will be falling asleep in a chair by the fire, after spending supper deploring the make of his boots.'

'Unkind,' Henry said. 'Very unkind.' But she was laughing.

'I should enjoy that,' Kate said firmly. 'I have very few ambitions, and if I knew my husband was asleep in a chair opposite me, I would cheerfully doze off myself. What I do not want is a husband who is out offering sugarplums to other women while I am at home alone.'

'Sugarplums,' Henry said. 'One could almost think that you meant something metaphorical, dearest Kate.'

'Kate?' Effie suddenly said, glancing over her shoulder. 'Are you calling Miss Daltry Kate? How sweet; is that a family name?'

'Absolutely,' Henry said, smiling at her with tigerish emphasis, all her teeth showing. 'I am her godmama, after all. I have pet names for all my dear ones.'

'She calls me her sugarplum,' Leo said.

Effie was tripping down the steps again, so he added: 'But I made her stop: altogether too soft and pillowy for, ahem, someone like me.'

Kate couldn't help laughing.

'Too small too,' Henry added proudly.

They had reached the bottom of the steps and

153

were greeted by Berwick. 'You are fortunate to have arrived so promptly; you needn't watch from the shore but can actually join the entertainment,' he said. 'If you would follow me.' He took them a short way around the lake and stopped before a gilded boat whose elaborately carved prow arched high in the air. The seats were padded luxuriously and set at an angle; presumably they would all recline.

'That looks like a very, very small Viking ship,' Leo said.

'I'm fairly sure the Vikings were an industrious lot,' Kate said, basing that on a book she'd read from her father's library. 'This looks more like Roman decadence to me.'

'The Vikings?' Henry asked. 'Who on earth were they?'

'Your ancestors,' Leo said. He whispered something in her ear and she gave him a little slap.

'What did he say?' Kate asked, following Henry into the boat.

'Something about rape and pillage,' Henry said. 'As if any of my partners ever lacked the proper enthusiasm!' She sat down in the carved seat that made up the stern of the boat and snuggled Coco onto her lap.

'If I didn't know you better,' Kate said, 'I'd think you were in love with that dog.'

'She and I understand each other,' Henry said loftily. 'Besides . . .' She scratched Coco under one ear. 'She's quite affectionate, isn't she?'

'She wasn't with me,' Kate said. 'You're making me miss Freddie. He looks at me with those same eyes.'

'I'm very fond of unquestioning adoration,'

Henry said. 'One can't have too much of it, from dogs or men.'

Lord Hathaway scrambled onto the boat and sat down next to Kate on one side of the boat. Algie, following him, sat next to Effie on the other side. Leo would have taken to the life of a Roman statesman; he dropped next to Henry, stretched his legs out, and said, 'I like this kind of military entertainment. So different from what one expects, i.e., violence and general hardship, not to mention hardtack.'

'What are we doing in this boat?' Effie asked, sitting bolt upright rather than reclining on the padded seat. 'Wouldn't it be better to watch from shore? The lake is so black at night.'

At that moment a footman leaned forward and lit a torch on the shore before their boat, and then a torch actually attached to the prow of their ship. They both leaped into flame—blue flame. Effie screamed.

'Don't worry, Miss Starck,' Algie said. 'It can't hurt you.'

'Why is it blue?' she whimpered.

That stumped Algie, leaving Leo to drawl, 'They've put some powder in with the oil. See, some boats are flaming red and others blue. There appear to be four of each.'

Algie was busily patting Miss Starck's arm. 'My fiancée is just the same,' he said. 'Ladies are delicate and frighten easily.'

'Your fiancée doesn't look frightened in the least,' Effie pointed out, narrowing her eyes at Kate.

Kate realized that was her cue to look timid, but couldn't manage. 'I do believe that we are part of a naval flotilla,' she said. 'Look! We're the blues.'

'What I can't figure out,' Lord Hathaway said, 'is how we're going to take our places on the lake. Unless we're meant to—'

But at that moment the boat rocked, very gently, and began to pull away from the shore, as if drawn by an invisible hand. Naturally, Effie screamed again. Algie had taken her hand now, and was patting it madly.

'You're going to give her a bruise,' Kate said.

'It's magic!' Effie cried.

Hathaway was craning his neck around the side of the boat. 'Though magic sounds very delectable, in fact, we're attached to a rope,' he reported. 'There must be a man on the other side of the lake, drawing us over.'

'And look,' Kate said, 'the other boats are all coming out too.'

From around the perimeter of the lake, boats flaming red or blue were slowly moving toward the center.

Effie asked the obvious. 'What if we all crash? I wish we weren't going backwards. I don't like sitting backwards in a coach either. I always make my maid do it.'

'I can swim,' Algie announced.

'Obviously we're not going to crash,' Henry said. 'Although, Leo, remember that if you have to tow me to shore, you'd better not forget my darling Coco or you'll wish you'd sunk.'

It was a good thing that Victoria had never appeared to care overly much about her dogs; it seemed likely that Coco would never darken the door of Mariana's house again.

A boat slid by them, red flame dancing over the

excited faces inside the boat. The prince wasn't among them, though it was a weakness of Kate's that she even noticed.

'About an inch to spare,' Leo said coolly.

'It's designed like clockwork,' Lord Hathaway said. 'The boats are all slipping past each other; it must look amazing from the shore.' In a few minutes all the boats had crossed the lake and reached the opposite side.

A grinning footman reeled them in. 'Well done,' Lord Hathaway said. 'You must have practiced for days to carry this out so well.'

'Weeks,' the man said.

'Why don't the boats collide?' Hathaway asked.

'I can answer that,' Leo said. 'The ropes are presumably just at the water's surface, so boats glide over each other's attachments. And the boats aren't going directly across the lake, because in that case a boat might crack into one coming from the opposite direction. They're going catty-cornered, and the lake's an oval, so they all just miss each other.'

The footman nodded. 'Now you'll be pulled back the other way, my lord, and this time you'll be able to see where you're going, so it'll be even better.'

It did look splendid. Kate stripped off her right glove and trailed her fingers in the water, silently scolding herself for wondering where Gabriel was.

'Have you taken off your glove?' Effie asked, sounding rather awed.

'Yes,' Kate said. She raised her fingers and flicked water into the blue light thrown off by the torch. 'Isn't it lovely?'

The boats were all moving slowly out from shore again, recommencing their orchestrated water

157

ballet.

Effie looked at her gloves but folded her hands in her lap.

'Go on,' Henry said rather kindly, for her. 'I won't tell your mother.'

'A lady—' Effie started, but stopped. She'd obviously just remembered that it would be impolite to suggest that Kate was not behaving in a ladylike manner.

'A lady should never feel anxious about her behavior,' Henry announced. 'The status is bred in the bone. To show anxiety is to lower oneself. Anxiety is *vulgar.*'

Effie digested that and finally pulled off one glove and consigned it to Algie's care. At first she squealed about how cool the water felt, but she seemed to gain courage as the boat moved silently out into the lake. When the first boat slid past them, she copied Kate and flicked drops of sparkling blue water toward them, giggling madly at the surprised faces in the boat.

No prince, Kate noticed crossly. He was probably on shore, cozied up to a rich baroness.

A second boat slipped past them, rocking a little. 'What are they up to?' Henry asked. She had her head on Leo's shoulder and was looking happily at the sky.

'They've got a bottle of champagne,' Algie said in a disapproving voice.

'Damn, got in the wrong boat,' Leo said softly.

His wife reached up and pinched his nose.

Algie was watching the red-torched boat retreat. 'They must be rocking it on purpose.'

'Silly,' Effie said, happily trailing her hand in the water all the way up to her wrist. One had to suppose that this was her first taste of freedom, such as it was.

Another boat approached, rocking even more wildly.

'All young men in that barque,' Lord Hathaway said. 'They need women to keep them sedate. And sober.'

'Don't tell me that we're the only boat consigned to sobriety,' Leo said, with mock sorrow.

'They've—yes!' Algie cried, peering ahead. 'A man's overboard. He's all right; he caught on to the rope.'

'What fools,' Lord Hathaway said with disgust.

'Wet fools,' Leo said. 'It might set a new fashion for castle entertainment. Enough with the motley, and on with the water.'

'He's swimming to shore,' Algie said.

'The problem is one of timing,' Leo said in a different tone of voice, sitting up. 'Are you dripping with diamonds tonight?' he asked his wife.

'No,' Henry replied. 'Well, I have the big emerald and I'm afraid my ear bobs aren't firmly attached.' She pulled them off in a businesslike fashion. 'You'd better take them.' She handed over her jewels and hitched Coco so firmly against her bosom that the normally quiet dog gave a little yelp of protest. 'Hathaway, you're in charge of my goddaughter. And Dimsdale, you have Effie.'

'Why?' Effie asked in alarm. 'What do you mean, Lady Wrothe?'

'Leo's very good at this sort of thing,' Henry said, 'and if he thinks—'

But at that very moment a boat loomed up, except that it didn't slide sweetly past their prow. Instead it slammed right into their side. For a

159

second, it looked as if they would be fine. The boat tilted wildly, but righted itself.

But then their boat jerked again, presumably because the footman was trying to pull them to shore, and it lurched over to the other side.

Effie screamed; Kate screamed too, for the split second before the water rushed toward her and she fell into the lake.

The water was cold but not freezing. She had a moment of terror thinking that the boat was on top of her, but then she realized she was facing the bottom of the lake and managed to kick her way to the top.

She broke the surface with a gasp and a cough, and looked wildly for the boat. She turned in a circle, kicking madly to stay afloat, and couldn't see it. The lake was covered with flaring torches that appeared to be bouncing up and down from her position on the surface of the lake, but her boat . . . her boat . . . There it was. Getting farther away by the second.

'I knew you weren't a lady,' said an amused voice at her ear. 'No lady even knows that word.'

She screamed and would have clutched at him, but Gabriel was behind her, slipping a strong arm around her waist. He pulled her back against his chest, so she was virtually lying on her back in the water. 'Don't be so loud,' he said in her ear. 'You don't want all those other rescuers to find you instead of me, do you?'

'What rescuers?' Kate said, spitting out a little lake water. 'My godmother told Hathaway to save me and he's obviously failed to do so.'

'I'd love to say he sank like a stone,' Gabriel said, kicking his legs so they started moving through the water, 'but it's unlikely. My whole boat went over as well, and I expect Hathaway rescued the wrong damsel in distress.'

'I like that,' Kate said darkly. 'I could have drowned. I hope Henry is all right.'

'Lady Wrothe managed to remain in the boat,' Gabriel said. 'Her husband lunged for the opposite side at just the right moment and righted it. I think Miss Starck may have escaped the water as well.'

'Henry must be worried about me,' Kate said. 'Could you swim a little faster?'

'No, I could not,' Gabriel said. 'This is my fastest when it comes to swimming on my back and dragging you as well. I don't think Lady Wrothe is worried, because she caught sight of me in the water and instructed me with one ferocious gesture to go after you. So I did.'

'I could kick too,' Kate offered.

'Your skirts are giving me enough trouble,' Gabriel said.

There was a moment of silence. 'Are we almost at shore?' she asked. The lights of the boat that she thought was hers were receding quickly.

'We would have been, but I must have got turned around,' Gabriel said. 'We're heading for the far shore.'

'There are no boats over there,' Kate said, peering over her shoulder.

'Don't complain,' Gabriel said. 'You're no lightweight, for all you've supposedly lost two stone.'

'Just be glad you're not rescuing Victoria,' Kate said.

'I am.' Then he gave a grunt, which turned out to be because he had swum straight into the marble lip of the lake.

'I can do it,' Kate said, twisting out of his grip and catching the marble.

He hauled himself up and then reached down and grabbed her wrist, pulling her up as easily as if he were landing a trout.

'Oh,' Kate said, shivering uncontrollably. 'It's so cold. You were brilliant, thanks.' She wrapped her arms around herself and peered across the lake. 'Damnation, we came up on the far side.'

Gabriel was walking away from her along the shore, so she stumbled after him, thinking that princes weren't all that gentlemanly when it came to it. He could at least have taken her arm. But then he bent over and started to pull on a rope.

Kate stood next to him, tremors going from the top of her shoulders to her feet. 'Are—are you getting us a boat?' she asked, feeling as if cold water had frozen her brain.

He was hauling on the rope so fast that it was spinning out behind him. 'Don't let this slap you,' he said with a gasp, and she suddenly realized how hard he was working. Sure enough, a boat was cutting through the water toward them. It was one of the red ones, its torch burning low now.

Kate could have sobbed with joy at the sight of it. 'Will they pull us back?' she asked. 'Don't answer that! Save your breath.' In the light of the approaching torch, she could see his muscled arms pulling, hand over hand, so fast that the rope raced past his shoulder.

It was . . . interesting. He looked like a farm laborer, but at the same time, not at all like a farm laborer.

The boat met the marble edge with a splintering

162

thud. 'Come on,' Gabriel said, breathing hard. He leaped in and held out his hand. She climbed on, almost losing her footing because of her wet slippers.

'Sit down; they'll pull us over directly,' he said.

'I—' she said, teeth chattering, but he pulled her down onto his lap, and that was the end of whatever she was about to say.

His body was huge and warm, and she was so cold that she melted into him with an entirely unladylike noise. He wrapped his arms around her and she almost moaned again from the pleasure of it.

'You're warm,' she said after a moment, feeling that they should be having some sort of conversation. 'Is the boat moving?'

'Yes.' He tucked her more firmly against the warmth of his chest. 'Are you still cold?'

'Not as much.'

'I have the solution to your chill,' he said, and his voice had gone dark and fierce. She turned her face up to his like a child seeking a good-night kiss—it was that natural—and his lips parted hers.

Their third kiss, she thought dimly, and it was already different from the others. They kissed now as if they knew each other, as if they were both leaping into a fire that they longed for. Raw heat scorched down her back-bone and she broke away with a little murmur, almost frightened by the force of it.

But his arms tightened and he wouldn't let her go, brushing his mouth against hers. Then she felt his tongue caressing her bottom lip until she gasped from the sweet heat. He took her gasp as if it were an invitation and gave her a little bite, nibbling on

163

her lip in a way that somehow had Kate pressing against his chest as if she wanted to get closer and closer.

He just kept teasing her, until she took her hands from his chest and wrapped them around his neck, pulling his head down to hers in a silent demand.

She could feel him laughing and then he was kissing her again and their tongues were tangling in a kind of rough explosion that made her feel dizzy and breathless.

This time *he* pulled back. 'We're coming to shore. They'll be able to see us soon.' He sounded a little drunk.

Kate nodded, looking up at him. His eyes were black in the torchlight, his cheekbones drawn, and his wet hair slicked straight back from his head. He looked like a Cossack warrior, the kind who pillaged villages and stole maidens.

Maidens like her, milkmaids and poor relations and women with few relatives.

She cleared her throat and quickly shifted off his lap to the seat next to him. 'Thank you for warming me,' she said, starting to shiver immediately.

An odd look passed through his eyes and she followed his gaze downward. Her gown was utterly soaked, of course, and unfortunately her wax breasts had not survived their bath unscathed. One was still in place, perkily holding up Kate's meager offering. But the one on the right, where Gabriel's arm had towed her through the water, had been squished. The misshapen remains had migrated down and were positioned just above her waistline.

She looked down, thinking desperately what to say. 'Henry calls them her "bosom friends,"' she blurted out, saying the first thing that came to her head. 'If you would please close your eyes . . .'

He did. 'A gentleman would not be grinning like that,' she scolded, plucking the freezing ball of wax from her ruined gown. The crushed one was a bit trickier, but she was able to pull her destroyed bodice down enough to pull it out through her stays.

The boat was close to shore by the time she had restored her bosom to its natural state. Luckily they were obscured from view by the fact that their torch had at last spluttered out, though she could make out curious faces lining the marble basin.

'All right,' she said, hauling her bodice into a reasonable approximation of its former self.

He opened his eyes.

'Take that expression off your face!' she said crossly.

'It's this or look at you in such a way that everyone would know *exactly* what I'm thinking about,' he said softly.

She glanced down and saw her nipples poking straight through the wct silk. Heat rose in her face. 'You'd better give the discards to me,' he said. 'If the servants find them, they'd never be able to keep it to themselves.'

She had them hidden at her side, but she reluctantly handed them over. Gabriel turned over the blobs of wax. 'You don't need these,' he said. 'But they're fascinating, all the same.'

'You may keep them,' Kate said. She could see Wick standing on the shore with what looked like a blanket in his hands. 'Now,' she commanded, 'go get me that blanket. I'm not standing up in this drenched gown.'

'Not without your bosom friends,' he said.

165

She gave him a fierce look, and it worked as well as it did with the French hairdresser; Gabriel got up, still laughing, and fetched the blanket.

Then he came back and wrapped her in it. 'Your wig is gone,' he said, looking down at her. 'You look like a drowned rat.'

He looked breathtakingly handsome, but she should retaliate for the benefit of his soul. The man raised confidence to the level of a deadly sin. 'You look—' she began. But there was something in his eyes that she liked, something lustful perhaps, but still . . .

'Thank you,' she said. 'I might have drowned without you and I'm very grateful that you towed me out.'

A strange look crossed his eyes. 'You should slap me for that kiss, for taking advantage of your chill.'

She moved around him, heading to the bow of the boat and Wick's outstretched hand. Just before disembarking, she paused and looked over her shoulder. 'Perhaps I took advantage of *you*,' she said, just quietly enough so that no one on shore could hear her.

He blinked and then said, 'I only wish you would.'

Twenty

The next morning Kate slept late, after a confused and mostly sleepless night in which she alternately tossed with fiery humiliation at the memory of Gabriel laughing down at her wax breasts, and flushed red at the memory of his kisses.

166

She was wakened by Rosalie, who told her that Miss Starck's maid was inquiring whether her mistress might join her for breakfast.

'Lady Wrothe says you're not to leave this room all day,' Rosalie said importantly. 'You're quite the heroine of the hour, I must say. Those youngbloods who caused your boat to capsize are properly ashamed of themselves and planning some sort of gift.'

'No!' Kate said. 'Surely not.'

'Yes, because you were the only one who wasn't plucked out immediately, but actually had to swim across the lake. Like a mermaid, that's what everyone is saying.'

'I wasn't in the least mermaid-like,' Kate objected. 'The prince towed me along like a dead fish.'

'No need to get into the particulars,' Rosalie said.

'Now Miss Starck and Lady Wrothe, they were saved by the quick thinking of Lord Wrothe. He righted the boat, and the only ones to fall in were yourself and the dog.'

'Is Coco all right?'

'Lord Dimsdale dove straight off the boat to save you, but I gather you came up on the other side. So he saved Coco, because the prince had already swum after you. By all accounts, Lady Wrothe was screaming so loudly that they could hear her on shore.'

'So Algie saved the dog, rather than me,' Kate said grumpily, sitting up.

'Lady Wrothe wasn't very pleased. And she was very sharp with Lord Hathaway this morning,' Rosalie confided, pulling open the curtains to reveal a beautiful sunny morning. 'She told him at breakfast—where anyone could hear!—that she'd instructed him to save you, and her husband to save her dog, and he could have had the courtesy to make an effort to follow her directions instead of just staying in the boat.'

Kate couldn't help smiling.

'And then Lord Wrothe said that for his part he was dashed pleased that Dimsdale had gone for the dog, because he didn't want to ruin his new boots. And then she bonked him on the head with a kipper.'

'*Very* exciting,' Kate exclaimed. 'I had no idea married life was so entertaining.'

'Lady Wrothe's maid says it's always like that in their house. They squabble something terrible. Until he buys her a ruby, and it's all over. They're that fond of each other; anyone can tell.'

'I suppose I should get up, if Effie wants to pay a visit,' Kate said, yawning again.

'I'll just put a wrapper on you and brush out your hair,' Rosalie said. 'She wouldn't expect you in a proper gown, not after the terrible shock you've had. Do you feel as if you have a fever, miss? The prince offered to send the castle's doctor.'

'He has his own doctor?' Kate said, swinging her legs out of bed.

'Came over with him on the boat,' Rosalie said. She started giggling. 'The "ship of fools," that's what Mr Berwick calls it. Because the duke over there in foreign parts, he tossed out half his court, including the fool himself.'

'I don't need a doctor,' Kate said, washing her face. 'I'll have breakfast with Effie, but then I want a bath, Rosalie, and I mean to get dressed. I don't

168

feel in the least bit chilled.'

'You mustn't bathe yet!' Rosalie said, alarmed. 'You were shivering so last night that I thought the bed might crack in half. Please sit down, miss, and I'll brush out your hair. I'll tie it back with a ribbon for your breakfast with Miss Starck, and then you must pop straight back into bed.'

*   *   *

It was immediately clear that Effie considered their midnight adventure to have made them the best of friends. She sat down opposite Kate at a small table Rosalie set before a roaring fire (never mind the balmy air coming through the window), and proceeded to give a breathless rendition of what it felt like as the boat drew away in the black, black water, with Kate nowhere to be seen.

'We knew then that you were *dead*,' she said with thrilling emphasis. 'Killed by that freezing water!'

'Luckily for me, I wasn't,' Kate said, taking another piece of buttered toast. She had ridden out, shivering, on a hundred chilly mornings, which likely inured her to the cold, though she didn't think Effie would understand if she tried to explain her hard-earned immunity.

'Lady Wrothe was on her feet,' Effie continued, 'desperately searching the waters.'

'Could you see Coco?'

'She was splashing alongside the boat, paddling really well. You should have seen how small that dog was after Lord Dimsdale rescued it, no bigger than a kitten with its wet fur. Lady Wrothe acted as if her own child had fallen in.'

'So where was I?'

'You finally came up on the far side. You were very lucky not to have hit your head on the other boat. Everyone from that boat was in the water, though they came out again quickly, all but the prince. Lady Wrothe was the first to spot you, and she shrieked at him to fetch you, *this instant*.' Effie giggled. 'I'd never have imagined that anyone could order a prince to do something the way she did. And of course he obeyed and swam over to get you.'

'How odd,' Kate said. 'I felt as if it was just a moment before I found my way to the surface, and the boat was already moving away.'

'It probably was,' Effie said, considering it. 'We were pulled off by the footman, of course, who didn't know what was happening. But at the time it seemed very slow, I assure you. When you didn't come back up, and the red and blue torchlight was bouncing off the water . . . even the prince looked horribly distressed.'

'How could you see? Wasn't he in the water?'

'Yes, but Lady Wrothe called out that you were missing and I saw his eyes. My mother says that I'm never to go anywhere near the lake again. Not even during the ball.'

'Don't tell me they're planning to do it again!'

'No one is to be allowed in the boats but servants who know how to swim,' Effie said. 'But it is already planned, so they're going ahead with it. The boats are going to be shooting off fireworks, which I must say sounds very pretty. I shall have to watch from the steps, though, because Mama is quite overwrought.' She sounded wistful.

'Will you have the last piece of toast?' Kate asked.

'No, thank you,' Effie said. 'I eat very little. You have it. You are at such risk of getting sick; everyone is talking about it. After that terrible illness you had a few months ago, and now the shock and cold.' She paused. 'Though you look very well.'

Kate smiled at her. 'I feel just fine.'

'I didn't know you had such long hair,' Effie said. 'Why do you always wear a wig? Don't you find it terribly hot? I can't bear them myself.'

'I like wigs.'

'I hope you don't mind a comment,' Effie said, 'but I think your hair is lovely. All those different colors of red and gold . . . it's just like a sunset. Better than that red wig, even though it *is* fashionable.'

'Red sky in the morning,' Kate muttered.

'Sailors take warning,' Effie said. She twiddled her fork for a moment. 'It was so romantic when Lord Dimsdale went into the water after you. I wish you could have seen it. The boat righted itself and he shouted your name and then dove straight off the side. Though of course you weren't actually on that side.'

'Who did that? Oh, Algie,' Kate said. 'It does sound romantic. My fiancé apparently has hidden depths.' Frankly, she was surprised.

'They're all in love with you,' Effie stated. 'Lord Hathaway as well.'

'He's all yours,' Kate said promptly.

'I'm not sure . . . you're so amusing. You say such witty things.' She looked across at Kate with her sweet seriousness and said, 'I don't want you to think that I'm in love with Lord Hathaway because I'm not. And I'm not desperate to marry anyone.'

171

'Neither am I,' Kate said, getting up to ring the bell. 'You don't mind if I call for more cocoa, do you? I think that dunking made me ravenous.'

'We didn't meet during the season,' Effie continued, 'though I heard about you, of course. But no one told me you were so funny. I think that's why they're all in love with you.'

Kate burst into laughter. 'What on earth are you talking about?'

'They're all in love with you,' Effie repeated. 'Lord Dimsdale, and Lord Hathaway, and the prince too. I saw his eyes, remember? They were wild with fear.'

'*You* have a natural gift for melodrama,' Kate said. 'Oh good, there's Rosalie.' She sent the maid to bring another round of cocoa and some more buttered toast as well.

Then she sat back down. 'I've got the shivers just listening to you talk about the black, black water and the torchlight bouncing everywhere.'

'It was awful,' Effie said. 'I kept imagining that a hand draped in seaweed had come up and dragged you into the murky depths.'

Kate laughed again. 'That lake doesn't even have fish in it; it's just a pond fed by an underground stream. There aren't many weeds!'

'You never know what lives in an underground stream,' Effie said, her big eyes growing even bigger.

'Minnows, maybe,' Kate said. 'No one's in love with me.'

Her tone must have been convincing, because after a second Effie said, 'Well, Lord Dimsdale is, of course.'

She'd forgotten her fiancé again. 'Except Algie,'

Kate agreed.

'You're so lucky. I would love to have a fiancé like Lord Dimsdale. He's so considerate, and young, and handsome.'

'Well, so it is Lord Hathaway,' Kate said, rather surprised.

'Actually, he is older.'

'But he is very handsome, and kind. Steady,' Kate added.

Effie nodded. 'I know. My mother says that too.'

'But you're not excited by steady and kind.'

'He'll make a good husband, I'm sure. He didn't dive in after you, though.'

'A black mark against him,' Kate agreed.

'He said afterwards that he couldn't see you, and so what would have been the point? Which is logical, but not what a woman wants to hear, particularly if she were dead.'

'Maybe he would have plunged in for you, just not for me,' Kate offered.

'I doubt it. I think he feels sorry for me, which is not the same as the kind of mad adoration that Lord Dimsdale obviously feels for you.' She hesitated. 'Did you hear what . . . what happened to me?'

Could she mean the fork? 'No,' Kate said. 'Your mother did speak of your father in the past tense . . .'

'First he died, just before my first season, and then my aunt died the next year, and then my great-aunt died.' Effie's soft little face took on an edge. 'They ought to make an exception for mourning when a person just has to make her debut. People talk about me as if I'm an old maid, and I had barely one season!'

173

'Nonsense,' Kate said, pushing away the memory of Henry's casual description of Effie as an octogenarian. 'I'm—' She just caught herself before she confessed her age. 'I look older than you do. That's all that matters.'

'Things were going very well last year,' Effie said, sipping her cocoa, 'and then an awful thing happened with Lord Beckham. Have you met him?'

Kate shook her head.

'My mother was so affronted that she took me to the country after I'd been to only two balls. So then I had to start all over this year.'

It had to be the fork. 'What happened?' Kate asked.

Effie rolled her eyes. 'He's barking mad. He said . . . You may not understand this, Kate, but he told everyone that I *pawed* him. In a private area!'

'No!'

'Yes, he did. And the truth was that he had tried to kiss me. I wouldn't have minded so much, but he pressed against me in the most revolting way. I twisted away and told him he was a repellent slug. It made him angry and he grabbed me down—down there, with his *hand*.'

Even given Effie's talent for melodrama, the man was odious. 'What a toad,' Kate said. 'We had a baker in the village like that once. My father had to throw him out of the county.'

'He wouldn't have done it if my father was alive,' Effie said. 'Because my father would have skewered him. At any rate, we had carried our plates of apricot tart onto the balcony, so I snatched my fork and stuck him in the hand. Since my father wasn't around to skewer him, I suppose you could say I did it myself. But next thing I knew, his story was everywhere.'

'You should have stuck him in the breeches,' Kate said.

'He was telling a lie, but no one believed me except my mother, of course. So we had to retire to the country. And this year'—she looked rather miserable—'well, someone like Lord Hathaway is so logical and kind that of course he doesn't listen to that sort of rumor.'

'Horrible,' Kate said. 'That is horrible. I knew the moment I met you that it couldn't be true because—'

'So you did hear it too!' Effie said, and she burst into tears.

Fortunately Kate was inured to tears after living with Victoria, so she poured her another cup of cocoa, and gave her a pat on the hand. And left her to it. With Victoria, every expression of sympathy just prolonged her weeping.

Sure enough, Effie wiped her eyes and apologized. 'I'm nervous,' she said, 'because Beckham arrives today, and I haven't seen him since last year.'

Kate narrowed her eyes. 'He's coming to the castle?'

'Yes, today,' Effie said damply. 'Isn't that bad luck? I managed to avoid him all season because my mother bribed one of his footmen, so we always knew what he was doing. But now my mother says we can't leave because Lord Hathaway is close to proposing to me.' She didn't look terribly happy about that prospect.

'I like Lord Hathaway,' Kate said.

'So do I, of course,' Effie said, sighing. 'It's just—well—he's not exactly romantic, is he? He would never bring me flowers unless they happened to be in his garden and he tripped over them.'

'You have quite an imagination,' Kate said.

'I can just see his poor wife,' Effie said. 'She'll be waiting expectantly for her birthday to arrive, hoping that he'll bring her a diamond tiara or at the very least, an Indian shawl, and he'll turn up with a tea cozy. Tears will come to her eyes, but since she really loves him—and it's not his fault—she'll swallow her sadness.'

'And buy herself an Indian shawl, I would hope,' Kate put in. 'You're a superb storyteller! I could almost see her weepy eyes. Why don't you just put about the real story of Beckham? I'm sure you could convince people.'

Effie shook her head. 'My mother feels strongly that a lady should never mention such matters. She feels everything so deeply. In fact, she's not getting out of bed today because she feels so distressed over my near death last night.'

Kate raised an eyebrow.

'I know . . . most people think you nearly died instead of me.' Effie sighed.

'If you told my godmother, Henry, she could squash Beckham,' Kate said.

'Does she really like to be called Henry? It's such an odd name for a woman.'

'Her name is Henrietta, but she prefers Henry.'

'I love the way she calls her husband sugarplum,' Effie said. 'It's just so—'

'Romantic,' Kate said, laughing.

'I read too many novels,' Effie said shamefacedly.

'I haven't read many, but the villain always gets his come-uppance, as I understand it. And that's what's going to happen to Beckham, I promise you.

Think of Henry as being like a fairy godmother: She can wave her magic wand and take care of that nasty little toad.'

'How I'd love to see him turned into a turnip,' Effie said.

'Just watch,' Kate said. 'She'll make turnip mash out of him.'

Twenty-one

'You will be taking a large party rabbit hunting this afternoon,' Wick said, catching Gabriel by the arm after the luncheon meal.

'That I will not,' Gabriel said instantly.

'What's got into you?' Wick demanded. 'You've never been the most biddable person, but I'd prefer you didn't go stark raving, if you wouldn't mind. I have a castle full of people, and your aunt's reader has already driven half the ladies into fits by handing out fortunes like confetti, and all of them depressing.'

'You want depressing, go talk to my uncle. I had to listen to him for an hour last night as he sobbed—sobbed!—over the failure of his naval spectacle.'

'It's my fault,' Wick said. 'I'd watched them practice it over and over, and I simply didn't picture the timing's being altered by drunk passengers.'

'Well, no one drowned,' Gabriel said. 'I have it from Miss Starck, who breakfasted with Kate, that the lady is just fine. So no harm done.'

'That being the case, would you get on your bloody shooting gear and take some of these men

177

off my hands?'

'No. Ask Ferdinand to take my place, will you?'

'I'll see if I can drag him out of the pigsty,' Wick said, turning away.

When Gabriel was sure that Wick was well out of hearing, he snatched a young footman and gave him a number of explicit, rapid instructions.

Then he went to his study, locked the door, and walked over to a small painting hanging on the far wall. In the picture's background, a battle raged; in the foreground, a songbird perched on a low branch. On the ground below lay a suit of armor, abandoned just where a knight had managed to kick it off. All there was to be seen of him was a lifeless foot in the lower right. And the bird sang on, his hard, alert eye showing total disregard for the crumpled warrior foolish enough to die under his tree.

It was the only painting that Gabriel had brought with him from Marburg, the painting that summed up his hatred of the patterned violence and sporadic warfare that marked all small principalities, including his brother's.

With an easy crook of his finger under the frame, he pulled the painting out from the wall. Behind it was a simple lever. One yank, and a door opened in the wooden paneling, revealing an extremely dusty corridor.

Wick and he had decided that the benefits of ordering someone to clean the corridor were not worth the potential consequences, inasmuch as the existence of a corridor that ran inside the thick walls of the castle was not so terrible in itself, but the fact that the corridor offered peepholes into most bedchambers?

178

Dusty it was, and dusty it remained.

Gabriel set off, dismissing from his mind the fact that Wick would be infuriated to learn that he had decided to reveal the existence of the corridor.

He kept pausing, peering into bedchambers to orient himself. Gold hangings meant the so-called queen's bedchamber, now consigned to Lady Dagobert. He walked past four more peepholes, calculating his location, and then looked again. He blinked and then hastily walked on. If his guests were choosing not to nap after luncheon, it certainly wasn't his affair.

He skipped four more, tried again, and knew he had the room, because there was Freddie, curled in a tight ball in the middle of the bed. He didn't hear anything, which suggested that Kate's maid was not in attendance.

He put his mouth to the peephole and said, 'Kate.'

Nothing.

He said it more loudly. 'Kate!'

There was a muttered curse word that made him grin, and then the sound of someone walking over to the bedroom door and opening it. He couldn't see her, but he imagined her staring into the corridor.

She closed the door again, rather more slowly than she had opened it, and he tried again. 'Come to the fireplace and look on the right side.'

'I hate people who spy,' she said in a loud voice.

'I'm not spying!' he protested. 'All I can see is your bed.'

A withering silence answered him.

'Freddie looks comfortable.'

'Freddie is always comfortable. Why are you

179

spying on a lady's bed?'

'I came to ask you to go for a drive with me. In secret.'

'I gathered the secret part. How many people traipse through that corridor at night?'

'No one,' he assured her. 'Ever. You're the only person other than Wick who knows it exists.'

'This is England,' she pointed out. 'You didn't build the castle yourself. Probably half your guests know of its existence.' Suddenly an eye presented itself before him. It was a beautiful eye, pale green like the light that comes through a stained glass window, and ringed in brown.

'Is that you?' she asked suspiciously.

'Of course it's me.'

'Should I pull a lever to let you out?'

'There's no entrance to any of the bedrooms.'

'Just for peeping,' Kate muttered. 'How distasteful.'

'I've got a carriage downstairs, and a picnic. I told the footman that I would take one of my aunts to see the old nunnery.'

'A nunnery sounds like a barrelful of monkeys,' she said, turning away. All he could see was Freddie again. She continued, off to the right. 'And your aunt, will she enjoy this excursion?'

'Just the two of us,' Gabriel said, and held his breath. No proper young lady would do it. Ever. No chaperone, no maid, no aunt?

Kate's eye reappeared. 'Are you planning to seduce me in the carriage?' The green looked a little darker with displeasure.

'I'd love to,' he said regretfully, 'but I wouldn't be able to live with my own conscience, so I won't.'

'Have you a conscience when it comes to people

180

like me? I thought you and Wick had summed up my circumstances.'

'You may be illegitimate, though I don't think you're a swineherd's daughter, for all your intimate knowledge of piggeries.'

'I'm not,' she said, and disappeared again. He could hear her walking about. 'If I were a swineherd's daughter would you seduce me?'

'I've actually never seduced a maiden,' he said.

'How virtuous of you.'

'It's likely not a reflection of virtue,' he admitted. 'Princes hardly ever manage to be alone, you know. When I was younger, I would have gladly cavorted with a maiden of any variety, but I wasn't given a chance.'

The eye reappeared. 'As long as you promise on the shambles of your princely honor that you won't kiss me. I find your kisses distracting.'

That was a facer. '*You* could kiss me,' he suggested.

'I won't. I need to find a husband, and your fiancéc—is she arriving today?'

'She has landed in England,' Gabriel said reluctantly. 'Probably she'll arrive tomorrow.'

'No kisses,' Kate stated.

He nodded and realized she couldn't see him.

'The truth is that I am going mad in this room. Effie brought me some dismal tripe to read. I don't care much for novels. And Henry won't let me go out because she says if I appear too healthy people will start questioning the illness that made me thinner.'

'I brought a veil, so no one will recognize you.'

'A veil?'

'My aunt wears them all the time. A mourning

veil. I'll meet you at your bedchamber door in five minutes.'

'Can I bring Freddie? I could hide him under the veil.'

'Absolutely not. My aunt never yaps.'

Twenty-two

The woman who emerged from Kate's bedchamber was swathed in black from her head to her toes.

Gabriel offered her his arm, feeling a ridiculous pleasure run through him. 'Be careful not to trip,' he said as they walked down the corridor.

The veil trembled as Kate shook her head. 'I'm having trouble walking; I can't see where I'm going. How does she manage this?'

'She's been in mourning a long time,' Gabriel said.

'How long?'

'Forty years, give or take ten.'

Silence.

'You're thinking she's overly mournful.'

'I would never characterize a princess in a negative light,' Kate said primly, though he knew damn well that was a lie.

'It was actually very clever,' he told her. 'My father would have found her another husband, but she fell into such a cataclysmic fit of grief that no one would have her.'

'I gather her grief wasn't all it could have been?'

'My brothers and I loved to go to her chambers. We would play speculation and bet each other with cherry stones. She gave me my first taste of cognac,

182

and lots of very good advice.'

'Such as?'

'She loved to think of improbable scenarios. For example, what if Noah's flood happened again? How would we survive?'

'Good question,' Kate said. 'Did she have the answer?'

'We decided a good boat with a hold full of nuts would save us. When I was small I used to steal filbert nuts from the table so that she could build up a store. I suppose she ate them privately; she never disillusioned me. Every time it rained I would happily think about the vast reserves of nuts stowed under her bed.'

'Very kind of her,' Kate said. 'What would she have to say about swineherds' daughters?'

'Stay away from them,' he said promptly.

'My father would undoubtedly say the same of nearly married princes,' she said.

They were coming down the grand stairs now. 'A last cluster of footmen and we're free,' he whispered.

'Should I hobble?'

'No need. Wick isn't here, and he's the only one who might notice. I'm going to put you in the dog cart and take the reins myself. I'll tell you when we're out of sight of the front door. We'll leave the road immediately.'

The moment he gave the word, Kate pulled up the veil and wrestled it off her head. 'That is *hot*,' she cried. She had a high flush and—

'Another wig?' he asked, disappointed. The night before, she'd been so drenched that he hadn't been able to tell exactly what color her hair was, but he thought it was yellow, like mustard or old wine.

183

'I always wear a wig,' she said primly. But then she looked at him and laughed, and he felt a bolt of desire so fierce that he almost dropped the reins. 'My hair is my only glory, so I'm saving it for when I can truly be myself: Kate rather than Victoria.'

'You're Kate today,' he said.

'No, I'm not. The only reason I'm out driving with you is that Victoria is a bit of a trollop,' she said with a wicked little smile. 'I myself would never do anything like this.'

'What *do* you do instead of trolloping?' he asked with not a little curiosity.

'This and that,' she said lightly.

There was a bit of silence as he negotiated the dog cart off the road and onto a little track that wound around the castle, just under the walls. 'What sort of things?' he asked. 'Taking care of pigs?'

'Actually, no pigs,' she said. 'That's a cheering thought, isn't it? If I get to feeling downtrodden I can just contemplate what might have been, in short, the pigs.'

'Do you feel downtrodden?'

'Now and then,' she said airily. 'I have such a ferocious temper that people tread on me at their peril. Besides, my godmother is taking me in hand, and next time you see me, I'll be respectably living in London with Henry at my side.'

Lady Wrothe must be giving her a dowry, Gabriel thought, which was decent of her. Though he hated the idea of Kate flirting with cretinous Londoners; in fact, it made him want to snatch her and—

Act like the bad prince in a fairy tale.

Christ.

'You look a bit hot,' Kate said. 'Where is this nunnery, anyway?'

'We're not actually going to a nunnery. We're going around the side of the castle, and we'll enter one of the gardens, a secret one.'

'A secret garden . . . how on earth did you find it? Don't tell me that a fairy led the way.'

'I was given a key. It's a secret merely because the gate opens out to the castle grounds, rather than the courtyard, so no one bothers to go there. Even Wick hasn't investigated it.'

They drove in a circle around the castle for a few more minutes. Then Gabriel pulled up the pony and jumped out, throwing the reins over a small bush. He grabbed a basket from the cart and turned to give Kate a hand, but she was already out of the cart.

He wanted—what he wanted was ridiculous. He wanted to be blatantly possessive, to pluck her from the carriage, carry her to the gate. He wanted to throw down a blanket and pull up her skirts right there in the open air where anyone could see them.

He wanted to—

He'd lost his mind.

That was the explanation, he thought, walking after Kate, who was hopping about and picking flowers like a five-year-old. Wick was right. The whole question of marriage, of Princess Tatiana's imminent arrival, had rattled his mental state.

He was about to marry. *Marry.* Which made it all the more unfortunate that—he stopped and rearranged his breeches—there was no one he wanted to be with but one illegitimate daughter of a swineherd, gathering daisies a few feet away.

It was just like a fairy tale, except that life wasn't

185

like fairy tales, and princes didn't get to be with swineherds' daughters, not unless they broke every social convention they had learned in their life.

And he wasn't going to.

Even though the look of Kate's body as she bent over to pick another flower made him so hungry and possessive that he found his fingers were shaking. He put the basket down and let fly a volley of silent curses, his favorite method for regaining control.

It had worked in his brother's court; it worked now.

'Let's go in, shall we?' he called, walking to the door and unlocking it. The brick wall was high and very old, so old that he could see it crumbling in places where ivy was pulling it down.

He pushed the door open to a tangle of yarrow, butterbur, and purple comfrey. Mixed in here and there were the nodding heads of cabbage roses, petals thrown to the ground as if a young girl had been scattering birdseed.

'Oh!' Kate said. 'It's wonderful!' She ran forward, holding up her skirts. 'It really *is* a secret garden. There are secret statues too. See, there's one, almost hidden in that clump of sweetbriar.'

'Probably a goddess,' Gabriel said, as Kate pulled back the ivy trailing over pale stone shoulders. Together they pulled down a clump of ivy that hung over the statue's face.

'Oh,' Kate said, her voice hushed. 'She's beautiful.'

'She's crying,' Gabriel said, surprised.

Kate reached forward and wrenched at another tangled strand of ivy. 'She's an angel.'

The young angel's wings were folded; she looked

186

down, her face white as new snow and sadder than winter.

'Oh Lord,' Gabriel said, backing up a step. 'This isn't a secret garden, it's a graveyard. They might have told me that.'

'Then where are the graves?' Kate said. 'Look, there's nothing at her feet but a pedestal. Wouldn't the family be buried in the chapel?'

'Yes,' Gabriel said with relief, thinking of the tombs of the lords and ladies Pomeroy neatly lined up in the castle's chapel. 'But why on earth is she here otherwise?'

Kate was bending over and pulling ivy from the pedestal. Suddenly she started giggling.

'What?'

'It *is* a graveyard,' she said, laughing even harder.

'Remind me never to escort you on holy ground,' Gabriel said, bending over. He started reading aloud. '*In loving memory of . . .* who? I can't read it.'

'*My dearest Rascal*,' Kate finished for him. She pulled aside a bit of sweetbriar and moved around the pedestal. 'And not just Rascal either. Here's Dandy and'—she moved again—'*Freddie*! Oh my, I have to bring my Freddie here. It'll be like visiting the tombs of one's ancestors in Westminster Abbey.'

'It appears that I have my own dog graveyard,' Gabriel said. 'If I had a pack of them, the way you do, I could measure out their little graves while they were still alive. I'd start with Freddie, since he's likely to die of fright any day now. I'll show this place to my uncle; maybe he'll feel better if we plant a statue out here of a pickle-eating dog.'

She poked him. 'You're ridiculous.'

He reached out and pulled off her wig. It came

187

with a scattering of hairpins and a shriek. He plopped it on top of the long-suffering angel.

'Nice,' he said with satisfaction, not meaning the angel, who had taken on the look of a tipsy trollop in the pink wig.

The sun slanted over the rosy old bricks and loved Kate's hair, every buttery, angry strand of it.

She was yelling at him, of course. No one ever yelled at him. No one but Kate . . . and that was because she was a different class, a class that didn't know that you could never scold a prince.

He hadn't even been reprimanded when he was nothing more than a princeling. His nurse, and his brothers' nurses, knew their place. He used to push, when he was a lad, and try to make the servants angry. No one rebuked him, even when he set the nursery rug on fire. When Rupert got one of the upstairs maids with child, his father just laughed.

Only Wick had looked at him in disgust when he saw the rug and told him he was a right fool. He had struck him, of course, and Wick hit him back, and they ended up rolling on the ground, and afterward he felt better. Because a child knows when he deserves a scold, and if he doesn't get it . . .

Well.

If someone had raked his brother Augustus over the coals once in a while, Gabriel thought, he wouldn't have been so vulnerable to that infernal friar who happened by with his promises of gilded halos. Augustus knew inside—as they all knew—that he didn't deserve all he had.

The truth of it made you distrust people, because they lied . . . In Augustus's case, it made him afraid about what would happen after his death.

Kate didn't lie. It was fascinating to hear the real

188

anger in her voice.

And that anger, perversely, caused a rise in his breeches.

Or perhaps it was her hair. It shone as if strawberries had been woven into gold. 'I just wanted to see your crowning glory,' he explained, breaking through her diatribe. 'You're right. It's beautiful.'

'I *told* you,' Kate said, but he broke in when she took a breath.

'I know. You were saving it for the moment when you meet Prince Charming himself. Rubbish.' She had her hands on her hips and she was glaring at him like a proper fishwife. Gabriel felt a surge of happiness.

'It may be rubbish to you,' Kate said fiercely. 'But I told you my reasons and you—you simply rode over them roughshod, because you think that anything you do is acceptable.'

He blinked at her, her words sinking in.

'Don't you?' she demanded. 'In your narrow, arrogant little world, you can snatch off a woman's wig simply because you want to, and you could tear off butterfly's wings too, no doubt, and father children on milkmaids, and—'

'For Christ's sake,' Gabriel said. 'How did we get from wigs to milkmaids and butterflies?'

'It's all about you,' she said, glaring at him.

The ridiculous thing was that even though she was saying terrible things about him—all true, except for the butterflies and the illegitimate children—he just felt stiffer, more like snatching another one of those kisses and not stopping there, but tumbling her onto a patch of grass.

'Don't think I misunderstand that look in your

189

eye,' she said, and her own eyes got even sharper.

'What am I thinking?' Damned if his voice didn't come out of his chest in a rumble, the kind of husky sound that a man makes when—

'You're thinking that you're going to break your own promise,' she said, folding her arms over her breasts. 'You're about to persuade yourself that I really *want* you to kiss me, even though you promised you wouldn't. Because in your world—'

'I've heard that part,' he said. 'About my narrow world. Do you want me to kiss you?'

He felt as if the whole world held its breath for that second, as if the aimless sparrows shut their beaks, and the bees hovered, listening.

'For Christ's sake,' she said with disgust, turning away. 'You'll never understand, will you?'

He understood that the curve of her neck was somehow more delicious than that of any woman he had seen in years. As she had her back turned, he quickly rearranged his breeches again. 'You think I'm a jackass,' he said helpfully. 'You're probably right too. Because I promised, I won't kiss you. On the other hand, I never promised not to remove your wig. You instructed me, as regards your wig, which to my mind is something quite different from giving my word.'

'You're splitting hairs.' She kept her back turned to him, obstinate thing that she was. Yet somehow the delicate line of her back was even more seductive than the curve of her bosom. He would like to fall on his knees and trace each bump of her spine with his tongue.

He shouldn't be thinking that, Gabriel realized dimly. She wasn't for him. Not for him . . . not for him. Kate bent over to peer more closely at

190

something hidden in the grasses, and his mind presented him with a picture of himself kissing her waist, then slipping down, down . . .

'Shall we have our luncheon?' he said, growling out the words.

'There's another marble here,' Kate said, pulling at a tangle of ivy and weeds.

He grunted and came to her side. He wrenched so hard that a great bunch of ivy came loose, roots and all, sending dirt and leaves flying into the air.

'A statue of a child this time,' Kate said, dropping on her knees.

The irresponsible, lustful side of Gabriel's body approved of that. Yes . . . on her knees . . .

He turned away and stamped back outside the garden to fetch the picnic basket, cursing his lust.

Wick was right. He was chasing Kate only because he couldn't marry her, and he couldn't bed her either. Because he was an idiot, in short.

And probably she was right too. He was a self-important ass who snatched off her wig just to suit himself. He was getting as bad as Augustus. As Rupert. Wick had kept him in line for most of their lives, belting him when he started to believe that his title meant anything . . .

But had he turned into an ass anyway, when Wick wasn't watching? Probably.

Twenty-three

Kate cleared the last weeds from the statue of the child. She was a chubby toddler, sitting on the ground in a smock, and laughing. 'Hello there,' Kate murmured to the little stone girl. 'I wonder . . .'

She pulled ivy from her pedestal and found a simple inscription: *Merry, Darling.*

'Your gloves are ruined,' came a voice over her shoulder.

'My maid brought along boxes and boxes of gloves,' she said. 'Look, Gabriel. Isn't she a dear? She has ringlets.'

'And wings,' Gabriel pointed out. 'She's a baby angel.'

'Do you suppose that she was Merry—or was Merry a beloved kitten, perhaps? She reminds me of the cupids in the north corridor. Perhaps she was made by the sculptor stolen from Italy, the one who escaped in a butter churn.'

'Does one erect a statue just for a kitten? My guess would be that this is a memorial, if not the actual grave itself.' He bent down and brushed away a head of yarrow that nodded against the child's cheek.

'That's so terribly sad,' Kate said.

'There's an instinctive wish to remember the child playing and laughing,' he said. 'When we were excavating Barbary two years ago, we discovered that the tombs of children were full of toys so that they could play happily in the afterlife.'

Kate nodded. 'Not so different, I suppose, from

putting a statue of Merry actually playing in the garden.'

'I have a little pot upstairs that I've been working on. It came from a tomb, and it originally held knucklebones. Presumably they were the boy's own toys. I'll show it to you someday.'

'It sounds fascinating,' Kate said, meaning it.

'My old professor, Biggitstiff, is an arrant blockhead, and threw out the pot, knucklebones and all. In fact, he had the men simply throw dirt in the tomb after he discovered there wasn't any gold inside.'

'Is he interested only in gold?'

'In truth, no. But he's interested in fame. He wants the big find, the exciting discovery. Something as trifling as the grave of a poor child would never interest him. That's what bothers me about his excavation of Carthage. He'll be rampaging about, looking for Dido's grave, and doubtless destroying all sorts of interesting artifacts.'

His voice had moved away again and she looked over her shoulder to find that he was spreading a blanket in a relatively clear spot of grass.

'Come and eat,' he called.

She scrambled to her knees and came to join him. 'It's a feast,' she said with satisfaction.

'Take off those filthy gloves,' Gabriel said. He waved a chicken leg at her.

'Mmmm,' Kate said, stripping off her gloves. 'Things smell so much better in the outdoors; have you noticed?' She bit into the chicken.

He didn't answer, just handed her a glass of wine that slid, light and faintly sparkling, down her throat.

193

She didn't notice until she'd eaten the chicken leg, a meat tartlet, a piece of mouth-watering cheddar cheese, and a pickled quail's egg that he hadn't answered. In fact, he wasn't even eating; he was just propped up on his elbow watching her. And handing her food.

She narrowed her eyes at him over a piece of almond cake. 'What?' she demanded.

Gabriel raised an eyebrow. 'Nothing.'

'What are you up to?'

'Trying to fatten you up,' he said readily enough. 'You're too thin, even though you weren't sick in the spring.'

'I've never been plump,' she stated.

'Ah, but you need more than that gorgeous mop of hair to catch a husband,' he said infuriatingly. 'The best Englishwomen are soft. Luscious, really. Look at Lady Wrothe, your godmother. She's like a gorgeous overbaked loaf, even at her age.'

Kate ate the rest of her cake and scolded herself silently for minding that, apparently, he didn't find her luscious.

Gabriel had rolled over and was lying on his back, legs crossed, eating a chicken leg. His breeches clung to muscular thighs; her eyes drifted to broader shoulders. His eyes were squinted shut against the sun, and his eyelashes lay on his cheeks like an invitation.

'I didn't mean to say that you ripped the wings off butterflies,' she said abruptly, pulling her mind away from the prince's princely attributes.

'What about the illegitimate children I had with fields of milkmaids? Did you mean that?' he asked interestedly, though he didn't bother to open his eyes. Instead he just reached out a hand. 'May I

194

have one of those little pasties?'

She put a meat tart in his hand. 'I would imagine that princes might have any number of bastard children,' she said. 'What woman could resist you? And I didn't mean that as a compliment to your charms.'

'I heard you,' he said. He was silent for a moment.

'Not that I mean you would have to employ force,' she added, feeling a qualm of conscience. He was so beautiful that he didn't even need a title to have women at his feet.

'I know.' He held out his hand again, broad but slim-fingered, a powerful man's hand. She put a second tart squarely on his palm.

'My brother Rupert,' Gabriel said, 'has any number of bastards. He's a pretty fellow.'

'You're—' She broke off just in time.

'Not as pretty,' he said. 'Rupert is more of a prince than I am. You should see him when he's ruffled and bewigged. He'd drive you into a blind fury, no doubt about it.'

'Really?'

'He looks like someone in a fairy tale, and he acts like someone in one of Aretino's books,' Gabriel said, turning over and propping himself up on his elbow.

'Aretino? I seem to remember the name, but I'm not sure . . .'

'You definitely don't remember the name; he's not an author known to ladies. Aretino was an Italian who specialized in books of naughty drawings that taught me a great deal as a lad. My father had a copy translated into English, though I have to say the language is fairly irrelevant. Ask

195

your husband about his work someday.'

Kate swallowed a grin. She knew exactly where she remembered that name from. She'd discovered Aretino's *School of Venus* in her father's library two years ago. The illustrations were revelatory.

'Here, have some more wine,' Gabriel said. It poured into her glass like stained glass turned liquid, golden, fragrant, heady. 'Rupert's looks, together with his title, have had a bad effect on him.' He smirked. 'I know you'll have a hard time agreeing with me that a title could be an evil influence on a man.'

She laughed aloud. Gabriel making fun of himself and his title was devastating. She felt a ping in the area of her heart and pushed it away.

'He practiced on the household women from the time he was fourteen, until he started practicing on the countryside at large. My father thought it was funny.'

'You didn't.'

'Rupert could never get his mind around the fact that there was the chance that the women were afraid of losing their positions if they didn't comply. It's all fun to him: He sweet-talks them and undoubtedly gives pleasure in bed. But . . .'

'What has happened to his children?'

Gabriel shrugged. 'We have a few of them in the castle with us. Along with their mothers, of course. When Augustus castle-cleaned, he threw fallen women out regardless of who tripped them up.'

'That's just wrong,' Kate said, biting down hard on a piece of candied pear. 'But you don't have any children of your own.' She knew it instinctively. Gabriel was as arrogant a male as a male could be—but the whole castle stood at his shoulder as evidence that he didn't duck responsibilities.

'Wick would kill me if I started producing false pennies,' he said lazily. 'Otherwise I'd be seducing a milk-maid right now.' And he gave her an exaggerated leer that left no space for misunderstanding about the milkmaid in question.

Kate reached over and snatched another bit of pear from his hand. 'So Wick has kept you on the straight and narrow. I like it. He's a good man.'

Gabriel drained his glass. 'Believe it or not, Katelet, I like to make love to women who won't be hurt by my seduction. Otherwise . . .' He gave her a smile that the devil would love to imitate. 'Otherwise I'd have you flat on your back in the grass, and you, my girl, would let me have my wicked way with you, title or no. Even if I was a swineherd.'

Her mouth fell open. 'Charming! You arrogant beast!'

'I'm falling into the habit of honesty.' He leaned closer. 'You're the one who told me that English people favor uncomfortable truths.'

'I fail to see what that has to do with anything. *You* are not English. And you're not irresistible either.'

'Let's play English and trade uncomfortable truths. You can tell me one first. Or rather, since that's your stock-in-trade, tell me another.'

'What are you talking about?'

'Tell me something that you think I don't want to hear.'

'There's so much that you don't want to hear,' she said, letting a touch of mockery edge her voice.

'If you're going to tell me that I'm outrageously handsome, I know it's not true.'

'You did say *truths*,' Kate said. His nose was too large for outrageous beauty, anyway.

He laughed. 'True enough, hard-hearted little Katelet. So go on, then.'

'I think you're . . .' She hesitated.

'Arrogant?' he supplied.

'You know that.'

'Worse?'

'I think that you will break your wife's heart,' she said, coming out with it.

She surprised him. He turned his head, and hair fell out of its queue, and curled by his shoulder. 'Why?'

'Because you intend to leave her, and go dig up this ancient city that you told me about. I can see, anyone could see, that you're just biding your time here.'

'I told you that myself. You can't claim particular insight into my character.'

'You're going to leave for Carthage,' she said steadily, 'and that's not right. It's not honoring the vows of marriage.'

He raised an eyebrow.

'To have and to hold,' she said. 'In sickness or in health. With you off in Carthage, how would you know if your wife fell ill? If she died in childbirth?'

'Her name is Tatiana. And I wouldn't leave her if she were breeding!'

'How would you know? Women often don't know for months. To be even more blunt, are you planning not to bed Tatiana for three months before you skive off for Carthage? Because that's problematic in a different way.'

He sat up. 'There are women who don't want a husband sniffing around their petticoats all the

198

time, you know. You seem to have a very romantic view of marriage in mind, and believe me, it's not one that I see among royal families.'

'I've read about dynastic marriages. Look at our own King James. He never loved his wife; they lived separately, and by some accounts, he loved the Duke of Buckingham better than she.'

'Now you're shocking me,' he said lightly. But his eyes avoided hers.

'You won't do it,' she said, suddenly realizing where she'd been blind. 'You won't be able to leave her.'

'To leave?'

She nodded.

'I certainly will leave,' he said, with all the stubbornness of a very small boy insisting that he wants to ride his pony again.

'No, you won't. It's not in you, Gabriel-the-Prince.'

'Sods to that,' he said, and with one quick move, he pounced on her, flattening her onto the blanket.

'Ugh!' Kate said, as the breath escaped from her lungs.

He just looked down at her as if the heat of his body wasn't burning into her limbs.

'This is shocking,' Kate said, sounding like a silly, bleating lamb. But it was taking all her energy not to curl up against him and purr. Rather than wrap her arms around his neck, she made herself shove at his shoulders. 'You, sir, are a regenerate!'

He bent his head to one side and she felt his breath against her cheek. 'Regenerate? *Regenerate.* Hmmm.'

'Get off of me,' she said between clenched teeth. 'You promised.'

'I promised not to kiss you,' he agreed readily. 'And I won't.' His head dipped as she pushed against at his shoulder. 'We *de*generates don't bother with kisses.' Then softly, wickedly, a wet tongue slid across the plane of her cheek. 'Or did you mean that I'm a *renegade*?'

'Oh!' A shiver went straight down Kate's body, a kind of warning, followed instantly by a sweep of warmth. 'Get off me!' she squeaked. 'You promised not—'

The tongue swept to her neck and she couldn't help it, she squirmed against his hardness and a little whimper broke from her lips.

'Are your kisses like your hair?' The question was so soft that she almost didn't hear it, lost in a sensual haze. 'For one man only . . . saved for the man you'll marry?'

'Yes, I'm saving both of them,' she said, gasping a bit, trying to pull herself together. Somehow her arms were caught between them so she couldn't push him away the way she meant to.

'What about licks?' he asked.

She scarcely heard him over the wild beating of her heart. The very smell of him was intoxicating. Who knew that men—or was it only princes?—smelled like this, like secret spice with a touch of leather and soap?

'It's preposterous to think that my seeing your hair will delay your future domestic bliss,' Gabriel was saying into the curve of her neck. 'It's absurd.' His whisper burned her skin, sending little quakes down her body.

'Isn't it?' he said, raising his head and looking down at her. His eyes shone with a kind of dangerous pleasure. She knew it was dangerous, and yet—

'I suppose,' she said, wondering what exactly she was agreeing to.

'Rank superstition,' he said. His lips feathered along the curve of her cheek. 'And don't think this is a kiss, Kate, because it's not. It's rot to feel that you can't show your hair to anyone until you're trotting about under your own name.'

She gasped. He was, his lips were, caressing her ear. 'Oh!' She couldn't help turning her head to the side so he could . . .

'You like that,' Gabriel said, his voice husky, melodic. The voice of the devil, Kate thought dimly, but she didn't care. 'If I promise not to corrupt you, Kate, may I kiss you? Please?'

He was all enticing male weight and sweet voice, but Kate fought to think clearly. Did it matter if she kissed a prince in a garden? Would it change the fact that she was going to find a good man and marry him?

She didn't think it would. Not a kiss. If it stopped with a kiss.

'You mustn't seduce me,' she said, and then stiffened at the sound of her own voice, somehow dropped into a deep and sensuous register that she'd never heard before.

He reacted to the sound too. His body seemed heavier on hers all of a sudden. He pushed up on his elbows, and her arms were free, but she didn't strike him, or push him away. Instead they just stared at each other, there in the sunlit cloister surrounded by tangles of wildflowers and a few half-eaten meat pies.

'I do not want you to seduce me,' she said, drawing on years of striking clear bargains with

201

tradesmen. She had to make it clear so that he didn't just swoop over her with all that princely beauty. 'I am—I am a *virgin* and I intend to be so on my bridal night.'

Gabriel nodded, and a lock of hair fell over his eyes again. He was so beautiful, so starkly masculine, that her throat closed and she couldn't remember what else she had to say.

'I will not take your virginity,' he said, his deep voice steady. Then his mouth quirked and he brushed his lips over hers again. 'Even if you beg me to.'

'Arrogant pig,' she muttered. 'I'm not your entertainment, Gabriel. I can't imagine why you're here with me, but I know that you should be in your castle with your guests.'

'For some reason, I'm mad about your kisses, Kate.' His eyes caught hers, and she stilled the way a rabbit does in front of a cheerful fox. 'I don't know what it is. I can't stop thinking about you. Kissing you was the first thing I thought about this morning when I woke up,' he said conversationally.

She blinked at him.

'I had been dreaming about our kiss in the boat, when you were wet and cradled in my arms.'

'You make me sound like a prize trout!'

'I would have liked to lick off every drop of lake water,' he said, his lips feathering along her cheek again. 'If you were mine, I would have bundled you up and then slowly unwrapped you by the fire.'

Kate tried to find words, but they seemed to be lost in a storm of sensation: the rough timbre of his voice, the thrilling pressure of his body, even the random tune of a lark woven together into a spell that kept her still.

'I woke up this morning,' Gabriel said, 'thinking of nothing more than rolling over and pulling you into my arms and kissing you again. Kissing: only kissing. As if I were a green boy of fourteen. In case you don't realize it, Kate, kissing is not a man's usual inclination in the morning.'

She frowned at him.

'Oh for Christ's sake,' he said, 'what a virgin you are.'

'There's nothing wrong with being a virgin,' she said stoutly. 'Now if you're done with reminiscing over your bawdy nightmares, would you mind getting up? You're treating me like a feather mattress.'

'If I were treating you like a feather mattress, Kate—and believe me, there's nothing I'd rather do—you'd be crying out with pleasure.'

Kate snorted. 'Is there no limit to your vanity?'

'Are you daring me to prove myself?'

'No!' she said instantly, and gave such a decisive shove that he rolled to the side and she managed to scramble away.

Twenty-four

Gabriel didn't bother to rise; he just sprawled at her feet, a boneless, laughing man. He didn't look like a prince at the moment. He looked as eager and alive as any Englishman gone a-courting.

'You—' she said, and stopped, shaking her head.

'Lost my mind,' he supplied. 'Wick says so too.' He put his hands behind his head and grinned at her. 'All I think about is you.'

'Absurd.' She bit her tongue rather than point out that she was skinny and old. 'I don't mean to concur with Wick's assessment, but your castle is full of women who are ten times more beautiful than I. I'm sure your bride will rival them. Why aren't you thinking about Princess Tatiana?'

'Because there's something wickedly seductive about you, Kate. I'll bet you're more beautiful than the plump and powdery Victoria. And she was the most beautiful girl on the market this spring; everyone has told me so.'

'In the midst of lamenting over how poor Victoria has lost her looks,' she pointed out.

'They're fools. You're ten times more lovely than that angel over there. It's not just because I snatched off your wig either. Do you know that your lips are the precise color of a raspberry?'

'Very nice,' she said, pretty sure that she ought to stop his compliments, but unable to do so. They felt like manna after the humiliations and fears of the last years.

'I love raspberries,' Gabriel said dreamily. 'I like to nibble them, and suck them into my mouth until they explode in a burst of flavor. I like them every way, fresh, baked, in a pie.'

'Are you suggesting that I would taste good in a pie?' she asked, laughing a bit. She sat down on the very edge of the picnic cloth and picked up her wineglass.

'You would taste good in any fashion at all,' Gabriel said. 'I am particularly fond of raspberry syrup.' There was sinful laughter in his voice.

Pictures from Aretino's book poured into Kate's mind, but—what could he mean?

Cold wine slid down her throat. She couldn't let

herself be overthrown by desire. For that's what it was, this sharp heat between her legs, the wish to throw herself on top of him, the easy way in which the morality of a lifetime was being replaced by an ache instructing her to—

'No,' she stated.

He opened his eyes. 'Had I asked you something?'

'*Why* have you lost your mind?' she asked. 'Is it because I've allowed you such liberties?'

'Perhaps.'

She scowled at him. 'Offer me a post as your mistress and I'll stab you with a fork, just as Effie stabbed Beckham. Except the fork won't go in your hand. I am not to be trifled with.'

'I like my mistresses fat and juicy,' he said, slanting her another of his wicked looks.

'If I ever became a man's mistress, not that I would ever do so, he would have hair the color of sunlight, and eyes as blue as—as blue as sapphires.'

'A Jack-a-dandy of that sort will care more for his own beauty than yours.' He reached out and picked up an apple.

'Absolutely not,' Kate said, warming to her imaginary gentleman friend. 'He wouldn't be vain about his looks. He would be a perfect gentleman: humble, thoughtful, and utterly honorable. He would be so in love with me that if I threatened to leave him, he would—'

'Build a funeral pyre and hop onto it,' Gabriel interrupted.

'Never. He would throw himself at my feet and beg my forgiveness.'

'There's the problem, Kate. He should have been there in the beginning, rather than paying for the pleasure of your company.'

'You're right; I shan't be his mistress. I'll marry him instead.' She picked up a lemon tart and contemplated eating it. She was not in the least hungry, but it looked delicious. And it would keep her from looking at Gabriel, who looked even more delicious.

'So you're planning to marry a man with golden hair, blue eyes, and the personality of a pudding? Sounds like Hathaway to me.'

'I'm considering him,' Kate said. 'May I have some more of that wine, please?'

Gabriel reached behind him and picked up the bottle, then propped himself on one elbow so he could pour wine first into her glass and then into his. 'He's not bad.'

'I know,' Kate said, feeling a bit hollow. 'The only problem is that Effie would quite like to marry him as well.'

'Effie is that girl who was in the boat with you last night.'

'Yes.'

'And she's the one you're offering to imitate, who nailed someone with a fork when he asked her to be his light-o'-love?'

'It was worse than that. Beckham kissed her in an improperly intimate fashion.'

'Do tell,' Gabriel said. 'Were they kissing the way we do?'

He had pulled off his cravat, and his shirt revealed a triangle of chest. It was vastly improper. Kate pulled her gaze away. '*We* don't kiss in any particular way,' she corrected him. 'We may have exchanged a few kisses in the past, but—'

'We kiss as if the bloody room had burst on fire,'

he interrupted. 'We kiss as if making love didn't exist and kissing was all there was.'

'Stop that!' She swallowed. 'Beckham rubbed himself against her.'

'I do that,' Gabriel said, satisfaction ripe in his voice. 'I'd like to do it again too. Have you lifted the ban on kissing? I can't remember.'

'No, I haven't,' Kate said, a fugitive shred of self-control emerging. 'So Effie told Beckham he was a toad, or something along those lines.'

'*Not* part of our kissing,' Gabriel said. 'You succumb. All I've heard are little murmurs, the encouraging kind.'

She decided to ignore him. 'That made Beckham angry, so he reached out and simply grabbed her.'

'Grabbed her? Hadn't he already done that?'

'With his hand,' Kate said, scowling. 'Between her legs. Poor Effie was so overset by it that she could barely explain it to me now, a whole year later.'

'I want to do that too,' Gabriel said, sighing.

Kate picked up a fork.

'But I haven't,' he said hastily. 'So that's when she forked him?'

'Yes, except he told everyone that she had groped him under the table and that's how the forking happened.'

Gabriel looked up at her from under thick eyelashes. 'Will you please grope me under the table, Kate mine?'

'I'm not your Kate,' she said, feeling her lips curve. Her treacherous heart was no match for a flirtatious prince on a summer's day.

'That's the odd thing,' he said, lying on his back

again and shading his eyes with an arm. 'You are, you are, you are.'

Kate put her glass to her mouth because if she didn't, she would reach over and put her lips on his.

'So she forked him,' Gabriel said, after a second.

'And he deliberately destroyed her reputation in retaliation. Hathaway is a decent man. He has obviously seen through the rumors and realized that Effie would never grope anyone.'

'It wouldn't be kind of you to take Hathaway from poor Effie under the circumstances,' Gabriel said. 'Unless you are fond of the man, in which case you might keep in mind that matrimonial life with Hathaway promises to be boring. Those overly decent men don't approve of groping.'

'Wives do not grope their husbands under the table,' Kate said, giggling.

'I shall make it part of the marriage settlement,' Gabriel said. 'I need a grope once a week or I'll wilt like a lily.'

'You wouldn't wilt, you'd—' She broke off.

'What would I do?' Gabriel asked.

Her eyes fell, but after all, she had nothing to lose. 'You'll be off to another woman.'

Something flashed across his face so quickly that she couldn't read it. 'Ah, my title rears its ugly head again,' he said, a bit of chill in his voice.

'It's nothing to do with your title. Husbands stray. They have mistresses, and they take *friends*.'

'Not everyone is as friendly as your godmother.' His voice was still cool.

She fiddled with her fork. 'My father was—friendly.'

Gabriel nodded. 'So was mine, as evidenced by Wick.' He got to his feet in one easy movement.

208

'Shall we see if there are other statues hidden in the garden?'

She took his hand as he helped her up, feeling a pulse of relief. This conversation was uncomfortably intimate. More intimate even than kissing, which was odd.

'I see a couple of mounds of ivy that might hide statues,' Gabriel said, hands on his hips. 'There, and over against the back wall.'

One of the mounds of ivy turned out to cover a pile of fallen bricks. 'I wonder what it was originally,' Kate said.

'There's no way to tell since it's all to pieces. I think I'll get some men to build a very small folly here. It would be a delightful place for a dinner *à deux*.'

'Do princes ever get to have intimate dinners of that fashion?'

'Of course!'

'But the castle is full of people demanding your attention,' Kate said. 'Are you ever alone?'

'Of course,' he said again. But there was an odd expression on his face.

'When you go on archaeological digs, does everyone know you're a prince?'

Gabriel pulled down a bit more ivy and inspected the fallen bricks. 'They don't care. I'm the foreign devil who's odd enough to want them to excavate carefully, rather than simply tunneling toward the gold.'

That explained a great deal about Gabriel's hankering for Carthage, to Kate's mind.

'You'd better find another blue-eyed prig to marry,' he said, moving over to the vines clinging to the back garden wall. 'It sounds as if Effie needs

209

Hathaway or she'll end up tatting baby bonnets for other people's children.'

'Hathaway is not a prig!' Kate said, coming over to help. 'He's honorable, and decent.'

'So you said.' Gabriel sounded bored. 'Perhaps what Effie needs is someone to take a skewer, rather than a fork, to Beckham.'

'It wouldn't help Effie if you skewered him, unless Beckham confessed what happened so that everyone knew it was all a lie. I'm going to ask Henry to take care of it.'

'Lady Wrothe is undoubtedly a formidable knight, but what do you intend her to do?'

'I don't know,' Kate said. 'You know, this might be a portico. I think you're wrong and there is a door into the castle courtyard. It only makes sense.'

'We looked from the other side,' Gabriel said, wrenching at a mass of ivy. It came down on top of him, trails and strands of ivy all around his shoulders. 'There are no gates in the outer walls.'

'You look like a satyr,' Kate said, laughing.

'Give me my wine and my dancing girls,' Gabriel said, leering at her.

'Beware!' she said, dancing back. 'I'll stamp on your tail.'

'How do you know what satyrs look like? I thought you were so ill-educated.'

'I can read,' Kate said. 'My father had Boyse's *Pantheon*, so I read that.' She glanced over mischievously and couldn't resist. 'His library was quite thorough. He had Aretino as well.'

Gabriel was bending over, shaking his head to get the last leaves out of his hair. He straightened, and the look in his eyes sent a bolt of heat straight to Kate's stomach.

210

'You're trying to drive me mad,' he said conversationally, moving toward her with the grace of a predator.

'Well,' she squeaked, sounding like a bleating lamb, 'I—I—'

Their kisses were everything he had described them to be: like a room on fire, like a house with no air. She melted into his arms and the pressure of his lips stole every sensible thought in her head.

And replaced them with lewd images from Aretino's naughty book, pictures of male bodies that were all muscle and smooth skin, men with wild expressions on their faces—only they weren't merely men; the face she saw in her mind's eye was Gabriel's.

His hands were sliding down her back now, moving slowly in a direction that they shouldn't move, down . . .

But he shouldn't be kissing her either, faithless man that he was.

'You promised,' she said, breaking away from him.

His eyes were black. 'Don't,' he said, and the word was like a groan. It weakened her knees.

'We agreed not to kiss.'

'That was before you admitted to ogling Aretino's art, if one can give it that name.'

'I fail to see what that has to do with anything.'

He leaned back against the wall and laughed. 'It means, my dear Kate, that you are that rare thing amongst young ladies: a woman with curiosity. And, to be blunt, lust.'

Kate's cheeks started to turn pink; she could feel it.

'I didn't study the book,' she said haughtily,

though she had. 'I merely leafed through it and ascertained that it was inappropriate before putting it back on the shelf.'

'Liar.' He moved one lazy step, so he was just next to her again, though not touching. 'What were your favorites, Kate o' my Life? Did you like those naughty ones with more than two people in a bed?'

'No,' she said, refusing to give in to the molten invitation in his eyes. 'I think I should return to my chamber now.'

'Good; I don't like those either,' he said conversationally. 'I've got no wish to have two women at my beck and call or, God forbid, another man inspecting my willy.'

'Willy?' She giggled. 'You gave it a *name*? Why not Petey? Or Tinkle, for that matter?'

'*Willy* is a term, like *rod*, but not as descriptive,' Gabriel said. 'And you, Kate, are like some sort of cursed mythological woman in a story.'

'That's not very nice,' she said, frowning at him. 'Next you'll be saying that my hair is turning to snakes.'

'Not Medusa. One of those goddesses whom no one can resist.'

Despite herself, she smiled at that. But the sun was slanting lower over the old brick walls and tipping his hair with gold. 'I really should return to the castle. Did we determine what this is?'

'It's a door,' Gabriel said. He pulled the last swath of ivy to the ground.

It was a huge arched door, painted dark red, with elaborately wrought hinges in the shape of fleurs-de-lis. 'This is not just any door,' Kate said, awed. 'It's like the door to a cathedral.'

Gabriel's brow cleared. 'Of course! It must enter

212

the back of the chapel.' He pulled on the huge knocker, but the door didn't budge. 'Locked,' he muttered. 'And no key that I recall.'

'It's probably in the chapel,' Kate said. 'I want you to promise something.'

'Anything for you,' he said, and foolish woman that she was, her heart gave a silly thump.

'No more traveling through that corridor behind my bedchamber. I'll cover over the peephole, but I don't want to feel as if people are peering at me at night.'

'If you have trouble sleeping, I'd be happy to rub your back,' he said wolfishly.

She wrinkled her nose at him and set off toward the picnic things. 'You have to make me a promise too,' he called, staying where he was.

'What?'

'If I manage to skewer Beckham in such a way that Effie's reputation is restored, then you . . .'

Kate narrowed her eyes. 'Just what would I have to do?'

'I am helping you,' he pointed out. 'Purely virtuous on my part. If Effie's reputation is salvaged, she'll have her choice of beaux, and you'll have a better shot at snagging hoity-toity Hathaway.'

'He's not—' Kate began and gave up. 'So what would I have to do if you achieve this miracle?'

He was next to her in one long stride. 'You'd have to let me kiss you.'

'Hmmm,' she said. 'Let's count the kiss you just stole, and then you're already in my debt.'

'Not that kind of kiss.' His voice was dark and thick.

Kate stilled, uncertain what he meant.

His arms closed around her. 'I'll keep you a virgin, Kate. I promise on my word of honor. But let me discover you, give you pleasure, love you.'

'L—'

He took the word from her lips. Their kiss was as untamed as the garden they stood in. It was the kind of kiss that skirted the edge of propriety even though his hands stayed at her back, and hers around his neck.

It skirted propriety because they both knew the kiss was like making love, that there was an exchange, a possession and a submission, a giving and a taking, a forbidden intimacy.

Kate staggered away, her knees weak. She turned rather than meet his eyes, knelt at the corner of the picnic cloth, and began to put silver back in the basket.

'I'll send a footman out to clean up, you foolish crea-ture,' Gabriel said.

'I'm not a creature, and there's no need to create work for someone that we could easily do ourselves.'

'I'm not creating work.' Gabriel reached down and pulled her to her feet. 'It *is* their work. And if you don't think that a footman will leap at the chance to escape Wick's eagle eye, then you don't know my brother well enough.'

'Still,' Kate said uncertainly. She glanced over to see him frowning at her. 'Don't start thinking I've been toiling as a maid instead of a swineherd,' she told him, turning and walking toward the gate. 'I've never been a maid.'

'Of course not,' he said, taking her arm. 'You're a lady.'

She glanced suspiciously at him, but he was

smiling down at her as innocently as if he'd commented on the weather.

Twenty-five

Clearly, Beckham was a scoundrel. And scoundrels, in Gabriel's experience, generally showed their true colors when drunk.

He consigned that part of his plan to Wick, telling him to ply his guests with too much champagne. Wick rolled his eyes at this dictum, but at dinner Gabriel noticed the footmen whizzing around the tables refilling glasses, as busy as ants at harvest time.

The plan certainly had a marked effect at his own table. Lady Dagobert's daughter Arabella stopped throwing him longing, if half-hearted, looks, and bent her attentions entirely on young Lord Partridge, to her left. By the fourth course, she had turned a charming shade of pink and was sagging gently toward Partridge's shoulder.

Her mother, on the other hand, turned a less-than-charming shade of puce and remained strictly upright.

Still the courses, and the champagne, kept coming. The countess loosened her corset, metaphorically speaking, and told him a meandering tale about an ailing aunt who lived in Tunbridge Wells. 'Illness,' pronounced the countess, 'should not be encouraged. My aunt has made a lifetime habit of it, and I do not approve.'

Gales of laughter from Kate's direction seemed to suggest that the conversation at her table was

215

rather more lively than that at his own. The one time he looked over his shoulder, Hathaway was leaning so close that the man could certainly see down Kate's bosom, and having the opportunity, likely was doing so.

That thought apparently caused an expression of such savagery to appear on his face that Lady Dagobert inquired whether he was having a spasm. 'My aunt,' she confided, 'claims to have spasms on the quarter hour precisely. I told her that if so she would surely die of apoplexy when the clock struck noon.'

'One has to assume that she did not comply?' Gabriel inquired.

'I meant it in a helpful manner,' the countess said. 'If the spasms do not lead to apoplexy, then they are not worth regarding, and should be ignored.'

'I am curious about a guest of mine,' Gabriel said, recklessly abandoning the aunt in Tunbridge Wells. 'I know that you, dear lady, are abreast of everyone in London . . . what can you tell me of Lord Beckham?'

She responded to his lowered voice and request for gossip like one of Kate's dogs faced with a lump of cheese. '*Well*,' she said, 'he's a nephew of the Duke of Festicle, as you probably know.'

'Festicle?' Gabriel said, rolling the name over in his mind. 'A suitable name.'

'Suitable?' Lady Dagobert asked dubiously. 'I don't follow, Your Highness.' Then she pronounced: 'He's not good *ton*. I don't hold with that young man.'

Now they were at the heart of it. 'My judgment is precisely the same,' he told her, ignoring the fact

216

that he hadn't actually met Beckham yet. 'There is something of the voluptuary about him.'

'He's a shabster,' the countess said, twitching her turban, which was in danger of plopping into her salmon. It was white satin with a diamond crescent that threatened to scratch Gabriel on the cheek every time she leaned close.

'Do tell me an instance or two of his perfidy,' Gabriel said, giving her the kind of smile that invited secrets.

'I wouldn't let him near my daughter,' the countess said, poking her salmon with a knife. 'He's ruined more than one reputation, you know. Young ladies aren't safe around the man.'

'A bad hat, as your Duke of York has it,' Gabriel suggested.

'Don't know about his hat,' the countess said, pursuing her own train of thought. 'But all these ladies—the ones whose reputation he ruined—apparently acted the jade around him. Now I'm not saying that we don't have some young ladies who aren't better than they should be.' She paused.

'It is so in all the world,' Gabriel said encouragingly.

'But if I were young and foolish, and prone to act the mopsie, which I *never* was,' the countess said, 'it wouldn't be with him, if you catch my meaning.'

'Precisely,' Gabriel said, nodding. 'You are very perceptive, my lady.'

The countess blinked at him. 'Continental flummery,' she pronounced. 'I've had enough of this salmon.' She summoned a footman.

'More champagne,' Gabriel told the footman. He was curious to see whether Lady Arabella would actually col-lapse into the young lord's arms.

217

After most of his guests had toddled out of the dining room (and those who couldn't toddle were supported thence by footmen), he tracked down Beckham in the billiards room.

The man was lounging at the side of the room, watching Toloose defeat Dimsdale, or Algie, as Kate called him, with mathematical precision. It seemed that Toloose, if no one else, was untouched by the sea of champagne that had sloshed through the dining room.

There was a general stir as Gabriel entered the room, of course. The group watching the game began a twitching appraisal of their breeches and coats. As if a prince—or anyone else with a title, for that matter—cared if their breeches bunched around their rods. Toloose looked up from the table and snapped him a bow; Algie's was deeper, and definitely unsteady. One had to hope that they weren't playing for money.

Gabriel greeted all the gentlemen in turn. Lord Dewberry, bluff and hearty, chomping on his cigar; Henry's Leo, Lord Wrothe, holding a glass of champagne, naturally, but looking none the worse for it; finally, Beckham.

Beckham, it turned out, was a man with no chin.

None whatsoever.

His head rose in a smooth curve from a slim neck to a mustachioed mouth, and then up to a wide and rather graceful forehead. The unfortunate absence of a chin meant that his head resembled a squat bowling pin. He was around thirty; he smelled like a civet cat and had dyed his whiskers. One had to appreciate that the mustache was an attempt to widen the bottom half of his face, but the effect was unfortunate.

Really, Effie was generous when she called him a toad, Gabriel thought, lavishing a smile on him, the kind a mongoose gives a cobra.

'When will your betrothed arrive?' Beckham was asking.

'One hopes before the ball,' Toloose said, carefully wiping down his billiard cue. 'Every flower in England is here, hoping to be plucked by His Highness, and they won't give up until the bride actually arrives. No one even deigns to flirt with the rest of us.'

Beckham laughed. 'You insult our host, Toloose, old fellow. The Continent is more formal than we are amongst ourselves. You must forgive the man,' he said, turning to Gabriel and lowering his voice. 'Ribald but well-meaning.'

Gabriel met Toloose's eyes over Beckham's shoulder. 'In this case, Toloose is correct,' he said. 'I do not know the bride whom my brother has chosen for me. Yet we have—how do I say?—a few weeks, a period of time in which to reflect on each other.' He deliberately added a certain awkwardness to his speech. Englishmen invariably underestimated those who did not speak their language with fluency, a foolish habit that would get them in huge trouble someday.

'And in the meantime you can survey our English beauties,' Beckham said, giving him a jolly tap on the shoulder.

Gabriel stopped himself from swatting the man like a gnat. 'The young English ladies are so exquisite in their . . . exquisiteness. A garden of delightful flowers, as Mr Toloose has called them.'

Toloose snorted, over where he was chalking his stick, so Gabriel threw him a warning glance. 'My

219

dear Toloose introduced me to a charming girl this very morning,' he said. 'Miss—what was her name?—Effie something. With lovely blue eyes. I am quite taken with her.'

Toloose's eyebrow jerked up; of all the men in the room, he knew for certain that he had not taken Miss Effie Starck anywhere near Gabriel.

There was a little silence in the room, as the cluster of men presumably tried to figure out how to deliver the nasty bit of gossip Beckham had put about.

'Ephronsia Starck is a bit old,' Beckham himself said, with a tittering laugh. 'Must be well into her twenties.'

'She hasn't the best reputation,' Dewberry said, 'but I've never cottoned to it myself. Think there was some misunderstanding.' He chomped on his cigar and looked straight at Beckham.

'Yes, because who could believe that little Effie would choose Beckham?' Lord Wrothe said softly, coming closer. By that point in the evening, he had to have drunk a few bottles of champagne, but miraculously he was steady on his feet. '*We* love you, of course, Beckham, but . . .'

Beckham's color rose above his high collar and he tittered again. 'I've had my admirers,' he said.

'What was the story?' Algie asked, in his usual bumbling fashion. 'Did she kiss you or something, Beckham?'

'Dear me,' Gabriel said. 'I trust she didn't give you an unwanted kiss, Lord Beckham? Though one must ask whether there *is* such a thing as an unwanted kiss from such a delightful young lady.'

'More than a kiss,' Beckham said, a trifle sullenly. He seemed to have grasped that the

220

atmosphere was not entirely charitable.

Gabriel turned around and gestured to the footman stationed at the door. 'Champagne for everyone.'

Dewberry was the sort of man who wouldn't tolerate unfairness; Gabriel could see that at a glance. Wrothe looked like the sort who might drink himself into a stupor, but even inebriated wouldn't lose his sense of himself as a gentleman.

'From what I heard,' Toloose called from the billiard table, where he was setting up the balls again, 'she was so overset by your indescribable charms, Beckham, that she attempted an intimate caress.'

Gabriel let his eyes drift from the top of Beckham's head, pause in the area where a chin should have been, down to the padded shoulders, pinched-in waist, and buckled slippers. 'Odd . . . Not that I mean it as an insult, my dear Lord Beckham. But young ladies are generally so frivolous, are they not? So prone to look to the outside, rather than ascertain the inner worth of a man.'

'The odd thing, to my mind,' said Dewberry, 'is that Miss Effie ain't alone. One of my cousin's gals, visiting from Scotland, had a similar type of story bruited about. Except that the little gal, Delia, supposedly dragged Lord Beckham into a closet.'

Beckham glanced toward the door, but Gabriel was standing squarely between him and escape.

'So adventuresome, these English lasses,' Gabriel commented. 'Yet they look as if—how do you say?—butter wouldn't melt in their mouths.'

'That's just it,' Dewberry said, coming to stand at Gabriel's shoulder. 'Delia weren't an adventuresome sort of girl, and she had a different tale about what happened.'

'Really?' Gabriel said. 'You were lucky that her father didn't take up a disagreement with you, Lord Beckham. But of course on the Continent we are so much more prone to turn to a rapier to resolve our differences.' He rested his forefinger on the handle of his rapier, and Beckham's eyes followed the movement.

'Delia was betrothed already and now she's got two little ones of her own,' Dewberry said. 'But she had no father to take after His Lordship. The same as Miss Starck, though I didn't think of it until now.'

'I fail to see what any of this has to do with the prince's original question,' Beckham said in his light, high voice. 'Elegance will always awaken a woman's ambitions, you know. If you gentlemen would like a few tips on how to heat up a woman's appreciation, I'd be happy to pass some on.'

It was a masterly attempt. 'You think that Effie Starck was overcome by lust for your costume?' Toloose said, drifting over to stand at Gabriel's other shoulder. 'Odd, because, if you'll forgive me, Beckham, she's never made the slightest approach to *me*.'

Toloose was without doubt the most elegant man in the room. He didn't have a pinched waist or a waxed mustache, but Gabriel judged that even his brother Rupert would have lusted after Toloose's swallowtail coat and French cuffs.

'Well,' Beckham said, 'ladies generally prefer an air of refinement, Toloose. If you'll forgive me,' he added.

There *was* something aggressively masculine

222

about Toloose . . . perhaps it was the look in his eye. Or the way he was holding his billiard cue. It was amazing the way a man in an embroidered coat could take on the air of a dockworker.

'I'm not following,' Algie complained. 'Either Effie dragged Beckham into a closet or she didn't.'

'She didn't,' Beckham stated.

'No, Delia did that,' Gabriel put in.

'Oh, so there were two of them,' Algie said. 'I thought the one girl had done it all. Effie Starck is a bit small for dragging men about, don't you know? Not up to the task, I would say.'

'Seems to me there was yet a third,' Wrothe put in.

He was lounging to the side, looking highly entertained. 'Wasn't there a story going about, years ago, Beckham? Some lusty wench took after you in Almack's.'

'No!' Gabriel exclaimed. 'But this is remarkable. A man so fortunate as to have driven three ladies to the point of an indiscretion.'

'But here's the question,' Algie said, slurring his words a bit. 'Did the third gal have a pa, then? Well, I suppose we know she had a pa, but was he living?'

'Good point, my dear nephew,' Gabriel said. 'A very good point. Lord Wrothe, do you remember the young lady's name? Or'—he turned back to Beckham—'surely you must, my lord. Even though these events seem to happen to you with distressing regularity . . . still you must remember the ladies in question.'

Beckham shrugged. 'All this questioning . . . so unpleasant, gentlemen. Am I expected to remember every coquette whom I've met in my

223

years? Almack's is full of dissipated fair ones.' He drained his champagne. 'I really must retire to bed.'

'No, no,' Gabriel said gently. 'There is no reason for flummery amongst ourselves, Lord Beckham. Do you or do you not remember the name of the third young lady whom you accused of making an unwanted advance?'

Beckham set his teeth.

'I've got it,' Wrothe said. 'Her last name was Wodderspoon, though I'll be damned if I can remember the rest of it.'

'Sir Patrick Wodderspoon,' Dewberry said, drawing his brows together. 'Died years ago; we were at Eton together.'

'No pa,' Algie said mournfully. 'She had no pa either.'

'Dear me,' Gabriel commented. 'England seems to have suffered a rash of trollopy young ladies without fathers.'

'All *right*,' Beckham snapped. He jerked his chin at the footman. 'You. More champagne.'

There was silence as the wine gurgled into his cup. He drank, and looked up, a fugitive sort of courage burning in his eyes. 'They wanted it anyhow,' he said. 'They're all nothing but cattle in fine clothing. Scratch the surface of a supposed lady and you find nothing more than a slattern, opening her legs to any spark of the first stare who happens by.'

'But you are no spark of the first stare. An obscure phrase, but clear enough,' Gabriel said. He turned and nodded to the footman. 'Please fetch Berwick. Lord Beckham will be leaving shortly.'

'He could have done that to my Victoria,' Algie said, staring at Beckham with a kind of blurry

224

horror. 'She ain't got no pa either. And then she'd have been ruined.'

'At this point it's too late to help Miss Wodderspoon,' Dewberry said, folding his arms over his chest. 'And Delia is married, snug and tight. But Miss Effie Starck—now that's a problem. Because I would guess that the young men aren't taking to her, not after your story.'

'He should marry her,' Algie said. 'And he should promise on his word of honor that he'll never do anything like this again.'

'He hasn't got a word of honor,' Dewberry said, at the same moment that Wrothe said, 'I doubt Miss Effie would take him. He's too ugly, among other things.' He said it coolly, over the rim of his glass.

Another blotchy flush was rising up Beckham's neck. He turned his back on Lord Wrothe and snapped a bow to Gabriel. 'I ascertain that you'd like me to leave this moldering pile of bricks, Your Highness, and I will. Gladly.'

'Not just yet,' Gabriel said. 'You will be leaving; my inestimable Berwick will help you along on your journey. But first . . . we really do have to discuss the question of making amends to Miss Effie Starck.'

Beckham's titter had a virulent undertone to it now. 'I'll go out there and tell the pack of them, shall I? I'll tell them that I had a kiss off the wench and she kissed like a dead fish, so I saved other men the trouble.'

Gabriel's fist slammed into Beckham's jaw. He flew backward, smashed into the edge of the billiard table, and caromed to the floor.

'Is he out?' Toloose asked, after Beckham didn't

stir.

'No,' Algie said, carefully pouring his champagne over the man's face. 'I think his eyelids are twitching.'

'Waste of good champagne,' Wrothe observed. 'Though I want to congratulate you on your forbearance, Prince. I thought you were going to have at him when he ventured into barnyard talk.'

Gabriel walked over and hauled Beckham to his feet. The man blinked and swayed, but kept upright. 'Do we need to have further conversation, Lord Beckham?'

'I'll begad if you didn't break my jaw,' Beckham said, putting a finger in his mouth to feel his teeth.

'Shall we practice what you are going to say about Miss Effie Starck?'

'I'll tell them that the prince wanted me to clear the name of his little canary bird, shall I?'

Over he went again, this time sprawling on the billiard table itself.

'Don't throw any champagne on him,' Toloose cried, alarmed. 'You'll ruin the felt!'

Algie pulled Beckham to a sitting position on the edge of the table. His eyelids fluttered, but then his head rolled over and he slumped back down on the table.

'Tiresome,' Gabriel observed, 'but I believe that he is likely ready to tell the truth.' He turned to another footman. 'Go to Lady Dagobert's chambers. Give her my compliments and request that she attend me here, in the billiards room, on a matter of utmost urgency.'

Dewberry's mouth fell open and Toloose laughed aloud.

A few minutes later Beckham blinked, gave a

yelp, and sat up. 'My tooth!' He spat a little blood and said, with something of a lisp, 'You've taken out my tooth, you bloody foreign—' He stopped short, catching Gabriel's eye.

'Lady Dagobert will arrive in a moment to hear your confession,' Gabriel told him. 'Confession, so they say, is good for the soul. In your case, it is your only chance of keeping the rest of your teeth. Do you understand?'

'I can't. You're going to make me a pariah,' Beckham panted. 'You don't understand England, or the English.'

Algie reached over, picked up a yellowed tooth on the billiard table, and dropped it in Beckham's hand. 'Wouldn't want you to leave this behind. Bit of a souvenir of your visit to the castle, one might say.'

'No one will invite me anywhere,' Beckham bleated. 'You have no idea what you're doing to me. I'll have to rusticate.'

'For life,' Dewberry put in grimly.

'I'll—I'll marry the girl!' Beckham said, looking wildly from face to face. 'That's the best I can offer, and she'll leap at the chance, you know she will. I'll do it just to show what a gentleman I am because she—'

'Effie won't want to marry you,' Gabriel stated. 'Especially not with that big gaping hole where your tooth used to be. It makes you look like a degenerate, which is appropriate.'

'I've got a nice estate,' Beckham said, starting to blather. 'She'd be lucky to have me. It's unentailed and—'

The door opened behind them. 'Pardon me,' came an imperious voice. 'I expected to find a fire

227

at the very least, but I see merely a gaggle of tipsy gentlemen, and I fail to see how *that* can be termed an emergency.'

Gabriel turned about and bowed. The countess had apparently been caught on her way to bed. She was dressed in a voluminous cap and swathed in enough ruffled white cotton to outfit an entire village.

'You do me too much honor,' he said, kissing her hand.

'I feel bound to tell you, Your Highness,' said Lady Dagobert, 'that I do not consider the time of night salubrious for encounters with the opposite sex, nor do I appreciate requests of this nature.'

'I entirely understand, and yet you are the only person in the castle to whom I could make this appeal,' Gabriel said, drawing to the side so that the countess could see Beckham for the first time.

She sniffed in disgust. 'Fisticuffs, I see.'

'Lord Beckham has a confession to make,' Gabriel explained, 'and as an arbiter of the *ton*, I felt that you were the best person to hear it.'

'I trust you're not implying I'm of a Romish disposition,' the countess said. 'Lord Beckham, say what you wish. But only, if you please, after you wipe the blood from your chin. I am quite squeamish.'

Beckham did as commanded, gave a kind of shudder, and blinked several times.

'Get on with it, man,' Lady Dagobert commanded.

'Effie Starck—'

'That's Miss Ephronsia Starck to you,' she interrupted. 'I don't hold with these relaxed manners among the younger set.'

228

'Miss Ephronsia Starck did not, ah, welcome my advances,' Beckham said. 'In fact, she stabbed me with a fork after repulsing an unwanted intimacy on my part.'

The countess nodded. 'You're a blackguard,' she said. 'Knew it the moment I saw you, and I'm never wrong about a character. I hope never to see you again in my natural lifetime.'

Beckham swallowed and looked as if he very much hoped her wish would come true.

'I'll take care of Miss Ephronsia's reputation tomorrow,' she continued, and no one in the room doubted but that Effie's name would be as unblemished as that of a newborn babe by noon. 'I shall ensure that she has her pick of the *ton*. I fancy that people give my opinion some weight.'

'Where you go, others will always follow,' Gabriel said.

'We'll follow,' Algie piped up.

The countess gave him a disdainful look but managed to stop herself from delivering a judgment of his character. She turned to Gabriel. 'Surely you said that Lord Beckham will be traveling for his health.'

'Yes,' he said, smiling at her. 'He will.'

'I believe that Jamaica is a nice place,' she said. 'I heard tell that one in two people there are eaten by sharks. That leaves fighting odds, as I see it.'

Gabriel bowed. 'Your wish is my command, my lady.'

She snorted. 'Continental flummery.' And with that, she exited the room.

'What did she say? I'm not going to Jamaica,' Beckham said, her words filtering through his mind. 'I might rusticate for the fall. Or perhaps even for next season. Though that would be a sacrifice, I tell you. I would be missed.'

Gabriel glanced over his shoulder. Wick was lounging in the doorway, a phalanx of footmen at his back. A moment later Lord Beckham was escorted from the room, and all that was left of him was a wail dying away down the corridor.

'I knew enough to put two and two together, and I didn't stop to think,' Lord Dewberry said, thumping the edge of the billiard table with his fist. 'I'm ashamed of myself.'

'Perhaps it took a man with an interest in one of these young ladies to look straight at the problem,' Lord Wrothe put in. 'Miss Ephronsia Starck is lucky to have met you, Prince.'

'Oh, I haven't met her,' Gabriel said. 'I'm afraid that I merely pretended an interest, the better to smoke him out. Would you give me a game, Toloose?'

'You took out Beckham from the goodness of your heart?' Toloose said, raising an eyebrow. 'Such virtue . . .' He handed over a billiard cue. 'I feel near to melancholy at the fact that I'm honor-bound to slay you at billiards.'

'Oh you are, are you?' Gabriel asked, chalking his cue.

'For the honor of my country,' Toloose said, nodding. 'Who would have thought the Pomeroys had such a magnificent table, by the way?'

'They didn't,' Gabriel said, leaning over to sight down his cue.

'Really?' Algie asked, cheerfully propping his elbows on the side of the table. 'So where did it come from, then?'

'It's the only piece of furniture I brought with

me from Marburg,' Gabriel said, giving Toloose a wolfish smile. 'You did say that you play for high stakes, did you not?'

His opponent broke into a bellow of laughter.

Twenty-six

As it turned out, Lady Dagobert's information offensive was considerably more efficient than predictions of the noon hour. Kate learned of Beckham's disgrace when Rosalie brought hot cocoa in the morning, and it was confirmed when, on Lady Arabella's invitation, she met a small group of ladies in the rose drawing room for a demonstration of how to shape a reticule from a swansdown muff, to be given by Effie's maid.

No one bothered to tinker with a muff, let alone shape it into a reticule. They were too busy agreeing that they had never trusted Beckham, and assuring Effie that she was a dove and a saint.

'Show us how you held the fork,' Henry said, snatching one from the tea tray. 'I'd rather learn how to poke holes in a loose fish like Beckham than turn my favorite muff into a reticule. Like this? Or like this?'

Kate burst out laughing, watching Henry thrust her fork into the air like a man learning to fence.

'I really couldn't say,' Effie said, her cheeks pink with excitement. 'It all happened so fast. I just knew that I had to save myself and so I did.'

'I only hope that I'm not of an age where gentlemen might hesitate to offer me an impropriety,' Henry said. 'I think I have the grip down perfectly. I'm sure I could do considerable damage, if only someone would give me the opportunity. Perhaps I could convince my husband that I need to practice.'

Lady Dagobert looked up from a small escritoire, where she was penning missives to, as she put it, everyone who mattered. 'I consider forking husbands to show a lack of moral fiber,' she pronounced.

'That's because she'd out-and-out bludgeon Dagobert if she wanted to,' Henry muttered to Kate.

'Let's talk about the ball tomorrow,' Arabella cried after a hasty glance at her mother. 'Miss Daltry, what will you wear? You have such exquisite taste . . . will you wear a pair of glass slippers?'

Kate opened her mouth, but Henry jumped in. 'Glass slippers? What are they? Something I missed because of that dratted trip abroad last spring, I warrant.'

'They're the most delicious slippers in the world,' Arabella gushed. 'And Miss Daltry brought them into fashion. I only wish I could have a pair, but Mama is quite heartless on the subject.'

'Might as well be made of diamonds, for the cost of them,' Lady Dagobert said, raising her head again. 'A waste of money.'

'Likely to splinter and cut your toes off, are they?' Henry asked with interest. 'I think I'm probably too curvy to trust myself to glass.'

'They're not really made of glass,' Kate said, wracking her brains to try to remember what Rosalie said about them. 'And yes, I will be wearing a pair.'

'All the best fashion is frightfully expensive,'

Henry said. 'My dressing chamber was positively littered with ostrich feathers after that craze last year at court. They cost a pretty penny, and the weight of seven of them gave me a terrible headache.'

'I shall wear a white satin petticoat with gold Brussels drapery to the ball,' the countess announced. 'With eight white ostrich feathers. I seem to suffer no ill effects at all from such plumage.'

'White, white, white,' Henry muttered. 'You'd think she was a bride. Someone should tell her that an expanse of snow always looks ten times wider than a plowed field.'

'Henry!' Kate said, giggling madly.

'You are right to correct me,' Henry said. 'That field hasn't been plowed in years.'

'I am wearing a draped tunic to the ball,' Effie said. 'Do tell me what you're wearing, Victoria? I find you such an inspiration.'

Kate hadn't the faintest idea. 'I brought three or four costumes with me,' she said airily. 'I never make up my mind until the very last minute.'

'Will you wear your hair in the Grecian or the Roman style?' Lady Arabella asked.

'I really couldn't say,' Kate said, elbowing Henry in a silent entreaty that she change the subject of conversation. 'At the moment I am enamored of my wigs.'

'I brought a gorgeous wig with me,' Arabella said.

'Gentlemen don't care for wigs on a gal,' the countess said, looking up again. 'I've told you time and again, Arabella, that a gentleman looks to a woman's hair to see what sort of breeder she'll be.'

233

There was a moment of silence. 'It's a good thing that I like wigs,' Henry said. 'Otherwise my three husbands might have looked elsewhere.'

'I apologize for my mother,' Arabella said quietly.

'I hear you, daughter,' the countess said. 'If there's any apologizing to do, I'll do it myself.' She looked over at the settee. 'I'm sorry, Henry. I had no call to be talking about breeding in front of you.'

'It's years in the past,' Henry said with a little shrug. 'But do you know, Mabel, I believe that's the first time you've addressed me by the name I prefer?'

'I shall not do so again,' the countess said, returning to her letter. 'It's dreadfully vulgar to use first names in conversation, let alone a pet name of that variety.'

'I knew I had some particular reason for liking the name,' Henry said. 'It's my incurable vulgarity.'

'I'll tell you what is vulgar,' the countess said. 'Vulgarity is the way that Miss Emily Gill makes eyes at that prince. Admittedly, he *is* a prince.'

'A particularly luscious one,' Henry put in.

'He isn't objectionable,' the countess said. 'But he's a foreigner, and a prince, and our host. And there's a princess supposedly arriving this very day to marry the man. Emily Gill has been staring at him as if he were a god or something of that nature.'

'Surely not,' Henry said, much shocked. 'Those gods never wear a stitch of clothing, at least none of Lord Elgin's marbles do. I spent a great deal of time examining them, so I know.'

'Take it as you will,' the countess stated.

'She is enamored,' Arabella said. 'She told me

234

that the prince smiled at her last night and her heart beat so that she almost swooned on the spot.'

'Even if he didn't have a princess on the way, he'd never marry her. This castle must cost a fortune to run,' the countess said, glancing about. 'The cost of maintaining staff alone must be thousands of pounds a year.'

'I wish I had a fortune,' Arabella said, sighing. 'He's so handsome.'

'I'm not marrying you to a fortune hunter,' her mother said, finishing her last letter with a flourish. 'Here, you—' She beckoned to a footman. 'Have them out in the evening mail, if you please.'

'It's very kind of you,' Effie said shyly. 'I know my mother would say the same, but she was so overset by the news of Lord Beckham's departure that she took to her bed.'

'Your mama has the fortitude of a chicken in the rain,' the countess said. 'This should do it.' There was a grim certitude about her tone. 'Even if that ne'er-do-well escapes from whatever ship the prince bundled him onto, he won't dare show his face in polite society again. I've written everyone I know. And anyone I don't know ain't worth knowing.'

'Truly most kind,' Effie said.

'Including,' the countess continued, 'the former Miss Wodderspoon. She was one of the first ladies he accosted. Luckily her betrothal was arranged in the cradle . . . do you know who she is now?'

Henry frowned; Arabella, Effie and Kate shook their heads.

'The Duchess of Calvert,' the countess said triumphantly. 'I wrote her *and* the duke as well. I knew him when he was a boy, of course. I thought he'd better know the truth about his wife.'

'In my opinion,' Henry said, 'the truth about one's spouse becomes clear after a mere few weeks of marriage. If not a few hours.'

'I agree,' the countess said. 'But it can't hurt. If Beckham dares to show his nose in England, the duke will cut it off. There's just one thing I'd like to know.'

They all regarded her in silence. The countess had a way of convincing a room that she knew everything, so a disclosure of ignorance was fascinating.

'Why'd he do it?' she asked.

'Men of that stripe can't stop themselves,' Henry said with distaste. 'I've run into them before. Beckham had no luck on his own merits, so he destroyed those who had the character to reject his advances, such as our own Miss Effie.'

'Not *him*,' the countess said. 'The prince. Why did the prince take after Beckham like that?'

'His Highness is like a king,' Arabella said worshipfully. 'He saw an injustice and he addressed it, like King Solomon.'

'I think he has a moral nature and can't stand a wrong-doer,' Effie said, her voice taking on a dramatic tone. 'Like an avenging angel, he came down with the sword of heaven and smote the evildoer.'

'You're not picking up that tripe at St. Andrew's,' the countess said, frowning at Effie. 'Don't make me think that I should speak to your mother. She'll have you reading the Bible this evening.'

'Please don't say anything to Mother,' Effie said, alarmed. 'She has already expressed concern that the dancing tonight will be too strenuous for me. I can't wait to see the Russian princess. Apparently she's due to arrive before supper.'

'Dancing tonight, is there?' the countess said. 'And the ball tomorrow. We'd better retire for a good rest, Arabella. I'm quite worn out by scratching all that down on paper over and over. Ephronsia, you come with me as well.'

Effie and Arabella obediently rose to their feet, and they processed from the room like the queen's barge attended by two small tugboats.

Twenty-seven

Henry watched them leave, and then turned to Kate. 'I don't suppose *you* know anything about the prince's unlikely digression into knight-errantry?'

'I may have mentioned Effie's plight,' Kate said cautiously.

'And he set off like a knight in shining armor to do your bidding. Curious, my dear. Very curious. If I were you, I'd be wary. When men start behaving like members of King Arthur's court, they're generally planning to shake the sheets, if you'll excuse the phrase. *Your* sheets, in this case.'

'Oh no,' Kate said weakly. Her blood heated at the picture that presented, of Gabriel, tangled in her sheets, his hands pulling her to him, his . . .

'Oh yes,' Henry said. 'Don't bet your fortune on a card game, m'dear, because your sins are written on your face.'

'Sins? I haven't—'

'Sins to come,' Henry said. But there was a smile in her eye. 'Just don't make a fool of yourself. Do you know how to prevent a babe?'

237

'Yes,' Kate said, a blush hot in her cheeks. 'But I don't need to know. I told him—' She shut her mouth.

'Fascinating,' Henry said. 'Unfortunately, his wife-to-be will apparently arrive on the premises at any moment. Would you take her place, if you could?'

Kate shook her head, taking a dainty little teacup that Henry offered her. 'No.'

'Why not? He's personable, he's got a fine leg, and he doesn't smell. You could do much worse.'

'He's my father all over again,' Kate said flatly, 'down to the fact that he has to marry for money. It's not his fault, exactly, nor was it my father's. But I'm not going to lie in a darkened room while my husband is out wooing other women.'

Henry bit her lip. 'I feel an unwelcome pang of guilt. I have to tell you that generally I never entertain the emotion.'

'I didn't mean you,' Kate said. 'Frankly, I'd much rather that my father had cavorted with you than with Mariana. My point is merely that he didn't love my mother. He didn't honor her, or even truly care for her. I want a *real* marriage, Henry.'

'A real marriage . . . It's hard to know what you mean by that, love. Marriage is a complicated beast.'

'Surely it's less complicated if one starts out with respect and affection,' Kate said.

'How do you know the prince doesn't feel that for you?'

'He feels lust,' Kate said bluntly. 'Which doesn't mean much.'

'There's nothing without lust,' Henry said. 'Between men and women, I mean. Just think about

238

your purported fiancé, Lord Dimsdale. If a woman was lucky enough to feel lust for him, affection might follow. Otherwise . . . I'm not so sure.'

'Gabriel doesn't like the idea that he is, perforce, marrying for money. It doesn't suit his character, and so he's wooing me in his spare time, as it were. Toying with the idea of making me his mistress. Playing the prince enamored of the swine girl.'

There was a second of silence. 'That's a cold assessment of the man,' Henry said, finally. 'I see him as a more passionate type, the kind who would throw his heart over a windmill if he met the woman for him.'

'No prince can do that,' Kate said. 'His marriage is a matter of royal protocol and treaties and that sort of thing.'

'You can't say he's like your father in that regard,' Henry pointed out.

'My father should have married you.'

'Then you wouldn't be here,' Henry said. 'What's more, I loved my first husband. And I love Leo, too. My second husband wasn't terrible, though I can't say I was quite as enthusiastic. I don't want you to think that Juliet just keeps pining her whole life, because she doesn't. Or rather, I didn't.'

Kate laughed. 'I can't imagine you pining.'

'Precisely,' Henry said. 'There's no use to it.'

'I would simply like to marry without regard to money.'

'The more important point is not to fall in love with someone who *is* marrying with regard to money.'

'I won't,' Kate promised.

'I wish I believed you,' Henry said, rather gloomily. 'I would have fallen in love with the

239

prince myself if I were your age.'

'I'll find a man who loves me for myself, and then I'll fall in love with *him*.'

'I'm trying to remember if I was ever as young as you are, but if so, the memory is lost in the mists of time.'

'I'm not young,' Kate said, grinning. 'Practically an octogenarian, as you characterized Effie.'

Henry sighed. 'I suppose that poor Dante is no longer in the running? I think he's taken a great liking to you.'

'He's a wonderful man,' Kate said.

'Too boring, the poor sweetheart, with all his talk of blackbirds and vicars. He'll end up with Effie after all. Though I do like her considerably better than I did before.'

'He'd be lucky to end up with Effie,' Kate said. 'She would keep him on his toes. She has a madly dramatic streak, you know.'

'Did you see the countess's face when Effie described the prince as wielding the sword of heaven? She definitely has a way with words.' Henry rose. 'This will be a very, very interesting evening. I hope that the Russian princess is beautiful indeed . . . for her own sake.'

Twenty-eight

As she followed her godmother out the door, Kate couldn't bring herself to agree with Henry about the *interesting* evening.

Was it normal, could it be normal, to be absolutely in the grip of something as fierce as her anticipation of the evening seemed to be?

From the moment she'd awakened in the morning, she hadn't been able to focus on anything other than Gabriel's promise to kiss her, discover her, give her pleasure. And didn't he say—didn't he say *love her*? What did that mean?

Her obsession had only grown worse once it was clear that Gabriel had fulfilled his side of the bargain. Beckham was dispatched to parts unknown; Effie's reputation was repaired and she would likely be married off within a fortnight, if Lady Dagobert had her way.

Kate had to fulfill her side of the promise, and let Gabriel do with her as he willed.

Henry went off to find her husband, and Kate continued up the stairs, desperately trying to pull her thoughts in order.

Give her pleasure sounded . . . it sounded wonderful. Every bit of her body tingled at the thought, turned warm and soft. It was like a fire in her blood, a kind of madness. She couldn't help looking everywhere for Gabriel, thinking he might come around the corner any moment.

It took all her self-control not to walk back down the stairs and loiter in the drawing room, waiting for him. Or worse, humiliate herself by asking Wick where his brother might be found.

The very thought of it stiffened her backbone, and she started walking more quickly down the corridor that led to the west wing.

She had to allow his kiss, whatever that was. But she didn't have to humiliate herself by allowing him to know the feverish state she was in.

She would simply get through whatever it was he had planned . . . with her dignity intact. Her heart was pounding at the thought, and she began to walk faster and faster.

It shouldn't have been a surprise when she rounded the corner into the picture gallery and barreled straight into someone.

It wasn't Gabriel. She knew that instantly because her whole being was attuned to the spicy male scent of him. This man smelled faintly like a pigpen, with an overlay of soap.

'Your Highness,' she gasped, dropping into a deep curtsy before Gabriel's uncle, Prince Ferdinand. 'I do apologize. I wasn't watching where I was going.'

'Miss Daltry, isn't it?' he said, peering at her, his eyelids fluttering madly. His gray hair was flying straight up at the top of his head, and he wore a pair of pince-nez on the very tip of his nose. 'No harm done, m'dear. I've been examining these paintings, trying to put together a bit of Pomeroy history. History is terribly important, you know.'

He was standing before a long-nosed patriarch. 'This is the first of them,' he said. 'Looks like this fellow built the castle back in the 1400s.'

'How long has it been since there was a Pomeroy living here?' Kate asked, curiosity replacing her embarrassment.

'Centuries,' Prince Ferdinand said. 'I consulted some sort of peerage book that was hanging about in the library this morning. The line died out with the Tudors.' He moved down the line. 'You see this lady? She's the last of them.' He was standing before a sweet-faced woman with a little girl on her lap. She wore a stiff ruff, and a small dog poked its nose out from under her chair.

'She was the last duchess?' Kate said, wondering if the dog was Rascal, Dandy, or perhaps Freddie.

'They weren't duchesses,' the prince corrected her. 'Nothing higher than barons, actually. Well set-up barons, one has to assume. With a castle this size, they likely were of help to the crown, supplying an army and the like. England was a roustabout type of place back in the day.'

'Do you know her name?'

Prince Ferdinand took out a sheet of foolscap, covered with notes in shaky handwriting. 'Eglantine,' he said, after a moment. 'Or perhaps that was the child. No, it's Lady Eglantine. Let me see if I can find her daughter's name . . . I know I wrote it down here somewhere.'

'Could it be Merry?' Kate asked, reaching out a finger to touch the painted cheek of the smiling little girl.

'That sounds right,' the prince said, turning his sheet upside down. 'Yes, I wrote it just here. Born in 1594, died in 1597. Only made it to three years old, poor scrap.'

'There's a memorial for her in the garden,' Kate said.

'She's likely buried in the chapel,' Prince Ferdinand said. 'I'd look, but I can't seem to find the key. My nephew must have it secreted

243

somewhere; Berwick doesn't know where it is. We haven't got a chaplain, you know. The religious folk all stayed in Marburg, and we sinners took the boat to England.'

Kate dragged her eyes away from Merry and her mother. 'To whom was Lady Eglantine married? This gentleman?' She gestured to a fierce-looking lord with his hand poised on his sword.

'Rather scandalously, it seems that she never married,' the prince said, pulling a hand through his hair, which made all the gray fluff stand up straight. 'That gentleman is her brother, the last Lord Pomeroy. Died in a brawl, by all accounts, leaving no heir. He had never married either, and of course Eglantine wouldn't have inherited. So the castle devolved to some distant cousin, a gentleman named Fitzclarence, and they lived here ever since. Two years ago, it came into the possession of the Duchy of Marburg.'

'How on earth did that happen?'

'My brother, Grand Duke Albrecht of Warl-Marburg-Baalsfeld, was attached to the Fitzclarences through King Frederick William II of Prussia's first daughter, Princess Frederica Charlotte, to the Duchess of York and Albany . . . and through my second cousin, to Caroline of Brunswick,' he said, rattling off the names like a catechism. 'Somehow in the middle of all that, Albrecht ended up with the castle. Sort of thing that does happen, more often than you'd think.'

Since Kate would never have thought about it, she kept silent.

'Likely no one would have bothered with the castle,' Prince Ferdinand continued, 'and it would have just moldered away, but Augustus was looking

244

for a way to send his rascally relatives packing.'
There was a growling undertone in his voice that
touched Kate.

'England is a comfortable place to live,' she
offered. 'It rains quite a lot, but we're all decent
folk.'

'I can see that,' Prince Ferdinand said. 'And I
didn't mean to disparage it in the least, m'dear. We
all feel the slings and arrows of outrageous fortune
now and then. The one I feel sorry for is young
Gabriel. You wouldn't know this to look at him, but
the fellow is brilliant. Absolutely brilliant.'

'Really?' Kate ventured. Thinking of Gabriel's
fierce eyes, and the set of his jaw . . . you *would*
know that he was brilliant, just by looking at him.

'Took a top degree. Set all the heads
a-squawking at your Oxford. He published some
sort of paper that forced them to think about how
they excavate old places. He cares, you see. Lot of
them don't.'

Kate looked at him and suddenly realized that he
was talking on two levels: Augustus, clearly, hadn't
cared for his rapidly blinking, elderly uncle. And
Gabriel, who did care for his relatives, cared for
history as well.

'I think the prince is happy to be here with you,'
she said.

'Rather be off in strange lands mucking about
with the tombs of kings and extinct cities,' Prince
Ferdinand said. 'But there, I'm old enough to know
that life doesn't give you what you wish.'

'Would you rather be in Marburg?'

'Not at the moment,' he said. 'Not with things
the way they are. Mighty unpleasant, those religious
types can be. Always asking a fellow to memorize

245

this or that Bible verse.' He gave her a small smile. 'Another thing I've learned in m'life: You don't learn kindness from memorizing even a whole book of the Bible. And that's the important thing, to my mind.'

And without further farewell, he bowed and wandered off the way that Kate had come, leaving her standing before the portraits.

She looked once more at Eglantine and her daughter, Merry, and then set off again for her room.

When would Gabriel claim his kiss? Presumably before his bride-to-be arrived. It was all too ridiculous; the very idea of kissing a betrothed man was scandalous. Somehow she didn't care.

Fire danced over her pulses again.

She would take a perfumed bath. After all those years working for Mariana, she still found the luxury of a bath to be the greatest pleasure in being a lady.

Then she meant to have an argument with Rosalie. She didn't want to wear her bosom friends. She was sick of jutting out in front like the prow of a ship, and of the feeling that she had her breasts presented on a platter for men to ogle at.

Though of course it mattered most who was doing the ogling.

The very thought of Gabriel's eyes and the way he had looked at her wet bodice after saving her from the lake . . .

She wrenched open the door to her chamber, thinking of pulling the bell cord to summon her maid. She darted into the room, reached her hand out—froze.

She wasn't alone.

246

Twenty-nine

He was seated in a chair by the window, reading, and the sun was making bronze streaks in his hair. 'I wouldn't pull that cord, if I were you,' he said, turning the page, a wicked little smile hovering at the edge of his mouth. 'Your maid might be shocked.'

'Gabriel,' she said, feeling blood pound through her body and a terrible, strange joy take hold of her. 'What are you doing in my chamber?'

'Waiting for you,' he said, finally raising his eyes. 'You owe me. In case you had forgotten.'

'I have heard something of the matter,' she said, drifting away from him toward the other side of the room. It felt too small with him in it. 'Where's Freddie? He usually sleeps on the bed while I'm gone.'

'The one to ask about is Caesar,' Gabriel said. 'That dog is as short-tempered as my aunt Sophonisba, and that's saying quite a lot.'

Kate frowned and looked on the other side of the bed. 'What have you done with them?'

'Freddie is here,' Gabriel said. 'Lazy sod.'

She looked over and saw Freddie lying between the arm of the chair and Gabriel's leg. His chin was resting on the prince's thigh and there was a look of utter bliss on his face. She laughed. 'Well, what of Caesar, then?'

'Locked in your dressing room,' Gabriel said. 'I believe that mongrel thought I was an intruder.'

'You *are* an intruder,' Kate said, plucking open the door to her little dressing room. 'There you are,

247

Caesar. Did you try to warn me that my room had been invaded?'

'I thought he'd have an apoplectic fit,' Gabriel said.

Caesar seemed chastened now. He growled at Gabriel's boots but otherwise kept his mouth shut.

Kate got down on her knees and gathered him up. 'You're a good dog,' she told him. 'You knew this rascally prince did not belong in my room because he might ruin my reputation, and you did your best to tell the world, didn't you?'

Caesar gave a little woof in the affirmative.

'One would almost think you're fond of that animal,' Gabriel said, putting down his book.

She looked at him over Caesar's silky head. 'You must leave my room, Gabriel. If anyone knew you were here—'

'I know,' he said, pulling out a length of black lace. 'I brought along the veil. No one will see us leaving together.'

'I'm not going with you anywhere,' she said instantly. 'I want a bath, and then a rest before tonight. Has your princess arrived yet, by the way?'

'She's on her way,' he said. 'Should be here in a few hours. Wick has all the servants in a pother over it.'

Kate looked at him dubiously. 'You must be . . . Are you excited to meet her?'

'Enthralled,' he said flatly. 'There's dancing tonight, and you can't dance.'

'I can try,' she said with dignity.

'Not until you've had lessons. Not unless you want everyone to know that you're not Victoria. The lucky thing is that given the arrival of Princess Tatiana, no one will even notice if you don't make

248

an appearance. They'll be too busy ogling her.'

'They'll notice if *you* don't,' she pointed out.

'I'll have to come and go,' Gabriel said.

'Come and go from where?' she asked suspiciously. 'I only promised you a kiss, Gabriel. You're making this sound like an event.'

'I took my life into my hands last night, fighting that blackguard,' he said, his eyes innocent. 'Of course I expect you to spend some time with me.'

'Spend time where?' she said. 'Were you really in danger?'

He held out his hand. Still kneeling, with Caesar on her lap, Kate leaned over and saw a tiny cut on one knuckle. 'Dear me. I'm like to swoon just thinking of the peril you were in.'

'Wretch,' he said. 'I think we should leave Freddie here, don't you?' He ran a finger over the dog's sleek head. 'We wouldn't want to embarrass him.' Freddie gave a luxurious sigh. 'Wick will send up a footman to give the dogs an airing later.'

'I'm not going anywhere,' Kate stated. 'As I said, I am planning to take a bath and a nap.'

'I approve,' he said. 'It'll be a sacrifice, but I'll leave you to take a bath alone, I promise.'

'I like it here,' she said, stubbornly.

'My chambers are in the turret,' he said. 'Please, Kate. I'll show you that pot, the one that held the knuckle-bones.'

She opened her mouth to say no, but there was just a shadow of uncertainty in his eyes. Something else too, something that she'd never seen in a man's eyes before. 'Tatiana isn't yet here,' he said. 'Not in my castle. Please.'

Her eyes dropped to his mouth, and she was lost. 'What about my maid?' she asked helplessly. 'She'll come to dress me soon.'

'I told Wick to keep her occupied.'

'You told *Wick*?' She got off her knees, Caesar scrambling to the floor. 'Just what did you tell Wick?'

Gabriel rose to his feet. 'Believe me, I was in more danger from Wick than from Beckham. He was livid when I told him you would—'

'I can't believe you told him that!' Kate cried. 'Don't you know what you've done? Everyone in this bloody castle will think I'm a doxy before the evening is out!'

Gabriel's jaw set. 'Wick is my brother. He's my right hand and my closest friend. He would *never* tell a soul, if only because he deeply disapproves.'

'And well he should,' she flashed. 'I can't go to your rooms! Even to be seen on the way there is tantamount to ruin.'

'You won't be seen,' Gabriel said. 'My aunt is housed in the same tower as I am, and you will be wearing her veil.'

'This is too dangerous,' she said. 'We might well run into an acquaintance of the princess's. What if we meet Lady Dagobert? She told me a short time ago that she knows everyone. Algie will wonder where I am.'

'Wick has already informed Lady Wrothe and your supposed fiancé that you are suffering from a stomach upset,' he said promptly.

'You take a great deal upon yourself,' she said, glowering at him.

'Please, Kate.'

The sad truth was that his *please* was irresistible. 'I suppose I would like to see the little pot. I could visit you for an hour. At the most,' she added.

He held out the veil. 'If you please, love.'

'Don't call me that,' she said, shaking down the veil so that a muffling layer of black lace stood between her and the world. 'I'm not your love. I'm merely—I'm merely—'

'Do tell,' he said, taking her arm. 'To ask my earlier question a different way, what *are* you? Wick wanted to know the same thing and threatened to lay me out cold when I said that to my mind you were the most beautiful woman I'd ever dream of seducing, not that I plan to.'

'I almost wish he had laid you out,' Kate said. 'I'm sure this will all end badly.'

'Well, just think of this: Everyone would think that I was trifling with Miss Victoria Daltry, not with you,' Gabriel said.

'They already think that,' Kate said gloomily. 'Victoria will be furious with me.'

'Because you've marred her reputation?'

'She didn't even have the fun of the flirtation,' she pointed out. 'Not to mention the fact that Victoria is truly in love with Algie.'

'I find that hard to imagine,' Gabriel said. 'He was with us last night, you know. He told me that he would have gone to Oxford, but he judged it a waste of time.'

'Yes, that's Algie,' she said, resigned. 'I'm sorry.'

'A sharp right turn ahead, and we haven't seen a soul yet. Why are you sorry? He's apparently a sprig from *my* family tree.'

To her horror, at that very moment she heard a cheerful, familiar voice somewhere in the vicinity.

And that voice was singing. '*That very morning to the spring I came,*' Algie sang, rather tunefully. To her horror, he sounded a bit tipsy. '*Where finding*

251

beauty culling nakedness—' He broke off, obviously seeing them.

Kate tried to peer through the veil but all she could see were people-shaped mounds that looked like moving piles of coal.

'Princess Maria-Therese, may I present Lord Dewberry and Lord Dimsdale,' Gabriel said. She sank into a tottering curtsy, mumbling something.

'It's a great pleasure to meet you,' Lord Dewberry said. Algie was undoubtedly engaged in one of his floor-scraping bows.

'Step back, for God's sake, man,' Dewberry said. 'You're going to topple over if you bow forward like that.'

Kate's heart was pounding so hard that she felt as if they must hear it. If Algie discovered her, it would be one thing, but Lord Dewberry . . .

'I hope you are in good health, Your Highness?' Algie said cheerfully.

'My aunt is undoubtedly shocked by your song,' Gabriel said before she could say anything. 'Have you imbibed of the grape, Viscount?' He sounded more pompous than she could have imagined.

'We've been on a tour of the wine cellars with Berwick,' Algie said. Yes, he was definitely tipsy, if not three sheets to the wind. 'Lovely wine collection you have, Your Highness.'

'I am escorting my aunt to her chambers,' Gabriel said. 'If you gentlemen would please excuse us.'

'I suppose she's my aunt as well, in some degree,' Algie said. 'Shall I take your other arm, Your Highness?'

Kate shrank back against Gabriel and shook her head violently.

252

'The princess is quite particular about those with whom she associates,' Gabriel said. His voice rang with authority, as if he were the Grand Duke himself.

'Of course,' Algie said hastily. 'I meant no disrespect, Your Highness.'

With huge relief, she heard the clatter of their heels as they continued down the corridor. And then, just as the sound died out, she heard Algie say, 'Woman looks like an awful goat in that get-up. Someone should tell her we don't hold with nuns over here.'

There was a murmur from Dewberry and a last word from Algie. 'All I'm saying is that she reminds me of the Grim Reaper. Could use her to frighten children at night.'

The hand on her arm was shaking. 'Stop laughing!' Kate hissed.

'Can't,' Gabriel said, his voice choked. 'One shouldn't ever know one's relatives socially. It's so lowering to one's *amour propre*.'

'What does that mean?' Kate asked. 'Are we almost there?'

'Just the stairs left,' he said, taking a firmer grip on her elbow. '*Amour propre* is a man's sense of himself. The very idea of Algernon gracing my family tree takes the edge off my self-esteem.'

'Good,' Kate said firmly. 'It's likely the first time in his life that Algie's been so useful.'

Thirty

Great stone steps curved up the inside wall of the turret. Kate concentrated on not tripping over her floor-length veil, trying not to think about the foolish mistake she was making even climbing those steps.

Gabriel meant to seduce her. She knew it in her bones. So why, why was she taking step after step into his lair, so to speak? Was she to be the second of her father's daughters to disgrace his memory by finding herself unmarried and with child?

Not that her father's memory could be disgraced, she reminded herself. What disgracing there was to do, he had done himself. The very memory of her father and his philandering made her jaw set.

She would see Gabriel's little pot. And she would let him kiss her. But nothing further, and that much only because—it would be stupid to deny it to herself—she had the most terrible infatuation with the man.

Which probably happened to the prince at least every other Tuesday, and unless she wanted simply to be grist for the mill of his arrogance, she would never let him know. So, as she threw off the veil, she put a nonchalant look on her face, as if she visited gentlemen's chambers on a regular basis.

As if those same gentlemen planned to kiss her into a wanton frenzy, and the only thing standing between them and her virtue was the strength of her will.

Unfortunately for Gabriel's plans, her will had gotten her through seven years of hard labor, humiliation, and grief. It would get her through this encounter unscathed.

'What a lovely room!' she cried, turning around. From the outside, the castle's two turrets looked squat and round, like baker's hats. But the rooms inside were high-ceilinged and airy. 'You've put in glass windows,' she said appreciatively, going over to look.

'They were here when I arrived,' Gabriel said, coming to stand at her shoulder.

'And what a view,' she exclaimed. The castle stood at the top of a slight hill. The window at which she stood looked to the back of the castle, and manicured lawns stretched before her, edged at the far end with a stand of beeches.

'The maze looks so simple from above,' she murmured, putting her fingers against the cool glass. 'Yet Henry and I failed to make it through and were dumped out there, by the ostrich's cage.'

'It is simple, but clever. I'll show you how to get to the center.' He was leaning against the wall, looking at her, not at the maze. His eyes touched her like a caress, sending a prickle of warning down her spine. At the same time, warmth drifted to her more intimate parts.

He wasn't supposed to look at her like that. Rank seducers didn't look like that. They didn't say things that assumed time beyond the present, space outside this small room.

'I can stay only a moment or two,' she said, as much to herself as him.

'You'll like the view over here,' he said, taking her hand and leading her across the room. The windows opposite looked down onto the dusty drive which she and Algie had traveled a few short days ago. From above, the road drifted along by twists and turns into a violet distance where dark groves met the late afternoon sun.

'It makes you think of a fairy tale,' she said, awed.

'The kind where a prince waits at your feet?' He said it lightly, but there was something there too.

'A princess is making her way up that road,' Kate pointed out. She turned away again and flitted rather blindly across the room until she was brought up short by an enormous carved bed. As if she'd been scorched, she swung about and walked in the opposite direction.

'Well,' she said, 'perhaps we should have that kiss now.'

'Not yet,' Gabriel said.

Kate sat down on a beautiful little chair, upholstered in coral velvet, and took time arranging her skirts. Then she looked up. She was tired of the game of wits they were playing. It was too sophisticated for her, too reminiscent of the sort of complicated and refined conversations that Henry likely had with her beaux.

'You asked the right question earlier,' she said. 'Who am I?'

He sat down opposite her, not taking his eyes from hers.

'I am the elder daughter of my father, Victor Daltry. He was the younger son of an earl, and had a snug estate, built from my mother's dowry. After my mother died, he left the entire estate to my stepmother, Mariana, who bestowed it on her own daughter, Victoria.'

'You are not illegitimate,' he stated.

'No. My parents were married.'

'And your grandfather was an earl.'

'I have almost no dowry,' she said. 'Mariana dismissed my governess and most of the household staff seven years ago, when my father died. I can bargain down the price of bread; I can mend a stocking; I cannot dance a polonaise.'

He took her hand, turned it over. 'I am sorry.'

'I should have left years ago, but that would have meant leaving my father's servants and his tenants at Mariana's mercy. I stayed, though my stepmother dismissed the bailiff. She could not dismiss me, you see.'

Gabriel put her palm to his mouth and kissed it. 'Go on.'

'There's nothing else to tell,' she said. 'Now I have decided to leave, which probably means that Mariana will throw out most of our tenants, who are hardly scrabbling an existence as it is. The harvest was poor last year.'

He nodded.

'The woman who is on her way to you . . . she is a princess.'

With a gesture so graceful that it seemed natural to him, he slipped from the chair to his knees beside her. 'True.'

'Your brother Augustus is an ass to have thrown out his family, and you have a castle to support. I know what it's like to have responsibilities of that sort.'

He closed his eyes for a moment, and the color of his eyelashes was like the color of regret. With a kind of piercing sorrow, she knew that she would never forget this prince.

It wasn't his dark head and fierce eyes, his unruly hair. It was the way he'd taken in his odd relatives, the menagerie, his aunt's reader, even the ostrich and the pickle-eating dog. It was the way he looked at her, the way he laughed, the way he brushed the weeds from Merry's face.

And she would never, ever forget the moment when a prince knelt at the side of her chair. When she was old and gray, and contemplating a life that she hoped would be richly satisfying, she would still remember this.

'If I were not a prince, would you have me?' He said it so low that she almost didn't hear. 'To put it another way, if you had thousands of pounds, Kate, if your estate was your own, would you buy me? Because that's what I needed, you know. I needed a woman who thought I was worth the price, and my brother found one in Russia.'

'Don't ask me that,' she whispered. 'My mother bought my father, and he never gave her a moment's happiness. I would *never* buy a man.'

He bent his head again. 'The question is irrelevant; I apologize for asking it.'

'Why did you ask it?'

'Do you have any idea what it's like to be a prince?' His head jerked back up, and his eyes were bitter, his mouth a hard line. 'I cannot do as I wish. I cannot be what I wish. I cannot marry whom I wish.'

She bit her lip.

'I am trained to put my honor and my house above all else. I think the pressure of it has driven my brother Augustus a little mad. He is an ass, as you say. But he's also crippled by the burden of having so many souls depending on him.'

'I'm sorry,' she whispered.

'I would like, just once, for a woman to see me

258

as other than a person with a coronet. Simply as a man, no different than other men.' The words wrenched from his chest.

She stopped him by putting her hands to his face. 'Hush.' His lips felt cool and soft under hers, and for a moment she just paused there, in an innocent kiss, the kind that maidens give each other.

But his skin was prickly under her fingers, and his smell, his wild masculine scent, came to greet her, and her mouth opened instinctively. One stroke of her tongue and his arms came around her, strong as steel bands.

She toppled forward against his chest and he swept an arm under her legs and just held her there, against him, his mouth slow and fierce at the same time. He kissed so sweetly that she could have wept, and yet the warmth building in her legs at the touch of his tongue against hers made her feel nothing like crying.

She gave some sort of inarticulate murmur and wound her arms around his neck.

'Yes,' he whispered fiercely. 'This is the way it is with us, Kate. Isn't it?'

She couldn't answer because she was waiting for him to kiss her again. 'Please,' she said, finally.

He laughed, a dark sound that felt like canary wine rushing through her veins. 'You're mine for the moment, Kate. Do you hear me?'

She raised her head and met his eyes. 'Not a prince, but a man,' she whispered, running her hands into his thick hair, so that his ribbon slipped over one shoulder and fell to the ground. 'Gabriel, not Your Highness.'

'And you are Kate, my Kate,' he said to her. His lips rubbed across hers as if they were young

259

wooers, too simple to know the ways of the wicked. 'I won't take your virginity, because that is yours to give and not mine to take. But Kate, I warn you now that I intend to take everything else.'

He looked down at her, and the expression in his eyes was pure sinful invitation. Kate felt her lips curl without her conscious volition. 'How do you know,' she whispered, 'that I won't do the same for you?'

Gabriel closed his eyes for a moment. 'I have no doubt of that.'

She leaned forward and licked, delicately, the strong column of his neck. A shudder went through his body and then he rose, still holding her. Kate thought he would lay her on the bed and tear off her clothes.

But instead he put her gently back into the little velvet chair. 'Stay,' he commanded, for all the world as if she were Caesar.

'Gabriel,' she said, conscious of the husky timbre in her voice. 'Won't you—won't you kiss me again?' And she stood up, because she was never any good at taking orders, as Mariana could attest.

'You're so much taller than other women,' he said. He put a finger on her nose and then drew it slowly down to her chin. 'You have a beautiful nose.'

'That's the compliment I was longing for,' she said wryly. 'This is my evening,' he said, 'and I have planned it very carefully.'

Kate put her hands on her hips. She felt saucy and sensuous and joyful all at once, as if desire and laughter were bubbling in her veins. 'Oh, so you think you can merely order me about?'

'I have to come and go,' he said, grinning back.

'But do you know what I have in mind, Kate?'

She shook her head. 'Devilry, no doubt,' she muttered.

'I'm going to drive you mad,' he said, conversationally. 'I'm going to kiss you and tease you and taste you . . . and leave. And then I'll come back and do the same thing again. And again.'

Her mouth fell open. 'You will?' Rather to her embarrassment, her voice didn't sound scandalized as much as curious.

He stepped away from her. 'You said you wanted a rest. Would you like a bath or a nap first?'

Kate looked around the great circular room. There was a curtained area to one side, but other than that, it was all one chamber. 'You want me to take a nap? Here?' He must have no idea how the blood was pounding through her, warming parts of her body that she rarely thought about. 'I'm not sure I can rest at the moment.'

'I understand,' he said, as courteously as if he had offered her a cup of tea. 'Perhaps later. Well, I'm afraid that I need to dress for the evening meal. Would you like to sit down? This won't take long.'

Kate blinked. Was he planning to undress in front of her? 'What of your valet?'

'My valet has been commandeered to help Wick this evening,' he said with a grin. 'So I have to dress myself.' He reached up and began to slowly untie his cravat.

'Do you need assistance?' Kate asked, mesmerized by the golden skin that appeared as he pulled the cravat free.

Looking at her, he shook his head and widened his stance. As if he had bade her, the movement made her eyes go to his legs. His breeches were tight, molded to his thighs. She jerked her gaze back up in embarrassment.

With an easy movement he pulled off his coat and tossed it on the bed. He was wearing a waistcoat of striped toilinette edged with crimson binding. It fitted close to his chest; a beautiful linen shirt billowed as he casually pulled it free of his breeches.

Kate watched as if she were entranced, not saying a word. She almost felt as if she were at the circus, at a special private performance. There was an air of theater to Gabriel, and the dramatic, laughing flare in his eye showed that he was exploiting every second of it.

'I need help with my cuffs,' he said. With an easy stride, he presented one cuff to her. She bent her head over the snowy linen, and pulled apart the small ruby buttons that held his cuffs together.

Without a word, he held out the other cuff. It was curiously erotic, the turn of his wrist, the way the shirt fell back on his arm. 'How did you get this scar?' she said, touching a white mark on his forearm.

'Excavating in Egypt,' he said. 'Two years ago. I was bitten by a barga snake; the only remedy is to slash the bite as quick as you can and let it bleed free. Luckily I had a knife to hand.'

'Awful!' Kate said. 'But it worked?'

'I was sick for a few days, but not much venom had reached my system.' He stepped back and his sleeves fell to his elbows.

She was thinking about Gabriel slashing his own arm, and not paying attention. 'Kate,' he said. There was a kind of deep timbre to his voice that sent a little quake down her legs.

He was toying with the top button on his waistcoat. Her eyes were drawn to those clever fingers. He slipped the first button free and moved to the second. Kate's mouth felt dry, watching as the buttons came free, one after another.

The linen of his shirt was translucent, giving just a glimpse of taut muscle underneath. Gabriel didn't say a word, just slowly slid from one button to the next.

As he undid the last button, he pulled off the waistcoat and threw it toward the bed. From the corner of her eye, Kate saw the garment hit the coverlet and slide to the floor.

But her entire being was focused on those teasing hands. 'It's rather hot in here,' Gabriel said, his voice darkly amused.

Kate made a shuddering attempt to maintain some sort of calm. 'I'm afraid I forgot to bring my fan,' she said.

'Here's one,' he said, reaching over to the large table to the right and handing her one. It was a lady's fan, exquisite, delicate, and obviously valuable. With a sudden thump of her heart, she realized that there had been other women in this room, that she probably wasn't the first to watch the prince undress himself.

But he was shaking his head. 'Not what you're thinking, love. That's a seventeenth-century German noble-woman's fan, with an interesting painting. I picked it up in Bamberg.'

'Of course,' she said, opening it carefully. 'That swan presumably represents Zeus?'

'Yes, Leda stands to the right, primly dressed in the clothing of a burgomaster's wife. It's one of the things that interest me about the piece.'

Kate fluttered the fan just under her eyes. For some reason it gave her a kind of impudent courage to hold it before her mouth. 'Weren't you about to take off your shirt?'

'Actually,' he said, pulling free the back part of his shirt, 'I generally take off my breeches first.'

Kate made a little sound.

'Boots first,' he said conversationally. He turned, bent over, and pulled off his right boot. Kate raised the fan to hover just below her eyes. The second boot was off, and he was facing her again.

'Breeches next . . . or stockings?' The sensual curve of his mouth was enough to make her squirm with a thirsty sense of power.

'Since you're asking me,' she said, fluttering the fan again. 'Stockings.'

He bent over again. Watching the hard-muscled curve of his leg made her pulse beat fiercely.

Then he stood in front of her, legs apart, hands on his hips. 'The breeches,' he said, with a primitive joy in his eyes.

She raised an eyebrow, as if nothing he could show her would cause particular interest. Of course she knew what the male anatomy looked like, if only from her embarrassed—but fascinated—study of Aretino's engravings.

But it was entirely different to watch Gabriel's hands swiftly unbuttoning his placket, under the shelter of his white shirt. He watched her intently.

'Shall I continue, lady?' he asked, as courteous as any medieval knight.

'Aye,' she said, and cleared her throat, met his eyes boldly. 'Do.'

His hands paused at his hips, his eyes sizzling into hers. 'I would rather you did this for me,' he said.

She almost dropped her fan.

'Kneeling at my feet,' he said, 'coaxing my breeches to fall to the floor so that you could touch me . . . taste me. . . as you will.'

Kate swallowed.

It wasn't Aretino's pictures that came to mind, but the image of herself, kneeling before him, pulling his breeches down just as he was doing now. Leaning forward and—

His shirt was tented in the front. She frowned, trying to remember the smallest details of those engravings. That was just it: They were small.

'It seems you see something that keeps your attention, my lady,' he said.

'Ump,' she said ungracefully. 'You may continue.' She waved her fan.

The white shirt rose, covered his face, fluttered in the air, fell to the side.

Kate's mouth fell open, but it was behind the fan, so he couldn't see it. Gabriel had to be three times the size of the men Aretino portrayed. 'You are a bit larger than the pictures would suggest,' she whispered.

'Italians,' Gabriel said, standing with his hands on his hips and obviously enjoying her fascinated gaze. 'Wait until you see the statues in Florence. Some of those statues have all the endowment of a small boy.'

'Well,' Kate said, forcing herself to look up, but that only gave her the chance to see what the rest of him looked like, the taut stomach, the muscled chest, the arrow of hair leading down to . . . to *there*.

'And now I must dress myself,' Gabriel said, casually turning. 'I asked my man to set out evening clothing. We're dancing tonight, did I mention that?'

Kate bit her lip at the look of him from behind, the powerful swell of his shoulders narrowing to his waist. Even his arse was muscled and powerful, as unlike Algie's plump round bottom as imaginable. 'Yes,' she said faintly.

He bent over to pick up a costume left for him on the side table.

'I don't always bother with smalls,' he said chattily. 'But when a man is wearing silk breeches, it stands to reason. Especially if there's the faintest possibility that his rod might make an appearance.'

She nodded like a silly doll as he pulled on his smalls, followed by stockings embroidered with clocks in gold thread.

'Those are very nice,' she managed to say, and cleared her throat again.

'I can't say I generally pay much attention to my dress.' Gabriel hauled on a pair of silk breeches so tight that they showed every bulge. *Every* bulge.

'You can't wear that,' she gasped, before she thought.

'Don't you approve?' He grinned at her.

'I can see—anyone can see—' She gestured toward his front.

He gave himself a careless pat. 'That's not going anywhere until I'm out of this room. I'll have to walk slowly down the stairs and think about something dreadfully boring.'

A billowing shirt went over his head, but this one was considerably more elegant than the one he had worn, with a gorgeous little frill at the neck.

'I must beg a favor, my lady,' he said, as grave as any courtier.

266

'Yes?'

'My cuffs.'

Her fingers slipped and trembled, pushing the rubies through the buttonholes on his shirtsleeves. If the truth be told, she felt ravenous. And that was no proper emotion for a young lady to feel.

'There you are,' she said. Her voice came out a husky rumble.

Gabriel moved to the glass and tied his cravat in a moment, his hands moving so swiftly, pleating, folding, and tying, that she could hardly follow.

'How are you tying your cravat?' she inquired, striving desperately to have a conversation. Any sort of conversation. Anything to stop herself from lusting after him like a veritable trollop.

'The Gordian knot,' he said. 'It's not too high or fussy and allows me to breathe.'

'Algie told me that he often ruins four to five cravats at a time,' Kate said. 'He tries to create a Trône d'Amour, but he calls it a trumpeter.'

The corner of his mouth turned down. 'He looks like a long-necked goose.'

Next was a silk waistcoat, a dark sea green with black embroidery. And finally he shrugged into a coat made of the same material, as tight as it was resplendent.

He pulled on a pair of buckled shoes. 'I suppose I might wear slippers,' he said, 'but they're bloody cold on these stone steps.'

Without pausing he moved back to the glass, pulled back his thick hair and pulled it tightly into a queue. 'Powder?' he asked himself, and then turned to her. 'Must I powder? It is my own castle, after all.'

'Surely most gentlemen will be in wigs,' she

managed. From being a naked, virile man he had transformed to a fairy-tale prince. 'Your—Princess Tatiana will expect you to wear a wig.'

'Loathe them. On me *and* you. This will have to do. My sword,' he said, looking about. He picked up his rapier and buckled it around his hips, under his coat. 'Gloves.' He snatched up a pair from the table.

Then he walked to just before her and put a leg forward, slid into a graceful court bow. 'My lady, I fear I must leave you.'

Kate took a deep breath. The man in front of her was the epitome of elegance, as gorgeous a piece of manhood as ever graced a castle. She rose to her feet, held out her hand.

He raised it to his lips, and she felt the touch of his tongue like a brand. Her fingers trembled and he rewarded her with a smile that would have made a saint swoon.

'I shall return as soon as I am able.' He turned, the wide skirts of his coat flaring behind him.

Kate stood in place, watching, feeling as if she'd been bewitched. He almost left, turned at the last minute. 'I forgot,' he said. 'Something to keep my guest occupied during my absence.'

He reached out, picked up a small velvet-covered book, and tossed it to her. Reflexively she reached out and snatched it from the air.

'There's my Kate,' he said, a wry smile quirking his lips. 'Do you know how many women would have squealed and allowed the book to drop to the ground?'

The door closed quietly behind him.

Kate stood for a moment longer, and then looked down at the book. Her fingers rubbed across the velvet and she slowly opened the front cover, read the title page.

The School of Venus.

Thirty-one

Gabriel stopped after the first turn of the steps descending from the tower and attempted to calm his pulse. His rod was threatening to rip through silk, and the only thing he could think about was the way Kate's lips parted in a gasp when she saw him in the flesh.

It hadn't frightened her. She was the kind of woman whom men dreamed about, the sort who wouldn't cower under the coverlet waiting to do her marital duty, but a woman with whom one could grow old, always discovering, never tiring, never less than enamored, bewitched, in lust.

He leaned his head back against the stone wall. His heart was thumping in his chest, tempting him to turn around, slam through that door, cover her mouth with his.

But she wasn't his. She couldn't be his. The chill truth of it slowly filtered through his blood, like the icy rain that Dante described in hell.

She couldn't be his because he had this bloody castle to support. And that meant he had to take his pretty arse downstairs and meet Tatiana, the woman gilded in Russian rubles.

He needed to put on a smile and charm her at dinner. Dance with her once, and then again. And tomorrow, at the ball, he should open the dance with her on his arm.

They were to be married within the month following the betrothal ball . . . if all went well. Of course it would go well.

There was no problem with his breeches anymore. He glanced down and smoothed a wrinkle in his cutaway, then walked down the steps.

But he still had this night, this last night.

He would go to dinner for a few courses, and then he would make some excuse to come back up, back to Kate.

A small smile curled his lips.

He had plans.

The moment Wick caught sight of him coming down the stairs he pulled the door to the drawing room shut behind him. 'Where in the bloody hell have you been? The princess arrived a good hour ago and you should have been here to greet her,' he said in a furious undertone. 'Her uncle was visibly displeased.'

'I'm sorry,' Gabriel said.

'Prince Dimitri doesn't seem to be a hothead, but it was a clear affront when you didn't appear, you lug-headed idiot.'

'I will apologize.'

Wick narrowed his eyes at him. 'Aren't you going to ask what your future wife looks like?'

Gabriel considered that, and shook his head.

Wick said something under his breath, and then: 'Prince Dimitri and his niece both speak fluent English, by the way. You will be joined by the Princess Sophonisba. Princess Maria-Therese will stay in her rooms this evening.'

'Bloody hell, Aunt Sophonisba is joining us?' Gabriel said with dismay.

'She's painted her eyes so heavily that she won't

be able to see her dinner,' Wick said. 'She's in there swilling brandy.' Then he lowered his voice. 'Just what have you done with Kate?'

'She's in my chamber, reading. Only reading.'

'I never imagined you'd do something like this,' Wick said, his voice tight with rage. 'If you weren't my brother, I'd leave this house.'

'I'm not doing anything,' Gabriel said between clenched teeth. 'For Christ's sake, Wick, do you think I'd take her virginity? Do you think I'm that sort of man?'

'Keep your voice down. Anyone might descend that stair,' he snapped. 'If not, what the hell is she doing in your chamber?'

Gabriel raised his right hand rather blindly and pulled on a glove. 'She's reading. I told you. Just reading.'

Wick stared at him. 'Damn it.'

'I did it,' Gabriel said, conversationally. 'I met the woman, the only woman for me. I met her, and now . . . I'm going to meet my wife.'

Wick made a sudden movement. 'No.'

'That's the way life is, Wick,' Gabriel said, pulling on his other glove. 'It's not always fair. You should be the first to know that. In case you're wondering, Kate understands why I must marry Tatiana. She just spent seven years working like an indentured servant for her stepmother, as far as I can see, because she could not countenance leaving the servants and tenants on her father's estate to her stepmother's mercies.'

'Then marry her. Bring her servants here and we'll add them to the crew.'

'We can scarcely feed the lion,' Gabriel said, straightening his rapier. 'Don't treat me like a

271

lovelorn maiden, Wick. I need to marry a woman with bags of money, and that's what I'm planning to do.'

'We can manage,' Wick said. 'Don't go through with it.'

'How would I support all of them? Who would buy Sophonisba's brandy, the lion's beef, the candles, the coal we need to get through the winter?'

'The tenant farms—' Wick began.

Gabriel shook his head. 'I've spent hours going over the books. In time, the farms will be profitable. But they've been neglected. The cottages leak, the steeple in the village church apparently collapsed last year. For all I know, the children are hungry. Not only that, but if I break the engagement, then I'd have to pay a forfeit. I need three dowries, not just one.'

Wick's comment was short but heartfelt.

'I'll forget about Kate in time.' He looked Wick straight in the eyes as he said it.

He would never forget her.

Wick knew it too. 'I've never said how much I appreciate the honor of being your brother,' he said now.

Gabriel quirked a smile. 'The feeling is mutual.'

He had barely walked into the drawing room when the doors behind him opened again and Wick's voice boomed out. 'Her Royal Highness, the Princess Tatiana. His Royal Highness, the Prince Dimitri.'

Gabriel squared his shoulders and turned to face his future.

Tatiana was poised in the doorway. She wore an exquisite gown of cream silk, embroidered all over with sprigs of flowers. Her eyes were large and dewy; her lips were a perfect rose pink. She was like a sweet drink of strawberries and cream, her skin a perfect milk, her dark curls satiny.

Gabriel advanced and gave his best court bow. She curtsied with all the grace of a member of the French court. He kissed her hand and she smiled at him, a bit shyly but very sweetly.

If the clouds had opened up and a booming voice had said, *This is your bride*, he wouldn't have been surprised.

Tatiana was eminently beddable. Demure though she was, her low décolletage displayed her status as a desirable woman. She had no need for 'bosom friends.' She was everything Kate was not: beddable, biddable, and rich.

He had vaguely expected to hate her, and he couldn't even do that. It took only a quick glance to see that she was very nice. She would never shout at him like a little shrew; it wasn't in her.

Her uncle Dimitri was smiling broadly and rocking back and forth on his heels. 'I've been to this castle,' he announced, in a thick accent. 'I visited as a lad, when Lord Fitzclarence had the castle. Told my brother that the castle was worth having to come to England.'

The damned castle, Gabriel thought, even as he bowed again and smiled.

'Expected I'd see you this afternoon,' Dimitri said, giving Gabriel a shrewd glance.

'I apologize,' Gabriel said. 'I wasn't aware of your arrival.'

'This little girl is the apple of her father's eye,' Dimitri announced.

A tiny sound escaped Tatiana's lips; she was pink

with embarrassment.

Gabriel bowed again and gave her a reassuring smile.

'I have to say my piece, chicken,' Dimitri said. 'We're from the Kingdom of Kuban, Your Highness. Don't suppose you've heard much of it.'

'I have not,' Gabriel said, 'but—'

Dimitri interrupted him. 'My brother helped settle Cossacks next to the Sea of Azov. So we haven't been princeling about for generations.'

Gabriel nodded respectfully. Over his shoulder, Wick was motioning that he should begin the procession to the dining room.

'What I'm getting to,' Dimitri said, 'is that her father didn't want her pushed into this marriage. If Tatiana likes you, she stays. If she doesn't, we'll be leaving, dowry and all, and none of this talk of broken betrothals.' His smile showed his teeth, and all of a sudden Gabriel saw, for just a flash, a Cossack warrior behind the man in blue velvet.

He bowed yet again. Thank God, at that moment Wick touched him on the shoulder, so he turned to Tatiana and offered his arm. 'Your Highness, may I accompany you to the dining room?'

She smiled at him, and he noticed that though she was shy, she wasn't paralyzed by it. Someday she would be a composed and doubtless articulate woman. A perfect princess, in short.

Prince Dimitri fell in behind, with Gabriel's aunt, Princess Sophonisba, on his arm, and they led the way to the dining room, followed by a great train of jewels, velvets, and silks. The women were exquisite, like delectable pillowy sweets. The men were groomed and polished, like the sleek aristocrats they were.

274

The only person he wanted to see, the only person he wanted to eat with, was upstairs, wearing a simple gown, a pink wig, and a pair of wax breasts.

Prince Dimitri was quickly swept into an argument with Lady Dagobert about whether the Portuguese court should remain in Rio de Janeiro or eventually return to Portugal, which left Gabriel to make conversation with Tatiana.

Except that his aunt Sophonisba was too old to care about rules dictating who spoke to whom, and so she barked a whole series of questions across the table at Tatiana. Sophonisba was a bad-tempered termagant, by anyone's measure. His brother Augustus loathed her, and had thrown her onto the boat with the same satisfaction with which he discarded the lion.

'Youngest of four, are you?' Sophonisba said, as the first course was being cleared away. She paused and reached under her wig to scratch her scalp. 'There were eight of us. Nursery was a madhouse.'

Tatiana smiled and murmured something. She was obviously kind-hearted, and if a little taken aback by his aunt's abrasive manners, wasn't letting it affect her courtesy.

'You're a pretty little thing,' Sophonisba said, picking up a chicken leg and waving it as if she'd never heard of a fork. 'What are you looking at?' she snapped at Gabriel. 'If it's good enough for Queen Margherita, it's good enough for me.'

Tatiana was giggling.

'La Regina Margherita mangia il pollo con le dita,' Sophonisba told her. 'Can you translate that, girl?'

'I'm not very good with Italian,' Tatiana said, 'but I think that Queen Margherita eats chicken with her fingers?'

275

'Good for you,' Sophonisba said. 'How many languages do you speak?'

'My brother and I sent our children to be educated in Switzerland,' Prince Dimitri said, catching the question. 'Tatiana's one of the smartest in our brood; up to five languages, aren't you, dumpling?'

'Uncle Dimitri!' Tatiana cried.

'Not supposed to call her dumpling anymore,' the prince said, grinning so widely that Gabriel could see every missing tooth. 'Though she used to be the most adorable dumpling baby I'd ever seen. We love dumplings in Russia; they're more precious than rubles.'

Tatiana rolled her eyes.

'I never married, you know,' Sophonisba barked.

She poked Gabriel and he jumped. His mind had drifted to Kate once again. 'This fellow's rascally father, my brother, never accepted an offer for my hand. I could have had anyone!' She scowled at the table, as if daring someone to disagree.

The truth was that Sophonisba had been betrothed to a sprig of a princeling in Germany, but after she had arrived at his court and he had spent a day or two with her, he fled. She'd been sent home in great disgrace, and the Grand Duke never again bothered to try to fix a marriage for her.

'Her Highness,' Gabriel told Tatiana, 'was a famed beauty.'

'I still am,' Sophonisba said promptly. 'A woman's beauty isn't just a matter of youth.'

Tatiana nodded obediently. 'My grandmother always said that the greatest beauties in her day were so covered with powder and patches that one couldn't tell if there was a woman or a horse

276

underneath.'

There was a moment of silence. Sophonisba had four or five patches stuck onto her powdered face; one was coming undone and hanging from her cheekbone.

Tatiana's mouth fell open and she turned pink as an autumn sunset. 'Not that I meant to indicate anything of the sort about *you*, Your Highness,' she gasped.

'Wasn't around when your grandmother was young,' Sophonisba said with patent dishonesty, since she had to be seventy-five if she was a day. 'I wouldn't know what she was talking about.'

She turned her head and barked down the table at Dimitri. 'That's utter nonsense, what you're sayin' about the Portuguese. Not a drunk in the bunch of them.'

'I do apologize,' came a quiet voice at Gabriel's right elbow.

'My aunt took no offense,' he said, smiling down at Tatiana. She was bloody young.

'Sometimes the wrong thing just comes out of my mouth,' she whispered.

'Prince!' his aunt said, interrupting this charming, if tedious, revelation. 'Not to put too fine a point on it, my bladder is about to burst.'

Gabriel rose to his feet. 'If you will all excuse me,' he told the table, 'the princess is experiencing a malady and I shall escort her to her chambers.'

'It isn't a malady; it's just old age,' Sophonisba said, waving her stick at Wick. He came immediately, drew back her chair, and helped her to her feet.

'You're the best of them,' Sophonisba told him, as she always did. She pinched his cheek and then

277

looked triumphantly around the table. 'Born on the wrong side of the blanket, but he's just as much a prince as his brother here.'

Lady Dagobert turned purple with indignation at this breach of decorum, but Prince Dimitri looked as if he was biting back a smile, which was a point in his favor.

As Wick was helping Sophonisba straighten her skirts and get her stick in the right position, Gabriel bent down at Tatiana's shoulder. 'You see,' he said quietly, 'nothing you could say would ever embarrass me.'

She looked up, dimples in evidence. She'd make a lovely princess; even close contact with Sophonisba wouldn't shake her composure. Plus, she knew languages.

She was perfect.

His aunt's chambers were on the bottom level of the tower. It took them a good twenty-five minutes to reach the door of her room, as she constantly paused to rub her ankle and complain about the flagstones, the damp, and the way he held his arm—too stiff for her liking, she pronounced.

The moment the door closed behind her, he turned about and bolted up the stone steps.

He'd been gone for almost two hours. At this rate, Kate had had more than enough time to absorb each picture in Aretino's book.

Thirty-two

Meanwhile, in Gabriel's chamber, Kate had opened the salacious little volume, peered just long enough to ascertain that, yes, Aretino's men provided little comparison to Gabriel in the most pertinent area, and closed it again. She didn't have any wish to examine engravings of men and women intertwined on a bed. Or on a chair, or anywhere else.

She had the living, naked body of Gabriel in her mind, and nothing could interest her besides that.

She put the book down and walked over to a large table set up before the window. Gabriel had forgotten to show her the pot that once held a child's toys, but she guessed it was represented by a carefully arranged collection of shards. To the right of these was a piece of foolscap, covered with precise, beautifully written notes about the pot.

But that wasn't all the table held. There was another fan, besides the one he had tossed her. It looked even older, and the paper was peeling from its delicate spines.

There was a small book entitled *The Strangest Adventure That Ever Happened, Either in Ages Past or Present*, a little pile of copper coins, roughly formed and obviously very old. A chart appeared to calculate the motions of seven planets, and a little vial was marked 'Diacatholicon Aureum.' Kate picked it up curiously, pulled the cork, and sniffed, but couldn't tell what it was.

Finally she picked up a much-thumbed journal called *Ionian Antiquities*, moved back to the velvet chair, and began to read. Twenty minutes later, after an exhaustive and probably learned discussion of Desgodets's *Les Edifices Antiques de Rome*, she moved to the bed.

She told herself to wake the moment Gabriel's feet sounded on the marble steps, the very moment the door opened. She could leap off the bed and it wouldn't look in the least as if she was inviting him to join her.

When Gabriel opened the door to his chamber Kate was curled like a small kitten in the middle of the bed. Her wig was askew, and bright strands of hair had fallen over her face. She'd taken her slippers off, but otherwise she was dressed as when he had left her.

She was bloody beautiful. Her skin was honey; Tatiana's was cream. Tatiana's cheeks were dimpled and round; Kate's cheekbones were just this side of gaunt. Tatiana's lips were pillowy and soft; Kate slept fiercely, her lower lip ruby red, as if she had bitten it in her sleep.

After one glance, his rod was straining his breeches again. Gabriel turned away with a silent groan.

He had the one night, only this one night.

Walking silently behind the screened area of his chamber, he opened a little wooden door that stood about waist-high, reached in, and rang a bell that sounded in the kitchens.

A moment later he heard the trundling, bumping sound that indicated the lift was on its way up. He waited until it was at the top of its journey, then reached in and grabbed the pail of boiling water and dumped it into his bathtub, released the rope, and sent the bucket back down to the kitchens again.

He almost splashed himself with the next bucket and realized that he couldn't get his coat wet, as he had to return downstairs, if not for dinner, then for the dancing.

Neatly and quickly, with the sort of fastidiousness that he gave to every task, he stripped off his coat, waistcoat, shirt, and breeches, draping his clothes over a chair. He left on his smalls; it was Kate's turn to be naked.

A few moments later he looked at the bathing room with satisfaction. He had lit candles on every surface, and placed a glass of wine within tempting reach of the bath.

A length of toweling on his arm, he returned to the bed and sat gently next to Kate. Her face had smoothed out now, and her lips were curled in a little smile, as if whatever had worried her earlier had stolen away, leaving her in a happy dream.

He pulled a pin from her hair. She didn't stir. He pulled another, and another, until he had all the hairpins he could see. Then he tried a gentle pull on her wig, but nothing happened.

Her eyelashes fluttered and he thought she was waking up, but she merely rolled over so her shoulder and back were presented to him.

In fact, Kate was carefully regulating her breathing and wondering desperately what to do. She had seen with a flicker of an eyelash that there was a naked chest bending over her.

Aching desire made her want to open her eyes and wrap her arms around his neck. She wanted to pull that beautiful body over hers and let her fingers run over his chest and back. It was an all-consuming fever that pounded in her chest and sent licks of fire down her legs.

But the cautious part of her brain had her frozen in place, her eyes shut, trying to persuade Gabriel that she was still sleeping. She was afraid.

He was too tender, in the way he was carefully pulling her hairpins, as if frightened to wake her.

He was too beautiful, sitting beside her, nearly naked in the golden light of candles.

He was too much, too everything. With a pang she knew exactly what was frightening her: It was the terror that there would be no satisfying life without this prince. That he was everything to her, and that without him she might as well go back to Mariana and spend her life wretchedly protecting the tenants.

'Kate,' he murmured, and she realized that his lips were against her throat, pulling back her hair, drifting over her ear. 'It's time for your bath. I have a tub full of steaming water waiting for you.'

'Ah . . . hello,' she said foolishly. But she didn't turn over. He had pulled off her wig, and one hand was stroking through her hair. It felt so tender that she let herself drift, eyes closed, feeling only the sensual stroke of his fingers.

Then she suddenly realized what was happening and tried to stop him—but it was too late. His nimble fingers had unfastened all the buttons down the back of her gown. She sat up, clutching her bodice.

'Gabriel,' she said warningly, narrowing her eyes at him.

'You promised I could kiss you anywhere,' he said, hooking a finger into her bodice and giving a gentle tug.

'I don't remember saying that! And why aren't you wearing any clothes?'

'I am wearing my smalls,' he said. And then added wryly, 'Except for the part of me that isn't.'

She looked down, just long enough to see that, in fact, a part of him was jutting straight out the top of his waistband.

'You shouldn't,' she protested, but at that moment he bent down and pressed his mouth on hers. Even so, she kept talking, but the words fell away as his tongue traced the soft line of her lips.

'I could kiss your mouth all night,' he whispered.

Kate told herself that kisses were what she had promised. True, she hadn't thought that he would be naked . . . But at least he was wearing smalls. Even if they didn't seem to cover that part of him.

A small part of her will gave way, and she wrapped her arms around his neck. He responded instantly, taking her open mouth and pulling her against his bare chest. Kate melted, a sensation so overwhelming that she began trembling all over. He kissed her until wildfire danced in her veins, until desire slid like brandy through her limbs.

'Gabriel, I . . .' she whispered.

'Hush, sweet Kate,' he said, pulling back. 'I'm going to take your gown off now.' Without waiting for an answer, he slowly drew forward the gown, pulling it over the tops of her breasts, over her corset with the wax inserts, down to her waist.

'My arms,' she said, with a gasp. 'I can't move.'

'*My* kiss,' he said, and his voice made the wildfire burn higher. It was hoarse, as if he was holding on to his control as best he could. He didn't free her arms.

She watched as his hands deftly unlaced her corset and then pulled it wide. Her bosom friends were tossed to the ground; her breasts, pushed high and rigid by the corset, fell into his hands like ripe apples.

He froze for a moment, and then pulled her chemise tight across her bosom. It was silk, as frail as gossamer.

'Oh God,' he said, sounding as if the word was ripped from his lungs. 'I've never seen anything more beautiful. Never.'

Kate's lips parted to say something, but no words came out because Gabriel had rubbed a slow thumb across her nipple. The feeling smoldering in her legs burst into flame. A choked cry came from her lips.

'I have to taste you.' With one swift movement, he put his hands to her chemise and wrenched. The silk parted as sweetly as a sliced peach falls in two.

'Gabriel!' she cried, but she could tell he didn't even hear her. He was looking intently at her breasts, his eyes blazing.

In his hands, her breasts didn't look too small. They didn't look as if they needed bosom friends to plump them up. They looked lush and round, exactly the right shape.

Then he bent his dark head and she felt the touch of his lips on her breast. She'd seen it in Aretino's pictures—men suckling women as if they were babes in arms. She had wrinkled her nose and turned the page, convinced that the Italian was depicting some sort of ludicrous perversion.

But at the touch of Gabriel's mouth she felt a surge of pleasure that was unlike anything she'd felt in her life. She couldn't breathe, and a cry came from her throat. Gabriel sucked harder and a thumb rubbed across her other nipple; Kate's mind went completely blank and her body arched up, a

284

moan breaking from her lips.

'I knew it,' he whispered roughly. He raised his head just long enough for her to see the mad exultation in his eyes. 'I—' But his words were lost as he lavished attention on her neglected breast. And for her part, Kate had no ability to shape words, no power to do anything other than writhe under him, gasping.

When he raised his head again her body was throbbing, the blood singing through her legs. 'Gabriel,' she whispered.

He returned to her mouth, kissing her punishingly, making her arch against him, lost in a firestorm of sensation and desire.

When she broke away, she knew perfectly well that her will was sapped, the whole practical side of her dismissed, as if it didn't exist. 'Please let me move,' she begged huskily, her eyes wandering over his chest . . . the chest she hadn't been able to touch because her arms were still trapped by her gown.

He moved back without a word, but she saw the way he was struggling to draw in air.

With a swift movement Kate swung her legs over the edge of the bed and stood up. She shrugged her arms from the sleeves of her dress, but held it to her waist, letting his hot eyes appreciate her.

'What's fit for the goose is fit for the gander,' she told him, a smile stealing over her lips.

His eyes widened and she slowly, slowly let the gown drop to the floor. Gabriel had ripped her chemise to the waist, so she pulled it off her shoulders, but didn't let it fall, holding it to her breasts, pulling it slowly past her nipples, shuddering at the feeling of silk rubbing parts made tender by his mouth.

Gabriel made a movement, as if he were about to fling himself off the bed, but she stopped him with one glance.

'You undressed yourself,' she said, letting one hand slide from her collarbone, down over the curve of her right breast, down to the frail silk of her chemise as it clung to her hips.

'Please,' he said hoarsely.

Kicking her gown away from her feet, she turned her back on him and saucily walked over to the table. 'You look a little hot, Your Highness. Perhaps the fan will help.'

Picking up the fan he had handed her a few hours ago, she sauntered back toward the bed. 'I always use it when I'm overheated,' she crooned, flipping it open and fanning her face. Then a bit lower, her breasts. A bit lower . . . Her chemise rippled in the breeze.

'I don't know why it is,' she said, 'but I seem to be uncommonly overheated at the moment.'

'Kate,' Gabriel said, his voice a groan. 'You're no virgin. Tell me you're not a virgin.'

Her smile slipped, and the fan fell to the floor.

Gabriel lunged off the bed as if he were possessed, jerking her into his arms. 'I didn't mean that the way it sounded.'

Kate tried to say something but the feeling of his body against hers had stolen her logic again, sent her into a storm of sensation and desire. His body was hard and demanding against her, delivering an unmistakable male demand that made her knees buckle.

'You're a virgin; I know you're a virgin and I respect that,' Gabriel was saying into her hair. 'I would never imply otherwise, darling. It was just

286

the cry of a man who was wishing that fate was different.'

She curled against his chest, feeling his heart thumping wildly. 'You're wishing that I was the hussy I feel like,' she whispered. Excitement curled tighter in her stomach. She raised her head to meet his eyes. 'Tonight you're just a man, remember?'

'I don't know if I'll survive this night,' he said raggedly.

A smile curved her lips and she broke free of his arms. 'I hadn't finished undressing. Are you planning to expire before that happens?'

'No,' he choked.

Somehow her poor chemise had clung to her hips. With a little wiggle, Kate sent it sliding down her legs, over the butter-colored hair that covered her most private area.

Then she raised her arms and pulled the last pins from her hair. It fell below her shoulders, ringlets and curls, thick and silky. She ran her fingers through it, shaking her locks free, enjoying the way her breasts rose in the air.

'You are so beautiful,' Gabriel growled, his voice little more than a thread of sound.

'I believe it's time for a bath,' she said, turning her back on him. Then she paused and looked over her shoulder. 'You *did* say that there was a bath prepared for me?'

He didn't seem to be able to speak, but he leaped ahead of her and pulled away the velvet curtain that concealed his bathing area.

'How lovely!' Kate cried, seeing the huge iron tub full of gently steaming water, candles throwing golden specks of light over the velvet of the curtains, over the water, over her body.

She stepped forward and put in a toe, then, with a sigh of pure pleasure, relaxed into the curve of the tub, sweeping her hair behind her so that it hung over the edge.

The only sound in the room was the gentle plash of water and the harsh sound of Gabriel's breathing. She couldn't stop smiling. If she, Katherine Daltry, decided to be a wanton, she would be the best wanton this castle had ever seen.

'Soap,' she said, holding out her hand.

Gabriel put the ball in her hand without a word.

'Mmmm,' she said, sniffing it. 'Apple blossom?'

'Orange blossom,' he said. His voice was dark and sinful.

She sat up just enough so that she could soap her left arm. 'Shouldn't you be getting dressed so that you can go back downstairs?' she asked. 'I'm afraid everyone will be wondering where you are.'

His eyes were fixed on her hands as she soaped her right arm.

'Gabriel?' she inquired innocently, her hands straying to her breasts. 'I'm sure you said that you would come and go. That was your plan, wasn't it?'

His gaze was so hungry, so hot, that she was surprised the water didn't evaporate. He cleared his throat. 'Why don't you finish washing, and then I'll go. Unless you would like some assistance?'

She raised a leg from the bath and slowly, slowly washed her toes, letting her fingers stray up her leg.

'I suppose,' she said, stealing a glance at him under her lashes, 'someone might help me with this other leg.'

Somehow it felt entirely different when strong male hands stroked soap over her leg.

And Gabriel's interpretation of *leg* was not

288

exactly in line with her own. Kate was no sooner lying back in the bath, enjoying the tingling sensation of his strong fingers stroking her thigh, than they crept higher . . . and then higher still.

She sat up. 'Gabriel!'

'Hush, darling,' he said. And with that, his fingers slipped into a caress. This was no kiss . . . She should stop him.

Instead her legs fell farther apart in a silent plea that he continue. Whatever he was doing was fatal to her self-control. Kate's common sense, her willpower, all the parts that made her fierce and strong, deserted her. All that was left was a body that rejoiced in his touch, arched toward him.

His other hand wandered to her breast and she actually threw her head back and cried aloud. His hands were like fire, teasing, tormenting, stroking her . . .

'I—' she gasped.

A finger dipped into her most private place for one throbbing instant and she shattered, crying out, her arms flying around his neck, her body shaking as stroke after stoke of fire shot through her body.

Kate came to herself slowly, finding that her wet arms were locked around Gabriel's neck, that her eyes were squeezed shut. His fingers eased from her plump folds, giving them a little farewell pat that sent a final shudder through her body.

'God almighty, Kate,' he said in a kind of groan.

She didn't move. She felt sweaty—and she was in a bath. Noises had come from her mouth that she hadn't imagined any lady could ever make. Pleasure was replaced by a wave of embarrassment so violent that she would have preferred to die rather than open her eyes.

Plus—though it was a minor consideration—her legs were still throbbing.

'Kate?' he asked, his voice just as sinful as before. 'Are you ever going to open your eyes?'

She shook her head, keeping her face tight to his skin. It smelled warm and male and indescribably enticing.

A hand slid down her back, following the curve of her spine under water, slid around the curve of her hip. 'I want to kiss you there,' he said, conversationally.

Her body jerked in shock. 'No,' she said, the word muffled by his skin.

'I must go downstairs and begin the dancing, but Kate . . .'

He gently pulled her arms from around his neck and stood up. Perforce, she opened her eyes. He was all taut muscle, even the part that stood fiercely above the band of his smalls.

'Won't that be uncomfortable?' she asked, realizing instantly that her effort to make casual conversation was a failure. There was something aching in her voice, something that begged him to stay.

He couldn't stay.

He was rubbing toweling over his chest and staring at her as if he couldn't look away. 'Yes,' he said flatly. 'I'm going to have to wait on those stairs for a good ten minutes.'

Looking at his face, Kate suddenly realized that there was no reason for her shock of embarrassment. What happened between them, no matter how intimate, was not shameful.

So she pointedly let her legs fall apart, just as they wished to, and ran her hand down the inside of

290

her thigh.

'What if I want that kiss . . . *now*?' she whispered.

Her flesh throbbed under her light touch, at the very idea of it.

'You're killing me,' he said hoarsely. 'I have to go, Kate. You know that.'

She gave him a devilish smile. 'It's all right. As long as you remember that I'm here, waiting.' She let her head fall backward, and her breasts rose above the water.

He made a choked noise and disappeared through the velvet drapes. Kate heard the door close behind him.

A small smile curled her lips. She had learned something rather wonderful, it seemed to her.

Gabriel would go downstairs and do whatever it was he had to do . . . and then he would return.

Thirty-three

'You almost missed the first dance,' Wick hissed at him. 'I've delayed the musicians as long as I was able, telling everyone that Sophonisba was taken ill.'

Gabriel felt as if he were in a dream. His mind, his heart, were locked upstairs, with Kate, with the silky, honey woman waiting for him.

The only thing that got him to the threshold of the ballroom was the iron sense of duty in which he had been drilled since birth.

'I'm here,' he said tightly.

'Not a good night,' Wick said, looking at him. 'She's over there.' He nodded toward Tatiana and her uncle, in the middle of a small circle of gentlemen.

Gabriel walked across the room like a sleepwalker and apologized to Tatiana for missing most of the evening meal. 'My aunt is elderly, as you could see,' he said. 'When we reached her chambers she wasn't feeling well, and I'm afraid she is rather imperious in demanding attendance during those moments.'

'I admire a man who has a sense of his responsibilities,' Dimitri said, rocking back on his heels and smiling approvingly at Gabriel. 'Family always comes first in Russia. I don't care for the kind of fathering that you see in England, with a child scarcely recognizing his own blood relation.'

A little girl with Merry's name and Kate's face danced across Gabriel's mind as he turned to Tatiana and requested her hand for the dance.

Tatiana danced like a feather, her curtsies graceful, her sense of timing impeccable. And Gabriel, trained to dance from the age of three, was as good as she was.

Dimly, from behind a haze of sensual frustration, he was aware of the pleasure of having a partner with whom he was truly in harmony.

'Perhaps we might dance again?' he asked, as the music drew to a close. She bestowed a little smile on him. 'Indeed, Your Highness, it would be a pleasure.'

'A waltz, perhaps,' he said, knowing that he was putting the seal on his coffin. The moment a waltz began and he stepped onto that floor with Tatiana held in his arms, it would be a matter of days until he was signing a marriage contract. The dance was considered too sensual and disreputable by many sticklers in the *ton*; stepping onto the floor with an unmarried woman was tantamount to an announcement of their impending marriage. Not that anyone had any question about that.

She looked a little puzzled, as if a shadow of the bleakness that stabbed through his body had become visible in his eyes.

'I would be honored,' he said, getting a grip on himself.

Tatiana turned from him to take Toloose's hand, giving him the confident smile of a girl who is discovering her power over men. 'I should have to ask my uncle,' she told him, secret laughter in her eye showing that she understood the implication of a waltz as well as he did.

Gabriel took a breath. If he danced two or three more sets, and then told the orchestra to play the shortest waltz they had in their repertoire, then he could pretend to fall, or pretend to get drunk. Anything to get himself out of the room and back up to his tower.

A sharp rap on his arm brought him back to himself.

Lady Wrothe was standing at his side. 'The music's starting again,' Henry stated. The expression on her face was not entirely charming.

'Lady Wrothe,' he said, bowing. 'Would you be so kind as to—'

'Yes, I would sit out this measure with you,' she said, interrupting. 'Very kind of you, as I turned an ankle with these dratted heels of mine.' She headed directly for a secluded little alcove, just large enough for its padded settee.

'Now where's my goddaughter?' she asked, without preamble. 'I've been to her room, so I

293

know that's a tara-diddle about her stomach. Kate's not the sort to suffer any ailments; I'd be surprised if the girl spent a day in bed in her life.'

Gabriel's jaw clenched as images of just how he and Kate could spend a day in bed together crashed into his mind. 'I'm afraid that I can't assist you,' he said, through the roaring in his ears.

'Can't or won't?' Henry said, tapping him sharply again with her fan. 'I'm not a jack-pudding, you know. That girl's parents have both cocked up their toes, and so she's mine now. And I'—she smiled with all the charm of a mother tiger—'will not be pleased if her heart is broken.'

'I would feel the same,' Gabriel said.

'Who would guess that, seeing you circle the floor with that over-nourished Russian girl on your arm?'

'Princess Tatiana is a very . . .' He paused. 'She's a lovely girl.'

'But would Kate enjoy seeing you make sheep's eyes at a *lovely* girl?'

'Lady Wrothe,' Gabriel said. 'This marriage was arranged on the basis of my bride's substantial dowry and my title. It's an old tale, and one we've all heard before.' His words came out like hard little acorns, one to each beat of his heart. His eyes flicked to her face. 'I cannot marry Kate.'

'If you're planning to weave me some sort of lament, don't,' Henry snapped. 'You don't have to hide Kate away like some sort of doxy you hired for the night while you're out there dancing with your bride-to-be. *She* can be here too, because there are plenty of men who would love to marry her, substantial dowry or no!'

Gabriel took a deep breath. 'I cannot marry

294

where I will.'

'I'm not saying you should,' Henry retorted. 'There are men who throw the world at their lady's feet, and then there are the rest of you, who see the world as a ledger in black and white. I encountered one of you early in life, so I know just what you're like.'

He had never been so close to striking a woman before. 'If you'll forgive me—'

But her hand fell on his arm, and what he saw in her eyes stayed his tongue. 'You've got a choice before you, prince,' she said. 'You damned well better make the right one, or you'll spend your life cursing yourself. That gentleman I mentioned just now . . . I don't think the dowry he married made up for what he lost. And I believe he would agree with me.'

Gabriel turned, rather blindly, and walked toward the door. A gentleman lurched out of his way at the last moment.

Only Wick stepped in his way.

'I told Tatiana that I'd waltz with her,' Gabriel said in a low, harsh whisper. 'Find her and tell her something.'

'A *waltz*? I'll have to tell her that you've taken ill.'

'I have,' Gabriel said. 'Sick unto death, I think they call it.'

Thirty-four

Upstairs, Kate dried herself off, examined her ruined chemise, retrieved her crumpled dress and put it over a chair, and finally pulled on a dressing gown that hung against the wall. It was silk, and felt like an exotic caress against her skin. She wound the cord twice around her waist to keep it closed.

Still Gabriel didn't come.

She picked up the journal on Ionian treasures, leafed through it, and was amused to find a learned and aggressive letter from Gabriel featured in the notes. She picked up Aretino and put him down again immediately. Those engravings seemed to have nothing to do with the incandescent tenderness with which Gabriel had touched her.

And, like that, she realized that she'd made a decision.

She meant to sleep with Gabriel. She was greedy, mad with greed if the truth be told. She wanted this—him—for herself, to make up for the seven years in which not a soul touched her in a loving way.

She would give him her virginity, and then leave for London. Her legs trembled at the thought, and she felt her cheeks warming. It was the only thing she had wanted ferociously in years.

The door opened, and Gabriel walked through. There was something leaden in his face, in his eyes. 'What happened?' she asked, from across the room. And then, walking to stand before him: 'Gabriel, what happened? Are you all right?'

He looked down at her, eyes full of an emotion

that she couldn't read. 'Do you know what I've been doing in the ballroom, Kate? Do you have any idea?'

She put a hand on his coat, wanting to feel the solid warmth of him in light of the chilly rage in his voice. 'Dancing.'

'Not just dancing,' he said, precisely. 'I've been dancing with my future wife, Tatiana.'

Kate never thought that pain could rip through one's heart like a wound, but now she knew it could. She had managed to forget about Tatiana, to pretend that Gabriel was simply . . . elsewhere. Her whole body tensed and froze, just as it had when she had entered her mother's room and seen a body with no spirit.

Luckily Gabriel kept talking. 'I sat with her at dinner. She has dimples and speaks five languages. We danced the first dance. She is an exquisite dancer. I asked her to waltz.'

'I see,' Kate said unsteadily, reaching up to push her hair behind her shoulders.

'You don't *see*,' he said in a savage tone. 'You don't know enough about bloody society to *see*. Waltzing with a woman means taking her in your arms and circling the floor, leg to leg.'

'It sounds very intimate,' Kate managed, proud of the control in her voice.

'Very,' Gabriel said. 'If you and I—' He turned away and spoke to the black window. 'If you and I ever waltzed, everyone in the room would know we were lovers. You can't conceal anything, not with a woman in your arms and a waltz playing.'

Kate was confused and getting a little angry. It didn't feel right that Gabriel was pushing his betrothal in her face. 'It is likely not proper for me to offer congratulations.'

He swung around and stared at her, his eyes like black coals. 'Do you *dare* to offer me congratulations?'

Kate smoothed the front of the silk dressing gown she wore. 'I should . . . I should return to my chambers.'

He was on her like a predator. 'You will not leave me!'

And then she knew what the emotion in his eyes was. It was despair, and rage—and love. Love. 'Gabriel,' she said, with a little gasp.

'You dare—' he began again.

'Hush,' she said, putting a hand to his cheek. 'Hush.'

He swallowed.

'I probably wouldn't love you so much if you were not the man that you are.'

His throat worked furiously. 'You—'

'Love you.' She nodded. 'With all my heart.' She brought his face to hers, and gave him the sweetest kiss of her life. 'You are mine,' she whispered. 'In some way, in some part of my heart, you will always be with me.'

With a groan, he folded her into his arms. She wrapped hers around his waist, catching the faint odor of his orange blossom soap, together with a spicy wildness that was Gabriel's alone.

After a while, he stirred. She put a hand over his mouth before he could speak. His arms slid from around her shoulders and she stepped back, tearless, head high.

'You cannot marry me. You will marry Tatiana because she is chosen for you, but more than that, Gabriel, because you *deserve* someone who speaks

298

five languages, and who dances like an angel, and brings a king's ransom with her.'

'If the world were different—' His voice broke.

'It isn't,' she said steadily. 'The world is what it is, and you have a whole castle to feed and clothe and look after. Not to mention a lion.'

He didn't smile.

'You will never turn your back on your responsibilities,' she told him. 'You are not your brother, Gabriel.'

'But for you,' he said achingly.

'I would rather love you now,' she said fiercely, 'than take you as a man broken by turning your back on your family.'

'You are a rather frightening woman,' he said, a moment later. But his eyes had lost that wild despair.

She put her hands on the knot holding the dressing gown together. 'What do you call this garment?' she inquired.

'A banyan.'

'It is rather hot.' She slowly untied the knot. 'You see, Gabriel, while you were downstairs making a decision of one kind, I came to a decision of my own.'

He looked, rather unwillingly it seemed, from her hands to her face. 'You did?'

'Whatever happens with Tatiana,' she said gently, 'doesn't matter here, not tonight. Tonight is for us. Tomorrow is for the world, for Tatiana, for dowries, and all the rest. I shall come to your ball with Algie, and then I shall travel to London with Henry. I believe that I shan't go back to Mariana at all. There is nothing for me there, though it took me years to realize it.'

'Henry will take care of you.'

She smiled. 'Yes, she will. She fell in love with my father, you know. Truly fell in love with him. But he married my mother instead. So she lived her life without him. And it was a happy life.'

Gabriel made a sudden violent movement. 'I don't want to even think about the prospect of you with someone else.'

That was just like a man, to Kate's mind. He talked easily of Tatiana, but the parallel, her future spouse, was not such a straightforward subject. 'Henry sees me as the daughter she never had,' she said. 'You will be here, and I shall be in London. But tonight . . .' She untied the cord and let it slip through her fingers. It fell to the floor with a gentle slap.

'Tonight I want you, all of you.'

'What are you saying?' His face was dark with hunger.

She let the banyan ease apart, its silk falling to the side to reveal one breast.

'I'm giving you my virginity, such as it is,' she said simply. 'It's a gift, Gabriel, and one I have the right to bestow on whom I wish. It does not mean that I won't climb in a coach after the ball and leave this castle, because I will.'

He was shaking his head, so she let the other side of the banyan slide open, freeing both of her breasts to his gaze.

'I, and I alone, can bestow this gift,' she told him, drawing a hand over the curve of her breast. 'It will not change anything between us. I expect you to use a French letter.'

To her relief, the steel in his jaw eased a bit. 'You sound like the abbess of a particularly strict

300

brothel.'

'Not a very complimentary comparison,' she said, unable to stop her grin, 'but I'll forgive you.' The banyan fell down, to her elbows. 'Do we have an agreement, Gabriel? Do we have tonight?'

'I shouldn't,' he said raggedly. 'As a gentleman—'

'You're not a gentleman tonight,' she reminded him. 'You're a man, Gabriel. And I'm a woman. With no titles, or society, or nonsense between us.'

'You're killing me,' he said, snatching her to him so suddenly that the breath left her lungs. 'You unman me.'

From what she could feel, that was definitely not the case.

'Really?' she asked, her voice a provocative thread of sound. Then she deliberately rubbed against him. Her wrapper had given up the fight and fallen to the ground; there was something delicious about the contrast between her nakedness and his formal attire.

Not that she had long to enjoy it.

With a muffled groan, he fell back a step, his eyes eating her alive, and began wrenching off his clothes. Buttons flew; his cravat skidded across the desk and landed on the little pile of pottery fragments; his breeches disappeared while she was still absorbed with his chest.

'You're very muscled,' she said, striving for a casual tone.

'Hunting,' he said.

'Don't tell me you've been providing all the fowl that we eat at every meal.'

His mouth quirked. 'Hardly. Witness the gift of my mother, who kindly left me a Star of India emerald whose price will keep the castle going for another six months, even given the extravagances of this weekend.'

She sobered, drew closer, and put a finger out to his shoulder. 'Gabriel?' Her whisper had an aching hunger to it, and he responded immediately, scooping her up and striding over to the bed.

He put her down and then, without further ado, swung a leg over her and lowered himself, slowly, onto her body.

Kate let out an involuntary squeak at the weight of him, the heat, the curious feeling of a muscled body against hers. He didn't move, just waited there, elbows braced on the side of her head.

She opened her eyes and met his. 'Aren't you going to . . .'

'What?' he asked, obviously trying to look innocent but failing.

Kate licked her lips. She didn't expect to have to instruct *him*. 'You know,' she insisted.

'No, you tell me,' he said silkily. 'You had all the time to study Aretino while I was downstairs.'

'I didn't look at that book,' she said, wiggling around to get herself more comfortable. He was no lightweight, after all. A strange look crossed his face. 'What?'

'That—feels good,' he said, a hoarse little gasp escaping his lips.

'Ah,' she said, pleased. She wiggled again, testing how his hardness fit into the curve of her thighs. 'Would you like to know what I did while you were downstairs?'

'What did you do?' He had lowered his head and was licking her collarbone. The rasp of his tongue sent a little frisson over her nerves.

302

'I didn't look at the Aretino, but I read the journal about Ionian antiquities,' she said, running her fingers down his shoulder, slipping to his broad back, dancing down the line of muscle there. 'I read your letter to the editor. It was very intelligent. Very argumentative too. I thought you needn't have called the author a numbskull. Or said that he was writing nothing more than piffle.'

'Kate.'

'Yes?'

'Shut up.'

His head slipped lower and his mouth closed over her nipple.

She didn't shut up. She couldn't; when he took her nipple into his mouth, she gave out a startled cry. It felt as if a wire snapped inside; as if she were a puppet, her body arched toward his, feeling soft, warm, and desperate. Suddenly the erection pressing between her thighs felt . . . different. 'Gabriel!'

He sucked harder, and she forgot the words that formed in her mind before they could reach her lips. She clutched his shoulders, but he pulled away from her. Before Kate could collect herself, he braced himself on one elbow, freeing his right hand, which slid down her leg to—

There.

'I don't think that's—' Kate managed.

But his fingers were dancing in her curls, and he lowered his head to her other breast, and she couldn't answer, she couldn't speak.

Sparks started racing up her legs, and she writhed, her hands clutching him, desperately running down his arms, over his chest. 'I want,' she panted.

303

'What?'

He sounded entirely too lazy, too calm, and too in control. His voice penetrated her brain and she opened her eyes. She was just lying on her back like a ninny and letting him pleasure her.

Ignoring (with effort), what he was doing with his fingers, she started kissing his cheek. When he wouldn't raise his head, she licked him like a cat, just the way he'd licked her, and purred when he shuddered at her caress.

Finally he raised his head, so she licked the edge of his lips, and then nibbled at them, because the idea occurred to her, and they looked delicious.

Gabriel put up no objection.

She let her hands run down his back and over the curve of his arse, discovering the muscles, exploring hills and valleys and the small dimples that marked his left and right side.

She could feel him stirring against her, and it seemed to her that it was likely a good sign.

'Kiss me,' she commanded, licking his lips again. 'Please.'

He covered her mouth fiercely, and her arms flew back up to his neck, as if only holding him tightly would keep her steady in the firestorm of their kiss. Long drugging moments later, he broke off the kiss, only to say, 'I want to make this last all night, but Kate . . .'

'What?'

'If you don't stop rubbing against me like that, this is going to be a very short and disappointing first encounter.'

'I like it,' she said, smiling up at him and wiggling. 'It makes me feel . . . warm. And soft. And'—her cheeks turned rosy—'wet.'

He framed her face with his hands, brushing her lips with his, and suddenly she felt that part of him, nudging against her.

'Yes,' she breathed. 'Please.' Everything in her body strained, as if all her concentration had gone to that fiery place between her legs.

His eyes were black with desire. 'I need to put on a French letter, as commanded,' he said, grabbing something from the bedside table. And then, a moment later . . .

He was larger and hotter than she would have imagined. He slid partway into her, and stopped, whispered something that she couldn't understand.

She drove her hands into his hair and arched toward him. 'It's not enough,' she panted, and heard a groan that was almost a laugh . . . and then he drove forward again.

She screamed, but not because of pain. It was the feeling of being owned, possessed and taken, the sense of another person, not just any person, but Gabriel, *Gabriel*.

He pulled back. 'Does it hurt?' he asked. 'Talk to me, Kate. We don't have to continue. We can—'

'Please,' she panted.

'Please stop?' He was hanging above her, his jaw tight, his eyes black with passion. 'Does it hurt too much, love?'

'I can't—'

'You can't take it,' he said, withdrawing even more. 'I understand. I've been told I'm too large before.'

'Damn it,' Kate cried, finally finding her voice. 'Come back, Gabriel. Come—come now!' And she reached down and pulled him fiercely toward her.

His smile flared with pure wild joy. 'That's my

305

Kate,' he crooned, and he stroked forward.

She arched her back instinctively, coming to meet him. He was too full, too big, too perfect. It was the very edge of tolerable. 'Again,' she gasped, willing her body to accept.

Obligingly, he performed.

And again.

And again, again, again, again, again. He pumped into her until his breath was nothing more than a hoarse rasp, and sweat dampened both their bodies.

'Sweetheart,' Gabriel said, 'you have to, I need you to . . .' but he lost his voice and she didn't know how to follow the heat and the madness where her body wanted to go. Until . . .

Until she discovered that if she tightened . . . if she squeezed . . .

He let out a hoarse bellow, for one thing. Every time.

And she . . . it made flames lick down her legs and up her middle, and she arched her back again, welcoming the joy and the wildness, the sweat and the pleasure, and then . . . there it was.

Wave after wave of heat crashing through her body, until she cried with wanton pleasure, dug her fingers into him, and hung on.

Thirty-five

They had washed, and made love again, slow and sweet, cuddled under the blankets, as the night air grew chilly and then freezing. 'I should go,' she whispered, at some point in that long night.

'I feel like bleeding Romeo and Juliet,' Gabriel said. 'Don't start telling me about the lark, Juliet, because they don't fly up this high.'

'I have to go,' she said, feathering kisses on his neck.

'No.' He sounded like a stubborn little boy. 'No.'

She laughed against his neck and tucked her leg a bit more securely between his. She had never imagined feeling so happy, so safe.

'I will never forget you,' she whispered, because it had to be said. She had been brought up to make proper good-byes, to say her thank-yous, to take her leave. 'And I will always remember this night.'

His arms tightened around her. 'You're turning me into Romeo.'

'Romeo didn't swear as much as you do,' she said, tracing a pattern on his chest with one finger. 'It's not princely.'

'Nothing I do is princely since I met you,' he said. 'Not this night, not—not any of it.'

She couldn't stop herself. 'Just don't forget me.' He was silent, and her heart faltered.

'Do you know what Romeo says to his bride when she's lying there in the tomb?' Gabriel asked.

'I don't remember,' Kate admitted.

'He promises to stay with her forever. Maybe there's something else, and then he says, *Never from this palace of dim night will I depart again*. I have the palace, Kate, I have the palace, and still I can't stay with you.'

'Doesn't he kill himself at that point?' Kate asked cautiously.

'Yes.'

'I'd rather not be part of that,' she said. 'I must say, Gabriel, that the literature you fancy seems

307

very dark.'

'I suppose there's a parallel between Dido and Juliet,' he said.

'Ridiculous women,' she said, resting her chin on his chest. 'I adore you, but I'm not planning to build a funeral pyre in the near future.'

She felt his chuckle before she heard it, felt his smile in the kiss he dropped on her hair. 'That's my Kate.'

'I don't have a romantic bone in my body,' she said unapologetically.

'I would bet I could make you squeal in verse.' And then he started kissing her again.

But she didn't need a singing lark to know the truth. Years of rising with the dawn told her that it was near, that she had to make her way back through those corridors.

'Gabriel,' she whispered.

'No.'

She wriggled away. 'I must.' She toppled out of bed, and pulled on his wrapper again, curling her toes against the chill of the stone floor.

He was out of the bed too, his face set in bleak lines that made her heart hurt.

But she bit her lip and didn't speak. She couldn't help, she couldn't help . . . this couldn't be solved with another kiss, or a promise.

Two minutes later she was swathed in black lace and bundled up in his arms. 'You don't carry your aunt around the castle like this!' she gasped.

'If we encounter anyone, I'll tell them that Sophonisba suffered a fatal apoplexy after too much brandy.'

She would have reproached him, but his tone was removed, cold as ice. 'It's not her fault,' she said, leaning her head against his chest, and listening to his heart beat.

'What isn't?'

'That she never married, and ended up being thrown out like a piece of unwanted laundry. It's not their fault, Gabriel, and you have to keep that in mind.'

'I never said it was.' He strode along another corridor, turned again . . . they had to be close to the door of her chamber now. 'It's Fate, that bloody impudent devil who brought down Romeo and Juliet.'

It sounded very dramatic to Kate, but she understood what he meant.

'I love you,' she said, when he put her on her feet at the door to her room. Risking everything, she pulled up the veil and looked into his face.

'I—' But the words seemed to catch in his throat, and her heart slammed against her chest at his silence.

Instead he bent down and kissed her and then, quickly, turned and left.

Kate waited until he turned the corner of the corridor, then tumbled through the door of her room. There was Freddie, waiting in the middle of her bed. He raised a sleepy muzzle and gave her a loving little woof. There were candles, guttering low on the mantelpiece. There were her book, and her slippers, and her nightgown waiting for her.

There was real life in this room, and behind her was nothing more than a fairy tale, and she would do well to remember that.

She could train herself in the boundaries of reality in the morning. For the present, she tucked Freddie's warm little body under her chin and let him lick up the salty tears that slid onto his face.

Rosalie slipped through the door a few hours later, banging around the room, pulling open the curtains.

'No,' Kate groaned. 'Please, go away. I can't get up yet.'

'You don't have to get up,' the little maid said cheerfully. 'I have such wonderful news that you—'

'Out!' Kate said, sitting up, knowing that her eyes were still swollen. 'Take the dogs with you, please. I'll ring for you later.' And with that she fell backward, pulled a pillow over her head, and pretended to be unconscious.

She didn't rise until two in the afternoon. She drifted listlessly over to the bell, rang for Rosalie, and then stared in the glass. It was faintly interesting to note that a deflowered woman looks just like any other woman.

In fact, she thought, leaning closer, she looked better than she had a week ago. Her skin had a glow to it, and her lips—

It must have been all that kissing that made them look crimson and slightly swollen.

Rosalie entered with a breakfast tray, followed by a line of footmen with hot water. 'I have such a surprise in store for you!' she said again.

'Tell me after my bath,' Kate said wearily, sitting down at the dressing table and picking up a piece of toast.

'Drink this.' Rosalie handed her a cup of tea. 'You had a nasty stomach upset last night. I felt terrible, not being able to tend to you, but Mr Berwick said he just couldn't do without me. I *am* good with flowers. And he promised to send you a maid. Was she helpful?'

'Absolutely. She was—she was perfect.'

'There, this will make you feel better.'

It wasn't until she was out of the bath, dried, powdered, and dressed, that Rosalie said hopefully, 'Would you like to know your surprise now?'

'I apologize,' Kate said. 'Of course I would.'

'Your stepsister is here!' she said with a squeal. 'Miss Victoria's lip improved and she arrived yesterday late, but of course you were ill and not to be disturbed. Would you like me to knock on her chamber? She's just next door. Mr Berwick moved Mr Fenwick up a floor so the two of you could be together.'

'Victoria is here?' Kate said, sitting down. 'With my stepmother?'

Rosalie shook her head. 'No. And isn't that a blessing? Lady Dimsdale brought her, but her ladyship left immediately as she is preparing for Miss Victoria's wedding.' She bustled to the door. 'I'll fetch her this moment. I know she's longing to see you.'

Victoria entered the room rather tentatively, as if she wasn't sure of her welcome. Kate got up and went over to greet her.

They could not be said to have grown up together; they had lived on the same floor of Yarrow House for only a matter of months until their father died, upon which Mariana promptly moved Kate from the nursery to the garret.

At sixteen, Kate was too old for the nursery, Mariana said, and there wasn't any call for a poor relative to be housed on the main floor.

But Victoria had an intrinsic kindness about her that was missing from her mother, and had never joined in Mariana's taunts or humiliations.

311

'Rosalie, will you fetch us more tea?' Kate asked.

The maid whisked herself out the door and Kate sat down next to her sister, beside the fire. Freddie came over and sprang into her lap. 'How is your lip?'

'It's fine,' Victoria said, patting it. 'After being lanced, it was already much better by the next day.'

'It looks perfect to me,' Kate said.

'Isn't this castle an oddity? It's so huge. I thought I would expire from the cold last night, at least until Caesar came to bed with me.'

'Caesar!' Kate said, startled. Her hand froze on Freddie's head. 'I didn't even realize he wasn't in my chamber.'

'I could hear him barking,' Victoria explained. 'I couldn't bear it, so I finally slipped over here and brought him to my room. Freddie seemed perfectly comfortable so I left him on your bed.'

She fiddled with a fold of her gown, the color high in her cheeks. Kate looked at her and knew exactly what that meant. 'I didn't sleep in my bed last night,' she said with a sigh.

'I'm not one to judge,' Victoria said.

'Why did you come?' Kate asked, softening the question with a smile.

'Algie kept writing me.' And, when Kate's eyebrow flew up: 'He writes me every day. We both do, every day since we first met back in March, at Westminster Abbey.'

'You *do*?'

Victoria nodded. 'Sometime pages and pages. Algie,' she said with pride, 'is a wonderful correspondent. I didn't have a governess, you know, so I am considerably less—well—he doesn't mind very much.'

312

Kate had never really thought about how Victoria's education was affected by Mariana's propensity to dismiss the household servants; her sister didn't seem someone who greatly missed tutoring. But her cheeks were pink and she was still pleating her gown.

'I'm sorry. I should have fought harder to keep the governess,' Kate said.

'You did all you could. Mother is . . . well, she *is*. I thought—I've thought for years—that it was wonderful how you protected Cherryderry and Mrs Swallow and most of the people on the farms. You couldn't keep a governess on top of all that.'

'I could have tried harder,' Kate repeated. She just hadn't thought much about Victoria, the treasured, coddled daughter. 'So what did Algie tell you?' she asked.

'He said that I should come here,' Victoria said, eyes on her lap still. 'He said that you were—were falling in love with the prince, and it wouldn't end well, and that I should come rescue *you*.' She said the last word defiantly, looking up. 'I know you spent years saving all the people on the estate and in the house, and Algie agrees with me, that sometimes people like that need rescuing themselves.'

Kate sat for a second and then she started to laugh. Not a harsh laugh, but the healing kind of laughter, the kind that comes after years of being alone are over, and you discover that you have a family.

It wasn't a normal family: Henry had no pretensions to being a paragon of virtue. Victoria was illegitimate, if kindhearted, and Algie was genuinely foolish. Yet they cared for her.

313

Victoria perked up at her laughter. 'So you aren't angry?' she said hopefully. 'I was worried that you would be irritated by my arrival, but Algie . . .'

Kate reached over and gave her sister a hug. 'I think it was tremendously kind of you. I am happy to be rescued. Although I don't mean to stay much longer; will that be all right with you?'

'Oh yes, because we have to leave after the ball, this very night,' Victoria said. 'We need to marry.'

'Of course.'

'If we leave at midnight tonight, we can be in Algie's parish by seven in the morning. Would you—would you accompany us?'

'Driving through the night?' Kate exclaimed.

'Well, the prince told Algie that he has to attend the ball. But Algie told his mother, Lady Dimsdale, that he would be home in time to get married in the morning.' Victoria looked at her hopefully. 'My mother is already at Dimsdale Manor.'

Algie was not one to disobey a direct command, obviously. 'Of course I will come with you. Did he tell you that I have a godmother, Lady Wrothe?'

'Yes . . . she calls herself Henry, doesn't she? And will she take you to live with her?'

'She will,' Kate said, smiling.

'Because you could always come live with us,' Victoria said anxiously. 'Algie's mother is moving to the dower house and the two of us will be knocking about in that great house by ourselves. We'd love to have you.'

She meant it. 'I'm so glad to have discovered that you're my sister,' Kate said.

Victoria nodded. Her eyes were a little teary.

Kate squeezed her hand.

'I just wish that our father had been more

314

gentlemanly,' Victoria said in a rush. 'I wish—I wish that Algie didn't have to marry me under false pretenses.' A tear slid down her cheek.

'He's not,' Kate said. 'He's marrying you because he loves you, and because you love him. And that's all anyone has a right to know about it.'

Victoria sniffed, and somewhat to Kate's surprise made an obvious effort to stop crying. 'I always believed in my father, I mean, in the colonel that I thought was my father. She even has a portrait of him, you know. Except that he never existed.'

'It's awkward,' Kate said, considering that an under-statement.

'I'm *illegitimate*,' Victoria said again. 'I wake up in the middle of the night and think about that. That word. It's a horrible word, all those syllables and none of them good.'

'The circumstances of your birth are not your fault.'

Victoria bit her lip. 'But when my mother married your father, you lost your inheritance, and she gave it to me . . . it's not right! I keep thinking about it. It's as if I'm some sort of parasite. I look like a lady, but I'm really nothing more than an illegitimate, thieving *chipper*!' And with that she broke into genuine sobs.

'Chipper?' Kate asked, feeling rather dazed. 'What on earth is a chipper?'

'A baggage,' Victoria wailed. 'A trollop. I'm—I'm carrying a child out of wedlock. I'm just like my mother!'

'No, you're not,' Kate said firmly, reaching over and pulling a handkerchief from the dressing table and giving it to her. 'A wise old man in this very castle told me that kindness is the most important

315

thing, and he was right. You are kind, Victoria, and your mother, unfortunately, is not. You are not a thief. Papa wanted you to have that money.'

'No, he left it to my mother and she—she—'

'He left it directly to Mariana, knowing full well that she would give it to you. My mother left me a dowry, you know that.'

'I'm just so grateful that he married her at all,' Victoria said, with a sob.

Kate had wondered for years why her father married Mariana. But now, looking at her pretty, silly, sweet sister, she knew why. 'I want to show you something,' she said, jumping up and running to the little writing desk. 'Just let me write a note first.'

'What?' Victoria said, taking another handkerchief out of her reticule. 'I know it annoys you when I cry, Kate. I'm sorry. It's something about being with child. It's made me worse than ever.'

'It's all right. I'm used to it.'

'Algie says I'm a watering pot and he's going to put me out in the garden,' Victoria said dolefully.

Kate composed the note to Gabriel.

Your Highness,

May I show my sister the statue of Merry in the chapel garden? Your uncle thought that you might have the chapel key. I'm sure that Berwick would be able to help us find the door.

Yours & etc.,
Miss Katherine Daltry

316

'What are you going to wear tonight?' Victoria said, putting away her handkerchief.

'I hadn't thought about it,' Kate said. 'Rosalie has something chosen. I wish she'd bring up something more to eat. I'm positively ravenous.'

'You *have* to think about it,' Victoria said. 'This is your presentation to society, Kate! I'm here, so you can go to the ball as yourself.'

Kate blinked. 'I hadn't thought of that.'

'I bought a powerful corset,' Victoria said, 'so that I will look thinner. And I'll wear a wig, and take the dogs with me.'

Just then Rosalie entered with luncheon on a tray, so Kate sent her off to deliver the note to the prince.

'It's so odd to think of you exchanging *billets-doux* with a prince,' Victoria said, a forkful of chicken halfway to her mouth.

'Because I've been a servant in Yarrow House, you mean?'

'You were never a servant!' Victoria said. 'Mother can be harsh, but not that harsh. You were . . . you were . . .'

'The label doesn't matter,' Kate put in. 'I think it's odd that I'm writing to a prince as well. I wasn't even sure how to address the note, if the truth be told. What am I to do tonight, Victoria? I can't dance, you know.'

Victoria's mouth fell open. 'Of course you can't dance. Mother only got me a dancing master when we went to London for the season. And we haven't time for Algie to teach you either.'

'Algie?'

'Algie is a wonderful dancer,' Victoria said proudly. 'And he's such a good teacher, so kind and patient. He's taught me no end of things.'

'You two are—' Kate said, and the door opened.

'The prince is waiting in the chapel for you both,' Rosalie squealed.

'I want to show you something,' Kate said, holding her hand out to Victoria. 'Something that you'll like.'

'I've never met a prince,' Victoria kept muttering as she trotted behind Kate down the stairs. 'I wish Algie were here. I do wish Algie were here. I just wish that he . . .'

Thirty-six

Gabriel looked so beautiful, waiting for them at the door to the chapel, that Kate actually felt her head spinning a little. But if there was one thing Katherine Daltry would never, ever do, it was lose her head over a man. Or swoon. Or throw herself on a funeral pyre.

So she held her head high and greeted him with a curtsy, introduced him to her sister, and generally behaved as if they were no more than passing acquaintances.

And since he did the same, there was no cause for the pain she felt. It was as bad as an arrow to her side, she thought glumly as she followed Gabriel's brisk footsteps through the chapel to the back room, where a red door had been discovered behind a tapestry.

Wick was there as well, and of the two brothers, he was the only one who seemed to have a tongue to speak. 'We had no idea the door was here,' he

318

was explaining to Victoria, 'until His Highness noticed it from the garden side.'

'I found the key,' Gabriel said, speaking for the first time since they exchanged greetings. He pulled out a huge rusty key and thrust it in the lock. It turned, but the door didn't open.

He threw his weight against it in a surprisingly violent gesture that made Victoria squeak and jump back. Still, it didn't move. Then Wick stepped up beside him. When they both put a shoulder to the door it opened with a terrible screeching noise.

'Rusted shut,' Gabriel said, his voice as cool and distant as if he were addressing a group of village drunkards.

Kate walked past him without comment. After a wet morning, the sun was shining fitfully on the drooping branches of the garden's one oak tree.

'How messy,' Victoria said in dismay, as she picked her way through the door. 'Dear me, Your Highness. Perhaps you should put some gardeners to work here.'

'They're all busy in the village mending roofs,' Gabriel said. 'This is not the weather to leave people without cover.'

'Here,' Kate said, catching Victoria's hand. 'I'll show you the statue.'

'What statue?' Victoria said, trailing behind. 'Drat, there's my skirt caught on a rose bush. Wait for me, Kate!'

But Kate walked ahead, desperate to create space between herself and Gabriel. She stopped in front of Merry and then bent down to say hello, wiping a rain drop from her marble cheek.

'What a sweet baby,' Victoria crooned. 'Oh, just look at her adorable plump fingers and her dimples.'

'Her name was Merry,' Kate said. 'She was illegitimate, Victoria. Her mother's name was Eglantine.'

'Oh.'

'There's no record of her father ... but there's a record of one thing.'

'What?' Victoria reached down and pulled a leaf from Merry's shoulder.

'She was loved, you see? She has her own garden, her own memorial.'

Victoria's big blue eyes filled with tears. 'Merry *died*?'

'Merry lived in the 1500s,' Kate said, schooling her tone to patience. 'Of course she died.'

'But—'

'My point is that her mother loved her just as much as she would have loved any child. And my father loved you that way as well. So the ugliness of that word *illegitimacy* doesn't matter. Because my father loved you enough to marry Mariana, Victoria. He was the son of an earl, and he married his mistress, a woman who wasn't a lady. For you.'

'Oh,' Victoria said softly. 'I didn't think of—are you sure, Kate?'

'I'm absolutely sure. He knew I was taken care of, and that my mother had left me a dowry. He made sure that you were taken care of by marrying your mother, and leaving your dowry in her hands.'

Victoria's eyes overflowed, but the sky had started splattering tears as well. So Kate wound her arm around her sister's shoulders and led her back into the chapel, past the men standing silently next to the large red door.

She gave Wick a smile, and Gabriel a nod,

because one didn't smile at princes as if they were common folk.

And definitely not if the only thing one wanted to do was kiss him until the haunted look was gone from his face.

'He's so handsome,' Victoria whispered, on the way back up the stairs.

'Who, the prince?' Kate asked. 'Yes, if you like the dark and brooding sort of man.'

'Well, he's not Algie,' Victoria said, with perfect truth. 'But Kate, did you see the way he looked at you? His eyes were positively burning!'

'He opens the ball tonight with his betrothed, Princess Tatiana,' Kate said flatly. 'I would expect their marriage to be celebrated within the fortnight.'

'That's so cruel,' her sister said. 'I can't like it. Would you like to leave now, Kate? My maid is packing already. We could be gone in an hour or two.'

'I will *not* run and hide. We shall attend the ball, and I mean to dance with every man who has two good legs, even though I can't dance. And then we'll leave for your wedding, and after that, London. The prince does not care for large cities. I shall forget about him.'

'I could never forget about Algie,' Victoria said doubtfully.

'But you and he are betrothed. It's a different set of circumstances. You're going to be parents together. I hardly know the prince,' Kate said, trying hard to give her voice an airy ring.

Victoria didn't answer, but she slipped a hand in Kate's and gave it a squeeze.

Thirty-seven

Henry was waiting in Kate's chamber when she slipped through the door, having dropped Victoria in her room to begin the long process of dressing for the ball. Kate took one look at her godmother and her lip trembled. Henry started forward, arms open.

She was crying before Henry even reached her. Her godmother pulled her over to the settee, sat them both down, and rocked her against her shoulder, saying things that Kate didn't hear. She cried until her lungs burned and her stomach twisted.

Finally Kate lifted her head. 'Just don't tell me to stop loving him,' she said, choking out the words. 'I couldn't stop breathing, I couldn't stop loving—' She lost her voice in a sob.

'I'm not,' Henry said. She pushed Kate gently backward, so she was lying down. 'I am going to tell you to stop crying, though. You're making yourself ill.' She got up and went to the washbasin, bringing back a cool, damp cloth. 'Put this over your eyes.'

So Kate lay there under the wet cloth, feeling the sting of her swollen eyes, and the way her chest still hurt from the violence of her sobs, and the comfort of Henry's fingers twined in hers.

'I won't tell you to stop loving him,' Henry finally said, 'because I know it's not possible.'

'My father . . .'

'I cried for a week when I heard he died. I cried on his wedding night; I cried when your mother died, because I knew he would be hurt by it.' There

322

was a moment's pause. 'I *never* cry,' Henry added.

Kate gave a watery chuckle. 'I don't either. *Ever.*'

Henry's fingers tightened. 'I'm so sorry, Kate. I'm just so sorry. All I can tell you is that life can be joyful, even if one of the people you love isn't beside you. Because there will be others. I know it doesn't feel that way, but it's true. You'll marry—'

'That's the worst of it,' Kate burst out. 'How am I going to marry anyone now? Now that I know—I know . . .' She fell silent, unable to put into words what it was like to nestle in Gabriel's arms, to laugh with him, to relax against him, to make love to him. 'I couldn't,' she said flatly. His scent was imprinted in her skin, and the way he shook when she touched him, the way his face grew wild and needy.

'I know,' Henry said. 'I know.' She got up. 'I'm going to change your cloth. Your eyes look like raisins soaked in brandy.'

'Charming,' Kate said, her laugh cracking.

'Love is messy,' Henry said, pulling off the cloth and putting another cold one in its place. It was a little too wet, and a drop of chill water rolled down Kate's cheek. Even as Kate was reaching to wipe it off, Henry patted her dry. 'Messy, messy, messy.'

'I hate it,' Kate said, with conviction.

'Well, I don't. Because it's better to live like a flame, Kate, to know a man and love him, even if he can't be yours, than never to love at all.'

'There will be no one else for me.' She said it out of the quiet conviction that it was true.

'Do you think I believed your father was perfect?'

Kate gave a strangled half giggle. 'I doubt it.'

'He wasn't,' Henry stated.

Kate nearly took off her cloth to see Henry's

face, but at that moment she heard her godmother get up and walk across the room. 'He was not perfect,' Henry repeated. 'He was a fool who believed that money was more important than love, that the two of us would never be happy together because he couldn't provide for me as he felt he should.'

'Stupid ass,' Kate muttered.

'Maybe,' Henry said. 'I do like being well-fed.' There was laughter in her voice. The cloth disappeared from Kate's eyes and Henry peered down at her. 'Much better,' she said with satisfaction. 'I'll get one more.'

Kate heard her walk away again. And then, over the splashing of water, she asked: 'What does she look like, Henry?'

'The little Russian, you mean?'

'Gabriel's bride,' Kate said. 'What is she like?'

Henry lifted off the cloth and put a fresh one in its place. 'She's not you. She will never be you.'

'Yes, but—'

'It's not important,' Henry stated. 'Your mother was your mother. She loved your father, and I was glad of that. But I didn't think about the two of them together, because it wouldn't be helpful.'

'I suppose not,' Kate said.

'You can make yourself stop thinking of him,' Henry commanded.

Kate tried to imagine a world without Gabriel.

'Starting tonight.' Henry pulled off the cloth again. Kate opened her eyes. 'Very good,' Henry said, as if she were checking the progress of a baking loaf. 'You'll be just fine in an hour or two.'

'I don't think I want to go to the ball tonight,' Kate whispered. 'I'm just not strong enough. He took us—Victoria and me—he took us into the garden behind the chapel, and his voice . . . it was as if he hardly knew me.'

'Don't you *dare* start crying again,' Henry interrupted.

Kate gulped.

'You are going to that ball tonight. You are going to look more beautiful than you have ever looked in your life—because *I* am going to dress you. You are going to give that prince one last chance to be a man.'

'To be a man,' Kate said. 'He *is* a man.' An image flashed into her mind of Gabriel standing before her naked, his chest heaving, his eyes hungry.

'Your father couldn't imagine life any way other than he'd been taught. He'd been told since birth that because he was a younger son, he had to marry a rich woman. Your prince has been told that he has to marry the woman his brother chooses to send him.'

'He has the castle to support,' Kate protested.

'I'll give him that,' Henry said. 'He has far more responsibilities than your father did, and they're real ones. His uncle is a loon, and it's not as if those elderly princesses could start tatting lace to bring in money.'

'He has no choice,' Kate said, sighing.

'There's always a choice. And tonight we're going to make that choice brilliantly, absolutely clear to him.'

Kate sat up. She felt washed clean, as if all those tears had rinsed away some of the grief. 'He won't break his promise to marry Tatiana.'

'Then you'll know for certain that he's a fool,' Henry said. 'I have to admit that my understanding of your father's character was a great help in moments when I missed him. If Gabriel doesn't have the backbone to take you, Kate, then he doesn't deserve you.'

'I wish you could just tell him that,' Kate said, getting to her feet. 'It would make it all so simple.'

Henry smiled wryly. 'It *is* simple. You'll be at the ball, and so will Tatiana. And there it is: his life before him. He can choose.'

'Did you have a night like this?' Kate asked, drifting over to the dressing table. Her eyes were not terrible, all things considered, though she looked awfully white.

'Your father's betrothal ball.'

Kate turned around. 'The very same occasion?'

'The very same. I wore yellow ribbed silk, trimmed with flounces and silk tassels. My skirts were so large I could hardly fit through a door. I wore a wig that night, and three patches. I painted my lips, which was far more scandalous in those days than it is now.'

'You must have been beautiful,' Kate said. Even now, Henry was absolutely luscious.

'I was,' Henry said. 'You may not like this, darling, but I'm going to say it anyway. Your mother was very frail, like a tulip that had been out of water. She spent most of the night reclining on the side of the ballroom.'

'Please don't hate her,' Kate began.

'Oh, I didn't,' Henry said. 'Anyone could tell she was a lovely person who was deeply unlucky when it came to her health. She longed to be up and dancing.'

Kate's mouth wobbled. 'Poor Mama,' she said. 'She always wished she had the energy to get up

. . . but if she tried, she would end up back in bed for days on end.'

'I can imagine,' Henry said, nodding.

'Did my father dance with you?'

'No.'

'And yet you were there.'

'I was the most beautiful woman in London that night,' Henry said flatly. 'I received four proposals of marriage in the week thereafter, and I chose my first husband from that group. And I did not look behind me.'

'I—'

'You will do the same as I, if it comes to that,' Henry said, fixing Kate with her eyes. 'I sincerely hope that the prince has more backbone than your father, but if he does not, you will leave this castle with your head held high.'

Kate nodded.

'And now,' Henry said, 'we must begin to dress. Where's that maid of yours?' She pulled on the cord.

Rosalie rushed into the room a few minutes later. 'Oh, miss, we're that late!' She caught sight of Henry and bobbed a curtsy. 'Excuse me, my lady.'

'We are indeed late, and it's my fault,' Henry said, smiling. 'I'm sure that my maid Parsons is shaking with anger. May I see what you have planned for my god-daughter's attire this evening?'

Rosalie obediently trotted over to the cupboard and then returned with a pale yellow ball gown reverently laid over her outstretched arms. 'It's edged in gilt thread,' she said, 'and there's the yellow wig that goes with it just perfect. And there are some diamonds—'

'No,' Henry said. 'That won't do. She'll look

jaundiced. Did you bring any other ball gowns?'

'Well, yes,' Rosalie said, alarmed. 'But I didn't—'

'Let's see those.'

'There are two more,' the maid said, running back to the cupboard. 'I could only choose three from Miss Victoria's wardrobe. They each take a trunk of their own, of course.'

'We understand,' Henry said.

'There's this silk damask,' Rosalie said, turning around. 'And the wig.' She nodded toward a wig that was tinted a distinctly bilious shade.

But Henry was already shaking her head. 'Green will swear at your hair,' she told Kate. 'Your mistress is not wearing a wig tonight,' she instructed Rosalie.

'No wig? Of course I don't need to wear a wig,' Kate said with relief. 'Victoria is here so I can be myself.'

'*She* has to wear a wig,' Henry said with satisfaction. 'You might as well send that green wig back to Victoria's room, because I'll not see that on your head as long as I'm living.'

'The last gown,' Rosalie said, hopefully. Over her arms was a great swath of gorgeous cream taffeta with designs in a delicate pale blue.

'Perfect,' Henry said, at the same moment Kate cried, 'It's beautiful!'

'If I don't return to my chamber Parsons will have an apoplexy,' Henry said. 'So, Kate: no wig, and put your hair up very simply, yes? I shall send Parsons to paint your face.'

'Paint my face?' Kate repeated, a bit dismayed. 'I'm not sure—'

'Parsons is a brilliant artist,' Henry said, overriding her. 'You won't recognize yourself. Now

328

be quick about it, my dear. We want to make a grand entrance, not enter after everyone has gone to bed.'

Kate nodded and then darted across the room to give Henry a quick hug. 'Thank you,' she whispered.

Henry gave her an odd half smile. 'I look at you, and I can find it in my heart to think that your father was not such a fool after all.'

By the time Kate had had a restorative cup of tea and emerged from her bath, she felt quite calm and almost happy. This night would decide the rest of her life. That was an odd and interesting thought.

She ran her fingers through her hair. It was tousled, and streaked with gold from all the riding she'd done in the sun. 'So what can we do with this, Rosalie?'

'I could do curls on top of your head,' Rosalie suggested. 'Or we could make coils, for a classical look, but that would be harder because your hair is so thick. I would have to use a curling iron to flatten it.'

Kate shuddered. 'Let's put it up, with some curls falling down the back as well. It weighs too much to pile all of it on top.'

'What would you like to wear as decoration?' Rosalie was poking around in a box on the dressing table. 'We have a silver net, but that would make your hair look brassy. There's a jeweled comb, but it's deep green and won't suit your ball gown.'

'I'll do without anything in my hair,' Kate said, shrugging.

'Oh miss,' Rosalie moaned. 'I'm begging you . . .' She rummaged about in the box. 'Here's a silver comb with emeralds,' she said in relief. 'I knew that had to be here somewhere.'

'It's only until midnight,' Kate pointed out. 'I'll hardly enter the ballroom before it will be time to run to Algie's carriage.'

'I'm almost packed,' Rosalie said, glancing around the room. Open trunks lined the wall.

There was a brisk knock on the door, and a maid so elegant that Kate could easily have confused her with a guest at the castle entered the room. 'It's Parsons, miss,' she said, dropping a curtsy. 'Lady Wrothe asked me to aid you.'

'Thank you, Parsons,' Kate said, seating herself before the dressing table.

Parsons opened a box and started rummaging through her various beauty aids. First she patted cream all over Kate's face. She opened a jar of rouge and then shook her head. 'Too pink,' she said. 'What I need is crimson.'

She tried crimson and then wiped it off. In a few minutes there was a tumble of jars on the dressing table.

'I had no idea this was such an elaborate process,' Kate said faintly. She had her eyes shut as Parsons did something to them.

'I finished Lady Wrothe before coming to you,' Parsons said. 'She's got lovely skin but even so, at her age it takes longer. I'm giving you only the slightest help, miss. I just need to find the proper lip color.' She turned over the various jars again.

Rosalie, who'd been watching while she pinned Kate's hair up, leaned forward and pointed to a little silk box. 'What about this?'

'Peony red,' Parsons said, investigating. She dipped her finger and painted Kate's mouth a deep red.

'It's perfect,' Kate said, awed. And it was. The color turned her honey skin from an abomination to a delight. Her cheeks were tinted with a pale peach wash, and her eyes seemed to have deepened and grown more mysterious. 'My goodness, Parsons,' she said. 'You're something of a magician, aren't you?'

Parsons laughed. 'You're beautiful, miss. Not a challenge at all.' She bustled out of the room.

'Your hair's almost finished,' Rosalie said, slipping in the comb adorned with emeralds. It glinted among Kate's curls. 'You do look wonderful.'

'Not young,' Kate said with satisfaction, drawing on gloves that went well above her elbows.

'It's not that. You really shouldn't talk about yourself as if you were a spinster. But you look—well—fiery.'

'I think a few more jewels are in order,' Kate said. 'We still have that box of Victoria's, don't we?'

Rosalie pulled out a pearl choker with a beautiful emerald in front, and fastened it around Kate's neck. 'And now . . . the glass slippers,' she said, with a tone of reverence that made Kate's eyebrows go up.

'Lady Dagobert said that they were a terrible waste of money.'

Rosalie was tenderly opening a wooden box and unwrapping a pair of slippers swathed in silk. 'Isn't that true of everything worth having?'

'Not really,' Kate said, thinking of lemon tarts, and Freddie's love, and even a prince's kiss.

The little maid knelt at her feet. 'Now put this on gently, Miss Katherine. They call it a glass slipper for a reason. It isn't made of glass, but it's still liable

331

to break.'

She slipped a gorgeous heeled slipper on Kate's foot. It had the sheen of polished glass, and gems flashed from the slender heel. 'Why, it's almost transparent,' Kate said, rather awed despite herself. 'What on earth is it made of, if not glass?'

'Some sort of stiffened taffeta,' Rosalie said, shrugging. 'The taffeta looks shimmery, a bit like glass. They're really only good for one night, because they never look fresh and new after being worn.'

Kate stood for a moment in front of the glass, surveying herself. With some satisfaction, she realized that no one would think she was the bewigged, bepowdered Victoria she had appeared to be for the last few days. The dark shadows under her eyes had receded, and rouge made her lips look pouty and undeniably sensual.

For the first time, she saw beauty inherited from her father in her face, the beauty that Victoria was famous for. She didn't look lush and pillowy, like Victoria—but she looked—she almost thought that she looked—*better*. More beautiful than her sister. If Gabriel looked at her like this, and decided he would marry Tatiana instead, then she had tried her best. 'Rosalie,' she said, turning to her maid, 'this gown was an inspired choice. Thank you.'

'It's the way it molds under your bosom,' Rosalie said, coming over to give her expert opinion. 'The way the fabric comes horizontal here, and then there's nothing but a bit of flimsy silk over your breasts . . . And your legs, miss! They look so long. You'll have all the ladies sighing with envy.'

Kate grinned at herself. As far as she knew, no one had ever sighed in envy over the way she

332

looked.

'Another thing is that it's just a little short on you,' Rosalie continued, 'which shows your ankle *and* the shoe. Some ladies shorten their gowns on purpose, just for that. Those with good ankles, of course.'

There was a tap on the door, and there was Victoria, with Algie at her back. She wore the famous cherry wig, offset by a delicious white gown trimmed in cherry.

'Lord and Lady Wrothe are waiting for us in the gallery,' Victoria reported. And then, catching sight of Kate's ensemble as Rosalie moved aside, she stopped and clasped her hands together. 'Oh! You look . . . You look . . . Algie, look at Kate, just look at Kate!'

Kate walked forward, hugely enjoying the surge of confidence that comes from feeling beautiful.

Algie's reaction was as satisfactory as Victoria's. His mouth fell ajar, though it couldn't go far due to his extraordinarily high collar. 'You look like someone . . . you look like . . . you look *French*!'

That was obviously his highest praise.

'You both look wonderful,' Kate said.

'I can't breathe,' Victoria confided. 'But luckily this ball gown is an old-fashioned shape, and the pleats mean that you can't see my figure very clearly.'

'You look delectable,' Kate said. 'Shall we go?'

Henry and Leo were waiting for them at the far end of the portrait gallery. Henry was magnificently dressed in plum-colored silk sewn with arabesques of seed pearls. 'Well,' she said, as Victoria and Kate reached the end of the portrait gallery. 'I must say that I'm glad that you two didn't come on the market when I was in my prime!'

'You would have stolen the gentlemen and left us brokenhearted,' Kate said lightly, giving her a kiss. 'Thank you again,' she whispered.

'For what?' Henry said.

'For coming to the ball with me.'

'You don't need us,' Henry scoffed. 'The prince will fall to the ground in an ecstasy of despair when he sees you. I just want to be sure that I don't miss the show. I love a good comedy.'

Wick's eyes widened as they approached the ballroom. He bowed deeply—and winked. Then he nodded to his footmen, and with a smooth, synchronized movement they each pulled open one of the great doors.

Wick preceded them to the top of a short flight of stairs leading down into the ballroom, and announced in sonorous tones, 'Lord and Lady Wrothe. Miss Victoria Daltry and Miss Katherine Daltry. Lord Dimsdale.'

There were perhaps two or three hundred people in the ballroom. Chandeliers caught the glint of diamonds and rubies, the sheen of iridescent silks.

Kate walked forward to the top of the stairs, and paused just long enough to make sure that all eyes were on her. Then she began slowly, very slowly, descending the stairs into the room. Naturally she held up her skirts, which brought the glass slippers—and her ankles—into view.

As she reached the bottom step, she heard the stir of voices, the shrill repetition of her name. But more than voices, she saw men's heads swivel in her direction.

She realized, with a start, that it was a bit as if

someone had tossed a bucket of oats into a pasture full of stallions. They all turned, almost as one, and headed toward the delicacy.

She greeted the nearest man with a smile. And she did not look to the right, or the left, to see if a prince might be watching.

Her pleasure was all the keener for years of watching Victoria prance off to local assemblies, and then to London for her season . . . always staying behind, always in plain cambric and sturdy cotton, with her fraying gloves and shabby boots . . .

Kate was in the grip of a particular kind of joy.

The first gentleman reached her, almost stumbling over his dancing slippers in his fervor. He introduced himself, in the absence of their host. 'How lovely to meet you, Lord Bantam,' she said sweetly. He was wearing two waistcoats, one of figured velvet over another of sky-blue satin, and he bowed with a flourish that caused the buckles on his shoes to flash like diamonds.

Which, she decided a moment later, they actually were.

Lord Bantam was followed by Mr Egan, and then by Toloose, Lord Ogilby, the Earl of Ormskirk, Lord Hathaway, and a Mr Napkin. Henry floated forward as naturally as if she were Kate's mama, tapping men on the arm with her fan, telling Ogilby that he certainly could *not* ask her goddaughter for a waltz.

It was a heady, delightful feeling, standing in the midst of the gentlemen, her emeralds glittering as brightly as Lord Bantam's buckles.

But it wasn't her emeralds that were attracting them. She knew that. It was the secret smile in her eyes, her peony lips, the sensuality in the way she moved.

She caught sight of Effie and introduced herself as Victoria's sister Kate.

'Kate?' Effie breathed, and then smiled mischievously, dropping a curtsy. 'What a pleasure to meet you! Why, I *adore* Victoria.' And then Effie was in the circle as well, the two of them laughing and flirting with all the men at once.

'I am a terrible dancer,' she said to the Earl of Ormskirk, whom Henry had decided would be her first partner. Interestingly enough, Effie had bestowed her hand on Lord Hathaway rather than the younger bucks vying for her attention.

He leaned forward as if mesmerized and breathed, 'Would you like to sit this dance out, Miss Daltry?'

Ormskirk had a strong chin and bright blue eyes. He looked like a man who was more comfortable on a horse than in a study. He would never read a journal about Ionian antiquities, whatever those were. Even after reading two articles, she still wasn't quite sure.

He was a man of deeds and not words. She favored him with a smile and was rewarded with another kiss on her hand. 'I should prefer to dance,' she told him lightly. 'But you, my lord, must take pity on me and tell me exactly what to do. I simply cannot keep these reels in my head.'

'Neither can I,' Ormskirk confided. 'I always find myself going the wrong direction. But this is a polonaise and that's easy enough. The trick is just to keep slowly promenading about until everyone stops. Quite boring, really.'

He was right; it was easy enough. Kate kept her

eyes fastened on him so that she wouldn't, by any stray chance, see Gabriel.

Even the thought caused a jolt of anguish, but her smile didn't waver.

The earl responded to her attention like a flower in the sun. At the end of the polonaise he surrendered her to Lord Bantam with obvious reluctance. But he reappeared a very short time later, when she was about to dance with Toloose, and plucked that gentleman by the sleeve.

Kate raised an eyebrow as Toloose made an excuse and walked away.

'My goodness, sir, you remind me of a court magician,' she said. 'How on earth did you frighten away poor Mr Toloose? I was looking forward to admiring his coat at closer range.'

'Toloose looks like a peacock, but he's actually a solid fellow,' Ormskirk said. 'I wanted to dance with you again, and so I arranged the perfect dance.'

She smiled at him, noting the way his eyes lingered on her lips and the curve of her bosom.

'A waltz,' Ormskirk said triumphantly.

Kate knew the answer to that one. 'My goodness, my stepmother never allowed me to learn the waltz! And I believe that my godmother explicitly instructed me *not* to waltz.'

'How lucky for us that your stepmama isn't here,' Ormskirk said. The twinkle in his eye made up, to some extent, for his high forehead. The poor earl was conspicuously going bald, though he was doing it in a distinguished fashion. It certainly wasn't his fault that his forehead shone so in the light of all these candles.

Kate frowned, trying to remember what Gabriel

337

had said the night before about the waltz. It was licentious, she knew that. 'Perhaps . . . Oh! There's my godmother,' she said with some relief. 'Henry, darling!'

'Ah, Ormskirk,' Henry said. 'I thought you'd be back.'

'It's a waltz next,' he said to her, with a curious kind of intensity. 'I've asked Miss Daltry if I might escort her onto the floor.'

'Ah,' Henry said, looking him up and down. 'Well . . .' She nodded and seemed to come to a decision. 'I haven't any objections as long as you don't cannon into me and Leo. I adore the waltz, but some couples act like a pair of horses spooked by a fly bite.'

Ormskirk grinned at that. 'I fancy I can keep within the traces,' he said lightly, and turned to Kate, holding out his hand. 'Miss Daltry?'

For some reason, she felt strangely reluctant to dance with him again . . . but that was foolish. It was just the crush, and the way Henry's perfume filled the air around her, and the heat of candles.

'The dance floor will be far less crowded than here,' Henry was saying to Leo, 'given as most of the debutantes will sit out unless that silly prince asks them to dance. I expect they'll all line up, the better to ogle him.'

Kate stiffened her backbone. She wasn't going to stand on the side while Gabriel circled the floor with his betrothed. She gave Ormskirk a smile, one guaranteed to make the pretty flush on his cheeks rise even higher. 'As long as you can steer me, my lord. For I must warn you that I am terribly inexperienced in this dance.'

He reached out, blue eyes steady, and took her

hand. 'Miss Daltry,' he said, 'it would be my honor and my privilege to lead you in your first waltz.'

Thirty-eight

Gabriel wore a coat of heavy embroidered silk that had been made for his presentation at the Austrian court. He knew what he had to do—and he would do it. Manfully.

No, royally.

He thrust a leg before Tatiana, gracefully extending a hand in a deep bow, a bow he had been taught by gentlemen who had spent their lives in the French court. The princess was pleasingly attired in a demure white ball gown. But it was adorned with real Brussels lace, and its sleeves were trimmed with swansdown.

Her delight quivered from every smile, every sideways glance at him, every shining glance she threw at other ladies.

Tatiana was confident, as well she might be.

He danced with her, he danced with others, he danced with Sophonisba, who cursed him for bending one of the feathers decorating her headdress. He had an odd little conversation with Toloose, who looked at him with something akin to rage in his eyes, and said out of the blue, '*She doth teach the torches to burn bright.*'

'Isn't that from *Romeo and Juliet*?' Gabriel asked, confusedly thinking of his goodbye with Kate.

Toloose nodded toward Tatiana, who was dimpling as she smiled up at Gabriel's uncle.

'Shakespeare might have learned everything he knew merely from a glance at her eyes.' And then he walked off without another word.

Gabriel shrugged and danced with Henry, who smiled at him with genuine amusement and said, 'I imagine you have seen my goddaughter by now.'

'I have not had that pleasure,' he stated.

'Well, then, you're the only one in the ballroom,' she said cheerfully. 'My goodness, Prince, your face is as white as marble. I do hope you're not feeling ill. Everyone is having such a wonderful time.'

'I'm glad to hear that,' he said woodenly.

'You probably were not aware of the fact. One is generally unable to tell if an Englishman is enjoying himself until he collapses in a drunken heap in the corner,' she added. 'There are a great deal more betrothals being fashioned here besides your own, Your Highness.'

He smiled, though he hated her for that comment. For the way her eyes assessed him, for the way she mentioned his betrothal, for the—

For the glinting challenge in her eyes.

He made it through the dance, bowed, straightened—and then he saw her.

His Kate. She was glowing like a torch, a gorgeous, sensual, strong woman. A princess, by any measure.

Her gown was magnificent, her hair delightful. He stared at the deep laughter in Kate's eyes, at the strength of her little round chin, at the angular slash of her cheekbones.

He saw both the inherent kindness in her face and the bone-deep sensuality in the way her lips curled.

He could fight his way through the throngs of

men around Kate, drive his fist into the chin of the man smiling down at her as if he was starving and she were manna from heaven.

But Tatiana was next to him, and Kate was not, and he had his duty, his duty, his duty. He turned his back, feeling his temples throb as they never had before, and at that very moment the opening strains of a waltz sounded in the ballroom.

Tatiana dimpled up at him. 'My uncle agreed that I might waltz last night, but after your indisposition, I chose to remain on the side of the room.'

He bowed; she put her fingertips on his shoulder; they swept onto the floor.

It was relatively empty; many of the guests either hadn't yet learned the steps, or eschewed it for its salaciousness, or chose to stay on the side of the room and gossip about those who dared.

Tatiana was like thistledown in his arms, anticipating every move of his leg. It was a genuine delight to dance with her. They found themselves at the top of the floor: He looked at her and raised an eyebrow.

'Yes, let's!' she said, laughing. Her cheeks were pink and her eyes shone.

And with that he let the music carry both of them, around and around and around, as they swept down the ballroom. As they turned in perfect circles, he caught the awed stares of his guests. He knew what they saw: He looked like the perfect Prince Charming, and she a fairy princess indeed.

They reached the bottom of the floor, and he looked down at his partner again. 'Perhaps we should be a little less flamboyant for the rest of the piece.'

'It was lovely,' Tatiana said, glowing. 'If I could, I would dance the waltz all night.'

He held her a bit more tightly, smiling. The length of her leg touched his; it felt as sensual as that of a goat. With a kind of cold detachment, he found himself wondering whether he would be able to perform on their wedding night.

What a scandal that would be . . . a prince found incapable.

'Oh dear,' Tatiana said, pulling his attention back. 'I'm afraid that not everyone is as skilled in the dance as you are, Your Highness.'

He followed her glance. It was Kate, of course. She was dancing with Lord Ormskirk. They too were making their way down the floor. But unlike the easy elegance, the silent grace, exhibited by Tatiana and him, Kate and Ormskirk were circling too fast. Her head was back, and she was laughing with infectious pleasure. Her gorgeous buttery hair swirled around her shoulders as Ormskirk pulled her in circle after circle.

When he and Tatiana danced, they held each other lightly. Properly.

But in order to keep up his outrageous momentum, Ormskirk was holding Kate against his body. Gabriel felt a surge of rage building in his chest.

The music ended. Kate and Ormskirk danced one final turn, in the silence, smiling at each other as if they had some sort of private agreement.

Tatiana's hand fell on his sleeve; Wick had thrown open the ballroom's great doors. It was time to retire to the gardens, where an exhibition of fireworks would be set off from boats on the lake.

He almost shook off her hand, but he didn't.

342

Instead he escorted the princess from the ballroom, out the great doors, down the long white marble steps.

The night was cool, and Wick had dotted about metal pots filled with burning wood in order to keep the guests warm. The licking flames competed with the moonlight and gave a yellow glare to the faces of people gathered at the lake's edge.

'I've never seen fireworks!' Tatiana cried with girlish enthusiasm.

Gabriel thought of the years he'd spent in various courts, of his first fireworks, at age ten. 'I'm happy to be with you at this occasion,' he said.

There must have been something flat about his tone. Tatiana glanced up at him and then pulled him coltishly toward her uncle and a large group. 'Uncle!' she called.

'There you are, dumpling,' Prince Dimitri said. 'Saw you making a right exhibition of yourself on the dance floor. Good thing your mother isn't here.'

Gabriel bowed. 'The princess is a remarkably graceful dancer.'

'She is, at that,' her uncle said. Tatiana had slipped to the front of the little group and was standing at the edge of the lake, watching the boats intently. 'So what you have planned for us, prince?'

'The boats will glide to the center of the lake and moor to each other,' Gabriel said. He saw Kate and the Earl of Ormskirk, to their left. 'On a signal from Berwick, they will begin to set off their fireworks, in such an order as to create a remarkable display.'

'Or so one hopes,' Dimitri said. 'Always tricky, these fireworks, aren't they?'

'They are indeed,' Gabriel said. 'If you'll excuse me, Your Highness, I want to make sure that all

343

preparations are in train.'

'Surely you needn't,' the prince said, but Gabriel was already slipping away. He walked to the back of his guests, clustered around the basin of the lake, and then started making his way . . . to the left.

Naturally.

She was standing toward the back of the group, thankfully, just in front of the entrance to the hedge maze. He silently walked up behind her and slipped one hand onto the curve of her waist, without saying a word.

She glanced at him, but it was dark and he couldn't read her expression. Without shrugging off his hand, she murmured something to the earl and backed away.

With one swift gesture, he drew her into the entrance to the maze and around the first curve. There were no burning pots here, no torches to illuminate the darkness. It was thick and velvety against their faces.

'Gabriel,' Kate said. To his relief, he heard an amused thread of laughter in her voice. 'What are you doing?'

'Come,' he said, and took her hand more firmly, turning into the darkness.

'I cannot,' she protested. 'My glass slippers . . . I can't walk on this grass!'

Without hesitation, he dropped to his knees before her and took one small foot in his hand. 'My lady.'

She raised her foot, and he slipped the shoe from her toes. Silently he touched her other leg, and took that slipper as well, placing them carefully on a bench that stood just inside the entrance to the maze.

'I feel like a child, dancing on the lawn in my stockings,' Kate said, a deep hum of pleasure in her voice.

With his left hand just touching the hedge and his right tightly holding hers, he paced the maze, seeing the turns in his head. It was really quite simple, if one knew the way.

Kate followed behind, stumbling a bit once, but he held her upright.

'We're here.' They turned the last corner and found the center. It was bathed in moonlight, and without the torch pots to compete, the air was silvery, washing the hedges and the laughing mer-horses with fairy dust. 'It looks like magic,' Kate said, drifting to the fountain. 'What keeps the water bursting from these statues?'

'It's a matter of gravity and the weight of the water held underneath. If I turn this crank'—he demonstrated—'the water turns to a mere dribble.'

'I would love to sit, but I'm afraid the spray has dampened the stone,' Kate said ruefully, 'and I mustn't crease my dress.'

She turned and looked up at him, but he had no words. He was afraid that nothing would come from his mouth but the most rudimentary words, the panting, thrusting gasps that men and women share in deepest intimacy.

Instead of speech, he reached out and ran a hand down the curve of her cheek. He felt the smoothness of her skin, the very edge of her curving smile. He replaced his fingers with his mouth.

'Gabriel,' she said, turning her face from his.

His heart jolted. 'I must.'

'You may not.'

'Kate!' It was pain to his heart even to say her

345

name. At the same time, it was like honey in his mouth, sweet and familiar, like a lullaby singing in his heart.

'Oh, Gabriel,' she whispered.

'Give me one last time,' he begged. 'Please, please. I beg you.'

'I—' She stopped and started again. 'I'm afraid, Gabriel. You'll break my heart.'

'Mine is already broken.'

There, the truth of it was out, between them. Her eyes glistened with something wetter than moonlight.

He kissed her in an act of possession. There was no other way to describe it, the way they fell together into some nameless darkness, some impudent fairytale space where he was no prince, and she no lady.

Just two bodies, aroused, warm, mad for each other.

'My gown,' she murmured, some time later. Her eyes glowed with a wicked kind of glee. 'This is so *wrong.*'

He reached out, wrenched the crank, and the gurgle of water entirely stopped. Then he showed her how to put her hands on the head of a wet, laughing mer-horse. Carefully, carefully, he raised layer after layer of fabric, throwing them over her back until her beautiful bottom lay beneath his hands, clad only in a pair of drawers so delicate that he could see her skin through them.

He hesitated, as if what lay before him was too beautiful for human hands. Then he bared her to the moonlight, leaned over, pressing against her, his hands curving naturally to her breasts.

She hadn't said a word, but the moment his

fingers brushed a nipple she let out a cry and pushed back against him. It was like being caught in a snowstorm and temporarily losing his sight; it felt as if all sensation came from his hands, his body only.

The sweetness of her breast, the tight bud of her nipple, the ragged pant that shook her body, the deep curve of buttock against him, the heaven that lay below.

He caressed her again and she cried again. He let his fingers drift down into her sweet valley and she sobbed and arched back.

His hand shook as he covered himself with a French letter. And then . . . they slid together as if they had made love like this a hundred times, as if their bodies were designed for this moment. He thrust deep; she arched with a cry that flew into the night sky.

It was almost too much. Gabriel clenched his teeth and concentrated on breaching her body without losing himself, letting her delicate perfume, the sweet honey of her skin, the ragged sound of her breathing come into his memory so that he could keep it—keep her—forever.

For a time there was nothing but the sound of their bodies meeting in silken, near violent pleasure, a sob from Kate, a groan from Gabriel . . .

But it was too deep, too greedy to last. He started pumping faster, and she was crying now, arching hard against him, and then they broke, together, shattering time and silence and any molecule of space between them, molding their bodies into one flesh, one heart.

He stayed like that, bent over her like any animal with its mate, until she made a small noise and

347

straightened against him.

At that moment, a hissing noise sounded in the distance and, as they both turned to watch, an explosion was fol-lowed by a rain of emerald-green sparks, falling back to earth.

Kate was shaking her skirts down but she stopped, her eyes meeting his. His heart thumped in his chest. 'I'm so glad,' she said, 'that those fireworks didn't happen a minute or two ago. It would have been absurd.'

Another explosion . . . Ruby sparks melted, turned to pink, and died.

He couldn't bring himself to answer her, to say a word. Instead he helped her put up her hair, his fingers lingering in its thick gold, stealing a last touch. Then he took her hand and led her from the center of the maze.

She raised her face to his as they turned the last corner. He didn't move, so she had to find his mouth with her own. She took—or was it a gift?—that last kiss with cool deliberation, as if she were giving him a message that he could not interpret.

In the last patch of darkness, he knelt again at her feet, genuflecting as would any medieval knight to his lady.

Her small foot rested trustingly in his hand as he slipped her shoe over the arch of her foot. Then the other, and he had to stand up. He couldn't stay there in the darkness forever.

'Kate,' he said, once standing. He reached out for her again, his grip tightening on her arms.

The orchestra began playing . . . they had moved down beside the lake, and the notes of a waltz swept into the quiet night like a joyful wind. He shifted his grip, one hand dropping to her waist.

348

'You said,' she whispered, 'anyone who saw us waltzing would know that we were lovers.'

'No,' he said fiercely. 'They will know only that I am in love with you. Please, dance with me, Kate.'

She put her hand in his, smiled, her eyes shimmering with unshed tears. Without saying a word, he held her hand high and swept her into a slow waltz. She didn't follow perfectly, so he pulled her tight, showed her silently how to feel by the press of his body which way he was about to turn.

Sure enough . . . she learned, she learned. By a moment later they danced together as if the air had decided to embrace the wind, as if they were two blossoms caught on a warm draft.

The music came to an end. Gabriel had not taken his eyes from her face, never glanced over his shoulder to see whether they had an audience. He didn't care.

She curtsied, held out her hand to be kissed.

Gabriel stayed in the shadow of the hedge, watching Kate pick her way across the grass toward Henry, who turned toward her and gave her a swift kiss.

The evening seemed endless. Finally they were summoned back to the drawing room by Wick, who had footmen circulating with hot drinks for those who were chilled, and tiny, delectable pastries for those who were hungry. Gabriel stayed at Tatiana's side. He felt like an automaton, but there he stayed, escorting her from place to place, laughing when she giggled, smiling when she smiled.

Dragging his eyes away from the bright flame that was Kate. Suddenly he realized that Tatiana was addressing him. 'Your Highness,' she repeated.

'Forgive me,' he said, turning back. Ormskirk

was standing beside Kate next to the fireplace; he was leaning over Kate . . . It looked as if Kate was saying goodbye to Henry and Leo, but that couldn't be. She couldn't be leaving . . . he had to see her tomorrow morning, see her one more time.

Tatiana looked up at him. She was a tiny thing, but there was a firmness to her chin and a strength in her eyes. 'Would you be so kind as to escort me to my chamber?'

'Of course,' Gabriel said, turning his back on Kate.

Tatiana placed her fingers delicately on his arm and they began to walk from the room. She had exquisite manners, smiling and nodding at various guests, even as she said: 'There is a sadness in you, prince.'

He cleared his throat. 'I am sure you misinterpret—'

'No,' she said. They had reached the door, then the entryway. She drew him into the shadow, to the right of the great arched door standing open to the courtyard. 'I do not misinterpret. I see what I see.'

Gabriel had no idea what he was supposed to say.

'I saw you waltzing with that lovely woman. I suppose,' she said thoughtfully, 'that you have a story.'

He blinked at her.

'A love story,' she clarified. 'You have a story, or so we call it. Many, oh many, of my relatives have a story in their past. We are passionate, we Cossacks. We love to be in love. And it seems to me that you have such a story as well.'

There didn't seem to be any reason to deny it. Tatiana was not angry, nor was she particularly upset. 'Something of the sort,' he admitted.

Tatiana nodded. Her eyes were sympathetic, very kind. 'We in Kuban know our fairy stories,' she said.

'As do I,' he answered, knowing exactly what she was saying. 'All stories come to an end.' He leaned down and dropped a kiss on her nose. 'You are a very sweet person, princess.'

There was a faint sound, like a muffled sob, a scuffle of a jeweled heel . . . he raised his head in just enough time to see the flash of cream taffeta disappear through the arch to his right.

He swore and started after Kate, never thinking of what it must look like to Tatiana, to anyone who watched. She was flying across the courtyard, through the arch leading to the outer courtyard steps, without looking back.

He ran faster.

But he was too late.

The courtyard shone empty in the moonlight. In the near distance he could hear the trundling sound of carriage wheels starting down the gravel drive.

Too late, too late, too late.

He took one step forward, thinking to run after the carriage, to run mad, madder than he already was. His foot brushed something.

He bent down.

It was one of Kate's glass slippers. It shimmered in his hand, as delicate and absurd as any bit of feminine nonsense he'd ever seen in his life.

He said it aloud, because there was no reason to be silent. 'I am—undone. She has undone me.'

And his hand closed around the glass slipper.

Thirty-nine

Kate's godmother's house was exceptionally comfortable: cozy, expensive, and slightly dissipated. 'Just like Coco,' Henry pointed out. They were lounging in her dressing room, whose walls were covered in watered silk, hand-painted with rather improbable coral-colored primroses. 'She and I both have the air of a *très-coquette*. Leo says that my little darling graced a brothel in her past life.'

Kate looked over at Coco, who was perfectly groomed and ornamented, as of this morning, with a sprinkling of amethysts. 'She's too self-conscious to be a good trollop. A man could tell with one glance that she only wanted the coin.'

'That's the nature of the job,' Henry said, very sensibly. 'Now listen, darling.'

Kate got up and walked to the window, knowing from the tone in Henry's voice that she wouldn't want to listen. The dressing-room window looked to the front of the house, onto a small public garden, windswept and rather forlorn. 'Winter is drawing in,' she said. 'The chestnut trees are all tinged with gold.'

'Don't try to distract me with palavering about nature,' Henry said. 'You know I wouldn't know a chestnut from a conker. What I want to say, darling, is that you need to stop it.'

Kate stared out the window, her shoulders tight, hunched against the truth of it, against the warmth in her godmother's voice. Her head hurt. Her head always hurt these days. 'Chestnuts *are* conkers,' she said.

Henry ignored that feeble digression. 'It's been over a month,' she said. 'Wait! Even longer.'

'Well over a month,' Kate said drearily. 'Forty-one days, if you want an exact number.'

'Forty-one days of you in a vile temper,' Henry said. 'That's enough.'

Kate came and knelt by the arm of Henry's low chair. 'I'm sorry. I'm so sorry. I don't mean to be so sharp.'

'I know you can't help it, up to a point.' Henry tapped her on the chin with one beringed finger. 'That point has come.'

'I don't mean to—have I really been in a vile temper?'

'Did you just imply that my darling Coco would fail as a night walker?' Henry demanded.

Kate couldn't stop a weak chuckle. 'I did.'

'I can assure you that she would be in the *highest* demand, as indeed would I be, should we have taken up such an insalubrious occupation. And last night at dinner, did you not inform Lady Chesterfield that her daughter was as adorable as a *newborn calf*?'

'She is,' Kate said feebly. 'Same absurd expression on both of them.'

'And finally,' Henry concluded, 'did you not advise Leo that his sister's hair was now the exact color of horse manure in the spring?'

'But I didn't say so to *her*.'

'Thank God for small favors.'

'It's just that particular shade of olive green,' Kate said. 'I've never seen it anywhere else in nature.'

'It wasn't a question of nature, as any fool

353

would know. The poor woman wanted to turn her straw to gold and it didn't work out. I'm not saying you haven't been a pleasure to live with, in some respects. I particularly enjoyed your characterization of the regent as Aaron's rod with a bend in the middle. Though really, one shouldn't joke about royalty, no matter how limp they are reputed to be.'

'I'm sorry,' Kate said, kissing Henry on the cheek again. 'I've been horrible to live with. I know it.'

'It would be better if you would at least leave the house now and then. I miss going to the theater.'

'I will,' she promised.

'Tonight,' Henry said, folding her arms. 'Tonight you are re-entering society, Kate.'

'I've never really been *in* it, have I?'

'All the more reason that you start now.'

Kate clambered up from her knees, feeling very old and sad. She walked back over to the window, where twilight was drawing in over the chestnuts, and the last rays of sun were slanting through the boughs. Oddly enough, there was a bit of bustle in the park, which was generally as lonesome as a stone.

'You did the right thing,' Henry announced, from behind her.

Kate turned around. Her godmother hadn't said a word about Gabriel, not since . . . not for forty-one days.

'You gave him a chance to man up, and he couldn't do it.'

'He had responsibilities.'

Henry snorted. 'You're better off without him. And you were definitely right not to tell him about the possibility you had a dowry. Just look how large that dowry turned out to be. I expect that you could sense intuitively that it would make all the difference to him, and I can't imagine a worse reason for him to break his betrothal.'

'I didn't sense it. I just thought . . . I hoped. Stupidly, I suppose.' It had been forty-one days, and she was stupid to keep a tiny flame of hope alive, merely because there had been no marriage announcement for Princess Tatiana. But who knew when that marriage was supposed to take place?

For all she knew, they had returned to Russia to consecrate their union there.

'One should never hope that men will rise to the occasion,' Henry said sadly. 'They don't, as a matter of course.'

Kate looked at the window again. Her shoulders were stiff and achy from holding in the pain and the tears. But she was so sick of weeping, so sick of wondering why Gabriel was the way he was.

It was like some sort of puzzle box. He was the way he was because he was a prince . . .

The line went drearily around and around in her head.

Henry's arms came around her shoulders and she was enveloped in a little cloud of perfume as sweet as treacle. 'You'll hate me for this, but some small part of me is glad that Gabriel turned out to be lacking the courage to break his engagement.'

'Why?'

Henry turned her around. 'Because I got to spend this time with you,' she said, tucking one of Kate's curls behind her ear. 'You are the child I never had, sweet Kate. You're the best gift that Victor ever gave anyone.' Her eyes were shiny with tears. 'I love him all over again for that, because I love you. And though I hate to see you so sad, the greedy part of me is terribly grateful for the time we've spent together in the last few weeks.'

Kate gave her a wobbly smile and pulled her into an embrace. 'I feel the same way,' she said, hugging Henry tight. 'It makes up for all those years with Mariana.'

'Well,' Henry said, a second later, 'I'm actually getting tearful. You'll think that I joined Leo in a pre-prandial brandy. I didn't really mean it about Gabriel. I wish he'd been the man you hoped he was, darling. I truly do.'

'I know,' Kate said.

'Men come and men go,' Henry continued. 'They're like icicles.'

'Icicles,' Kate said stupidly, turning back to watch the men in the gardens bustling about. Their shapes were black outlines against the dark blue sky.

'They hang beautifully, and look all shiny and new, but then they break off with a crash and the really bad ones melt,' Henry said with a sigh. 'What on earth are those people doing in the gardens? It looks as if they're setting a Guy Fawkes bonfire. Is it Guy Fawkes Day?'

'Isn't that November?' Kate asked. Mariana had hardly been one for honoring public holidays.

Henry gave her a last squeeze. 'We'll go out to the theater tonight and you can lap up some lovely attention from Ormskirk. His notes are getting more and more frantic. I think he believes you to be wasting away. You've lost Dante as a prospect. I had a letter from Effie's mother just now, and she accepted him.'

'Good for her,' Kate said. 'I'm so glad Lord Hathaway fought off all those young men and won

356

her hand.'

'So it's time for you to disprove Ormskirk's fears of your imminent death,' Henry insisted.

'I am certainly robust,' Kate said. The shadows under her eyes and the hollows in her cheeks were gone. It wasn't fair that pain in the heart should feel so much more debilitating than mere exhaustion.

'I'm going to send a footman over there to inquire what on earth is going on,' Henry said, stepping closer to the window frame. 'Look at all the birds. They look as if they're having a proper gossip.'

The trees were full of blackbirds, flying up in little groups and landing again in clusters.

'Maybe they're having a roast of some sort,' Kate suggested, 'and the birds are waiting for them to break out the bread.'

'A roast?' Henry said. 'In this neighborhood? I highly doubt it. Look, they're lighting the bonfire. It's a big one, I must say.'

At that moment there was a scratch at the door and Henry's new butler entered with a silver salver. 'My lady,' he said, 'a note has arrived.'

'Has arrived,' Henry asked. 'From whom? Do you have any idea what's going on in the park, Cherryderry?'

'This note comes from the gentlemen in the park,' he said. 'But no, I am not certain of the nature of the activity.'

'Would you mind asking Mrs Swallow to send more tea, Cherryderry?' Kate asked.

He bowed and departed; Henry tapped the note against her chin consideringly.

'Aren't you going to open it?' Kate inquired.

'Of course I am. I'm just wondering if I should

357

send a footman for the Watch. I wish Leo was home; he would know what to do. Look how those sparks are going up into the trees. What if it all catches on fire?'

'Open up the note and see what on earth is going on,'

Kate said.

'I can't,' Henry said.

'What?'

'It's addressed to you.'

Forty

I would prefer not to throw myself on a funeral pyre.
Please come back to me.

The note fell from Kate's fingers and she took a step toward the glass, straining her eyes through the gathering darkness.

And now she could see . . . a man. A tall man with wide shoulders standing before the bonfire. He had his arms crossed.

He was waiting.

Henry was picking up the note from the carpet, but Kate didn't pause.

She ran, ran down the stair, across the marble entrance hall, through the front door, and across the street. There she fetched up short at the iron railing, her hands curling instinctively around the icy metal.

'Gabriel,' she breathed.

'Hello, love,' he said, not moving. 'Are you

358

coming to save me?'

'What are you doing? Here? The fire?'

'You left me, as Aeneas left Dido,' he said. 'I thought this would get your attention.'

'I didn't leave you. We couldn't—you have to—'

'You left me.'

It was typical male foolishness, so she asked the only question that mattered: 'Are you still betrothed? Are you married?'

'No.'

She released the railing and ran to the door to the garden, caught herself about to dash through like Freddie responding to an offer of cheese, slowed down. She managed to walk until she was close enough to see his face, and then he was running and she was running . . .

'God, I've missed you so much.' He growled it and then he found her mouth. He tasted like wood burning in the outdoors, like winter air, like love.

Time, minutes, hours passed as they stood in front of that bonfire locked in each other's arms, not talking. Just kissing, forty-one days' worth of kisses, nights' worth of kisses, morning kisses, luncheon kisses, twilight kisses.

'I love you,' he said finally, drawing back.

Kate felt her lips, bee-stung, ripe like a peach. She wanted more of him. Her hands skated over his broad shoulders, buried themselves in his hair, drew his head to hers again. 'I do too,' she whispered. 'I do too.'

He fell back a step, and her arms uncurled from his neck. He took off his hat, and the fire cast dancing lights on his hair. Then with a simple gesture he fell on one knee before her.

'Will you, Katherine Daltry, do me the great

honor of becoming my wife?'

Kate had been dimly aware that there were men in the garden, that Henry had crossed the street, that servants and bystanders and likely most of London were gawking through the railings. She heard a little rumble from them now, like the sound of laughter infecting a whole city.

She put out a hand. 'You do me too much honor,' she said.

He stayed where he was.

'Yes,' she whispered. 'Yes, yes, yes!'

He bounded up and swung her in a circle, and the golden sparks flying away through black boughs swung crazily in the air as she laughed. Henry was laughing, and Leo was in the park too now, and last of all, Gabriel was laughing. A deep, joyful laugh with an edge of triumph and possession that made her heart beat quickly.

'I have,' he said a moment later, 'a special license.' And he drew it out of his pocket.

Then Henry was there, hugging Kate, and Leo too, smelling like spicy brandy.

'Tomorrow morning,' Henry dictated. So it was to be.

To her shame, Kate didn't even remember to ask what would support the castle; they were all seated around the supper table when Henry broached the subject. Kate was trying to ignore the fact that Gabriel was rubbing his leg against hers.

'So, prince,' Henry said, 'how do you plan to keep my goddaughter, not to mention that castle of yours, in the manner to which she has a right to expect? Now that you're not marrying for money,' she added, throwing Kate a wicked glance.

But Kate had her own ideas about when she

360

would inform Gabriel of her dowry.

'I sold a book,' Gabriel said calmly. 'I got a whopping advance, enough to support the castle and Kate for well over a year, even if she indulges in glass slippers. By that point, the surrounding estate should be profitable enough to support the castle in plain fashion, if not a princely one.'

Kate's mouth fell open. 'A book about archaeology?'

'About the archaeological excavation of Carthage,' he said. 'With plentiful details about the life of daily people at the time.'

'That is Gabriel's particular interest,' Kate said to Henry and Leo. 'He is one of the very few archaeologists who thinks that an ordinary man's life is as interesting as that of a king.'

'It depends on the man,' Henry said. But her eyes were fascinated. 'I didn't realize publishers even paid people to write books. I thought they just did it'—she waved her hand—'for the love of it, or something.'

'Even I know that!' Kate said, laughing at her.

'I haven't read a book in years,' Henry replied, unperturbed. 'But I'll make an exception.'

'Gold lettering in a three-volume set,' Gabriel said. 'By subscription only.'

'In that case I will definitely read it,' Henry said. 'I will buy it in duplicate. And so will everyone else I know,' she assured him.

'You're brilliant,' Kate said, beaming at him. 'I'm just so—I'm so proud.'

'What on earth happened to that little Russian girl?' Leo asked.

'Fobbed her off on Toloose,' Gabriel said proudly. 'It took me two weeks of throwing them together. After all that, he came to me and said he had to return to London, because he couldn't bear it any longer, so I yanked him into the maze and told him to do his damnedest. A day later Tatiana's uncle pulled me aside with all sorts of lavish apologies.'

A hand slid onto her thigh, under the tablecloth.

'You're practically my wife,' Gabriel said in her ear. 'That means groping is allowed.'

'Amazing how even a prince can take on the look of a naughty curate,' Henry said to her husband.

But Kate wasn't listening.

*　　*　　*

At midnight Kate told herself again that Gabriel was a gentleman. A *prince*. Of course he wasn't going to sneak along the corridor of Henry's house, as if he were indeed a naughty curate.

She was the one with the depraved imagination, clearly.

There was a noise.

But it wasn't from her door.

She ran over to the window and pulled open the sash. 'Thank God,' Gabriel said, hauling himself up and swinging a leg over. 'I nearly toppled into the garden.'

'Hush,' Kate whispered, pulling him into the room. 'I'm not sure Henry and Leo are asleep yet.'

'They aren't,' Gabriel said. 'They're down there in the library, and we really should tell them tomorrow that disporting themselves on the hearth rug ought to be done with drawn curtains.'

Kate started giggling madly. 'No!'

Gabriel's mouth quirked too, but there was an

intent wildness to his gaze that didn't leave much room for laughter. Without saying another word he began to untie his cravat.

'Oh,' Kate said nervously. And then, 'Aren't you going to tell me more about the book?'

'No.'

'Did Tatiana mind losing you?'

'She saw my mad dash when you left. I think she had doubts about the happiness of the marriage, and rightly so. Plus Toloose is so much more elegant than I am. They're pretty as paint together.'

'You ran after me?'

His face took on a drawn ferocity. 'Don't ever leave me again, Kate. I couldn't take it.'

'I didn't leave you,' she protested. 'That is, I had no choice. Are you taking off your coat?'

'I'm taking everything off. And unless you'd like me to undress you, you might consider doing the same.'

'Shouldn't we wait until tomorrow?' she asked, feeling an unaccountable burst of shyness.

'No.'

He was down to his smalls.

'Oh,' she said faintly. 'I forgot . . .'

'I didn't forget anything,' he said with satisfaction, reaching out and pulling free the tie to her negligée. He pushed it off her shoulders, and she saw a glint of appreciation in his eyes. When Kate hadn't felt like going in society, Henry had ordered half the modistes in London to attend her at home.

She was wearing a creation so delicate and yet erotic that it could only be made for a princess. Gabriel swallowed visibly. 'That's a wicked, wicked gown.' There was a ring of admiration in his voice.

Kate reached for the simple little tie that kept the whole confection of lace and transparent silk floating around her body. He didn't say a word, so she untied it, and then, very simply, stepped forward, letting it fall in a cloud around her toes.

Gabriel picked her up and carried her to the bed, putting her down as delicately as one of his broken pottery shards. 'I didn't forget anything, not a detail, about the times we made love,' he told her. 'But there was one thing that I never had the chance to do during those times.'

'What?' Kate asked, hearing her voice catch.

'This,' he said. And with that he ran his hands down her body and without hesitation took full possession of her most intimate parts.

'What are you doing?' Kate cried, rearing up. But as his mouth followed his hands, she stopped asking, because all she could do was gasp. And then cry aloud. And finally, shriek.

It wasn't until hours later that she remembered what it was she had to tell him. By then she was lying half across him, her hair spread across his chest, his hand absent-mindedly playing with her curls.

They were both drugged and drunk on love and pleasure, and yet neither of them wanted to sleep yet.

'I have to tell you something,' she whispered.

He was winding her curls around his finger. 'Your hair is like spun gold,' he said. 'Like the stuff Rumpelstiltskin wove from straw.'

'I have a dowry,' she said, raising her head so that she could see his face.

'That's nice,' he said, winding more around his finger. 'Did you know that the Greeks used to leave a little pile of hair in the burial—'

'Gabriel.'

'—tombs,' he finished. 'You have a dowry. That's wonderful. Wick and I worked everything out, but every little bit helps. Do you know how much everyone in the castle wanted me to pick *you* over Tatiana?'

'No,' she said, smiling.

'Ferdinand told me that he would sell his gun collection. Sophonisba said she would give up her brandy, though I'm bound to tell you that she later reneged.'

Kate was laughing delightedly.

'And Wick,' Gabriel said.

'Wick?'

'Wick said that he would hire himself out as a butler.'

Kate felt her smile wobble. 'Oh, Gabriel, that's the nicest thing anyone has ever offered to do for me. Or for *you*, in this case.'

'For us,' he said, gathering her against him so that he could brush her mouth.

'The wonderful thing is,' Kate managed, 'that I have a dowry.'

Her breasts were rubbing against Gabriel's chest and he seemed to have stopped listening, so she pulled herself up and suddenly found herself sitting on his chest.

'Mmmm,' he said, pushing her back so she slid lower on his body.

'No!' she said, blinking.

'Oh, yes,' he said, his voice a silky promise.

'Listen to me first.'

'Anything.'

But he wasn't listening. She bent over, feeling

365

bold and beautiful, and said, 'Gabriel, I am . . .' But bending over had put her in a vulnerable position. His hands deftly nudged her this way and that, and a second later she clutched at his shoulders for balance, a cry breaking from her lips.

'No shrieking this time,' he said, thrusting up.

'No,' she gasped.

'I heard Henry and Leo make their way to a much-deserved bed a few minutes ago.'

'No, I won't,' she gasped. 'Please don't stop, Gabriel.'

He was grinning. 'I think we should have that conversation. Weren't you about to tell me something, darling?'

Kate narrowed her eyes at him and experimentally tried a few moves of her own. She rose up on her knees.

His eyes took on a wild sheen.

'Don't you want to hear what I have to say?' she asked, rotating gently, just enough to make his face clench with something like agony. It was his turn to gasp. 'Not at the moment. Could you just . . . yes . . . like that.'

'I am—'

She sank onto him, deeply, greedily and then rose on her knees again. 'I am one of the richest—' He wasn't listening. His hips arched but she avoided him. 'Tsk, tsk,' she said.

'Kate!'

'I am one of the richest women in London,' she told him, sinking down, letting the pleasure of it flood her body.

He moved so suddenly that she squeaked, flipping her over, pounding into her in a thirsty, deep convulsion that swallowed both of them in a rich, warm darkness where there were only the two of them, wanting, loving, possessing.

Sometime later they slumped beside each other, boneless and happy.

Silence.

'Did you say what I thought you said?' Gabriel suddenly demanded.

She pretended to be asleep but he managed to wake her.

And his celebration woke up Henry and Leo.

Forty-one

Four years later

It was the fifth year of the excavation of Carthage. Despite the fact that Professor Biggitstiff claimed to find evidence of Dido's city at least three times a month, to this point no solid proof had been found.

Biggitstiff had not given up. He was determined to find that evidence, and failure only solidified his resolve. 'It's as if he expects to find a big sign some day,' Gabriel groaned, lying back and putting his arms behind his head. 'A plaque: *Dido Slept Here.*'

His wife gave a consoling little murmur. She was drifting into an afternoon nap.

Much more important than Biggitstiff's failures, from Gabriel's point of view, was that the dig had painstakingly brought to light fascinating facts about the inhabitants of ancient Carthage, about everything from their toiletries to their burial practices, from their betrothal gifts to their birthday celebrations.

Even though he and Kate attended the dig in person for only four or five months each year, during the winter, his methods had prevailed. Though Biggitstiff had fought him at first, the overwhelming success of his book, with both a scholarly and popular audience, had made Gabriel's techniques for approaching an archaeological site the rule. Thus the Carthage dig was proceeding with painstaking carefulness and full attention to every scholarly question.

Though nothing was happening at the moment. It was the hot and lazy part of the afternoon, when every sane man was lounging under a canvas, sipping a cool drink, and fanning himself.

Not everyone in Carthage was sane, as evidenced by the rapid pattering of feet around the pile of shards waiting in the sun to be catalogued.

'Oh Christ,' Gabriel moaned. 'He's at it again. Nanny must have let him loose.'

'Do something,' Kate murmured. 'I can't move.'

'Don't move,' he said, pressing a kiss onto the nape of her neck. 'You lie there and let that baby girl grow fat and happy.'

'Little Merry is baking,' she said, rubbing her rounded tummy. It wasn't a complaining groan, since Kate had discovered that she much preferred the sunny warmth of Tunis to the chill of an English winter.

'We'll be back in England in a couple of months and you'll be telling me how cold the castle is.' He gave her another kiss. 'I'm sure you could use a massage . . .' He gave her a little nip, right at the smooth part at the back of her neck, then soothed it with a kiss.

Whatever Kate might have replied was lost when

a small form burst into the tent, waving a shard. 'I found something wonderful, Papa! Look what I found!'

A very small princeling named Jonas ran over, followed by a small yapping dog, and put the broken pottery piece in Gabriel's hand. He was named for his favorite uncle, Mr Jonas Berwick. 'See, Papa,' he cried. 'It's a bird. I found a bird!' His stubby finger traced an arch that might well have been a wing, a dent that might have been an eye, a crack that looked something like a beak.

'That's amazing,' Gabriel said slowly.

Something in his voice made Kate raise her head.

Without speaking, but with a very solemn face, he handed her the bird. But, like Gabriel, her eyes didn't fasten on the beak, but on the ancient Greek letters.

She puzzled over it for a moment. She had spent the last few years devouring the languages and books that she never had access to when younger, but her knowledge of the Greek alphabet was still shaky. 'Oh my God,' Kate whispered. 'It says DIDO!'

Gabriel burst out laughing.

'What is it, Papa?' Jonas called, jumping about on one leg. 'Why are you laughing? Have you seen how good I am on one leg?'

'You're just like Biggitstiff!' Gabriel chortled.

'It says *Dido*,' Kate protested, lying back down and holding the shard up in the light so she could see it better. 'It does have a wing, darling.'

'That's not the wing,' Jonas said disapprovingly. 'That's the bird's bottom. See, it's been dropping poop right there.' He pointed to a tiny mark at the bottom of the *o* for Dido.

'And *that*,' Gabriel said, 'is an alpha, rather than an omega, as you assumed, m'dear. Jonas's poop is the wiggle that turns an alpha to an omega.'

'So what does the word mean, then?' Kate asked sleepily.

'My guess is the shard spells half of *didascalos*,' Gabriel said, 'meaning pupil or disciple. Which is interesting in itself, given that we were speculating over whether there might have been an organized school on the grounds.'

'It's a *bird*,' Jonas said disapprovingly, taking it back.

'Fly the bird outside and find Nanny,' Gabriel said, giving him a little push. 'Mama needs a nap. Take Freddie with you.'

Barring the fact that he couldn't seem to stay out of a shard pile when he saw it, Jonas was a fairly well-behaved boy, so he trotted away, leaving a dusky tent, an amorous prince, and a drowsy princess.

Who found herself tempted . . . and woke up.

Epilogue

In the wondrously various world of *Cinderella*s, the prince always manages to find his cinders girl, and carries her off to his castle. Sometimes the evil stepsisters are banished, sometimes they become housemaids in the castle, and once in a blue moon, they transform into house fairies. The wicked stepmother is never seen again, the pumpkin rots in the garden, and the rats are set free to wander whither they wish.

This particular *Cinderella* ends a bit differently. Of course, the prince did manage to find his cinders girl and carry her off to his castle, except for those months when they happily migrated to warmer, less rainy climes. The evil stepsister, who wasn't really evil at all, moved to a country estate with her inestimable husband, where they raised eight children. None of Lord Dimsdale's offspring was very bright, but they were cheerful and extraordinarily beautiful. Even more important, they were very kind, taking after their papa and, indeed, their mama as well.

They did not take after their maternal grandmother, the wicked stepmother, perhaps because they rarely saw her. Mariana sold her estate to Gabriel, who bequeathed it to his brother Wick. She promptly moved to the city and married a prosperous banker. In a short time she acquired three times as many gowns as she had owned before. She died abruptly, of a lung ailment, leaving her banker impoverished and rather less bereft than he would have thought.

Kate and Gabriel settled down together in the messy, charming castle full of relatives, assorted children (they had three), and animals. Freddie lived to a ripe old age, traveling back and forth from archaeological sites with aplomb. The elephant lived even longer, though the lion unfortunately ate two shoes one day and expired the next.

And now I shall borrow from an author of some of the world's best tales, Rudyard Kipling, to say, O Best Beloved, that every story must come to an end. I leave you with the final, crucial point of fact: They all lived happily ever after.

Even the pickle-eating dog.

Historical Note

A fairy tale exists in a kind of timeless hour, caught between today and yesterday. For that reason, I allowed myself more freedom with language than I have in previous historical novels. *A Kiss at Midnight*, I cannot emphasize too firmly, is a fairy tale, not an historical novel. There are many ways that princes found wives, but it is doubtful than any of them ended up with a castle and an English bride in just this way. If I had to suggest a date, it would probably be somewhere around 1813, during the Regency.

My biggest literary debt lies, obviously, in Perrault's version of *Cinderella*. Scholars generally think that Perrault mistook the word *vair* (fur) for *verre* (glass); I reimagined his slippers as translucent, due to being created from stiffened taffeta. A similar literary mistake is that *The School of Venus* was wrongly attributed to Aretino for years, and published in England under his name; it was actually written by a student of his, Lorenzo Veniero. Besides those gentlemen, I owe a debt to E. Nesbit's *The Enchanted Castle*. While I had no magic ring to transform my characters into living marble, I tried to give Pomeroy Castle some of the delicious joy of Nesbit's castle.